Girl Desecrated 1984

Vampires, Asylums and Highlanders

Cheryl R Cowtan

I0525554

---

1. http://www.cherylcowtan.com

Dedicated
 To all the girls
who've been hurt before

Disclaimer
All persons in this novel are fake.
Fake, I tell you!
True fakers.
Fake products of my imagination.

Names of locations, and my efforts to recreate the 1980s, are used in a fictitious manner, and are not meant to represent the company, actual setting, or current physical business practices of any property or person.

1 Peter 5 King James Version (KJV)

Be sober,
be vigilant;
because your adversary
the devil,
as a roaring lion,
walketh about, seeking
whom he may devour.

Virginia Colony: A Dark Heritage

Although Scarlett was dead, I was convinced she would open her beautiful eyes and pierce me with a dark glare of sinful desire. May God forgive me, in some deceitful corner of my corrupt soul, I desperately wanted her to. And that is why I had to entrust her to the guard of others the night before her burial.

The carriage wheels tore ruts in the wet earth with a loud sloshing noise, as they brought me ever forward to the place Scarlett would be laid to rest for eternity. We passed through the cemetery's black iron gates, and though my hands started to sweat as we approached the gravesite, my eyes remained dry, for I had buried my tears with my soul.

My heart withered, a neglected fruit that would never again sweeten, now that my love was dead.

The wheels slowed. Without waiting for the footman to open the carriage door once we were stopped, I alighted and handed my daughter down from the carriage. She stepped gingerly into the turned mud. She looked down with delight at the rainwater squelching up bubbles around the bottoms of her leather, button boots.

She was too young to truly understand our loss, and she was too old to hold in my arms. Yet, I wanted nothing more than to clutch her against me as we faced the burial of her mother.

I risked a glance toward the grave. A magnolia tree spread its leathery green leaves above the ground where my love would be laid to rest. I could not see the gaping hole dug around the tree's roots for my neighbours stood in a ring around it. Shoulder to shoulder like trunks they stood, their funeral clothes blending together to create an imposing wall of social judgement. But they were no better than I, or my love, for the toes of their shoes ringed the same fate that awaits us all.

I drew in a lungful of the humid air, hoping to add fortitude to my waning courage. I had to be strong. Every man and woman in our fair community was here to witness my grief, some with satisfaction, and some with relief. No matter their purpose, all would gather an accounting of the events here today, to be relayed at future balls and parlour teas as a comeuppance for my betrayal in marrying an outsider.

I clasped my daughter's gloved hand in my own and made my way forward. They watched us approach, not in silence, but without welcome or gesture to make it easier. The soft humming of their murmurs was for their ears only. The only other sound in the graveyard was the soft plops of the last raindrops, and the mud sucking at our boots.

There was no place for us at the edge of the maw, but I walked on, my chin high, my eyes resting on each face before moving to the next. I would not let them make me feel an outsider at my own wife's funeral.

Then to my surprise, the left and right flanks tightened to make space for us in their circle. It was a small sign, but one that brought me hope for the future acceptance of my little girl.

Silence hung. I should have spoken a few words, but the sight of the slender coffin at the edge of the grave turned my thoughts into cold, sluggish clay. I released my daughter's hand and wiped my palms down the front of my thighs.

My woollen pants were much rougher than the memory of the smooth-grained wood of the coffin. I had rubbed the grain soft with walnut oil until it shone, each stroke a loving apology to the woman inside.

The magnolia tree's branches had protected the wood well from the morning rain. Only a spattering of drops shimmered on the little oval window, not enough to obscure the view of Scarlett's face within. Her splendour was framed as if she were a painting hanging above the mantel, instead of a lifeless woman being viewed for the last time.

In contrast to the dark grain of the coffin, her skin shone alabaster white, unflawed and as smooth as marble. And her mouth... My fingers twitched to trace those lips that were still full and dark like wine. Closing my eyes, the memory of her lips on mine caused a heady rush. Soft... as soft as rose petals against my skin. My loins warmed beneath my funeral pants, jolting me to an awareness of my surroundings with a horrific sense of shame.

Gritting my teeth, I contemplated the magnolia's grey trunk to defuse my passion. It was dark from rivulets of rain. The trunk was as much a betrayer as her lips. For it too took me back to the recent past. This tree had been a silent witness to my hands gripping the bark above Scarlett's hair as I had turned her mouth into a little circle of surprise with my heated thrusts.

Someone coughed delicately into their kerchief. My blood started at the sound. I did not want to be existing in this place, yet I must. I must hold together for the service. I must stay alive, face life without Scarlett.

I shifted my stance to hide my flush from the prying eyes of those ladies best known in the community for their chin-waggin'.

"Je-sus!" Pastor Smith's voice boomed with exuberance.

All eyes turned expectantly to the pastor who was finally prying open his Bible with soft hands.

"Jesus Oh Lord, we do not ask for your forgiveness, but thank you for your guid-ance."

His meaty jaws snapped on the syllables causing his chin to quiver above his white collar.

"We do not ask you for your blessing, but thank you for your clemency, for we are but sheep in your colossal flock, and we are often tempted to wander astray."

A few murmurs of agreement caressed the warming air, but I could not join in with true repentance. The Lord's name had shaken loose from my faith, driven out by the depraved trail I had embarked on with Scarlett.

The loss of my soul rattled the ragged sobs lodged deep in my chest, threatening to thrust my grief out through my tight lips.

"And thank you, Oh Lord, for the good book which tells us to be sober, be vigilant, when faced with the roaring lion. Today, we wrestle not against flesh and blood, but against principalities, against powers, against the rulers of the darkness of this world, against spiritual wickedness in high places."

I was not the only man to darken my brow with a frown at the pastor's choice of words. Skirt hems whispered at the edge of the yawning grave as the womenfolk shifted against his unconventional sermon.

"Jes-us! Luke wrote of how you healed Mary of Magdalene of seven devils." He held up five fingers, for the fingers on his other hand were holding steady his black, leather-bound book. "Seven! Oh Je-sus, Our Lord. Seven evil spirits and infirmities!"

The sun's golden rays broke through a misty cloud and brushed the grey stone shoulders marking the dead. I could have chosen a spot in the open grass for Scarlett's burial. I would have, if Ebba had not warned me of the need for tree-root binding. Ebba with his voodoo tales, which seemed conclusive, considering all we had survived.

Still, I had to wonder what would happen if I ignored Ebba's frantic advice, if I buried Scarlett under the carpet of green. Would she dig her way through the warm earth to roam wild under the night sky? Over time, would her flesh slip from her bones as she scoured the villages?

A shudder coursed through me at the thought. I was thankful I'd had the foresight to listen to the man, as he, Ebba had stuttered his way through slaughtered English to swear the magnolia roots would hold Scarlett's impaired soul fast within the earth. It was on his advice, I had selected the base of the only tree in the cemetery for her everlasting rest.

It had been a crude business, standing side-by-side with my overseer, as my finest field hands dug carefully around the base of the trunk, digging and refilling until they had exposed a cradle among the roots big enough for my darling.

The looks the ladies now cast at the stark hole affirmed what I already knew. It was in poor taste to have the grave lying open for the service, but I could not walk away until I was sure Scarlett was tucked securely beneath the tree. And after that, I could never come back, for I could not trust myself not to dig her out with my bare hands.

"Jesus, as it is written in the Scriptures of Mark, we know this kind cannot be driven out by anything but prayer, and so we will pray! Oh Lord! How we will pray..."

I removed my hat, pressing it tight against my chest waiting to follow his words of devotion. But, the silence dragged on and finally, it came to my mind that Pastor Smith was not pausing for effect. He had stopped speaking.

His mouth gaped without words, his voice stuck somewhere behind his bobbing Adam's apple. The good book trembled in his hands adding to my unease.

Afraid the pastor had seen the unthinkable, I cut my glance to the coffin to note the angle of Scarlett's chin. The leaf-dappled sunlight cast new shadows on her cheek, and I was unexpectedly unsure, thinking her head had shifted slightly. From where I stood, it was difficult to see through the partially reflecting coffin window, but I squinted, searching for any moisture on the inside of the glass to prove she still breathed. The longer the moment held, the more chills crept along my arms, little tickles of fear suckling on my anticipation of her rising.

One of the men standing by the grave's edge cleared his throat. I tore my gaze from the coffin and searched for the sound. It was my cousin, Zebadiah. He stood like me. All the men stood like me, with their black hats in their hands, heads lowered to hide their thoughts from the women. Their features were adjusted with appropriate lines of grief, but the tension had moved through their shoulders like a string yanking them upright into a watchful stance.

Zebadiah gave me a meaningful look beneath his black brows. He knew. All the men knew we had to get Scarlett into the ground before the day wore on. Ebba had said night must find her in the wooden embrace of the magnolia.

I addressed the pastor, my deep baritone rumbling with emotion, "Good man, please continue".

He jolted out of his reverie, and his voice broke through the tension, higher in pitch than before.

"Lord God..." He blinked the sweat from his eyes. "Lord God, you spared not the angels that sinned. You cast them down into fiery hell, to the chains of darkness to wait for judgment day."

The magnolia roots had to be the chains of darkness around Scarlett, for the Lord had not rescued us. We had been left to our own devices to deal with this unearthly occurrence. And like all men below God, we had made mistakes.

During the digging, a main root had been scored by the shovel, and I worried the tree would weaken and die. I had had a mind to cut the throat of the slave who had let the shovel's blade slip, for if the tree died, what would hold Scarlett down? I had almost convinced myself to commit the careless slave to the earth alongside of her, when I recognized the sense of influence, that familiar shadow of compulsion persuading me. I can't be sure it was Scarlett ensuring she would have an eternal servant to see to her everlasting needs. For if I put him down, she would not be alone in the earth, and the thought comforted me. And the slave's body would provide the nutrients the tree needed to thrive and repair the score, ensuring its survival.

Oh, yes, my logic, whether mine alone, or tethered to her will to survive even past her demise, had almost been the death of one of my best field workers.

An Indigo Bunting let out a trill, a cheery song, reminding me of better days, of hope and happiness and all the lofty promises a blue canary can sing about.

I searched within myself for the man I once was.

That man, I once was, did not enact lascivious activities with women, or so easily cut another's throat. That man would never have listened to the words of Ebba, much less have given credit to his voodoo superstitions from the Dark Continent. Before Scarlett, the slaves' mumbo jumbo had never made my eyes water in fear.

That man I once was, I must endeavor to become again. I would have to learn to be content to be part of one world only—this world. I had to forget that other world of pleasure and temptation for it was the path to hell, and yes, I believed that now. After what I had been through with Scarlett, I believed in the unfathomable world of spirits. I accepted the immoral and vigorous malevolence of Satan and his sycophants. And it would be Ebba's mumbo jumbo that would save us all.

The pastor's next words pulled me from my thoughts with apprehension.

"Lord forgive us for we had fellowship with the devil," he said, his voice sunken to a whine worthy of a helpless ninny.

I spoke his name roughly, drowning out the distressed whispers of the ladies. Pastor Smith jumped at my reprimand and raised his bleak eyes to mine. His head shook at the end of his neck like a bone rattle, but the good man heeded my warning, slowly closing his Bible.

Our moral shepherd did not have the religious constitution needed to provide salvation for any of us who'd had a hand in this tragic event. We had put on the armour of God, and there was no undoing what we had done. My faith, my belief in myself as a good citizen, everything I had thought was truth was scattered to the wind, and no one on this earth could put that to rights. Things weren't as simple as living and dying. I understood that now.

"Let us pray." Pastor Smith lowered his head, as did the rest of us. *Soothe my soul, man!* I silently begged.

"Brethren, whatsoever things are true, whatsoever things are honest, whatsoever things are just, whatsoever things are pure, whatsoever things are lovely, whatsoever things are of good report; if there be any virtue, and if there be any praise, think on these things."

A gloved hand brushed my arm with the light flutter of a dove, drawing me gently from the prayer. I looked down to see Miss Anne, the woman I had been pledged to before Scarlett had arrived on the ship of brides. A warm Southern wind flipped the edge of Anne's pretty bonnet, revealing her innocent, cornflower blue eyes.

"I am so sorry, William. We ah all weepin' for your loss," she whispered, softly.

I gave Anne a tight-lipped smile and looked away from her self-less compassion. Her lady-like fragility should have moved me. It would have once. And I did not feel I deserved her sympathy. I had acted the cad, jilting her, and breaking my wedding promise to her father. I should not be forgiven for that.

Anne slid her hand from my arm, the movement evoking a memory of Scarlett's nails digging trenches in my shoulders as I drove her deeper into our feather bed. The effect of that vision on my constitution made me suck in a breath so sharply it whistled against my teeth.

Anne ran a concerned glance over my face. And Lord help me, I locked her into my intent stare, which I know burned with inappropriate thoughts. Her lashes fluttered, and her gloved hand crept to her throat as a blush rose from her lace collar to brighten her apple cheeks.

I closed my eyes and pinched the bridge of my nose with my fingers.

Even dead, Scarlett seemed able to graft my thoughts onto yearnings a gentleman should never ever contemplate. But then again, no gentleman had ever lived a night wrapped in her smooth limbs, savouring such sordid and delightful affections as I had.

Scarlett's attentions had raised me above God, but so help me, in no time she had thrown me down to the devil. And then, the killings had begun.

The damp air of the afternoon clogged my already constricted lungs. I held back a cough and loosened my grip on my hat before I accidently tore the brim off.

Across the open grave that awaited my love, one of the women raised a black lace hankie to dab at her dry eyes. She gave a sly look beneath her raised brow.

Oh no, do not... do not lure me.

I turned away from the temptress to study the other women, my eyes darting from a black crepe veil to a shaded face beneath a bonnet, to the disapproving grey hair of my betters. They were unread-able, cloaked as they were, but I was sure none were shedding tears for me or my wife. These ladies had all despised Scarlett, from the very day she had arrived with her strange and foreign ways. They did not hate her because she was an abomination, for they were ignorant of that, and so they would stay. No, they hated her because she had been beautiful and alluring.

Scarlett was not beholden to the laws of communal man. She had followed her own path, and if there was one thing these ladies could not abide, it was a fine-looking outsider who did not follow their rules, and who ensnared their unattached men.

As harsh and unforgiving as the ladies of the Southern Colonies could be, their finer sensibilities and lack of intellect clearly left them unaware of the fact that Scarlett's coffin would never fit into the bower between the tree's roots. Any boy with measuring sense could see we would have to pluck her cold body from the coffin and lower her into the earth on her side.

The thought of lifting her from the coffin and holding her in my arms again left me eager as a young boy faced with his first chance at a kiss.

I would be the one. No one would step in and carry her to her bower in the earth. It was my right. Just as I had carried her over the threshold of our home, so I would carry her over the threshold of her final resting place.

Would her skin be cold? Or warm, as warm and pliant as the last time we had loved one another. I decided, then and there, I alone would be present when I moved Scarlett to the cradle of roots await-ing her eternal repose.

It would be hard to convince the others to leave before the task was complete. The men, like me, had coveted her, and feared her. In our secret meetings, they had voted to burn her on a funeral pyre worthy of *Homer*.

After seeing what she had done to those poor unfortunates, I would have tossed everything she had touched, every horse she had ridden, and even her personal slaves into those all-consuming flames. I would have burned my entire plantation if it would ensure she never hurt another soul. But I couldn't burn her. I couldn't defile that smooth, flawless skin with blisters from the overheating of her flesh.

Burning her would be turning my hope into ashes. I knew she was dead, but I could only survive that reality by hoping she would rise. Secretly, I yearned for her to return from the dead and be mine, again, and if she did... I wanted her body to be unmarred by flames.

The degraded thought scared the blood from my heart. I wiped a hand down my face and shook my head like a dog, trying to loosen the disgusting threads of grief-filled thinking.

Burying Scarlett would not be enough to clear her from my sick mind. I needed prayer, just like the good pastor said. And I needed punishment.

Tonight, I would seek out my overseer and have him whip the unnatural cravings for Scarlett's dead flesh out of my own. It had to be done before I could find that man I once was. Before I could begin to live a God-fearing life again.

"Papa?"

Abitha, my golden-haired angel, stood beside me, prim and proper in her little leather boots and white gloves. My daughter was the reason for my courage, the hope for my future. She was a true daughter of the New World, and the only blessing from this entire sordid affair.

Squatting, I placed my arm gently along her delicate back. "Yes, mah dahlin'?"

"Magdalynne Rolfe said ah was go'an to be the lady, now that Momma's gone."

Abitha wrinkled her button nose above a shy little grin. I wanted to crush her to me.

"Is it true, Daddy? A'm ah go'an to replace Momma?"

"Yes, honey pie." I smiled at her, tears of pride filling my eyes. "You're go'an to be the lady, now."

Abitha smiled ear-to-ear with a child's excitement, clutched my hand in hers and pressed it to the velvety flesh of her cheek.

"A'm go'an to make you so happy, Papa, 'cause A'm go'an to be just like Momma."

The words twisted a strand of fear around my windpipe. I wanted her to be everything but what her momma was.

As I considered telling her so, her smile slid away from her face like it was wiped by the devil's broom.

A sense of dread pinched my shoulders, and I wanted to pull my hand away from her sweet face, but this was my darling daughter... my flesh and blood. Surely...

"Just like Momma in every way," Abitha whispered, with a look in her eyes that was far beyond her years.

She turned my hand and nipped the inside of my wrist with her pearly white teeth, and my world went black.

Chapter 1: Colonial Unrest

I t was September 12th, 1984, and I, Rachel Cara Anam, was turning eighteen.

Eighteen was a big deal. Like every kid, I had looked forward to becoming an adult for years. I had imagined a wild college party with hundreds of friends on my day. My big day! It should have been so exciting. It should have been awesome.

Should have, so sad, too bad.

Who cares.

My eighteenth was a life marker for failure. I was single, still hadn't found a way to get to college, and I didn't have the kinds of friends who throw birthday parties. My dead-beat dad was perpetually absent, and my mother was locked up for life in the local loony bin.

I learned the hard way that life doesn't always turn out the way you'd want. The important thing is to keep trying to make it go your way. So, family or not, I was still going to party because this birthday was a victory of sorts. I could have cut out of this shitty life long ago, but I'd stuck it out, and surely that was worth a slice of cake. Or a warm beer.

I HAD STARTED DRINKING early in the Albion Hotel, a dark, local dive that squatted in the shadow of the most magnificent church in Guelph. I liked it there because the bar only had two windows, which created the perfect dim atmosphere for guilt-free, day-drinking and best of all, the bartender never checked ID for legal drinking age.

It only took me 'til six to burn through the last of my birthday budget. I tried not to wallow in self-pity at being out of booze cash, but the disturbing lyrics of Floyd's "The Final Cut" pressed out of the neon jukebox and fed my dark thoughts.

I needed a distraction and cast a look around the pub. It was the first time I noticed the people sharing my space since I'd arrived. A few men were perched on time-scarred, wooden stools along the bar, regulars by the look of their defeated posture. Experience had taught me men are cheap and easy, so it wouldn't take much to get a free beer. Normally.

Problem was, I had made a birthday resolution to not have sex or engage in any physical interactions or altercations with members of the male gender for one week. Sounds a little uptight, but those are the exact words Patrick used before pressuring me to agree.

Patrick tricked me into agreeing, really. He knows how much I want to get better and go to college. He felt it would be a helpful part of my therapy to swear off men for a week. He seemed to think drying out the well so to speak, would almost cure me. That seemed a little farfetched, considering my psychiatrist thought I was certifiably crazy, but hope is a valiant chum.

I needed all the help I could get, even if it was from my mother's male nurse at the Homeward Asylum. Of course, while I was making this pledge, I was wondering if I could bend Patrick's holier-than-thou attitude and get one last screw in before day one started. It was a useless thought. Patrick never responded to my flirting. He was a stickler for keeping it clean between us.

He did slip in fifty bucks to sweeten the deal, with a promise of another fifty at the end of the seven days. I thought the whole thing was a gas until I drank away my first half of the bribe. It was a stupid thing to do—to give my word. I'm no saint, but I have a few codes I live by and keeping my word is one of them.

TODAY WAS DAY ONE OF my sex-free resolution, which meant the only option left for free booze was to call up my friend, Lene. I slipped my fingers into the front pocket of my skin-tight jeans and touched the dime I always kept there.

Every girl carried the just-in-case-you-need-to-phone-home dime, because every mother put it in their pocket. I kept mine in case I wanted to call the asylum.

I left the dime where it was. Better not to use my emergency coin. I'd just wait to see how the night would unfold here at my favourite drinking hole. The old bar generally didn't provide a solution to my problems. It just provided beer. But that can be enough for some girls.

"Cheers to that," I said aloud and tipped up my last brewskie, just to make sure it was empty.

Trying to look flush with cash, I held up my hand until the bartender caught my eye and gave a sullen nod. I grabbed a wrinkled newspaper from a nearby table. Before I had read halfway through an article about Prime Minister Trudeau retiring, a new beer was placed before me. I reached for it, not taking my eyes from the picture of Pierre and his toothy smile.

"Put it on my tab, Chief."

I tried to sound sure of myself.

"Better to pay up front," the bartender replied, in his slow-paced, gravelly voice.

I looked up past the paper and smiled sweetly at him. "It's my birthday..."

The bartender pushed his tobacco wad deeper into his lower lip, which made his Harley moustache jitter like a mouse on his face. His eyes held no empathy, and I figured I was going to lose this one. To my amazement, he walked away, leaving the beer on the table.

"Imagine that," I said in wonder, realizing I didn't always have to spread my legs to get what I wanted. Things were looking up.

Spurred on by the thought of some better luck, I downed half my beer and leaned back over the newspaper, scanning the pages in the hopes of finding a job, or a classified ad from a Prince looking to sweep me off my feet. The ink-smudged pages began to blur, as I flipped through them at an ever-increasing speed.

"Nothing... nothing... noth-"

A spasm gripped my hand, twisting the newsprint with a loud crinkle. I dropped the page and shook my wrist out. The paper had settled open at an article on Pope John Paul's Canadian tour.

"Oh, how Mommy would love that," I mumbled, while massaging the cramp out of my hand.

My mother's Protestant hatred of Catholics was almost as rabid as her Satan paranoia. I tried to laugh at her ridiculousness, but horrid childhood memories rivaling scenes from Stephen King's *Carrie* choked my tongue.

Yes, I knew how it felt to be dragged by my hair into a cramped, dark closet. I remembered the bite of wooden floors under my knees. I understood only too well what happens to a child's mind when they are forced to believe they are the reason for the unexplainable, that they are an abomination to God, and to the woman who gave them life...

Whoa! I slammed a mental door shut on the thoughts that threatened to sweep my sense away. A quick glance at the men across the room quelled my worry they might have noticed I was slipping down to crazy town. They were busy with their booze and man-talk.

A familiar tug jiggered the fleshy walls of my intestines. Sometimes, I'd get the strangest sensations deep in my guts whenever I got close to any form of zeal, like a church my mother dragged me into, or a Bible waving threateningly at the end of her arm. My childhood had done a number on my stomach as well as my psyche. So, I tried to keep the memories locked up to avoid whatever ulcer-like reactions kicked in when I thought of Mom or God. The two were so intertwined: I couldn't be sure which would cause a reaction.

I put pressure on my stomach with my hand and tried to avoid looking directly at the picture of the white-skinned liaison of God on the table in front of me.

His domed forehead wrinkled under a conical, peaked hat seemed to be pointing at me from the newspaper. According to the article, the Pope was supposed to be a good man, a godly man. I tried to see inside of him, but no matter how I adjusted my head, his benevolent eyes would not meet mine. Still, I was sure I needed to be wary. Why else would my internal alarm be going off at the sight of his black and white image?

If he was a threat, my mind reasoned, having his scent would be useful. I leaned closer to the paper and drew some air in through my flaring nostrils. All I sucked up was the bar's damp-towel reek. So, I pressed my face right to the Pope's picture to capture his spoor. The newsprint felt cool against the end of my nose, yet sniff as I might, there was no odor of flaked skin to be had. Only the sharp oily scent of fresh printer ink filtered in, making my eyes water.

"You're not doing a line of coke, are ya? Cause it's a little obvious right here in the open."

A pair of grey, acid-washed jeans was standing beside my table.

Great. Caught doing something socially unacceptable. Again.

Cloaking my sheepish blush behind a hard-lined mouth, I peered suspiciously at the witness to my madness.

A fresh-faced, man-boy looked down with a hopeful grin. When I didn't respond in kind, he stepped closer to my table. The movement startled a cockroach into a mad scuttle across the disfigured hardwood floor. The jukebox had dropped a new 45, and "Hotel California" added an eerie complement to the bug's flight.

The man-boy said, "Don't worry. No one saw."

"What do you want?"

He shifted his weight to his other foot. "I just wondered..."

I raised my eyebrows, urging him to finish his sentence.

"I've seen you..." he swallowed and started again. "I work at the Homeward. I'm a part-time janitor there."

My mouth formed a little "O", but I didn't say anything. I listened carefully to the Eagles' lyrics about willing prisoners.

He cast his glance at the empty chair beside me three times before he managed the courage to ask, "Can I sit?"

"No."

The hand reaching for the chair stopped in mid-air. His other hand held a bundle of sharp instruments sporting multi-coloured feathers. He gripped the darts in his thin fingers, as if hoping they could replace his lack of plumage and win him a mate.

The sharp points, and the Eagle's lyrics fused with my reality.

"Hoping to kill the beast?" I whispered.

"What?"

A confused frown crossed his brow, reflecting the age-lines waving across the Pope's forehead. The urge to catch John Paul's scent tugged away at my self-control.

He rubbed his palm on his thigh and tried again.

"So, like I said, I know your mom." His voice had dropped with his confidence.

I opened my hands and shook my head as if trying to understand why this was relevant.

Yet, I was worried he might tell me, 'Your mom howls like a banshee when the moon is full'. Or he might say something like, 'Your mom whips her food trays at the wall when anyone mentions your name' or worst of all 'Your mom thinks you're the devil's spawn, and she'd love another chance at killing you.'

Yeah, I didn't need this crap. "Get bent."

He moved his head from side to side, slowly. "No, listen, I have a note from your mom."

"What?" I sat up straighter and looked at him with disbelief.

"Your mom." He dug in his back pocket and pulled out a piece of paper that looked like it had been used as sandpaper. "She asked me to find you."

I stared at the paper held in his narrow-tipped trembling fingers and set my teeth on edge.

It was probably a bullshit sermon where she would quote scriptures about Jesus casting demons out of pigs. Hell, what else could it be? It certainly wouldn't be words of love or a short sentence about regretting not being there for me... no, not from my mother.

I wanted to tell him to shove the paper where the sun don't shine. I wanted to get up and leave, and never think about the note again. But the truth was my eyes were filling up with tears because it was my birthday, and my mom had sent me a letter.

"Drop it on the table," I rasped.

He did.

"Now, go away."

He hesitated, and I know he wanted to use the note to connect with me, maybe get a little on the side. He was a man, after all.

My face stiffened into a granite-like expression. The climbing strains of the song led up to his defeat. He sighed and trudged back to his bar stool.

I watched him, making sure he didn't turn back. The other men in the room offered him sympathetic looks as he returned to his side of the bar.

THE CREASED, YELLOW foolscap note had landed on the Pope's picture, creating a tent above his nose. Cautiously, I extended my nails towards it. Touching the edge of the fold with a timid fingertip, I hesitated.

My heart was bursting with hope. Hope that my mom had come through. My hand started to shake, causing my finger to tap against the letter.

What would she have to say to me, anyway? Happy Birthday? Birthdays weren't celebrated in my house. Hell, they were mourned. Every year I turned older, my mother lost a little more of her mind. It was as if my aging drove her into a freak-out of religious zeal.

A burst of mocking laughter from across the room drew my mind from the hurtful memories.

At the bar, a fat-handed guy wearing a red plaid Muskoka dinner jacket leaned back on his elbows and spoke loudly enough for me to hear.

"That's not how you bag an ice queen, pup."

He was speaking to my dejected cast-off, but his red-rimmed eyes were boring into mine from across the room. His accent gave him away as American.

"You gotta let her think she's in control. Let her believe she's the boss," he said.

I never took my eyes from him as I picked up the note, folded it carefully, and shoved it into my jean pocket.

A few of the other men murmured in agreement. The American's beer was up, and he was sucking on the bottle to wet his lips for his next blasphemy. Unwrapping a fat finger from his beer bottle, he pointed up at a faded portrait of Queen Victoria hanging crookedly on the wood paneling above the bar.

"See that bitch?"

Queen Vic looked regally down her nose at the late afternoon drunks in the room.

His friend joined in with a mocking tone, "Careful Donald, Canadians still kiss up to the Monarchy."

Donald stumbled as he slipped off the stool and pushed his fat belly out into the open space between the tables and the bar seats.

I pushed my right foot up onto my toes to release the uneasy energy that was building inside of me.

"Bossiest bitch queen that ever lived, that one." He sauntered over to the cheap framed print and stood beneath it. "But we showed you royal bastards. You thought us Bostonians were toasting your tax-sucking rule with that backwater you call tea."

His friend laughed nervously.

I decided I should also get Donald's scent.

He left Queen Victoria's regal contemplation and sauntered none-too-steadily in my direction. The creases at the corners of his eyes deepened as he squinted at me with intent.

I stopped shaking my leg, flattening my foot against the floor in case I had to stand up quickly.

"These ice queens, they're just dying to melt. All ya gotta do is burn a little hole in their tender parts."

I needed to draw Donald a bit closer if I was going to sniff him without being noticed, and I knew exactly what would egg him on.

I raised one eyebrow, "Well if it isn't Yankie Doodle Dandy come to preach the American way."

"If it wasn't for America, there wouldn't be a Canada, you cu...."

"Whoa!" Donald's friend interjected, with a nervous laugh. "I think we're done here. Time to head out, Bud."

Man-boy stood up, took a step forward and then one back, his eyes riveted on the backs of the men.

"Oh no," I said, "Please don't go. I'd love to hear more about that War in 1812 you lost."

Donald's face mottled up with reddish blotches, and I released a little bravado on a fake chuckle. A chair scraped against the floor as another man in the room tossed down a few bills and walked out. Somebody whistled the Spaghetti Western notes to a showdown, *whoo-ah whoo whoo wha.*

Donald stepped forward until his thighs touched my table. He banged his beer down onto the newspaper I'd been reading. My shredded nerves betrayed me, jolting. He leaned over until I could see the chicken pox scar on his crooked nose.

"You ain't no different than us." The hot words filled the air between us.

"How so?" I opened my eyes wide and turned my head to the side as if I was interested in what he had to say.

The table skittered forward away from the pressure of his legs, and he quickly flattened his hand on the table top to steady himself. A smile twitched at the corner of my mouth as the clueless fool smeared his paw print trail around.

Man-boy took three more slow steps my way, and the bartender stepped out from behind the bar.

"You're livin' in the 51st State, bitch. You just don't know it, yet."

I heard the scratch of falling dirt as my Upper Canada Loyalist ancestors rolled over in their graves.

I spoke softly, "My people came from the Southern Colonies with nothing but tar and feathers on their backs." I gave him a little smile. "They walked all the way to Canada to get away from buffoons like you, Donald."

"Why you..." Donny-boy tried to walk through the table to get to me, but his friend grabbed the collar of his jacket and held him steady.

I stayed seated even though every inch of my skin was screaming to stand up and defend myself. I could smell his yeasty breath hanging over my table, but this was only his mouth odor. I wanted his scent.

"Time for you boys to move on."

The bartender looked calm, standing beside Man-boy who was white as a sheet.

"We're going, we're going," his friend tried to say over Donald swearing at me.

They banged rudely into Man-boy on their way out.

He said, "Sorry," automatically and then pressed his lips together to stop any more culturally-triggered apologies.

The door shut behind them.

"I'm sorry, too," I conceded.

"You all right?" The bartender gave me a squinty-eyed look, running his hand down his long moustache.

I tried to soften the tension in my face, "It's Queen Victoria I'm worried about. Now everybody thinks she's responsible for the Boston Tea Party."

The bartender blew some air out though his nose in appreciation of my joke. The excitement was over, and the Albion's homey normality set in. The bartender went back to polishing glasses in the late afternoon sun streaming through the window above the door. The other customers went back to staring dejectedly into their foamy beers, and Queen Victoria continued to survey the Colonies with her heavy-lidded gaze.

Everyone except Man-boy. He was standing at the end of the table gazing wistfully at me, waiting for a reward for his gallant, if failed, attempts to intervene on my behalf. An impulse to crush his self-esteem, to make him pay for being the same gender as Donald, tempted me.

But that was my bad side, and I wanted to stop listening to my bad impulses. My psychiatrist, Dr. Casbus said I shouldn't be cruel to others, no matter how much I'd been hurt.

"Thanks for having my back," I offered, generously.

He grinned and put his hand on the chair beside me, making me immediately regret playing nice. I quickly hooked my biker boot around the rung and held the chair from being pulled away from the table.

His eyes clouded over. "Does this mean I won't get a chance to burn a hole in your tender parts?"

I let loose a bark of a laugh.

"Pretty much."

MAN-BOY WASN'T THE only one who'd changed from the exchange. I was jacked up with a purpose, and Donald kept flashing in my mind as the mark.

I'd had weird impulses before. It was all part of my 'crazy'. But tonight, it seemed to be in overdrive. I wanted to race out the door and hunt Donald down and finish what we'd started. My hand brushed the pocket of my jacket, fingering the reassuring bulge of my Rambo commando knife. The idea of a fight set my heart racing, and I had to shut my mouth to avoid panting aloud in anticipation.

Chapter 2: The Lure of Donald

I might have looked a little subdued after the ruckus, for my head was down, a riot of blonde curls shielding my face.

The truth was, I was studying the spot where Donald had laid his meaty paw. Despite my resolution to be good, I couldn't help feeling tempted by his big, greasy handprint. I had to touch it.

Dragging the back of my hand along the varnished tabletop, the cracks in my knuckles picked up the American's oily smear like little skin shovels.

It would take just one sniff of my hand, and Donald's scent would be imprinted on my mind, forever. It was a heady thought, but I forced myself not to inhale. Not yet. I would keep his scent nestled there, in between the dry folds of my skin, in case I decided he and I needed to get up close and personal.

Prolonging the excitement recalled a long-ago Christmas and a forgotten present I had discovered under the tree the next morning. That kind of gift can make the feeling of Christmas last forever, if you can just resist opening it.

I used my left hand to raise my beer, which was almost empty, same as my pockets, but not my future. Now, thanks to Donald, my future showed promise. He was only one sniff away. Maybe he had gone to the King Eddie to continue drinking. No, no, a man like him would turn left and head to the Chooch to watch women shed their clothes for his disdain. Yes, that was the man who was Donald.

The jukebox clicked as it changed records, and Cindi Lauper screeched her song "Girls Just Wanna Have Fun". The notes startled away my inner conversation. I had been disconnected from reality, and now was worried I had been talking out loud about what I would do to the American.

A glance at the other drinkers proved I had kept my thoughts to myself. The show was over. I needed to stop obsessing.

DURING MY COUNSELLING treatments, Dr. Casbus had said obsessing was not healthy. So instead of mentally tracking Donald in my mind, I thought about turning eighteen, and how I was going to change my life.

It had been five years since I'd started working with the good Doctor on my crazy impulses. I mean I'd always tried to act normal, but now with the doc explaining my mental state, I knew what I was up against. And, it wasn't pretty. If anything, sometimes I seemed worse, but the drinking kept most of my weirdness tamped down.

Donald popped into my head again.

I randomly thought of pineapples and dropped my right hand onto my lap to make sure I didn't accidently raise it to my face. Once I got his scent it would be ten times as hard not to rush out the door, turn my face to the wind, and wait for his unmistakable odor to lead the way.

The ability to track was what I called my sixth sense and it was freaky. I didn't use it... well maybe I had stalked a few guys in the past, but really, I didn't 'track' people. Besides, Dr. Casbus had said it was all part of my delusions. He said I couldn't track.

Only I could. It would take all of ten minutes to find Donald, if he was walking. If he'd gotten into a car, it would take longer. I'd still be able to connect him to the scent of whatever tires rolled his getaway vehicle down the road. It would just be a longer walk.

My eyes were drawn back to my hand that was now resting on the table. The cracks in my knuckle undulated like Hawaiian grass skirts, welcoming me to lean over and press my nose against my skin. The more I considered just letting go and taking a sniff, the more excited I got.

Shaking free of the temptation, I said out loud, "This is nuts".

I wasn't the only one surprised by my outburst.

The bartender raised one bushy eyebrow. I resisted the urge to wipe away the drop of sweat that was rolling down my temple. Looking beyond the bartender, my eyes locked onto the counter at the spot where Donald had been leaning.

A shiver of anticipation coursed through my body. I was bent on having a go—a hard-hitting, bloodletting sexy, thrilling all-out fight. I could feel it heating up my skin, streaming through my veins, burning in my guts. The possibility of a dangerous encounter egged on my wildly thumping heart.

I jumped up, knocking the table with my knees. It rocked, and a few heads turned.

"You're cut off," someone said amid laughs, while I steadied my beer.

Weaving my way in between the empty tables, I slipped through the open doorway that led to the other section of the bar where the washroom was. My legs felt stiff, and with each step, it seemed I was slowing down, each stride shorter, until I was moving with a wooden-legged gait. Thankfully, no one sat on this side of the bar to witness my bizarre movements.

I half fell into the washroom. The door hit the wall and bounced back at my face. I put my hand up to stop it before I was struck, and there it was—my scent-slathered knuckle right in front of my nose. I stopped breathing.

I pushed away from the impulse to snort Donald, staggered to the sink and leaned against the counter. The rusty faucet was cold and damp beneath my hand. It screeched out a complaint as I twisted it.

The water rushed out of the lime-plugged tap, gushing all over the stained counter. Drops sprayed my jeans, plastering the rough material to my skin. I slapped at the soap dispenser. It was empty.

"Shit!"

My mind betrayed me, saying it was an omen, convincing me I was meant to have Donald, not wash him down the drain.

My arm played dead, resting heavily against my side. I had a close relationship with the muscles that locked the elbow and the shoulder, knew them intimately after living with my mother. But, I wasn't working these muscles. I was only in control of half of my body and the other half seemed to have a mind of its own.

Staying alert in case Donald's scent slyly delivered itself to my nostrils, I grabbed my right wrist and tried to force my hand under the water. It was like grabbing a stranger by the arm.

After the initial shock, I went back to tugging with effort. A quick twist of my body forced my right shoulder over the sink. At the first touch of the water on my fingertips, the resistance in my arm let go and my shoulder slumped.

Relieved, I scrubbed my knuckle until it was red and sore and rubbed both hands under the rushing water to be sure the essence of Donald was washed down the drain and into the sewage system where it belonged.

SHUTTING OFF THE TAP, I leaned my forehead against the glass. It felt cool on my feverish skin.

"What the hell." My breath fogged the mirror.

I pulled back to look at my reflection. My face was flushed under my tan, my cheeks glowing from the excitement as if I'd just been wrestling. But who had I been fighting against?

The permanent frown line between my winged eyebrows deepened as I looked closer.

"What is going on with you?" I asked myself.

Buried in the reflection of my brown, almond-shaped eyes a shadow flickered. I blinked, and it was gone.

Turning my arm to the side, I watched with relief as this time my arm responded, doing as I wanted. Digging a paper towel out of the rusty metal holder, I scrubbed at my knuckle again, just in case.

LOSING CONTROL OF MY body parts was new, and for the first time in a long time, I needed someone to talk to. But who could I trust with a secret so damning it could be used to put me away?

I was struck with a sentimental yearning for my mom. I embraced it for a moment, before brushing it roughly away.

If I were to tell my mother what had just happened, she would blame me for tempting Satan, and she would prescribe days of Bible reading and prayer for atonement. She was the last person I needed to talk to.

But that didn't mean I couldn't read her note, which was still tucked snuggly in my pocket. I slipped the paper out and slowly unfolded it in front of the mirror. My mom's 1950s penmanship flowed across the wrinkled paper with a grace and beauty her disturbed mind could never possess.

"Are you sure you want to do this?" I asked my reflection.

The letter was typical. No "Dear Rachel" at the top, or another term of endearment, just her getting down to business.

I have dreaded this day, since you were born...

Any sentimental feelings I might have felt were shattered by my hostile reaction.

"Happy f'ing birthday," I mumbled, then kept reading.

I know you curse me, I know you do not want to heed my words, but you must. For now, in your eighteenth year, you are ripe, ripe for the legion who wait to...

"Yada yada, blah blah," I skipped past the biblical quotes and paranoid bullshit.

You will be tempted to celebrate.

"No thanks to you."

But you must adorn yourself in modest apparel, with shamefacedness and sobriety. They will come from across the sea to walk among you. They will seek you out, tempt you with the evil ways of the City of Babel. They will seek to raise the familiar within you.

"Or we might get drunk and have a much better time than you're having in your straightjacket, Mom."

Regard them not, for they will defile you.

You must show restraint. You must be attentive. You must resist the lure of whoredom for the daughters will not be forgiven.

"Omigod!" I rolled my eyes and quickly skimmed the rest, longing to find one word of motherly love, like maybe "I'm proud of you" or "I'm sorry I strangled you and left you to raise yourself".

I was ready to crumple it up and walk away from my mother's 'love', but the word "darling" caught my hungry heart.

Remember your lessons, my darling. Remember Job. Now is the time of your trial. Remember God said unto Satan, "Behold, he is in thine hand; but save his life". God will not protect you. He will offer you up, but you must resist. Use the strength I have given you when Satan smites you with sore boils from the sole of your foot unto your crown...

The soft paper gave easily as I crushed it in my hand, choking the string of words into silence.

I tossed the paper into the garbage can. Then fought the temptation to drop a lit match into the garbage to erase the evidence of my mother's disappointment in me. A sharp pain cramped my heart, useless stabs of self-pity. I hammered a fist against my chest and blinked back the hot tears that threatened to spill down my face.

"Who cares!"

It didn't sound convincing. I said it again, in my head, over and over, and drew on anger to push the pain away.

"Who the hell gives a shit!" I barked into the empty washroom, and this time I sounded like myself. Pissed at the world and ready for a fight. Now I could go back out into the bar.

I wet my hands and scrunched them into my hair to pat down my mess of blonde curls. The black and gold case on my fire-engine red lipstick flashed at the mirror, as I twisted it open in my cold fingers. Drawing even higher peaks on my upper lip, I turned my naturally full mouth into a sharp vampish line. A few swipes under my eyes cleared away the smudged eyeliner and mascara, and I was good to go.

The cold metal grips of my Rambo knife kissed my fingers, when I slipped my lipstick back into my pocket. It was a reassuring promise that if life ever got too painful, I always had a way out.

Atlantic Ocean: The Scent of Menses

The great ship rose on the rolling swells, the wood groaning out in protest as the waves pushed against its belly. The sun was up with the wind, the sails catching the brassy rays as they billowed like the white chests of sea birds. The yellow sky sliced a horizon across the deep azure of the sea, inviting the ship forward with astounding beauty.

Despite the scenic allure, all eyes were turned inward to the small section of deck where the women took their walks. Ladies from all classes mixed in this place where social status mattered less than on land. Petite feet in delicate slippers whispered alongside well-worn leather cast-offs from older brothers. The sandy hues of coarse wool swayed alongside the brighter gemstone shades of silk and cotton hems sashaying like polishing rags along the deck boards.

The captain examined his cargo with reserve.

"Women." He scowled and shook his head.

There was a time when a woman would not have been allowed on a seafaring vessel. A time when the mere presence of the finer sex would have tapped the sailors' passions, made volatile by months at sea. There was even a time when it was believed that the scent of a woman's menses would draw up the giant squid from the black depths. Those times of ignorance and superstition were fading in the face of justifiable reasoning.

This captain's merchant ship carried spices from India, brandy from France, and timber from the colonies. Those were the cargoes the captain preferred. But ships had to be repaired, and men had to be paid, and it was the age of human cargo, which brought more profit.

The captain wasn't a slaver. He hadn't sailed to the Dark Continent and traded with tribes selling their captives. No, this ship's human cargo was European and willing.

His callused hands felt the change in the ocean as it pressed against the great ship's rudder, seconds before the lookout in the crow's nest called out, "Land ahoy!"

The ladies' cries of excitement chimed over the strong winds. In disarray, their fluttering across his deck to see their first site of Jamestown further irritated the captain who preferred order above all else.

"First Mate," he spoke over the ship's wooden wheel, knowing John Allington was ever-listening for his command.

"Captain!"

"See that the females are taken below."

His first mate gave a curt nod, though the captain had still not looked at him. "Right away, Captain."

Allington leaned over the quarterdeck and called down to the sailors assigned to the care of the women.

"All passengers to the hold!"

"Aye, aye!" A sailor saluted in an offhand manner.

Changing winds were the captain's forte. He could smell a change in the cool breezes that pushed the crests into white peaks even before the sea responded. When bartering for cargo, he could sense the weakening will of a trader before the man himself knew he would lower the prices on his goods. The captain's senses were as sharp as they ever had been. Change was in the future of his ship. Change brought on by the slave trade. It was a distasteful affair, but for now he would ferry brides to the Southern Colonies, for his ship was fast and clean, and his crew was disciplined.

The captain's musings were disrupted by the image of a lone woman still standing on his main deck, the deck that would soon be crawling with sailors preparing for the journey up James River to Jamestown.

"Allington!" The captain released the wheel to point an accusing finger at the woman.

His first mate looked shocked that there was still a female standing there. "Captain!"

Allington's boots clattered down the quarterdeck stairs as he quickly made his way to the burly sailor standing by the woman's side. The young man's irritation grew as the sailor continued to fail in carrying out his orders, even as he marched towards the two.

The woman stood at ease, her gloved hands folded against the front of the long stomacher above her skirts. Her cap failed to contain the ebony strands of silky hair that escaped to whip about her comely face in the strong wind.

The sailor stepped up to meet Allington. "She refuses to go below deck, sir."

The refusal posed a problem for the first mate. This woman was not a sailor or a soldier to be struck about the head with a cudgel until she did what he wanted.

Allington stepped past the sailor, placing his body between the lady and the captain's view.

"My good lady." He removed his hat and tipped his knee.

She lowered her eyes, her lashes dark against her pale cheeks. "My good sir".

Her accent was unfamiliar to his well-traveled ears, but it mattered not. The women came from all parts of Europe as marriage chattel for the New World. It did not matter where she came from. All that mattered was where she would go, and that was down to where the captain ordered her to.

Satisfied with her demure behaviour, Allington continued. "It is the captain's orders that all ladies retire below deck."

She raised her eyes and Allington was struck at how dark they were. "I understand the captain's reasons, good sir, for this is not my first voyage at sea."

The first mate nodded in acknowledgement of the woman's prior experience. "Then you will retire with the others?"

The sailor moved forward, as if to take her arm.

"No," she said softly, and Allington leaned closer to hear her.

"It is my wish to see with mine own eyes the shore that will be my new home."

Allington was shocked at her disregard for the captain's orders. He blinked and tried to insist, but the words stuck in his throat as the woman's eyes darkened and forced him to consider their depths.

Any concern the first mate might have had for the captain, who was glaring from the quarterdeck, was washed away by the desire to please this woman, a desire greater than any duty he had ever felt in his service on board a ship.

"If it pleases you sir, I would express my wishes to the captain in person."

Dipping his knee, Allington tore himself from the woman's enticing presence to escort her to the wooden stairs that led to where the captain stood, wooden and unyielding.

The captain watched them come on, first, with disbelief that a woman was about to set her tiny boots on his quarterdeck, then with a resigned sense of grudging acceptance of the changes that carrying human cargo would bring.

The iron-spined seahawk did not look at the woman as she moved to stand at his side, preferring instead to gaze out onto the ocean at the waves, which were much more predictable than the female sex.

Arlington hovered behind her, as if afraid she would do something even more drastic than just speak to the captain. But in truth, he only wished to lean closer, perhaps even press his face against the back of her neck.

The woman spoke first. "My apologies for this intrusion on your very important duties, Captain." She paused, and the mainsail flapped at a sudden lull in the wind. "I hope you can find my request to remain topside during our approach to land a reasonable one."

The captain still did not acknowledge her presence. His eyes squinted within the lined leather of his face, watching the shoreline that was his destination, listening to the wind's change as they moved inshore. He made her wait until he was good and ready to speak, and then he released the tone that made men shiver to obey.

"This is my ship, and it is my command that you go below."

Arlington seemed confused as to whether he should nod or not. Instead, he looked down at the shine on the toe of his black boots.

"I understand," the woman said, her voice so soft the captain could barely hear it.

Triumphant, he shifted his eyes beneath his coiling grey eyebrows to observe the woman.

The first thing that struck him was her astounding beauty. Yes, beauty formed by curve of cheek, and colour of lip, but more than that, vital beauty—a glow of vibrancy that pulsed beneath the skin and shouted to the winds "I am alive!"

The second thing that struck him were her eyes. Once the captain had seen a cyclone ripping across the ocean. That's what her eyes reminded him of—deep swirling tunnels of dangerous water threatening to suck him down.

"I understand, sir. Now I say to you, I will remain on the quarterdeck and watch the land come."

To the captain and the first mate, this seemed a most logical request. The captain nodded and looked out across the water, thinking no more about it.

Satisfied, the lady moved to the railing and looked down behind the ship.

The great rudder strained against its hinges as the water swirled, cresting white behind the stern, and pushing them towards her new home.

The people on this ship were pliable like water, and she, hard and unswerving like the rudder could easily sway their will. And as it was on sea, so it would be on land.

Chapter 3: Speak of the Devil

Returning to my table, I pulled the collar of my biker jacket up to make myself appear relaxed and uncaring. I held the casual James Dean pose for fifteen minutes, while I finished my beer. Had Man-boy read my mother's note?

She was wacked and everything she said and did was crazy. I knew this, but I had so little from her, I couldn't completely disregard her words. Mom had written that a temptation would come from "across the sea". The States was only over the border, but still I wondered if Donald was the temptation. The one who would release my inner "familiar". And what the hell was that anyways? The only thing he had released in me, so far, was a little patriotic anger.

I stopped trying to make sense of my mother's lunacy and forced my attention back to the newspaper article about the Pope's tour that was still splayed out on my table. The man was the image of benevolence, his eyes reflecting unconditional love. His mouth set in the position of forgiveness. John Paul II held his right hand up to the crowd, palm out. It was meant to be an embrace, an acceptance of those gathered to view his holy presence. Yet gripped in the Pope's other hand was Christ, strung out like sinewy taffy along a staff-like cross. It was a cruel icon that drew my mind from my own problems. Christ's own father had allowed the Romans to stake him, when he could have easily wiped them out. I never understood the whole "sacrifice for the people" thing. To me, Christ's suffering seemed unnecessary and wasted.

At that bold thought, my heart kicked up a notch, and a truant string of words spewed out of my mouth like verbal vomit.

"You cain string up your own image but you cain nevah erase your own sin."

I slapped my hand to my mouth to stop the words, for though the vocal cords were mine, the tune being played on them did not belong to me. The voice I had spoken in had a slick and silky Southern accent.

Oh, I should never have mentioned those Southern ancestors in my argument with Donald. For whenever I did, it was like speaking of the devil, and now I was going to see Satan's tail. I had to get the hell home.

I jumped up, almost tripping over my chair, and half turned to the door. Unexpectedly, it burst open, and I was struck by the final rays of the setting sun. I threw my elbow up over my face and shrieked in surprise as the blinding light pierced my eyes.

The sound of laughter and conversations filtered in behind my raised elbow. The after-dinner crowd were coming in. Normal sounds. Normal people. They didn't notice me, even though I was not acting normal.

The exit was blocked, so I turned and headed into the darker back room. My eyes had not adjusted from that initial sunburst, and half-blinded, I stubbed my toe and almost fell into some empty chairs.

"You're definitely cut off," taunted the same voice.

Followed by the bartender's gentle order, "Leave her be."

SUPPORTING MYSELF WITH my hand on the back of a chair, I stopped and got my bearings. The back room shimmered as if heat was rising from the floor. I rubbed my face, but it didn't do any good. This had nothing to do with my eyes. This was an 'episode'. I had to get out of sight.

I crossed through the connecting doorway, weaving like a drunkard between the tables to collapse into a chair, my back against the far wall.

Thankfully, no do-gooder had followed to see if I was okay. Granted only a few seconds of relief, my stomach lurched as the walls shifted against their frames, and then mushroomed out, distorting the space within.

A cramp in my guts tightened into a knot as the room pulled in at the middle, the furnishings squeezing into new positions like organs under a corset. Another loop-de-loo tried to spill my ingested beer onto the floor, but I gulped back the rising bile.

Gripping the table with my fingers, I watched my fingertips turn white as they grasped for grounding.

The shrinking of space within the room forced the air to wheeze out, leaving behind a draw that tugged like a black vacuum. I could not move my arms, could not call out, as much as I wanted to scream at the top of my lungs for help.

The draw sucked deeper and deeper tunneling into a black hole. I had to stop falling, but all I had were visuals—pictures to replace action. So, I imagined myself a lizard with a wide fringe of neck skin. As soon as the image was clear, I flicked my tail and flailed my legs. My bone fan burst open with the sound of a web umbrella springing into place. The sharp edges caught, and a jarring drag shuddered through my jaw. I hung, suspended for a few seconds as the image held me at the edge of the abyss. Suddenly, reality slapped back, and I understood I had no lizard's jaw, no clawed feet to dangle.

Cold threads of dismay wove diagonally through my mind shattering the image of the lizard into a thousand sharp-edged pieces. An echo of shattering glass tipped me over into that ever-waiting darkness.

The feeling of falling, spinning end over end, shredded at my sanity like claws on silk. The more I tried to hold onto what was real, the more frayed I became. Then I did what I always did to survive. I invoked my anger.

Rallying my will with curses, I silently charged myself to action, because there was no damn way I was going to lose it in my favourite drinking hole.

Get control, bitch!

"Holy gloom and doom," a voice spoke from the murkiness.

I clutched the sound wisps, manipulating them like cat-in-the-cradle strings until a fractured sense of my friend, Lene, materialized in front of me. I concentrated on her presence, recalling the olive shade of her skin, the metal shine of the filling in her back, left molar.

Gradually, her jet-black hair materialized, draped like an oiled fringe over a pale gold, reflective, half jacket.

She slipped away from me, impossible to hold for there were no facial features, no body, no backdrop to cling to.

I tried to focus on the blank, flat oval where her high cheekbones should have been.

Climb out of it! I demanded of myself.

Her perfume caressed my nostrils, and my mind decoded the scent. The translation ruffled the layers of time and place, spinning them away before they buried me.

Climb!

The Albion's wooden chairs popped, one-by-one through the negative space like stars being birthed in a new universe.

With a sense of gratitude that washed my eyes with hot tears, I saw Lene standing beside my table. A normal teenager in a normal world—everything I wanted to be.

She surveyed the bar. Conscious of the seconds passing since she had spoken, I knew time was stretching thin between her greeting and my expected response. She hung her shimmering jacket on a chair, while I licked my parched lips and worked at acting sane. I hoped to hell I wasn't going to speak with a Southern accent.

My voice split as I tested it. "H—ey."

"What's crackalackin'?" She grinned in her naughty way, giving off a golden, party energy. I let it flow over the darkness tugging at me.

Time ticked on, and I knew I should say something else.

"Done work?" I asked, puffing out the words as if I'd been running.

"Yeppers."

I clamped my mouth shut and silently counted to four, while drawing a slow breath in through my nose. I could do this. I'd had years of last minute, pulling-it-together practice from the many times Family and Children's Services had launched a surprise visit on our home. Thankfully, Lene was naturally self-absorbed and didn't notice I was struggling

I assumed a pose of nonchalance as the sweat cooled on my forehead.

She dropped her purse onto the table with a loud thump. Slipping a hand in past the open clasp, she pulled out three rolls of quarters wrapped tightly in brown paper. She wanted me to ask about her tips, so I did.

"How much tonight?"

"Fifty," she grinned. "I'm buying!" She pulled out another two rolls.

"Uhhh..."

I wanted to say I was going to go home, but a bead of sweat ran down to the fold in my eyelid and started to slip sideways into the corner of my eye. I fluttered my lashes, trying to disburse the salty burn.

"What are you drinking?" she asked, noticing the absence of a bottle on the table.

"Oh... I'm out."

Beneath the table, I twisted my hands, rubbing the numbness out of them.

"Didn't dip into your college fund, I hope?" Lene asked.

"You know the story. My paycheque was sucked up by rent. Nothing left over."

I wasn't about to tell her I had fifty bucks coming to me if I followed my resolution and kept my legs shut for seven days.

"You need a better job than that corner store shit."

"It won't last." My jobs never did.

She sighed. "Well don't worry. Like I said I'm buying."

I tilted my head to one side and then the other, cracking the tension out of my neck. The idea of getting good and drunk was tempting enough to forgive her comment about my job.

"But let's not drink here." She tossed her hair back. "There's no action, we should split."

If we moved to a busier bar, I'd be surrounded by people, and that would make it feel safer. But I wasn't sure what the limits of my sanity were, or how safe others would be around me. My 'crazy' had already gone beyond anything I'd experienced before, and I'd just had all the action I could take, but I wasn't about to confess my madness to my best friend. Everyone was probably safer if I stayed right where I was, in a half-empty pub.

Jerking my chin at Man-boy who was just visible on his stool through the open doorway, I asked, "What about mamma's boy, over there?"

Lene turned around in her chair to stare.

She dismissed him by delivering her verdict, "Wounded".

"Virgin," I countered, trying to make him sound more interesting so she'd stay.

"Not even!"

"Even!"

"Woun-ded!"

She was sticking to it.

I knew Man-boy was a virgin. When he had entered the bar, earlier, the light behind him through the open door had cast his shadow forward onto the hardwood floor, and it had been white as snow. That's why I called him Man-boy.

This was my seventh sense, and I didn't question it. I was used to reading people by the colours they laid out before them on the ground. But, it wasn't worth an argument.

"Okay, Lene. You win. He was wounded by my rejection an hour ago."

She let out a joyous laugh, and my stomach pitched as I joined in. I choked it off with a cough.

"I'll be right back." Lene grabbed a roll of quarters and left to order our beers.

Suddenly afraid to be alone, I squeaked, "Don't leave...", then shut my trap before she could hear me.

My eyes roved the empty room, the fear of slipping away again, pebbling my skin.

A burst of male laughter carried from the other side of the bar where she had disappeared.

I ran my tongue over my dry lips. I was in control for the moment, but I wasn't sure how stable I was. Calling my shrink would probably be best.

I slipped out of my seat and hurried to the pay phone that was screwed into the wall by the men's room. I dragged the handset to my face, ignoring the grating shriek of the phone's steel-wrapped cord as it scraped against the metal privacy edge. Digging out my emergency dime, I tried to get it into the slot, but my hand was shaking so much, I fumbled and almost dropped it. A few more tries and it finally clanked through the metal guts of the phone. I punched the square zero button with Donald's knuckle, and tried to ignore the smell of stale beer on the plastic mouthpiece.

A nasally voice answered my call with, "Operator."

"This is an emergency..." My words poured out. "I need to speak to Doctor Casbus at the Homeward Asylum."

"We have a new service, which requires you to dial 411 for phone numbers."

Lene walked back into the room, and I adjusted my expression, waving at her from the phone booth. She sat down and checked under her nails.

Lowering my voice, I cupped my hand around the receiver.

"But, I just used my only dime, lady."

"Well, that's *your* problem, isn't it?" The operator hissed.

I pulled the phone handset back and frowned at it. She sounded suspiciously like the TV comedian, Lily Tomlin.

"What did you say?"

Dead air sucked at my ear.

"And it's not your only problem!" The words were garbled as if her mouth was full of marbles. "Is it?"

Lene met my eyes from across the room. She lifted her eyebrows. I gave her a reassuring smile and turned my back to the room, hunching over the phone.

"Listen, bitch..."

"You need to hold onto yourself," the voice snickered, and another voice joined in, snorting in perfect synchrony.

The hairs on the back of my neck stood up.

"Only you have nothing to hold onto," they sang out, their shared tone rising to a pitch of excitement. "You don't know yourself..."

I sucked in a trembling breath.

"...and you can't hold on to what you don't know."

I was immobilized with fear. The breathing on the other end became more heated until they were panting out ragged masculine grunts. The voices sounded in pain, then a drawn out, orgasmic moan wriggled through the ear piece.

I yanked the phone away from my face and slammed it down as Lene half stood.

Shaking my head, I held up my hand like the Pope.

"Is it your mom?" she asked, before I reached the table.

"No," I stopped myself from grimacing. "Thanks for the drink." I tipped up the bottle and guzzled.

She watched me, her eyes darting from my face to the phone.

"Tell me what's going on."

I conjured a lie as I wiped my mouth with the back of my hand. "Oh, the phone rang. I was stupid enough to answer."

"Get real!" Her eyes sparkled. "Who was it?"

"Fffff, I don't know. Some creep jerking off."

I sat down slowly, shifting my chair around to avoid her eyes.

"Gross!" She laughed, and I joined in, only I sounded like a hyena on speed.

"Yeah, totally gag me."

"Took you long enough to hang up," she teased.

"Who am I to deny a guy his satisfaction?"

I tipped my beer again, trying to drown out the urge to cry. My teeth chattered against the bottle. I needed to leave, but I was too afraid to go home alone.

Lene's laughter petered out.

Another guzzle on my beer, and a welcomed buzz chased my nerves away.

She was staring at me. A weird little silence settled in place between us. Lene picked at one of the coin rolls with a blue painted fingernail. I couldn't for the life of me think of anything to say.

She finally spoke, "I'm leaving Reg".

"What?" I tried to focus on her words.

"I said," she stopped to swallow, "I'm leaving him."

"For real?"

She didn't answer.

I tried to read her eyes, but she wouldn't lift her gaze from the coin roll. I didn't want to shock her out of this decision, so I adopted a bored look and asked, "What brought this on?"

"Oh, you know. He's a jerk."

I nodded slowly. Reg was a jerk. A jerk who left bruises on her body, a jerk who stole her beautiful light and replaced it with tears. A jerk who had somehow won her heart and then worked hard to rip it from her rib cage on a daily basis.

The idea of her saving herself was tempting me to jump into her problems with both feet, but Lene had "left" him before. And seriously, I had my own life to deal with. I couldn't get too jacked up about her relationship woes.

"Tomorrow's Saturday." She took out a smoke and offered me one. "Are you going to visit your mom?"

"Shit, yeah."

Popping the cigarette between my lips, I leaned forward to touch the end to her lighter flame. I sucked in a double lungful.

I was definitely going to visit, but it wasn't my mother I needed to see... it was her doctor. Sure, I could ask her about the yellow foolscap note she'd sent with Man-boy, but seriously, she'd been warning about demons and familiars and had been cursing my existence since before I could remember. Nothing new there.

After tonight, after the way things had gone before Lene showed up, my arm resisting the washing under the tap, the whole room disappearing into a black hole, and the voice on the phone, I needed to talk to Dr. Casbus. I needed help to be normal. I'd even be willing to take those pills he was always pushing, just so I could live my life without all this bullshit.

I also needed to see him, because until I did, my mother's Satanic theories were front and centre in my mind. Thinking about going home to an empty apartment without his reassurance was terrifying. I needed the good doctor to share his scientific theories and analyze me back into a sense of calm.

"I have an idea." My smile felt forced. "Why don't we celebrate your new single status with an all-nighter?"

Lene's face brightened, as I'm sure, she considered all the naughty business we could get up to. She raised her hand to order another round.

Jamestown: The Predator's Carnal Rule

C rowds of eager men had poured out of the colony's log gates and gathered on the single dock when the tall sails of the ship were first sighted. They knew on board was the bride pool and the men would get to choose a wife from the passengers. After the initial cheers of greeting, which included excited hat waving, a hushed anxiety travelled through the crowd, subduing the fellows as they waited for the women to disembark.

The first boot peeking from beneath a skirt touched the deck, and with that first woman's appearance, all nervousness fled in the face of excitement.

Few men stood alone, for how can one truly assess the value of property without another to share thoughts with? As the female passengers walked unsteadily down the ramp to the dock, the men discussed the positive attributes of each.

Once all were ashore, the women were greeted by the town's mayor, who generously gave them one night on shore to freshen up, followed by an ultimatum that they should choose a husband on the morrow or return to England on the ship they had just exited. Apparently, there was no place in Jamestown for single women who had no family to care for them.

It was not easy for the ladies to be faced with such quick decision-making after a sea voyage that had lasted almost five months. Some had found the journey agonizing and were shadows of their former selves, having lost weight due to sickness and despair. Others had started as shadows, taken from the gallows, the pubs, the alleyways, where they had plied their bodies for half-pennies or a meal to get them through to the next day. These were used to suffering and had found ways to get extra rations from the sailors to keep them fed. Some of the women had come from farms, unwed daughters whose arms were strong from milking and harvesting, women with the knowledge to make candles, to spin wool and work a loom—all skills needed in Jamestown.

And then there was She, the one who in twenty weeks had never shared her name. This one plainly had never milked a cow nor sold her body to survive. She wore fine gloves and her bonnet was trimmed with the most intricate lace. Not unnoticed by the others, her skirt hems had been clean when she'd first climbed the gangplank to the ship. Due to her strange accent, which was not English, not French, and certainly not German, some of the ladies surmised She might be a gypsy who had found her fortune, perhaps as the paramour of some wealthy gentleman.

There were many suppositions, and much time in which to debate these ideas among themselves throughout the long, arduous journey. The She walked like a queen with her head held high, and the grace of her movements was beyond compare. Her poise was one argument stated many times against the gypsy theory. Yes, She had been the topic of late night whisperings.

And now on land months later, this She was looking peaked, her cheekbones pressing sharper than before, but it was not from the continuous upheaval of the ship upon the waves. Packed within the dark hold with the others, She had tried to keep the scent of their bodies out of her lungs. No, not the smell of their sweat, nor the piss, and shit, and puke, but those other scents of ligaments and marrow, blood and bone.

She had also used much energy in trying to close out the noise of their thoughts, tried to ignore her growing awareness of their dreams and hopes, for in that way lay compassion, and one should never feel compassion for prey.

Even knowing this carnal rule could not help her, for the close quarters had overwhelmed the She who could sense deeper than the others. Yes, she shared their ability to walk on two legs, but that is where she parted ways as an enlightened being with a dozen more senses to draw upon, a dozen more centuries to remember, and a dozen more reasons why she could not reveal who and what she was.

Too long, too close, too immersed and rendered impotent by the boundary of the sea to take her place among them as huntress, for were she found out, there would have been nowhere to run.

Powerless to cull the herd, and restore her failing energies, she had resorted to acquiring a companion from among the sailors. It was easily done. The will of a rigging-crawler is weak. Weakened by a lifetime of taking orders aboard a ship. The sailor she chose bent willingly to her influence, so willing it was most unsatisfying to the She who preferred pursuit, and peril, and the possibility of failure, to the sloth of drawing sustenance from the eager.

Having to keep her sailor alive, she could only sip as if partaking of a rich brew of fermented fruit. The curbing of her appetite throughout the trip had taken its toll on the regeneration of her milky skin cells, but not on her spirit.

Here in this new land, she planned to build a better life for herself. She had plotted to get as far from the clutches of folktales and superstition chasers as she could. For it was these tale bearers who had tried and almost succeeded in eradicating her kind from the plentiful pastures of Eastern Europe. The She had one plan for the Jamestown colony and that was to survive.

THE NEXT MORNING, AFTER the ship's arrival, the women rose and tried to tidy their appearance before meeting the men who had once again congregated in the fort's common area. The excited rumbling of the men's voices filtered through the town hall's open windows, lighting little wicks of nervous energy in the women's bellies.

"Come quick!" One of the more enthusiastic girls gestured the others over to the heavy curtains that draped the ripple-glass windows. The windows looked out over the common outdoor area built on the inside of the fort.

In the muddy area below, the men of Jamestown gathered. Their excitement was obvious in the way they greeted each other, the rapid pumping of arms and the boisterous slapping of backs. Heads nodded as they conversed and waited to mingle with the ladies who would soon be their help mates.

These men had pioneer spirits and courage. They had travelled to an unknown land to make a new life for themselves in a country where even the climate could kill.

When these adventurers had first arrived, trade had been established with the Powhatans. Then the fort had been built. Then another, after the Indian raids. Then, the men of God came, and disease came, and the first two women, followed by families, and then winter. Cold, deadly winter followed by four years of Indian wars, and the hollow ache of starvation. Still, year after year, the settlement had survived and one year after the ship, *The White Lion,* brought the first black people, the settlement was thought safe for women—European women. Wives!

It was a glorious day, for now each hard-working man could claim his bounty in female flesh. Of course, there would be opportunities to talk to a woman before making a life-binding decision, and there would be a celebration meal, ale and, no doubt, a dance.

The women peeking from behind the curtains had similar thoughts of how the day would play out. They, too, exclaimed at the possibilities below, and shared comments on the men who came in every size, shape, and age. They cheerfully bantered, while worry twirled in their corseted bellies. None wanted to be unchosen. None wanted to be the last chosen. None wanted to make a bad choice.

Out of all ninety women, not one was more beautiful, more alluring, or more sure of herself than She. There was no doubt in her mind or in the minds of the others that first pick of the men would be hers.

Unlike the others, She wasn't choosing a husband. She already had one. She was choosing a male specimen intellectually and physically worthy to plant his seed in her belly. This was how she would survive on this northern continent. She needed to continue her line of daughters—two legged walkers, vessels to house her eternal light. Through their lives, She would attain her immortality.

But first, She must find a worthy man.

Chapter 4: Attempted Escapes

I didn't say any more about Lene's break-up with the abusive jerk-boyfriend, because a hot looking guy approached our side of the bar and distracted her. I eyed him warily, not ready to trust anything after the night's macabre events.

"Hey, lookie here." Lene's eyes sparkled with interest as she took in his glossy brown hair and wholesome looks.

I was more interested in his coat made from softened animal hide and lined with creamy wool on the inside. My hand twitched to caress it as he walked by.

He pushed open the men's room door, and the yellow light from within created a vintage outline around his head. I wasn't sure if it was a shadow, but if it was, it was the first I'd seen in that colour. I had no idea what it meant. The door swung shut, and Lene closed her eyes, no doubt savouring the image of his tight jeans and work boots.

"Clydesdale." She narrowed her eyes, wickedly.

Even though Lene had claimed to love her sorry excuse for a boyfriend, it didn't mean she was always true to him. Generally, she wanted every man to pay attention to her, and if any man showed an interest in me, she wanted him too. I was more willing than usual to play third wheel, because it would keep my legs closed and on track with my healing plans, not to mention my fifty-dollar reward.

Lene stared at the bathroom door with the concentration of a cat stalking a bird.

She didn't notice the waitress approaching our table. I was taken by the woman's hair that was styled like a beaver's coat, greasily slicked back from her face until there was no part showing. Her pocket apron jingled with coins as she leaned over and placed two beers on the table.

She pulled the copy of *The Mercury* I had been reading earlier out from under her arm. I leaned back when she placed it on the table in front of me.

"Bartender said this was your paper?" The waitress asked, barely glancing at me.

Donald's hand had pressed down onto the paper when he had leaned over my table to berate me. Now his red plaid jacket filled my vision like a target. My nostrils flared hungrily for a whiff of the American.

I gripped the arms of my chair tightly, refusing to let myself touch that spore. I didn't want to go through another round of fanatical thinking. So, I thought of rainbows and candy floss, and the fact I'd have to drink Blue all night because Lene was buying.

"Who's the hunk?" Lene asked the waitress about Mr. Sheepskin coat, as she passed a handful of coins to her.

"Never seen him before."

An unhealed cold sore, slathered with greasy medication, adorned the waitress's bottom lip. It made me think of Donald's oils.

"He's been sitting by the pool table with a bunch of buds," she offered, tipping her head towards the other side of the bar.

Mustering my courage, I slowly reached out and with two fingers gingerly folded up the paper, corner by corner. I kept my mind occupied with mathematical calculations and was very careful not to touch any part Donald had pawed. When I was sure I had buried his spore as deep as I could in newsprint, I held *The Mercury* up at arms length.

"Hey," I called out to the waitress, causing her to frown and come back.

Holding it gingerly, I passed it to her, "Take this out and burn it. Smells like puppy piss."

She carefully lifted it from my fingers, but then she fumbled and dropped the newspaper. Without thinking, I caught it right in front of my face.

The rough tumble released the scent of burnt meat into the air where it was drawn into my eager nostrils. At the first trace of aroma, my brain kicked into overdrive. Synapses fired like fireworks, classifying the American's DNA, computing his connections, calculating his demise, and encouraging me to go find him.

"Sorry about that." The waitress took the paper from my shaking hand.

"Puppy piss?" Lene asked.

"Not quite," I released a low growl, trying to suppress the growing desire to hunt American.

Grabbing the cold beer, I toasted Lene's confused look and took a swig.

The washroom door swung open. Mr. Sheepskin Coat was headed our way. Lene put on a sexy smile and stood up to block his path.

He was a good four inches taller than she was, but when she slipped her shapely body into the aisle, he stopped in mid stride, just as she'd planned.

"You're not going to walk by a couple of women drinking alone, are you?" She gifted him with a sexy pout.

An "I might get laid" realization spread across his face, softening his mouth.

"Och, I meant no offense, lassie."

He stared with interest at her bare midriff.

"Lassie?" His Scottish accent shocked the echo out of me.

Lene shot an annoyed look my way and weaseled herself back into the man's mono-vision. He forgot me in seconds, surrendering his attention to the vibrant beauty in front of him.

"Well, I won't take offense if you just fix the situation," she winked, and reached out her hand to stroke his coat lapel.

He stared open-mouthed at Lene's hand on his chest.

Just then, a shorter man came from the other side of the bar and strode across the floor toward us. He ogled Lene from the waist down with a smart grin on his face.

"Did ye get yerself lost, Duncan?" he asked.

Lene turned to greet him, her white teeth flashing. While Lene was putting on a show, I drank her beer. No sense in letting it get warm. And besides, she had just made sure we'd be in booze for the rest of the night.

The two men were giving Lene their complete attention and though I had agreed to play back-up, I was starting to feel a little miffed. Thinking I should go do something about Man-boy's virginity, I pushed back my chair.

"Well, then..." I said it like my grandfather trying to prematurely end a Thanksgiving dinner, and rose slowly from the chair, stretching my spine to its full length. The men's eyes moved to the top of my wild blonde hair then trailed to the two-inch heels on my biker boots. The shorter one winked at Duncan, and excitedly chirped, "Now, here's a Skinny Malinky Longlegs!"

I gave him the ice-queen-look and made to leave. Lene hooked her arm in mine, and with a smile over her shoulder at the two men, and a promise to return, she spun me around and half-dragged me into the washroom.

"For Judas' sakes!" I yanked my arm from hers before the door closed. "What are you doing?"

"You're not leaving."

My temper sparked at her attempt to control my choices. As I was about to give her what-for, a shocking vision of her head tilted at a gross angle assaulted my mind. Lene's broken spine pushed the skin of her neck out to the side like a tent pole. The horrifying image was so clear, it competed with reality. I retched and covered my eyes with my hands.

Seconds ticked by before Lene spit out, "Uhh... Rachel?"

I peeped out between my spread fingers to make sure all of Lene's body parts were still connected. Her hands were on her hips, elbows jutting out defiantly, as she narrowed her eyes at me. "Are you on something?"

I slowly lowered my shaking hands. "Maybe ... yeah..." I swallowed, trying to wet my tongue enough to talk. "Maybe I popped a bean or two."

This false confession was met with silence.

"I was just trippin'." I chuckled. "I thought there was a bat flying around the bathroom."

She immediately ducked and twisted her head to check for bats.

"No, I *thought* there was a bat..." I tried to explain but Lene didn't hear me over her screeches. She leaned over, flipped her hair down over her face and rapidly rubbed her hands through it to dislodge any flying rodents, while stamping her feet on the floor.

I laughed for real, this time.

"Cool your jets." I grabbed at her wrist. "There's no bat. I just kirked out, okay?"

She flipped her head back up, and as I watched the long black hair flying out in front of her, time slowed down. The strands divided, splitting apart and coming together like baby spider webs weaving in the wind. I was mesmerized by the detail, drawn into the patterns of those midnight threads crossing and uncrossing, floating in the air as they followed the pull of her scalp.

"Rachel!"

She was in front of me again and time had caught up to its normal pace. I tried to cover my eyes with my hand, but I missed my face and brushed along my ear.

"You're seriously messed up," she declared, with a disapproving shake of her head.

She turned away and set her turquoise purse on the wet counter. Digging out a fuchsia lipstick, she examined her reflection in the mirror.

"Yeah." I leaned against the washroom stall and tested my arms by crossing them. "I am messed up."

"Uh, Lene," I tried to sound calm. "Tonight, it might not be a good idea to grab my arm, okay?"

She rolled her eyes and continued to touch up her make-up.

I was still afraid to go home and be alone, but it was clear after seeing that image of Lene's broken neck, my staying put her at risk. I felt safer with the promised all-nighter, but I needed to distance myself from Lene for her own protection. The question was how to get out of hanging with her and avoid going home alone.

If I picked up a man to go home with, I'd break my resolution. Patrick had sworn I'd only push myself further into madness if I didn't stick to my resolve. The idea of tonight's weirdness being my future was too much to even consider.

It was past eight on a Friday night, so calling the Homeward to speak to Dr. Casbus was out of the question. The head nurse would never bother him this late.

A sly idea struck me. Just because I couldn't call the doctor, didn't mean I couldn't go see him in person. I'd gone to the Homeward at night before. On those nights when I'd been afraid for my mother, afraid she'd be scared, or missing me, or they would be hurting her with their treatments.

The head nurse, Mrs. Huds didn't like it, but Casbus always showed up to save me from her lecture on rules. He didn't let me have a room to stay in—it wasn't the Holiday Inn, but he'd let me stay long enough to dial down my fears a notch or two.

And sometimes, I learned more about myself, like the last after-hours session, when Casbus had explained why I had holes in my memories.

"YOU ARE UNDER EXTREME stress when you visit your mother," he had said. "You have developed a special skill, an ability to disappear within yourself to avoid unpleasant encounters."

I had frowned at him, trying to catch his point. "What do you mean 'disappear'?"

"During times of life-threatening duress, your conscious mind has gone inward, and allowed your subconscious to take control."

I stood up from his leather couch and paced the floor. "Can everybody do that?"

He watched from behind his thick, reflective glasses, as I wore a path in the carpet.

"You are not the only one, Rachel. Many children who struggle to survive do so through dissociation."

"But you said before I had multiple personality issues!"

"Yes, you suffer from the merciful adjustment a mind undertakes when it cannot deal with what must be endured."

I fiddled with my earring.

His squirrely eyebrows popped up above the rim of his glasses.

"Sometimes, over time, a young child who is dissociating will develop an 'alter', an alternate personality to deal with what is causing them pain."

I took my earring off and cleaned the post. Then, put it back in, trying to be nonchalant.

His explanation had sounded so right. I had another personality who spoke with a Southern accent, who spoke her mind at the most awkward moments. Worse yet, she had opinions and urges different from mine, and her demands had brought on trouble more than once.

After Casbus explained my lost memories, so many confusing things fell into place. It didn't make it easier—understanding and accepting are two different things. It was still frightening to admit the Southern voice was my alternate personality, but now at least I had a treatment goal.

Casbus was going to merge my personalities...help me become whole.

THAT WAS THE LONG-TERM treatment goal. Right now, I needed Dr. Casbus to calmly explain away the weird things that had happened in the bar. I needed him to use scientific words and logical reasoning to explain why my arm stopped obeying my brain, why I heard voices on the phone, why the rooms squeezed and changed shape, and why I was seeing Lene's body twist and break like a pretzel. I needed professional reassurance that I was not going to track down Donald, the American, and gut him with my Rambo knife.

But more than anything, I needed Dr. Casbus to prove I was not fighting off Satan and his hordes of demons.

I clawed my fingers through my hair, giving the roots a good tug. Lene snapped the lid on her lipstick and checked her teeth in the mirror.

"Listen," I started, "I probably should head out."

Lene shot a dirty look through the mirror, before turning around with a fake chummy smile plastered on her face.

"C'mon, I'll buy you another drink. All you have to do is sit at the table with us," she urged.

Her mention of the drink was tempting, but the doctor had better stuff to numb me.

"Don't you have a shift tomorrow? Shouldn't you go home?" I coaxed.

"I'm not going home. *He's* at home."

She faced the mirror to look at herself once more. Her eyes glittered like aluminum in the silver glass.

"Besides, I want to hang with you to help celebrate your birthday."

"How do you know it's my birthday?"

"Bartender told me."

"Traitor," I whispered.

"Com'on!" She made as if to grab my arm. I backed into the washroom stall. "We've got two good reasons to party! Let's do it!"

I chewed my lip.

"I'll pay for your cab home, afterwards," she added, sweetening the deal.

My brain put two and two together and came up with a paid-for ride to the Homeward and Dr. Casbus. That was good enough for me.

"Warning." I held up my finger, making sure she understood the danger. "If Reg shows up and tries to hurt you, I'm not responsible for what I might do to him."

The concern in her eyes for Reg's well-being proved this break-up wasn't going to last. Just like the other times.

Her voice was a breathless whisper. "I'll need you here to make sure I don't leave with him."

"Fine. I'll stay." I pushed the stall door shut between us. "But I'll need something stronger to drink than beer."

"I'll meet you out there," she chimed, patience not being one of her virtues.

I struggled to pull down my tight jeans. With my elbows on my knees and my face in my hands I tried to relax my mind and my bladder.

Toilet-poetry was scribbled on the inside walls of the stall. I had read most of the comments and had even penned a few myself, so I noticed the new line of precise printing, right away.

Welcome your fate with recognition, for your fate is your well-known life.

I had to read it a few times to figure out what the hell it meant, but once I did, I quickly disagreed.

"Bullshit," I announced and gave the toilet paper roll a good spin, taking off more than I needed.

If fate was life, then Lene should just stay with the "wife-beater", because every man she hooked up with would beat her. I couldn't believe that was true, for her or for me. I had to believe my shitty life wasn't some prearranged hell I could never escape. I wasn't doing the best with decisions, or money, or finding someone to love me, but I hoped I was finally on the road to controlling my 'crazy'. And just to prove I had control, I was going to turn this train-wreck of a night around.

I stood, zipped up my jeans, and kicked open the stall door. "I'm goin' to par-tay!" I sang out loud.

Party, but not get laid, I reminded myself.

Chapter 5: Highlander Invasion

While I had been contemplating my life in the washroom, Lene had succeeded in attracting a herd of men. I found her surrounded by six beefed-up Scottish hunks, all in their sexual prime.

"Might as well make it a party, Lene," I muttered, sarcastically.

The men dwarfed the two small wooden tables they had pushed together. I stood awkwardly on the outside of the ring of taken chairs. I might as well have been invisible, for all eyes were glued on Lene and her coy grin.

"Sae, whit's there tae dae in this town fur fun?" One of the Scot's asked.

"You're lookin' at it." Lene posed as if someone had pulled out a Polaroid.

Astonished laughter erupted, and I got sick of standing.

"Seriously, did you guys escape from the Fergus Highland Games, or what?"

The outburst of laughter trickled into silence and several strong jaws turned my way. A few of them leered and someone said something raunchy about a caber. A flutter of excitement erupted in the pit of my stomach, but I held my neutral expression and raised a judgmental eyebrow at the caber jester.

The Scot who had christened me a 'Skinny Malinky' jumped up and grabbed a chair from an empty table. He muscled apart two men.

"Move aside and make room fur the tall lassie."

The tall lassie who just wants to go home, I thought. An image of Lassie the TV dog pushed a giggle to the edge of my disapproving lips.

Setting down the chair, he touched his cap in an old-fashioned gesture. "I'm Colin, by the way."

His eager expression reminded me of those small dogs that like to hump legs.

"Hm." I nodded and avoided eye contact.

After some careful, no-touch-the-stuff shifting between the two big men, I finally squeezed in. The guy on my left blatantly checked me out, while I took in his short, fair-hair, blue eyes and muscular build.

Raising an eyebrow, he said, "Fits yer name and far yi fae?"

I had no idea what he meant but chuckled at the silliness of it.

He tried again, "Naeme's Lennox."

He was yummy and definitely off limits tonight and for six more nights.

"Hi."

I turned away to focus on my best friend who was seated directly across the table. She had her game on. Her voice was slick and sweet like warm maple syrup, and the men were caught by the promises in it.

"I know all the best places," she was saying in response to a suggested bar hop. "But this is the best place to be."

"Why's that?" Sheepskin coat asked.

"Cause I'm here, of course." She winked at him, and he grinned in appreciation of her boldness.

I was watching Lene, but I was focussed on the body heat coming off the two men sitting on either side of me. It was probably the worst place to be seated when I was trying to be celibate and control my 'crazy'. Lene's voice droned steadily, like a mosquito on a hot summer night, while I closed my eyes and concentrated on squashing the sensual pulse that was tightening up my hot spots.

Just as the Pope's picture had tempted my nose, the men at the table were awash with scents. The greasy odour of bone marrow and fat, the pungent sting of sweat, and the opaque thrust of cologne mingled with clouds of carbon dioxide. I could hear the leathery stretch of their lungs when they sucked in air; the click of their tendons when they shifted their feet beneath their chairs.

My carnal response was over-the-top, and it exhilarated and unnerved me at the same time.

I opened my mouth slightly to breathe without using my nose. It reduced the onslaught of odors but engaged my taste. I opened my eyes and shook my head to dislodge the urge to nip the inside of Lennox's wrist.

The guy on my right placed a cold beer beside my hand on the table. He held it lightly in his wide palm, just within my reach. I hadn't looked at him yet and purposefully still didn't turn. Out of the corner of my eye, I watched him tap his thick thumb three times against the side of the Molson label.

"Let's play a wee game," he said in a deep Scottish cadence that danced the suggestion out into the air.

Keeping my eyes forward, I tilted my head and pretended re-newed interest in Lene's shameless antics. But truthfully, I wanted to play a game. I needed a distraction from my fears, and the scents, and even my inside voice, which was now trying to join in on the conversation.

The man chuckled, not misled in the least by my apparent disinterest in him. He moved the bottle closer and left it there. I should have shown better manners, but I needed a drink, badly. I grabbed it and sucked back almost half of the beer before wiping my mouth with the back of my hand.

I couldn't help a little twitch at the corner of my mouth as I imagined his shock at my beer guzzling extravaganza. That display should turn him off.

"Lass," he said, softly, "Tell me yer name".

I finally turned to face him and was stunned into silence.

He was hot. Hot beyond Fabian-Harlequin book-cover hunky. His skin was lighter than mine, old fashioned European skin, but the sun had warmed it and scattered a few freckles along the tops of his cheeks. It gave his handsome face a boyish charm, but there was nothing boyish in the way he was looking at me.

His hair with its rich dark auburn shine was cut long. The ends curled in slightly to caress his wide cheekbones. A trim beard surrounded his kissable mouth.

I couldn't find my tongue to break the silence.

"Are ye done?" His dark, green eyes crinkled at the corners.

I swallowed. He was somewhere around thirty, which wasn't a turnoff. With looks like his, if he was over sixteen and under sixty, we were good.

He gave his head a little shake as he grinned. The movement made his long bangs slip down over his forehead, and he tossed his head to move them out of his eyes.

It might have happened in slow motion, and my tongue might have been hanging out of my mouth.

"What?" I asked, wondering if he had spoken.

The bangs slipped forward again, covering one eye. I was tempted to brush them back, but he finger-combed them. He smiled, revealing a dazzling row of strong teeth, and I was back in slow mo.

"Yer name." He tilted his chin up.

I raised my eyebrows. "What would you like my name to be?"

Instead of a flirty reply, he stayed silent and the edges of his smile dropped just a bit. I quickly shifted down.

"You said you wanted to play a game," I reminded him. "Guess my name."

"Hmm."

It was hard not to wiggle, while he titled his head to the side and looked all the way down my body and legs. I tucked my ankles away under the chair and straightened my back. His glance swept back up over my tight curves.

"Give me a hint."

Our eyes locked.

I gulped and tried to remember what we were doing.

Finally, I thought of something. I would give him clues to my initials. "R ye really Scottish?"

"Aye."

"No, A".

The silence stretched on, and I turned my head to the left to hide a smirk. Lennox started to say something, and I quickly turned back to 'Bangs'.

He leaned against the chair, his muscular arms relaxed. "Is yer name Rose Amy."

I gave him an impressed look. I hadn't expected him to catch on to the vague alphabetical clues to my initials.

"Wrong."

"Curses." He clicked his tongue against his teeth a few times, and I wanted to lean in and kiss him, hard. "Renee... Antoinette".

"I'd kill my mother if she named me Rene Antoinette."

I took another drink of my beer, wishing I hadn't mentioned my mother.

He gave a throaty laugh. "It's god-awful, that's fur sure."

"Quit stalling," I sighed in mock boredom.

"Rachel Anne."

My blood slopped to a halt in my veins.

"Uh-No." I lied, hiding the shock in my eyes. "And that's three tries. You're out."

Grabbing the half empty bottle, I tipped it up and emptied it, while struggling to figure out how he could guess so close to my name. Or did he get it right? Had he said Rachel Anam?

I shot a dirty look at Lene wondering if she'd been stupid enough to share my personal info with these Scottish throwbacks.

"Bet yer name's Ronnie. A nice soft name to go with yer manner."

Maybe he didn't know my name after all. Coincidences can happen.

"I'm no Ronnie."

His eyes dropped to my mouth, but they didn't linger.

"Well, I'm gonna call ye Kit, until I ken different." He raised his finger to order another round.

"Kit..." I repeated the name slowly, testing it in my mouth and feeling slightly liberated at the renaming.

Across the table, Lene tossed her black hair around her head like a runway model. She was completely aware of the slow burn she was building in the men as she teased them. Duncan-of-the-sheepskin coat was turned in his seat to face Lene, his face all puppy-dog eyes.

The booze had chased away the fleshy tints my nose had been picking up earlier. 'Bangs' now smelled earthy and spicy, like an evergreen forest. I closed my eyes to bask in his scent. Much more appealing than butcher shop aroma.

He leaned down to my shoulder and whispered, "They seem to be getting on."

I opened my eyes to see Duncan and my best friend's foreheads almost touching. They were talking in hushed voices, no doubt making plans for the night. Watching them made me feel a little anxious. Lene shouldn't be doing anything on the rebound. If anybody knew that piece of advice, I did, because I'd lived that mistake one time too many.

I tried to hear what they were saying by ignoring the sounds closest to me and watching their mouths intently. Along with the weird things happening, my 'spidey senses' were improving. The tracking, the shadows, and the ability to hear people who were far away was getting better, and I was getting used to using them.

I cleared Stevie Nicks' wailing "Rhlannon" from the air, peeled the murmurs from the late-comers at the surrounding tables, forced the Scottish brogue to slip into the background, and finally, I picked up Duncan's soft whisper.

"What about yer friend?"

Lene didn't glance my way, when she said, "She doesn't matter".

The dismissal was a little hurtful. After all, we had made plans to pull an all-nighter together.

"What do ye think they're talking about?" 'Bangs' asked.

I turned, surprised, "You couldn't hear them?"

"Nae. Ye could?"

I slouched in my chair. "Oh, I'm sure they're playing some sort of Scottish name-guessing game."

He was unfazed by my barb. "Oh aye, we Scots love our games."

I took another look at Lene, burned she was planning a tryst. Maybe the wrong girl was making anti-sex resolutions. A better friend would have dragged her into the washroom for a serious talk.

"Why the long face, Kit?"

I shrugged, even though I was worried about Reg's insane jealousy. "I was just thinking we reap what we sow, eh?"

"Nae." He continued to study my face from the side. "Our lot is cast."

"Our lot?" I turned to meet his eyes. "You mean, the results of our decisions?"

"Each of us has a place we ur meant tae get tae. Ye ken it as fate."

I gave him a searching look. "Have you been reading the philosophy in the girl's can?"

"Whit's fur ye'll no go past ye."

I raised my brows.

"Whatever is meant tae happen, will happen."

"Och," Lennox's voice close to the back of my head made me jump. I leaned back to let him make the third point in the triangle. "You'll no git me t'agree with thet."

His accent was much stronger. I could barely work out the meaning.

"So, you don't believe in fate?"

"I prefer tae be in charge of mah own future."

I laughed, "You sound like Doctor Who."

"Who?" Lennox said, but 'Bangs' cut over his words.

"Only a fool ignores the path set out fur him." A muscle in his jaw jumped. "Don't be a fool, Lennox."

Silence hung heavy around the table, except for Lene's whispers of encouragement. She was trying to drag Duncan back into some little tête–à–tête, but his attention was on the scene playing out in front of me.

The big boys appeared to be locked in a stare-down. I pushed my chair back a bit, not wanting to get in between the two big brutes if they decided to go head-to-head.

"I completely agree with Lennox," I said, giving the tension a little poke.

'Bangs' turned his face slightly my way, while still holding Lennox's glare. I could feel the anger sizzling in him. My body responded with a slight shiver.

"Hmm," he grunted, casting his eyes my way.

The familiar temptation to tame the bad guy tickled at my insides.

"If fate controls your life, what do you think is fated to happen tonight?" I blinked, innocently.

The tension left his shoulders. "Yoo're meant tae ken Angus a wee bit better." He gave me a wink.

I quickly scanned the men as if they could provide a clue. It took me a second, but I caught on. "Oh, you're Angus."

He put out his hand, a strong hand, the palm wide and calloused. I hesitated to take it.

"You know what they say about people who talk about themselves in third person, don't ya?"

"Tell me."

"Loony. Nutbar. Crazy beans."

I pushed my hand into his firm grip. The minute his warm skin touched mine, a spark lit inside my chest and rippled like lava deep into my belly. My eyelids flickered, and my lips parted, releasing a trembling "oh" of surprise.

The conversation died around us as all eyes turned our way. Angus gave Duncan a very obvious nod. I shut my mouth and composed my face.

Lennox cursed, pushed back his chair and stomped off to the bar.

Suspicious Angus had some sort of bet going with Duncan, I tried to slip my hand from his, but he held on.

"Let's try again, Kit. My name's Angus." He lifted his chin, encouraging me.

I wasn't going to share my name, but just to get my hand out of his, I intended to say, 'pleased to meet'ya'.

Only when I opened my mouth, I simpered, "Honoured, I'm sure," in a bloody Southern voice.

Angus' mouth fell open and out of the corner of my eyes, I saw a number of heads jerk up.

Not even bothering to look around for a clock, I blurted, "Whoops, look at the time. I gotta go."

Standing up abruptly, my thigh caught on the arm of my chair. It tipped up, and Angus hung on, standing with me and moving my chair to the side with his other hand.

I looked up. He was big. A big man who stood over me.

"Settle down there, Highlander," I warned, steadily pulling my fingers from his grasp.

He wouldn't let go. "I get the impression ye don't want me tae settle."

I cringed, wondering which of my voices was going to be talking when I opened my mouth to answer.

"It's never about what I want, friend." I cast a nervous glance toward the exit.

"Ah find that hard tae believe, lass."

I prickled. "What's that supposed to mean?"

"A woman like ye ur surely knows how tae get what she wants."

His eyes, like evergreens on fire, burned with a provocative invitation. A hot flush spread up my torso.

In that moment, I decided what I wanted for my eighteenth birthday. I wanted Angus the Scotsman. I wanted him like nothing I'd ever wanted before. His lingering gaze held me pinned with unspoken promises.

His friends were openly staring, strangely interested, as if they were attending a "Girl Pick-Up 101" class and taking notes.

I didn't care, I didn't want to step out of this moment to care about anyone other than Angus. My body was smoldering, and I wanted to turn up the intensity.

Angus gave my hand a gentle tug. The movement caused the greasy scent of bone marrow to glide into my sinus cavities. My nostril's flared like a stallion picking up the scent of a mare in heat.

Quickly, I turned my head to the side to hide whatever deviant look might have crept across my features. I had two choices: plant a kiss on those sensual lips, bringing our bodies grinding together, or shut down my raging hormones and dismiss him to keep my word to Patrick.

Lene caught my eye and frowned, which meant I should quit hogging all the attention. Normally, I would step down and let Lene take the stage, but she hadn't been keeping me in booze as she had promised. Right there on the table, my beer bottle stood empty, the last of the condensation drying from its dissolving label.

Ignoring the heat rippling off Angus' body six inches from my chest, I picked up the empty bottle with my left hand and tipped it upside down.

"Doesn't look like I'm very good at getting what I want, now does it?"

A twitch flickered in his cheek.

I shook the bottle again and grinned, "Hmmm?"

He gave a hearty laugh, released my hand, stepped back and waved the waitress over.

I had just bought myself more time to decide on my birthday present—a night heaving beneath the highlander or sacrifice what was sure to be glorious sex for the sake of my mental well-being.

Jamestown Fort: Training the Tongue

When She joined the other women by the window, they parted to avoid any companionable closeness with her. She took her rightful place in front of them, standing directly before the glass. The She was not one to hide behind curtains and giggle behind her hand. She stood proudly, her head held high, ignoring the whispers of the others. She perused the crowd below over her straight nose, her poise that of a Queen standing on the royal balcony looking out upon her people.

She scanned and measured the men, sorting them by their clothing, their walk, whom they spoke to, and how others reacted to them. During her inspection, her dark eyes alighted like a pair of crows on *the* man. Unknown to her, he was the man who, in the future of Jamestown, would harvest the richest tobacco crops. To do so, he would have to purchase the largest number of slaves, and he would rule all from the most opulent home.

She was not able to read the future, but on this day, the She judged him by his size and poise, which bespoke of health, his clothes of breeding and wealth, and even from this distance, he had the most handsome face a woman could hope to gaze upon.

She turned from the window to see a serving girl, a daughter of the colony bringing bread and cheese on a tray.

"You," the She said.

The young girl looked up in surprise at the beautiful woman's tone and gave an awkward curtsy. "Yea ma'am."

"Come," the She said.

The girl flushed with a willingness to please. This summons was a fortunate chance for her to prove her ability to be a lady's maid. She turned, once, twice, thrice before she found a flat, uncluttered surface on which to place the laden tray. Picking up her skirts, she moved swiftly to the lady's side.

"Yea ma'am?"

The She's nostrils flared in appreciation of the girl's natural disposition to serve.

"Who is this man?"

Finding the one man within the crowd who had captured the She's attention should have taken a pointed finger, and the asking of many questions such as, "Is it he?" or "Do you speak of that one?" Yet, the She had only to touch the girl on her shoulder, and immediately the girl's eyes were drawn to their target.

"Oh, that be William Cain, m'lady."

"William Cain." A growing smile spread the She's red lips revealing just the tips of her white teeth. "Tell me all you know about Master William Cain."

And as is the way in towns with small populations, the girl seemed to know everything about the man. Words fell from her lips about William's brother Edward and about their combined land, making them the wealthiest land owners in Virginia. On and on, the girl droned, listing his preference for pigeon pie, describing his prize stallion, laughing at his affinity for cards, and swooning over his manners, which made the few ladies in the colony fall in love every time he doffed his hat. Why the servant girl even knew his favourite bird in this new world, the Scarlett Cardinal.

Rather than being irritated by the incessant chattering of the lowly serving girl, the She listened carefully to the cadence of the girl's speech. Her sensitive ears were acutely aware of how some vowels were delivered high in the front of the girl's mouth, pushed out by her tongue as if it could not wait to release the words "bow" or "cow". She also noticed the girl used her nose to merge other vowel sounds making it difficult to determine whether she was speaking of "hem" or "him". During this intense study of the girl's language, the She cast off her strange Eastern European accent and adopted a new way of speaking.

"Oh, m'lady," the servant girl began, understanding now that this regal woman had her eyes set on William. Smartly, she lowered her glance before proceeding to say, "Every woman here would wish themselves his wife, but the lovely Miss Anne has been promised that honour."

It was at this point, the She finally spoke, sounding as if she had been born in the colonies. "He's married?"

No one in the room noticed the new drawl to the She's words. They were too busy picking their men.

"No, m'lady. But they are betrothed—has been since they were children."

The servant girl, having a new subject, started up again, tumbling more words from her mouth. She described Miss Anne as young, beautiful, accomplished, and a favourite of the colonists, but most of all, pure, as pure as a woman could be.

At the word "pure", the She regained her smile. "You silly girl," she drawled. "A man who has the fastest stallion, the largest parcel of land, and the richest crop does not want the purest woman."

This the other women did hear, and a backdrop of gasps followed the She's words. The other women forgot the men and joined in on their favourite pastime, judging another.

The She cared not. She turned back to the window and waited until William Cain lifted his head and saw her. She raised her hand to her lips and blew him a kiss that was helped along by those special senses. Her kiss floated on the wind, and she knew the moment his lips burned with her promise for he stepped back, his eyes wide, and lifted a gloved hand to his mouth.

The She did not say a word but whispered in William's mind, "You are mine," using her new Southern accent.

His nod was imperceptible to those men milling around him, those hopeful men waiting to be acknowledged by Master William Cain. Those men did not realize how lucky they were to not be chosen by the She. Or perhaps it was the She that was unlucky, for William Cain and his magnolia tree would eventually bind her life in the ground.

But first, there would be love.

Chapter 6: Elk Tripping

S till warm from Angus' attentions, I reminded myself that Patrick had said, "one week" of celibacy and my symptoms would disappear. He had explained it as some sort of developmental milestone, one last chance to train my brain. According to him, every time I slept around, disrespected myself, or gave in to violent impulses, I was blazing a trail to crazy-land. If I created too many ice slopes for my mental toboggan, I'd be crazy forever.

With a reluctant sigh, I slipped back into my chair and gave Lene a dirty look because she was having way too much fun flirting.

Lennox returned and sat beside me. He was trying to catch my eye by leaning forward on the table into my frame of vision. I sulked and fiddled with my empty beer.

"If ye gie tired of Angus, Ah'll be canty tae scratch 'at itch fur ye."

The offer jolted my seductive organs up another notch to sultry and slick. I turned and took a good look at him. His skin was so fair, it was almost translucent, the veins creating blue shadow lines at his temples. It was an inviting liquid map, though which I could see the throb of his engine, and I wanted to stroke and prod the blood moving beneath his skin. As Lennox met my heated glance, the soft tissue beneath my tongue picked up the quickening of his pulse.

Enthralled, I looked away to better concentrate on following his heart beats. I tracked my heart's rhythm playing next to his. It was a surreal counterbalanced symphony of two life-drums, his fast, mine slow. I wanted them to be one.

Angus said something to the waitress behind me, and they laughed together. But to me, his voice sounded hollow and dull at the edges as if he were standing at the end of a long culvert.

My hands blindly peeled the Molson Canadian sticker off my beer bottle, and carefully folded it six times.

Lennox spoke again. "Ah ken yer kind of woman, an' I kin what ye need."

His pulse raced mine to an inescapable finish line.

I dropped the dissolving label and looked at the silver scales spattered on my palm from it. Lennox shifted closer, his hand moving into my space on the table. He was gazing at my face, speaking softly, but I didn't catch the words.

My attention was on the little rips of silver on my palm. The pieces began to move in spasmodic jerks across my skin, timed to the beat of Lennox's core. The stop motion lurches drew the pieces together seamlessly to form a picture of a metallic heart with arching arteries.

I blinked.

Like an image viewed through the changing focus of a camera, the silver blurred, and a reflection of my eyes became clear. So clear, I watched black bleed like ink from the brown of my irises, spilling night across the white, right to the inner edges of my eyelids.

Lennox's nose brushed aside my curls. "What dae ye say, Lassie," he whispered hotly into my ear.

I turned fixing him with my black stare, and his pulse leapt in rhythm jumping over my ever-quickening beats. I harried the sound like a wolf chases a young elk, driving it to exhaustion until it falls to struggle in the snow.

His mouth popped open as his core's contraction was locked in place.

An excited gasp escaped my mouth to kick raggedly against my lips. I waited for my heart's pattern, for the exact millisecond to drop his beat onto mine. Then, I did. It created a moment of perfect synchrony.

Lennex struck his chest with his fist. A wet choking cough burst from his lax lips, and suddenly, all sound returned in an overwhelming crescendo of jukebox tunes, talking, laughing, and the blond man's thick-tongued gags.

"Chokin' on yer drink again, Lennox," Duncan interrupted Lene to ask.

Colin was also watching, "Awee bit too strong is it?"

I watched Lennox's struggles with fascination. His hacks tugged deep within me, triggering contractions in muscles made for wrapping. I squeezed my thighs together.

I could sense Angus behind me, waiting. I didn't want to stop watching Lennox struggle, but it was Angus that I desired, wasn't it?

"Ur ye all right, mukker?" Angus leaned past me and hammered his friend on the back, laughing with the rest.

Lennox took a shaky breath and murmured something to Angus. His face and neck were red, the skin of his neck pimpled above his collar. His lips had taken on a bluish tinge. Somebody passed him a whiskey, but it slopped in his trembling hand.

"Och! Don't waste it," Colin yelped.

Lennox pressed his hand to his chest and kept his bulging eyes averted from mine.

"He's fated tae choke tae death, that one."

Death.

Cold realization of what I had just done eroded my excitement, as his shaking hand spilled more whiskey on the table.

Stomach acid burned at my larynx. I rubbed at my eyes and licked my lips. They tasted like cigarette tar.

Had I really just done that to him? Or maybe I hadn't. Maybe it was just a coincidence, and Lennox had choked on his beer.

Angus settled back into his seat. "

I turned to him to avoid looking at Lennox. "Fated to choke?" I accused. "Who says it wasn't manipulation?"

"Maybe it was destiny!" His voice seemed loud in the sudden silence.

All eyes turned to Angus as Lennox wheezed like an old, leaky tire.

"How is it destiny to ..." I hesitated, not knowing how to describe what had just happened.

"Go on," he ordered.

"...to choke on your own spit?" I ended on a haughty note.

Lennox started to say something, but Angus' loud "Shhhh!" stopped him.

Angus leaned in, putting his hand on the arm of my chair. "Destiny is the force that propels us through life, lass."

He clutched my hand. I kept it closed tight, hiding the heart that had formed on my palm.

"Fate is the guide that helps us make our choices. Free will is the deception."

The others nodded and made noises of agreement. With his intent stare holding mine, he gently tried to pry my hand open.

I squeezed my hand shut over his thumb, trapping it within my clasp. "Free will is my superpower. Fate is the fairy-tale."

He caressed the side of my hand with his thumb and asked. "Don't ye believe we were fated to meet tonight?"

"Oh puh-lease."

I tried to pull my hand away, but his fingers clamped down on my knuckles. The waitress put two beers onto the table. Lennox cleared his throat. I stared at the booze thirstily.

Angus waited until I met his eyes with a guilty glance before reluctantly releasing me. I slid my hand into my lap keeping my palm facing down. He twisted off the bottle caps and passed a beer my way. Tipping his up, he drank deeply.

I tried to touch Angus' heartbeat, as I had done to Lennox. If I could do it again, it would be proof of another ability—a ninth sense. And, if I could control the beating of Angus' pulse, it would be proof I was getting worse, or better, depending...

I searched for the rhythm in the space between us. The hum of the dim lights became dominant in my mind. I peeled it away as insignificant. I peeled all the sounds, shredding the ambiance until I could hear a urinal leaking down the rust-stained wall in the men's room. Yet, try as I might, I couldn't hear Angus' heart.

When I lifted my head from his chest, Angus quickly adjusted his features into a neutral expression.

"Where are you from?" I asked, not meaning to sound so accusing.

"Can't ye guess?"

"You're from across the sea," I quoted my mother's letter. "I know that much."

"A prize fur the lady!" he shouted, and the others cheered.

I blushed at the attention. Why was I in the spotlight? What was going on?

"Why are you here?"

"Do I need a reason tae visit the friendly and welcoming country of Canada?"

"No, but it's a little unusual to find a group of men like you guys in the local bar, that's all."

Angus shoved at Lennox, "Did ye hear that, Lennox? She thinks we're unusual."

I cast an innocent look around the table at the others. "I never said that."

Lene pointed at the bathroom with an angry jab while she yanked on Duncan's coat trying to get his mouth back on hers. But he was looking at me. They were all looking at me, listening in on Angus and me.

Angus grabbed my left hand off my lap, and before I could stop him, he flipped it over to look at my palm.

I looked at his tilted head, and with a feeling of dread, I followed his gaze.

The silver heart was gone. There were no flakes of Molson label stuck to my skin like fish scales. It had been a delusion, a figment of my deranged imagination.

"Take no offense. In my family, we tease each other." He rubbed his thumb in a circle on my skin. "And yoo're an easy one tae tease, lass."

The doctor kept saying I was delusional. Everything I experienced felt like it was real, but the metallic image was gone. This proved it. I didn't have the power to kill people by stopping their hearts. I had never had any power. I was just nuts.

"And ye?" Angus asked, completely unaware of my internal struggles.

I quickly looked up from my hand. "What?"

"What do yer people do?"

"My people..."

What would I say?

My mom does shock treatment and my dad ... it probably wouldn't be 'what' he was doing, but 'who' he was doing.

It was time for some little white lies.

"Oh, I come from good people if that's what you're wondering."

"Duncan," Angus called across the table. "I think I'm gettin' roped intae a proposal."

"What?" I started to stand up. The others burst into laughter, and Colin slapped Angus on the back, offering to be his best man.

Angus gently pulled me back into my seat.

I shook my head at him. "This is some sort of Scottish humour thing, isn't it?"

He leaned in closer and lowered his voice. "This is some sort of thing, no doubt."

I let that dreamy line sink in, while he gave me his full and committed attention.

Angus put his elbow on his knee and moved in close to whisper. "Now we've met proper-like, I think it's time tae get down tae some serious drinkin'".

The last word rolled off his tongue, and I became very interested in his ability to flick the tip with such speed. One of the men yelled for whiskey. I lifted my head to take my cue from Lene, but she and Duncan were trying to swallow each other's faces.

Party on, then.

"Fated or no," Angus held up his bottle, "tae a night we won't soon forget."

The group's laughter echoed off the stained, plaster ceiling. I raised my beer, but before I clinked the bottles together, I challenged him. "You think you're a man I won't forget?"

"I'm nae any man ye've met before."

"Praise be," I smirked, "the others haven't been worth spit."

Then the whiskey came, and I was taken by the tawny light, forgetting to worry about my 'crazy'.

After what I had done to Lennox, I should have gone home and hidden until I had better control, but as the night wore on, I forgot about everything except the firmness of muscular thighs, hot pleasures hidden behind metal zippers, and the sharp burn of hard liquor.

Chapter 7: Tongue Twisted Truths

Lennox was standing by the wall between the washrooms and our table, and he was trying to get Angus' attention. At first, I ignored him, and kept Angus turned my way, but one of the other guys let Angus know he was wanted.

"Don't miss me," he grinned as he got up.

I openly ravished his body with my hungry glance. Angus was well over six feet and built thick with wide shoulders and hips topping muscular thighs. He wasn't a man who could be knocked down easily and that excited me. The old floorboards creaked under his weight, as he made his way over to Lennox.

I tore my eyes from his ass and dropped my glance to my palm where the silver heart had been. My lifeline was still unbroken by label bits.

I was always struck by the length of my lifeline. It ran over the edge of my palm, looping around the base of my thumb. My destiny line was extra-long too, stabbing up through the heart and brain lines, shattering them into segments beneath my middle finger as if telling death to shove it.

A tingle at the back of my neck drew my attention to Lennox who was casting furtive glances my way while he spoke to the big man.

"He has nothing to tell," I whispered to myself.

Lennox looked as terrified as he had when he had met my eyes before the choking started.

Angus slapped Lennox on the back and laughed out loud. Lennox shot another wary glance over Angus' shoulder at me, his face stricken with something close to guilt.

I stared at Lennox's mouth as it moved over the words he was spilling into the air.

"Mumble...mumble," and then, I could read his lips. "...If ye don't turn 'er, ye could end th' curse forever. Ye could free us from uir bonds, Angus."

His hand clutched the Scotsman's muscular forearm with a grip that left white marks on Angus' skin. I couldn't see Angus' mouth, but now I had their conversation, I could hear it.

"Listen tae me cousin. We're here tae do a job. If ye can't handle that, ye have tae return home."

"But Angus, if ye release 'er, think whit she will dae tae folk. Dae ye want 'at oan yer conscience?"

"Lene, what's takin' sae long?" Duncan's voice shouted on my left, shattering my concentration and just about deafening me into the bargain.

Lene was no longer seated beside Duncan. With a feeling of *deja vu*, I turned to look in the direction of his frustrated glare.

Damn! Lene was on the phone. I staggered drunkenly when I jumped up, quickly regained my balance and moved to intercept Lene's call.

As I passed the men, I heard Lennox say, "Ah'll not dae it!"

It was a strange comment, and maybe one a girl in a bar should pay attention to, but I didn't have time to think about what he meant. Lene saw me coming and turned her back, huddling over the phone piece.

"Who are you talking to?" I hissed at the back of her head, as if I didn't already know.

Suddenly, my paranoia kicked in. "What are they saying about me?"

She waved me away, placing her hand against her other ear.

My arrival didn't make her miss a beat. "I just got off work, Reg."

My boozed-up brain revved into high gear, when I heard the "wife-beater's" name. I tapped Lene's shoulder and when she turned to face me, a finger to her lips, I grimaced and shook my head at her. I knew better than to talk. If the number one loser in her life heard my voice in the background, Lene would pay later. He hated my guts, and the feeling was mutual.

"What are you doing?" I mouthed the words, exaggerating my expression of disbelief.

"Listen, I was thinking maybe we could have a drink and talk it out." Her chin trembled against the plastic mouth piece.

I shook my head side to side in an exaggerated "no".

He was shouting so loudly; I could easily hear him even without my special senses.

"I didn't mean it..." She turned away again, but not before I saw her tears. "Please, Reg, just give me another chance."

I couldn't stand listening to her grovel and apologize to the cretin. I pushed down the silver cradle, disconnecting the call.

Lene shrieked and spun around. "What the hell are you doing?" She yelled loud enough for the whole bar to hear.

"Lene, think for a moment. Think of all the times he's hit you."

Frantically, she started digging in her purse for another dime. "You don't know what you've done..."

I cupped my hand over the coin slot. "I just saved your ass."

"You have no right," she started to cry. "No right..."

"You can't go back to that bastard. He treats you like shit. Someday, he's going to kill you, Lene."

She kept rummaging in her purse, ignoring me.

"Listen to me!" I yanked the purse out of her hand, accidently ripping the strap.

Then she lost it. Sobbing loudly, she ducked her head and rushed past me, heading towards the can. I turned to follow but stopped short. Every person in the place was watching, including Duncan. He was frozen in a half sit, half standing position. I looked down at the purse in my hands, feeling like a bully. The last thing I needed right now was a misinformed hero.

I forced a slight smile and waved my hand at him as if we did this every night. To be truthful, we did this break up bullshit twice a year. Followed by her finding a man, getting him all turned on, and then running to call Reg. This was all part of Lene's weekend theatrical performance. I'd been through it a million times before, only tonight she was going to keep her word. Even, if it had to be at the expense of our friendship.

ANGUS GAVE A PUZZLED look, but I ignored him and entered the washroom. Lene was sobbing into her hands by the paper towel dispenser. The slick-haired waitress was in there trying to help. I told her to get the hell out and waited until the door shut before I spoke.

"Look, I'm sorry about your purse." I laid it on the counter beside her. It flopped to the side like it was injured.

She was sobbing her heart out.

I dipped my head trying to catch her eye. "Let him sit on it this time. At least one night?"

She stopped crying long enough to give me the stink-eye. "I'll lose him."

"Good! Good riddance."

She blew her nose loudly into the stiff paper towel. "Easy for you to say, you're not in love."

"If what you have is love, I don't want any part of it."

She fondled her purse, squeezing it between her fingers. "That's where you seem to be confused." Her tone was cold, "You aren't part of it."

"He's an asshole."

"I'm the asshole. He doesn't deserve me!" She shrieked, stabbing at her chest with her finger. I stepped back, giving her space. "He doesn't deserve a whore for a girlfriend."

"Don't use his words."

She turned her purse upside down and shook it. Make-up, tampons, and coins fell like consumer rain onto the chipped, grey counter.

I spouted out a line my mother's nurse, Patrick, had used on me. "We both know you're not a whore, Lene. You're just searching for love."

"You don't know shit." Tears were dragging her mascara down her cheeks in black rivulets.

"You can stay at my house. Reg won't know you're there and if he comes?" I pushed air out past my tight lips creating a pffft sound.

Her scrambling fingers found a dime and leaving her purse and all her things spread out on the counter, she tried to walk through me.

I put up my hands and stopped her. I had to because, unlike me, she could change her life so easily.

She stepped to the right.

"Lene," I said, and stepped with her.

She went snaky, hitting at my raised hands and screaming like a banshee for me to get out of her way. The force of her attack pushed me back against the wall.

I'd pretty much had enough when one of her hands got past by raised arm, and her nail scratched my chin. I gave her a good shove the other way. She stumbled, falling against the bathroom stall.

"Don't you hit me." I warned, pointing my finger at her.

I was mad, but I was also scared and cringed inside, waiting for the gruesome images, the Southern accent, the change in time and motion, but nothing happened.

A loud pounding on the door made us both jump.

"Lass!" Duncan's voice called out, then more softly, "Lass?"

We froze, staring at each other with wide eyes, looking as guilty as if we'd been caught robbing the joint.

"Lene, please come out and talk tae me." His soft brogue filtered through the small crack he had pushed open.

Normally, I didn't give a shit if Lene wanted to use and abuse the local men, but Duncan sounded like he was genuinely worried.

"You need to deal with him." I pointed at the closed door.

She twisted her hands. "You do it. I need to call Reg back."

Duncan was Angus' friend, and I could imagine Lene's slutty behaviour screwing up my chances with Angus. Someone had to limit the damage. I put up my hands in a surrender pose.

"Fine. Make your damn call."

I left first, pushing the door wide and making Duncan leap back to avoid getting beaned. I didn't bother clearing my scowl as I hooked my arm in his and half pulled him back to the table. "Something's come up," I said, drawing on a lie I'd used in the past. "Lene's grandpa is in a wheelchair, and sometimes Grandma tips him out. Lene is their emergency contact."

I didn't know a man could look infatuated and deflated all at the same time.

I sensed Lene slip behind me and head for the phone. I kept Duncan moving away. "She needs space to sort things out."

Angus was still standing by Lennox. He had obviously watched the entire drama, judging by his troubled expression, and he was still watching as I gave Duncan a gentle push towards his chair.

I didn't approach the table, choosing to stand in the middle of the three parties, a barrier to Duncan if he chose to access Lene. But it was awkward. The Scots were talking in low tones with Duncan at the table and casting furtive looks under their heavy brows. I avoided looking at Angus, and let my eyes skitter over Lennox's intense stare. Feeling uncomfortable, I stuffed my hands in my pockets, not really knowing what to do with myself.

Most normal guys would head for the hills at this point, and I couldn't blame Angus if he decided the drama was too much.

I stopped myself from looking at the floor. Adjusting my body language, I raised my chin and locked eyes with Angus, braced for his rejection.

"Come tae me," he said.

I was swept by an urge to run to him, but I hesitated. Lene was cowering over the phone, bleeding guilt all over it. I couldn't help her if she wouldn't help herself, and it hurt too much to stand by and watch.

I measured my pace as I approached the highlander. Angus wasn't smiling, but I could feel his satisfaction at my choice. It seeped out of him on a tide of self-assuredness. He held out his arm inviting me to slip under it, and though I would normally refuse, just to let a man know he didn't control me, I was only too happy to slip alongside him.

Held tight against his warm body, a sense of being coddled settled my nerves. The calming effect of his protectiveness felt natural, almost instinctual. Strangely, I didn't feel the need to destroy the moment. I basked in it.

But only for a second before Lennox said, "Ye should at leest tell 'er." And then he walked away.

Jamestown: Human Pairing

The ship-wives were beckoned to the square to listen to a representative of the Virginia Company of London. He seemed an unpretentious man, a clerk, if you will, who had some important points to make before the Jamestown colonists started mingling with the new members.

The man stepped up on a makeshift wooden box and spoke a "good morn" to the good people gathered for the day's celebration.

As he looked out at the more delicate gender, he released a sigh of satisfaction. The bride ship had come through, and it was hoped these ninety women would secure the colony's growth.

The clerk waved a document in the air and the crowd hushed, anxious to hear what he would say.

"Each woman," he called out, to reach the hearing of those standing furthest away. "Each woman, upon entering into marriage with a man of Jamestown, will receive as promised, one new apron, two new pairs of shoes, six pairs of sheets..."

He droned on, reciting the promises made by the Virginia Company of London. As each item was listed, gasps of delight flickered in the air. The gifting lent to the day even more enjoyment for these items were needed to set up a good home and many of the women were arriving with few possessions.

The representative talked at length about marriage licenses and how each couple would be married, one after the other, until all were satisfied.

When all was said, and done, there would be a lot of paperwork, but these contracts were the foundation of the colony, the building blocks that would ensure the birth of children on this new soil.

It wasn't just the Virginia Company of London who wanted the population to grow in the colony, it was also the wish of Scarlett. These people who would be her neighbours, these men who would make business deals with her husband, these children who would grow by her child's side, were the herd. From these people, would she harvest, and as they prospered, so would she.

The clerk stepped down off the crate and the human pairing began. Scarlett scanned the crowd of male faces, looking for the man she had already chosen.

Chapter 8: Gilding the Heart

I turned my face up to Angus. "What does Lennox think you should tell me?"

One side of his mouth lifted in that quirky expression I was getting used to. "He thinks I should tell ye that yer legs go on forever, and when ye glide across the floor, ye drive us all to distraction."

I snorted. "You didn't see me fall over my chair, then."

His eyes darkened. "I saw every inch of ye."

Angus hadn't made a move to go back to our seats, giving us more time alone. He was playing fast with his words, but he hadn't dropped his arm to cop a feel yet. He hadn't dropped his lips to mine either. He just let me lean on him and it seemed the most natural thing to have his arm wrapped around my shoulder.

He was warm. His chest and hips and thighs were a thick pillar of muscle and bone. I had seen men like Angus at the Fergus Highland Games, draped in their tartans and plaids. And I had seen what his type of build could do in the caber toss, stone put, and hammer throw. Angus' was an ancient build of brute strength. He was meant to plow fields, to walk in the place of oxen, to press his weight down onto a woman until she begged for air.

What would it be like to wrap my legs around him?

His cheeks were flushed, and it was obvious he was wondering the same thing about me. I caressed the short reddish hairs of his beard, but I didn't touch the throbbing pulse on the side of his neck.

"Do ye ken yer eyes are like Scottish honey?" His voice was husky and low, and a thrill stabbed the pit of my belly.

He turned me to face him.

"Like Scottish honey left in the jar until it's thick and sweet." He gently pinched my chin between his thumb and forefinger. "Left tae ripen intae the darkest gold."

Angus was courting with lines that stabbed deep in lonely, barren places, delivering his words in an accent that had me dreaming of castles and lochs, and strong thighs under rough kilts.

His lids grew heavy over his heated gaze, and he drew his bottom lip between his teeth before releasing it to sit full and soft above his strong chin.

Oh, I recognized this look. This was a man preparing for a joining of the lips, a sharing of the mouths, and a dance of the tongues.

I forced myself to step back.

"Settle down there, hero," I warned, hooding my own desire behind a hard-edged glance.

He hooked his thumbs in the belt loops of my jeans and steadily pulled my hips closer.

"But that's what I want, Kit. I want tae settle with ye."

The willful personality I was trying to project was laid bare by his choice of words. From the jukebox, Billy Joel sang "An Innocent Man", strangely helping Angus' cause.

His lashes dropped as he moved in to kiss the side of my neck. I trembled right down to my feet.

"Yoo're mine, lass," he whispered in my ear.

Oh, yes.

The fight hadn't even begun and now it was over.

I was his.

My lips parted for his kiss, but instead of a breathtaking moment of first joining, the Southern Belle took advantage of my weakened state and spoke through me. "I think you forget yourself, Sir."

I gasped in shock.

Angus pulled back to examine me, unmoving, unblinking, while an embarrassed flush burned my cheeks and stung my eyes.

A quizzical frown furrowed his brow, and I tried a shrug and a small smile, hoping he could forgive it.

"Hmm," he grunted and peered like a scientist discovering a new species.

I started folding up the soft edges of my heart, just like I had folded up the newspaper over Donald's scent. Pressing my mouth into a hard line, I raised my nose a notch higher than usual, just to let him know I didn't care.

The 'crazy' wasn't finished yet. It pushed another sentence out through my resisting lips. "What is it that you want, Fergus?"

His brows came down, pushing a wrinkle over his nose. "A good start would be for ye tae remember my name. It ain't Fergus."

"Oh, your repute precedes you, sir. I know exactly who you are."

I whimpered at the end of the line, because it wasn't me who was speaking. It was my bitch-alter personality, and she was way out of line.

He unhooked his thumbs from my jeans and ran his hands down the sides of my hips as if brushing something dirty off.

I wanted to brush my hands off too, brush off my whole body from the bizarre behaviour Angus had just witnessed.

Loss chipped away at the golden glow he had begun to put in my chest. I did a quick sweep of the bar. Lene was no longer on the phone. She was probably gone back to Dufus, and now I didn't even have a way home.

"Angus! Angus! Angus!"

From the table, the men had begun chanting, unaware of our awkward exchange. Even Duncan had become reanimated and was holding up a glass of whiskey. "A toast from Angus!"

I stepped to the side to let him pass, looking down at the toes of my boots.

"Kit," he pressed a light touch into my lower back.

The tendrils of depression that always awaited my failings, plucked away at me, trying to draw me in.

"Kit, come toast with me."

If I hurt this much now, what would it be like tomorrow morning when he was finished wasting his time? Or maybe we wouldn't even get to tomorrow morning. Maybe that voice would take over, or I'd have another black out. I couldn't handle tonight ending in a cruel dismissal the sane reserved for psychos.

Angus gestured toward our chairs. "One toast."

I chanced a glance at his face. He looked wistful, as if he were sorry.

It gave me the nerve to nod and lead the way back to the tables.

Angus picked up two glasses of whiskey and handed me one. The dim ceiling lights reflected in the fiery liquid. It reminded me of campfire flames and all the bush parties I had honed my guts on. Five years of booze and sex, and here I was, eighteen, falling in love with a stranger, and ready with an open throat.

The men raised their glasses, and Angus looked at each man in turn. Looking mighty serious, he boomed, "Alba gu brath!"

The group echoed the toast with enthusiasm and tossed back their drinks. After a few appreciative snorts and coughs, they waited, the room growing quiet, while I held my full glass in the air.

I hadn't tossed my drink back because this was the one that would tip me. Whiskey was my devil, and this was the one I shouldn't dance with.

Angus cupped the side of my face. His thumb brushed across my lips, igniting a throbbing pulse in my throat. A slow smile spread his lips, and he winked. The men sniggered and waited for me to finish the toast.

"Fiddle-dee-dee", I drawled and tossed back the whiskey in one tip, holding my throat open for the burn.

The liquid razed a path down my esophagus and into my guts, but I didn't choke. I slammed the glass onto the table, and the men cheered like I'd made a perfect 12 o'clock caber toss. One look at Angus' hungry glance, and I had to agree. I had just lined up a win.

We sat, and Angus pulled my chair toward him until my knees were nestled between his legs. Three whiskeys later, I lifted my right boot and planted it against Angus' shoulder, threw my head back and let out a Canadian bush-party whoop. The men nearly pissed themselves with excitement. Angus knocked my leg down, grabbed my hips with both hands, and effortlessly pulled me up onto his lap. My legs draped either side of his chair. I laughed low in my throat and slid my arms around his neck.

Nuzzling his ear, I whispered, "I've got two secrets."

"Let's make a vow," he said.

I pulled back and tilted my head.

"Nae secrets between us."

"It's my birthday, today."

There, it was out.

"Let me guess." He grinned.

"You with your guessing games," I laughed, tossed my hair and tried to look older.

He brushed my hair back with his hand. "Yoo're not old enough tae be drinking in this pub. Yer only eighteen."

I was a little put-out the game was already over. "And you're not!"

"Nae, I'm not some boy tae be played with, Kit," he warned.

I shifted on his lap, very aware it was a man I was sitting on. "You'll never guess my other secret."

He wrapped his hands around my waist and lifted me into a more comfortable position.

"We're gonnae hae a great nicht, Lass," he spoke in a thicker accent than I'd heard him use. "An' then tomorrah nicht, yoo're gonnae teel me th' other secrit."

"Tomorrow night..."

I lapped up his promise for a few seconds, but Lene shattered the spell. She appeared out of nowhere and grabbed my elbow, barking, "No, you're not, because we're not going to be here tomorrow night." With a rough tug, she pulled me off Angus' hot thighs, graciously taking my weight as I lost my balance.

"Let's go," she hissed up at my ear, as she dragged me toward the front door.

I could have flattened her, but I let her steal me away. I was secretly happy to see her, happy she wasn't with loserville. And, I'd gotten myself into a sticky wicket, acting like a whore, and about to break my vow to Patrick. Angus had acted better than most guys, especially when faced with my 'alter's' voice, but still, I had to get away from him. My 'crazy' was just skirting the edges of my control, and the more I saw of Angus, the more I didn't want him to see the real me.

Groans and cat calls rang out behind us, and someone yelled something about a party pooper. Lene tried to pull me around the corner, but I dug my heels in. Turning, I used my best Southern Belle gesture to throw a kiss at Angus. He was glowering like a bull, his fist clenched on his thigh. He didn't try to catch my kiss. Instead, he started to stand up, but Colin gripped his arm and said something to him.

I just had time to pout, before I was spirited outside and put into a cab by a furious, best friend who took the front seat. She hammered her door lock down with a fist and barked out her address to the cabby.

She turned her condemning eyes my way. "What were you thinking?"

I opened my arms, palms up, "Obvioushly..." The word slurred against my teeth as the last whiskey hit my bloodstream. "I wasn't."

I leaned back, the pressure of my body against the taxi seat releasing the smell of vomit and sweat into the stale air of the cab.

Trying to change the subject, I said, "Happy to see you in once... one piesh."

Her black hair flew out from her head like whiptails, as she rounded to face front.

"You never think past your own needs!" She yapped in her most exasperated mother's voice.

Depending on Lene's mood, I would either have to walk home from her place, or she'd pay for a cab to my house after she got out. Since she was playing wounded mama, I was pretty sure I was getting a ride all the way home tonight.

The cabby caught my eyes in the rear-view mirror and tented his bushy brows in disapproval. Always, the judgement. I ran my tongue provocatively along my upper lip. He quickly looked away.

The street lamps made yellowish globes of murky light against the dark night. I mourned my lost chance to ride the Scottish bull and sighed, fogging the window.

The cab pulled out into the street, but the red eye of the traffic light stopped the car in the shadow of the Church of Our Lady. The light of the full moon turned our foggy exhaust into white plumes that floated up toward the gothic spires of the church. The twin towering peaks lorded over the city of Guelph, and below, the ornate wooden doors whispered of the wonders within. I was tempted.

A hollow echo heaved in my stomach at the thought. The sensation was stronger than before, and I wanted to lift my shirt, see if I could catch movement beneath the skin lying taunt on my stomach. Another loud grumble rolled through my intestines.

The cabby cast a worried look through the mirror, "Are you going to be sick?"

I shook my head. Lene turned around and gawked at me, then faced front saying, "She's just trying to get attention."

The moonlight streaming through the window glowed on my shirt. Slipping my cold fingers under the black lace, I waited, holding steady while the seconds passed. Nothing. So, I turned my gaze to the concrete steps that led up to the Church's door. The bubbling pulse started, and I quickly yanked up my shirt. Right above my belly button, my skin twisted, as if someone had grabbed it and turned it counter clockwise from inside.

I gasped, then pulled my shirt down, checking to make sure Lene and the cabby hadn't seen what I'd seen. They were busy watching the street light ahead.

Sweat broke out on my forehead. I tried to rationalize what had happened. The doctor said I might start seeing things. Well, no shit, Sherlock, I had. In one night, I'd already seen more than my fair share of weird. This was just one more unexplainable event to add to my list of insane happenings.

I wanted to cross my arms, but I was afraid to rest my arms on my stomach.

The green light beckoned. The cabby put the taxi in drive at the same moment I heard heavy footsteps slapping the sidewalk.

"Wait!" I yelled at the driver.

He hit the brake, and I twisted in my seat hoping to see Angus rushing to rescue me from Lene.

A dark figure smacked his hands down onto the roof, his body blocking out my view of the church's tall stained-glass windows.

"Don't..." Lene's warning was lost in the squeaky descent of my window as I rolled it all the way down.

Before I could look up at his face, the man threw something at me. It hit my chest with a plastic rattle and tumbled into my lap. I grabbed at it, and when I looked up he was gone.

"What is it?" Lene asked, trying to see what I was holding.

The cab moved forward, and I held up a cassette tape for Lene to see.

"Weird."

The cold wind blew my hair across my eyes.

"I'd say," I agreed, and tossed my hair back. That made my head spin, so I stopped moving. The passing street light momentarily lit up the black square in my hand.

"Who's it by?" Lene asked.

I squinted trying to see the worn-out white letters on the cassette label. "I can't make it out."

The cabby took a turn, and I tipped drunkenly sideways, almost fumbling the tape out the open window. "Shit!"

We stopped at another light, and I rolled up the window before anyone else could throw junk at me.

"Who do you think that was?" I asked Lene.

"Who knows? Some hobo, probably." She turned back to face front.

"You don't think it was Angus?" I asked.

"Who's Angus?"

I slipped the cassette into my jacket pocket and leaned back against the seat.

"Never mind," I mumbled.

I no longer had the spins, but I was nauseous. Sickened by the thought that my friend didn't care enough about me to even know who I was talking to all night.

And I wasn't the only one who had talked to him.

I had to go see Dr. Casbus and tell him about the voice taking over. And while I was there, maybe I could see my mom.

I checked my pockets for the yellow foolscap letter Man-boy had delivered from my mother. But then, recalled I had thrown it into the washroom garbage.

Struck by daughter guilt, I decided when I went to the Home-ward, when I saw my mother in a straightjacket, her hair wild with knots, her condemning lips rolled in under her teeth, I would make a point to ask her about the letter, and her reference to the biblical Job. It would make her happy to preach at me for a while.

Another ripple moved under my shirt, and I slapped my hand down onto my belly, accidently knocking my wind out.

"Ignore her," Lene said to the cabby.

Jamestown: Cain of Arran's Field

William's brother, Edward, had been wary of the She from the beginning, from that first day at the Jamestown bride pairing. Edward had been struck by the majesty of the woman walking directly towards him, her steps as sure as if she already knew who she would choose as a husband. Edward's heart had leapt into his throat, and a fine sheen of sweat had broken out on his forehead beneath his golden hair, for he had thought the beauty was coming to choose him.

He had pulled his hat from his head and would have already been in a bow, if he could have torn his sky-blue eyes from her countenance. That's when his older brother had stepped forward. William swept his hat off his head in a flourish of grace and aplomb that coasted the corner of his hat above the ground without touching the dirt, before standing to present himself without regard for decorum.

"My lady, I am William Cain of Arran's Field."

"Honoured, I'm sure," she had simpered in the musical cadence of her newly acquired colony speech.

As Edward was occupied with composing himself enough to speak, William continued, "And might I have the honour of knowing your name?"

"Why, it's Scarlett, of course!"

The joyous lilt of her voice and the warmth of the smile she bestowed upon them left the two men desiring to hear more.

After a few halting seconds, William remembered himself and introduced his brother Edward. But for William's dark hair, the two could have been mistaken for twins, but Scarlett's sharp glance picked out the minor differences between them.

A flash of her lashes, and Edward barely resisted dropping to his knees in the dirt of the street and begging for her hand. An action that would surely have led to social embarrassment, if not total scandal.

The lady briefly took in Edward's trim figure before her eyes returned to conduct an unseemly appraisal of William.

"My darling, Scarlett," William said, taking liberties that set Edward to blushing, "have you by chance seen the red songbird that shares your name?"

The lady had the grace to look surprised. "You do not mean the Scarlett Cardinal, my favourite bird of all?"

"I do indeed!" William held out his elbow, and Scarlett stepped up to place her slim-fingered hand upon his arm.

"And what of these beauties?" She looked around at the women standing in conversation with would-be suitors. Some ladies were strolling arm in arm with lucky fellows who had succeeded in extricating brides from the crowd. "Do you have any feathered favourites among this flock?"

Edward, not to be left behind, took a few hurried steps to catch up. He moved to the lady's other side, and graciously offered his arm, of which behaviour, Scarlett approved. Placing her hand upon his arm, she walked between the two most eligible and sought-after men in the colony of Virginia.

Before William could think up a pleasing answer for Scarlett, Edward, attempting to be clever, said in a rush, "He's soon to wed the Indigo Bunting."

That stopped the lady's small boot steps.

"Oh!" Scarlett took her hand from William's arm to touch her throat. "Tell me it is not true. Quickly, before I succumb to my disappointment."

"It is not true." William performed another of his graceful bows.

"But..." Edward started.

William raised his eyebrows in warning. "My dear brother, how could I possibly be marrying Miss Anne when I am betrothed to Miss. Scarlett?"

Edward looked stricken. His eyes darted to Scarlett's glowing face, which was composed and peaceful. They seemed to enjoy Edward's confusion. With a sly grin, William even seemed to be daring him to challenge the subject.

Edward did what any fine gentlemen of the time would have done. He brought his heels together, reached out his gloved hand for the lady's and bowed over it, while saying, "Let me be the first to welcome you to the Cain family."

But inside that calm, socially trained exterior, one word was ringing an alarm in Edward's thoughts about his brother's easy surrender and deceptive jilting of Miss Anne.

William could only be *bewitched*.

Chapter 9: Calling on His Name

I opened my eyes and looked at the door of my one-bedroom basement apartment. It gave no clue as to the time of day, for the thick curtain was drawn on the window.

The darkness signalled I should sleep more. But, my bladder cramped out a toilet call. Throwing off my quilt, I staggered into the space that was my kitchen. In the pitch dark, I avoided the corner of the kitchen counter, but mistimed and tripped up the one step leading to my bathroom. Putting out my hand to stop my fall through the bathroom door, I rapped my knuckles on the sink and let out a yelp as my shoulder slammed the door against the wall.

"Shhhhhh," I warned myself and listened for movements from upstairs.

The new landlord and his wife lived above in the main part of the house. She wanted me out, and he just wanted me. I was careful not to give either of them what they wanted.

Satisfied no one had heard my less than graceful entry, I slid my hand up the wall trying to find the light switch. A flick of my newly bruised knuckle, and the bare bulb hanging from the stained tile ceiling flashed on. The harsh light stabbed my sleep-drunk eyes. I raised my hand and waited for my pupils to adjust.

As I stood in front of the mirror, my eyes sheltered from the glare, a familiar sense of dread crept over me.

What if I look in the mirror and it isn't me looking back?

I cleared my throat and tried to shake off the paranoia, but memories of other episodes crowded my logic. Many times, after waking from a bad dream, I would feel disconnected from myself. I would begin to think the feeling would manifest into flesh—that I would be replaced in the mirror's reflection.

I hoped the fear was part of my psychosis, confirmed by Dr. Casbus' diagnosis of my alternate personality. Reason said my 'alter' couldn't change how I appeared on the outside. But the idea of a part of me getting so strong it could take over my life and look at me through my own eyes left me quaking.

My raised arm began to ache, but that was only the beginning. If I didn't face myself soon, I wouldn't be able to look in the mirror, not now, not tomorrow, and possibly not ever. I had to face myself.

Slowly, I lowered my hand and looked at my reflection.

A riot of rebellious, pillow-shredded curls framed my oval face. My skin was a little pastier than normal. Lack of sleep and too much drinking can do that. Or maybe it was the dried-berry shade of long-lasting lipstick which still kissed my pouting lips. I leaned closer, peering into the velvety brown of my irises, which led straight to my tortured soul. But, nothing in that rich colour, nor in my Bette Davis lids drooping in sleepy invitation hinted of sinister doings. No duplicity, no threat. That wholesome-gone-trashy girl looking back at me was plainly me. I closed my eyes and dropped my head back. What a relief!

Pushing my layered bangs back off my face brought to mind the Highlander. With a thrill in my belly, it all came back—my birthday drink-a-thon, the Scottish invasion, Lene breaking off with her loser boyfriend, Reg. Hotter than hot Angus and his muscular thighs, glass after glass of whiskey burning through my guts. And... and Angus. The way he had thumbed my chin up, so he could look deep into my eyes, the way he had wrapped his arm around my shoulder.

Looking at myself now, I didn't see what made Angus so attentive. And thanks to Patrick and his demands of celibacy, my well-honed skills in the sack were going completely to waste.

I probably wouldn't see the Scot again.

More memories of the night before filtered in past my booze-soaked brain. Donald's greasy scent, the Southern slip-ups, the voice on the phone, the impulse to break Lene's neck, and the stranger who had thrown the cassette tape onto my lap through the cab window.

"What a weird kirked out night," I squeaked to the mirror.

At the sound of my voice, my pulse jacked up, pushing blood through my system and pounding in my ears.

"Stay calm, hoser," I whispered.

Sitting on the toilet, I finally released the hot urine that had irritated me awake. From where I was seated, I could see into the L-shaped hall that connected the washroom to the kitchen. Not much light leaked out into the hall, but there was enough to show something dark lumped on the lime green rug off to the side. I blinked to clear my vision. I hadn't seen it on the way into the bathroom, but then again, the lights had been off.

I stood up, flushed the toilet and cautiously stepped closer to the bathroom door. My body cast a long red shadow, my shadow colour, over the lump, which was red and black. And plaid.

A dark feeling slithered up my spine and embedded itself in the base of my skull with a dull burn.

The thing crumpled on the rug was Donald's Muskoka dinner jacket.

I braced my hands on either side of the door jamb and searched my memory for any reason why the American's jacket would be in my apartment. I came up blank. I had no memory of meeting up with the guy at any time last night. I had no memory past the cab ride, past the point when someone had thrown that cassette at me.

Had I been so drunk I'd had a blackout? What if I had brought the American home, and what if he was out there, in my apartment, waiting for me to leave the washroom?

I crossed my arms over my thin t-shirt and listened intently for any sound of movement. The refrigerator hummed, and the kitchen tap dripped with a plunk, every few seconds. The faint sound of a car driving by outside, its tires making a muffled swishing sound on the asphalt, carried to my ears.

If Donald was out there, I had to go out and face him.

As soon as I made the decision, the air seemed to pull out of the room sucking me into place. I tried to move my feet, but I was held fast by an unseen pressure.

Terror skittered over my limbs like rats leaving a sinking ship.

My senses went into overdrive. Nostrils flaring to catch a scent, the roaring of blood coursing through my system, thrumming in my ears. All normal fight or flight responses.

But then, something abnormal happened. My left arm warmed from the outside. It felt like someone was leaning against me.

My eyes shot to the mirror to see who was standing at my side. The only person in the reflection was wide-eyed with terror. And, that was me. I could still feel the presence, the pressure. I started to reach out with my right hand, intent on feeling the invisible form that was there. But I never got a chance to touch it.

It touched me, first.

The unmistakable brush of a hand against my breast shocked a cry from my mute throat. I fell to the side, my arm driving down into the toilet. Cold water splashed up into my face. Sputtering, I pushed off the toilet seat, and spun wildly trying to get to my feet, droplets spraying off my hand onto the wood-panelled walls.

I ran out of the bathroom, crossed my apartment in record time, and leapt the last few feet onto my bed. The old frame groaned, the headboard banged against the wall with a sharp slam, rattling the window above it.

Like a child, I scurried under the covers and pulled the blankets up over my head.

In my little den of safety, surrounded by my panting, I trembled. I was too much of a coward to even think of facing down whatever was out there.

Instead, I inhaled my stale morning breath which carried less oxygen with each gasp until my head started to throb.

My mother had said the demons would come and punish me like Job, with blisters and horrors and loss.

My childhood fears were running wild.

I tried to think logically. Dr. Casbus would say I was suffering a psychotic episode brought on by misfiring brain chemicals and neurons.

But, if my mother was right, I needed to call on God's name for protection.

If Casbus was right, I needed to calm down, dial zero, and get an ambulance.

Flapping my arms up like a bat, I flipped the ends of the blankets out to capture fresh air, then wrapped it around my body again. I sucked in a cool lungful.

"You're just my imagination," I whispered under the blanket.

Help me.

"I'm just being stupid."

The feeling of being watched trickled like ice water over my back. I pressed my lips together and waited for a hand to yank the blankets off my head.

Help me.

"You've just had an exciting nigh—."

My voice cracked. I cleared my throat and tried again.

"It's just another overreaction."

I calmed enough to remember my breathing exercises from Dr. Casbus.

Breathe in, two, three, four. Breath out, two, three, four.

"It was just..." I started to say, but a thought interrupted.

It was the valley of darkness.

My stomach growled as if I had not eaten in days.

The valley of darkness, waiting, while she eats at the table of my enemy.

The skin around my bellybutton tightened and twisted as if someone were grasping it from the inside.

My mouth opened without my permission, and the Southern voice spoke. "It is the shadow of death".

I reefed the blankets off my head releasing a shower of static electric sparks into the blackness. My hair clung to my face like sticky cobwebs, and I frantically swiped it away from my eyes.

There should have been light coming from the bathroom, but it had gone out. My apartment was as dark as a tomb.

"Who's there?"

The sound of my voice in the heavy silence spread my fear like a disease. I waited for an evil beer-belly chuckle from Donald, the American, but there was no sound except the pounding of my blood.

First, came a strange off-kilter feeling, an overall shift in the room around me. The air tilted, as if it had solidified into an invisible cube and then tipped itself inside of its boxed walls. All around me, everything felt skewed—on end.

I waited for the floor boards to creak, or the bed to growl, but nothing happened. My nerves stretched thin until I couldn't take it anymore. A scream built deep in my belly.

Slowly, the sound made its way to my ears—a strange tapping. I turned my head blindly toward the noise. It was coming from my front door. The only door that led outside to the street above.

I almost called out, thinking the landlord was finally coming down to investigate. But at the last second, a new feeling of dread caused me to cover my mouth.

Over my panicked gasping, I heard, *Shnk. Shnk.*

It was a metallic sound, not quite a tap. More of a—I connected the noise to the cause. It was the outside door knob being turned left and then right, left and right, the turn pushing the little metal latch in and out of the door jam with a *shnk, shnk* sound.

The landlord wouldn't need to try the doorknob. He had a key.

My limbs went numb. I whimpered and tugged the blankets up to my chest.

"Please let it be locked..."

I always locked the door, but I didn't remember coming home, last night.

Shnk! Shnk!

The noise became more frantic, the door pushing in against the frame.

Shnk! Bang!

The air moved again, and I finally believed whatever was trying to get in my door wasn't anything earthbound. My heart leapt up into my throat to choke me. It was time to call on God's name.

Rattle! Rattle! Rattle!

"Please God... protect me in my hour of need," I whispered the rusty words.

Bang! Bang!

My eyes filled with hot tears that milked my terror. "I am afraid."

A heavy body struck the door.

"God. Please help me."

And again, until I thought the frame wouldn't hold.

My voice cracked, as I yelled. "You're not welcome here. I did not ask you here."

As abruptly as it had started, the rattling and pounding on the door stopped.

I listened intently to the silence until my ears felt like they were swelling from the inside.

There was no sound of retreating steps outside, no more turning of the doorknob. I waited for another noise, another attempted entry, my skin alive with sensations as I stayed frozen on my knees on the bed.

Chapter 10: Recordings of the Dead

The unmistakable rasp of a zipper cut through the darkness from the direction of the kitchen table. The zipper clicked slowly, as if it were releasing its metal teeth one tick at a time. Then, I heard a plastic rattle and knew what I was listening to. It was the same rattle the cassette had made when it had landed in my lap during the taxi ride. Someone was unzipping my leather jacket pocket and removing the tape.

The black figure who had run up to the cab came to my mind and my bladder went weak. Maybe he had come back for it. Maybe he was standing, right this very moment, in my apartment staring through the inky darkness of the basement.

I peered through the darkness in the direction of the kitchen light switch. To reach it, I would have to get out of bed and cross the room.

"Screw that!"

Throwing myself to the right side of the mattress, I clawed at the front of the night table. I yanked the drawer open with such force the entire thing rocked. Something fell to the floor with a crash. My hand rummaged blindly in the drawer until my fingers connected with the metal canister of a flashlight.

Gripping it in both hands, I flicked it on and rapidly swung the circle of light past my kitchen counter, over the fridge door, and across the table top. No one was there.

I was terrified to look near the front door, but I had to. The dim beam of light barely reached that far, but it was enough to show the chain was on and the bolt was turned.

The springs inside my old couch squeaked. I whimpered aloud, stumbled out of the bed, and swung the light that way.

Nothing.

Frantically, I swung the light into each corner of my basement apartment trying to catch whoever was in there with me. I lit up the couch, then the washroom door, then back across the room to the closet, and back at the table.

I could see no one, but I was too terrified to stop darting the light, sure that an intruder was keeping one step ahead of the flashlight's beam. The room felt cold and empty and evil. Snot ran from my nose over my lip, but I couldn't take my shaking hand from the flashlight to wipe it away.

The rattle noise came again, and I spun like a cornered animal, flashing the light back to the kitchen table. The dim beam landed on a small rectangular shape on the table top. I panted out my fear, and though my eyes burned, I didn't blink or take them from that dark little square.

I was sure it was the cassette tape. It had been in my coat pocket, but now it was lying flat on the table top. Who had taken it out?

I swiped the room with the flashlight again, and returned the beam to the table. The cassette tape was no longer on its side but balanced on its edge.

Someone was in my apartment.

The hairs stood up on the back of my neck in warning.

I kept the beam pointed at the cassette and cautiously climbed back onto my bed to get my feet off the floor. Just as the springs squeaked with my weight, I realized I hadn't looked under it.

A slithering hiss from the direction of the table set my teeth chattering.

The wheel on one side of the cassette was rattling as it spun, feeding the tape out through the top of the case. A sob escaped my lips as I watched the shiny plastic ribbon-like tape rise up in a loop like an upside-down hangman's noose. The tape kept pushing the noose wider and wider, feeding out more tape until there was too much weight. The shiny ribbon fell forward, spilling onto the table, and the voice started.

"Yous got to bury her deep, Massa."

The wheel on the cassette tape turned some more, pushing out the words that were garbled and interspersed with static.

"You don't know what you ask of me, Ebba."

The man spoke in the same Southern accent as the voice of my alternate personality. But his words were soft with regret.

"Yous got to bind her in the roots of the magnolia so's she cain't nevah get out!"

Behind the two men's voices, background noises cluttered the static. It was the sounds of people talking, the clinking of glasses.

I listened intently, trying to understand what I was hearing, while I watched the ribbon spooling out of the cassette.

A child's voice stabbed the air, much louder in volume as it called out, "Mommy! Mommy?"

"Yous got to bind her, Massa," the voice insistent. "Or she will plant herself in your daughter, and in her daughters, and in your great-grandaughters."

"We are gathered here, in the eyes of God..."

"Yous got to trust! Trust your ole Ebba. Trust yoself."

"Mommy!"

I strained to hear what was being said, forgetting to be afraid. So many voices were speaking over each other, I couldn't make out all the words. The background static got louder, threatening to conceal the voices.

Someone shouted, "*Jesus*" with all the fervour of an evangelical preacher.

The wheel squeaked and rolled, and the tape ribbon spooled out, but the only sound left was the thick white noise of static, turning and spinning, and spooling into the silence.

The first voice shouted, "The roots of the tree will bind her!" so loudly, I screamed and dropped the flashlight.

It landed in the blankets, its beam shining directly up into my eyes. Blinded, I grabbed it and pointed it back at the cassette. Bright circles of light danced in front of me, and I blinked rapidly to see.

There were no more voices. The cassette was lying on its side on the table, the black mass of ribbon creating a shiny nest around it.

The air tilted, just as before, settling back into its space, releasing me from the eerie, distorted feeling.

The atmosphere drifted into the background where it belonged.

My ears popped.

Backing up cautiously on my bed, I reached above the headboard to slide aside the heavy curtain. The window looked out onto the landlord's laneway. It was still dark outside. The street light cast a white circle above the landlord's car.

My hand shook as I pushed the curtain all the way along the rod, allowing the streetlight to cast a white glow over my bed.

Turning, I slowly placed one foot down onto the linoleum floor before moving off the bed and warily crossing the room to the kitchen light switch. My hand was shaking like I was palsied as I reached for the light switch. The single grey florescent panel flickered its greenish glow into the room. The buzz of the light joined in with the refrigerator's hum.

I cut my eyes to the cassette lying immobile in its puddle of tape, expecting it to start up again. I was so junked up on adrenaline, I couldn't stop shaking.

Moving to the kitchen cupboards, I yanked out a large cooking pot. I turned the pot upside down on the table, trapping the cassette under it.

I wiped the sweat from my face and whispered, "That's better," just to hear something other than the rushing sound in my ears.

The light made me braver. I opened the closet door to search, cringing at the classic horror movie squeal of the hinges. In the washroom, I checked behind the door. Then under the bed and behind the couch.

When I was sure there was no one in the apartment with me, I faced Donald's jacket. Taking a pair of barbecue tongs from the kitchen drawer, I advanced on the coat and pinched it by the collar. Using two hands to hold the tongs, I lifted the jacket up, carrying it back to the kitchen to check it out under the brighter light.

Turning it one way and the other, I saw that it wasn't ripped, and there were no marks on the material—no blood stains.

I had my suspicions it was Donald's, but just to be positive, I let it drop to the floor, knelt down and used the tongs to dig in the pockets for identification.

A crinkle sounded as I pinched something soft with the tongs. Was it a map leading to my apartment?

I withdrew it slowly, revealing a pack of Marlboros. Breaking my rule of not smoking at night, and not smoking in the apartment, and not smoking American cigarettes, I shook one out with the tongs, lit it up and sucked as much smoke as I could into my lungs.

There wasn't anything in the other pockets to identify whose coat it was. And though the American cigs were a bit of a clue, it wasn't absolute. I didn't want Donald's scent, but I needed to know for sure.

Careful not to touch the material with my fingers, I leaned over and gave it a sniff. The inside of my nose tingled as it fed my brain the greasy charcoal smell of burnt meat that was Donald. My mind tracked the scent one hundred miles to the American border, and then across multiple European genetic strands, bridging the complexity of the man to this moment—to this coat.

I had my answer.

Standing up, I paced the kitchen, flicking ashes onto the white tiled floor. I couldn't understand how his jacket had made it into my apartment. If he wasn't here, if he hadn't been here, it meant I had brought it home. And if that were true, where the hell was the guy?

I stopped walking and looked at my leather jacket hanging on the chair. It might hold some clues. Averting my eyes from the cassette on the table, I squeezed the pockets of my coat. The cool material scrunched softly in my hands. My Rambo commando knife was missing.

"Shit!"

Expecting the police to knock at any moment, I walked in panicked circles knowing I had to get rid of the evidence. I had to hide it, but my one-bedroom apartment had no nooks and crannies for stashing proof of whatever crime I may have committed last night.

"Shit! Shit! Shit!"

Suddenly, I had a brainstorm. Each ceiling tile was maybe three feet by three feet and hung suspended on a rack frame that was bolted to the floor above, leaving a space of about a foot between the landlord's floor and my apartment ceiling. Moving a chair to the centre of the kitchen, I stood on it and carefully reached up to push aside a large, white tile.

This is where I hid my diary, and my mother's diaries, and my great-great-grandfather's diary. All the family secrets even I hadn't read were resting up here in the ceiling beneath the upper floor, sandwiched between the two boundaries of the house.

I gave the metal ceiling frame a tug to see if it would hold the coat's weight. It was screwed securely into the floor joists above. Using the tongs at this angle was impossible, but by wrapping my hands in a towel, I was able to hide 'Donald' away in my 'attic' without leaving my prints all over the evidence.

With a feeling of relief, I pulled the tile back in place and climbed down.

That taken care of, I sat on the end of my bed, stared at the overturned pot on the table and chewed my fingernail. Too much was happening too fast, but I was certain of one thing. No way was this an hallucination. The cassette tape proved it. But to admit this night of terror had not been in my head, meant acknowledging my mother had been partially right in her fanatical prophesies.

I was desperate to speak to Dr. Casbus. I still held out a vague hope he could explain away the supernatural. I had panicked and called on God earlier. My fear of spirits and demons was ingrained by my mother's fanatical worship of outdated beliefs. She had programmed me to recognize my own 'heretic thoughts' and to be terrified enough for my skin to crawl at any denial of the existence of God and Satan. Even to claim, in my mind, that demons didn't exist struck fear in my heart. There was always the hovering horror 'they' might think I was challenging them to prove me wrong.

I opened my mouth wide, cracking the tension out of my jaw. I didn't know what to believe anymore.

I had to see Dr. Casbus. Now.

Chapter 11: Asylum Adventures

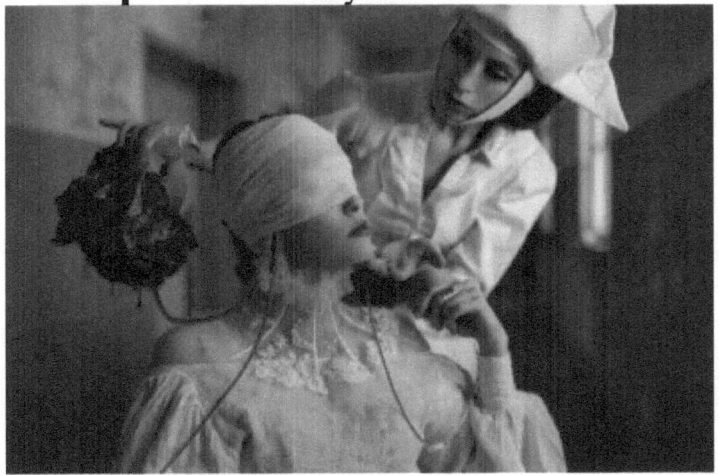

Outside the cab window, the darkened buildings flickered by beneath the streetlights. I used to joke about nights like this, dark, wet nights and journeys at ungodly hours. I used to say, "This is the moment when it all turns into a B movie" and then whoever was with me would join in on a 'B movie' scene game where we'd say things like: "Yeah, this is where we see a shadow run from behind the city garbage bin." "Yeah, and this is where the stupid, blonde, teenage girl walks over to check."

"Who would be that dumb?"

Now it seemed my life was the 'B movie', and I was the dumb blonde trying to stay one step ahead of the plot.

Bored with staring at the back of the cabby's head, I tried to make conversation. "Hey man, what time is it?"

"Four."

He didn't bother meeting my eyes in the mirror, which was fine by me.

So much had happened, and I had to think about what I was going to share and what I wasn't going to share. I knew I shouldn't tell him I met Donald at the bar. When that dick-head had left, I hadn't followed, but if his body showed up Casbus could testify about my connection to the American.

I decided to skip the account and only tell Casbus someone had thrown the cassette at me through the taxi window.

Before I'd left the apartment, I'd taken the pot off the tape cassette. I had expected it to be gone, evidence that it had been all in my head. It was still there, silent and unmoving. I had planned to put it in my pocket, take it in to Casbus as proof that more was afoot than my insanity. I squeezed the pockets of my coat. Still empty. Somehow, I had forgotten to bring the damn cassette tape. I needed it. The whole episode was becoming fuzzy, slipping off into the places I stuffed bad memories. I had to hold on to this one, because this was the one that countered science. The tape, and maybe Donald's coat. The coat I could never use. Just in case, the fool was...

I was tempted to deny I was capable of gutting and skinning the American like a Bison, but that would be a lie.

MANY YEARS AGO, I HAD been playing in the Elora Park, pulling my ten-year-old body up onto the monkey bars. I was wiry and strong and took risks with abandon. On that day, I had been taunting the neighbour boy, Timmy. He was a few years older, and Mom used to call him a holy terror because he loved to torment me. But on that day, I had the advantage.

I was on top of the monkey bars, and I had been going at him for almost an hour. I threw another pinecone down at his black brush cut, and that fired him up. He was almost foaming at the mouth as he climbed up the metal rungs to get me.

When Timmy came up one side, I started down the other. When he climbed down and ran across the grass, I climbed up out of his reach. We repeated this round about game, until he stamped his sandals in the dust. I found his frustration funny, and I laughed and laughed until I got a belly ache and had to go home.

A week later, in the park, Timmy got his revenge. When I got there, he was sitting on the monkey bars waiting for me. No one else was around.

At first, I tried what he had done. Climbing the ladder, then running back and forth to find an opening, but he blocked me. When I tried to swing across the bars, he stepped on my fingers. I dropped under the rungs and stood there, wondering how best to get him.

Unexpectedly, something hot and soft hit the top of my head. Instinctively, I grabbed at my hair, my fingers slipping on the strands and coming away greased with his feces.

My outrage splashed cold over my park-heated body. I sidestepped out from under the rungs and looked up at Timmy's white ass still aiming down at me.

I opened my mouth to call him a freak, but my words came out calm and airy.

"You, sir, are no gentleman."

My knees bent of their own accord, my thighs flexing to send me flying up. I pulled my body over the rusted rods like a gymnast, and without a sound, I landed beside Timmy before he could clap his asshole shut.

I SQUEEZED MY EYES closed against the memory of the boy plummeting head first to the ground. My mother's scream as she came upon us is forever etched in my mind. As is the memory of how her cry brought me to my senses. Timmy lay motionless, twisted in the hot dirt beneath me, while I sat on his body and played with his disjointed neck.

That's when she had tried to strangle me, her hands wrapping my scrawny chicken neck, squeezing the air from my throat. My eyes had bulged as I looked up at her, the sky big and blue over her shoulder.

Then the hands had come, and she was ripped off, and I was left sprawling in the dirt beside Timmy's lifeless body.

To this day, I don't know why or how I killed him. I only know the Timmy incident had put Mom in the Homeward. She'd taken the blame for his murder, and I'd been free to suffer guilt and regret, alone.

She was crazy anyway, so things had probably worked out for the best. At least she was getting the treatment she needed.

The cab stopped at a light, and I opened my eyes to see where we were. We passed a flickering Mac's Milk sign. I knew this route off by heart, so I knew we had only a few more blocks to go.

THE CAB PULLED UP THE lane to face the imposing Homeward gates. The driver put the car in park, and turned around, his elbow on the back of his seat. He squinted suspiciously as if seeing me for the first time.

"Seven." He held his hand out.

I dug a ten out of my back pocket while the guy drummed his fingers. By the sour expression on his face, he knew he wasn't going to get a tip. And he was right. I waited patiently for my three bucks while the cabby made a show of searching for a dollar bill. Those three bucks were going right back into my college fund jar.

Money exchanged, I had a moment of doubt. The car's lights lit only a portion of the tall gates making it look like a creepshow waiting to happen.

The driver turned front and placed his hands on the wheel. "I can take you back for another seven."

I swallowed. I couldn't spend fourteen bucks on a wasted trip.

Stepping out into the cool air, the pre-dawn crispness bit at me. The city was strangely quiet, and I was careful not to slam the cab door. The taxi rolled back onto the deserted street. I quickly stepped to the side to avoid being lit up. He shifted, the engine chugged with an irregular purr. I watched his red tail lights fading down the abandoned street.

During the day, traffic would be speeding past, but Guelph wasn't big enough to support 24-hour action. Nobody in their right mind was out at this hour. Nobody but me.

I turned and faced the eight-foot-tall iron rods. It was a bold gate, not hiding its purpose in caging people. It wasn't going to keep me out.

The rods were welded three inches apart, so there was no going between. And the tops were spiked with iron spears that would surely stab a piece out of my ass if I tried to go over.

Lucky for me, I had someone on the inside who had slipped me details for a late-night break-in.

I gave the gate the finger and slipped off to the left. Following the rusty, spiked wall until it ended, I found the cheaper, less elaborate prison fence. These chain links led the way into a ditch that was filled with brush growing wild along the Sanitorium's property line.

Moving through the neglected boundary between the road and the Homeward grounds, I was careful not to break the dry stems of Goldenrod. Only a fool would leave an obvious trail.

The bushes grew denser, and soon the thighs of my jeans were soaked by the dew on the wildflower stalks. As I pushed aside some branches and slipped between, the unforgettable tickle of a spider web slipped across the bridge of my nose. I tried not to think about how many spiders might be caught in my hair and pushed on.

A sharp jab in my finger caused me to yelp and pull back. I quickly put my finger into my mouth and sucked on the unmistakable bruised sting of a Buckthorn. The tang of my own blood confirmed I had reached Patrick's first marker.

"Stop at the first well of blood," he had said, when sharing his bizarre pointers on how to break into the asylum. I had thought he was being melodramatic or describing some creepy lawn ornament.

I spit on the ground. "Cryptic asshole."

He must have had something against plain speech for he was prone to speaking with sideways riddles. Usually, I never got his meaning until it was too late. He had better not have been riddling when he had said this was where I could get back to the fence, which was now completely hidden behind the seven-foot tall, thorny bushes.

I pulled my coat sleeves over my hands and used my elbows to force my way through the branches. The hard spikes dragged along the leather.

I tried not to cry out like a baby when a thorn jabbed my thigh. I turned sideways, slipping against the least resistant branches, and was relieved to get through to the other side where the branches gave way to a small clearing.

I stopped, took a couple deep breaths and listened for sound.

The fence ahead was gaping with a jagged hole right where Patrick had said it would be. I bent down, placing my hands on the cold, dewy grass. The fence jingled with a metallic shimmy as I slipped through, but no one came running to investigate. My respect for Patrick went up a notch.

Standing up on the other side, I slipped my hands into my jacket to warm them in my armpits. I looked around at the shaded mounds

of sculpted shrubs and the ribbon of grey road stretching out under
the early-morning sky until I got my bearings. I took off in a jog along
the winding road that led to Casbus' building.

When I could make out the metal door and the bars on the windows, I slowed. Patrick hadn't said which window to throw rocks at
or where the hidden entrance was, if there even was one. I figured I
was going to have to use some good old-fashioned charm to get in.

Blowing out a breath of white air in the chilly morning, I pressed
the after-hours button with my thumb. In the grass behind me, a
cricket chirped while I waited impatiently. I pressed it again and
vowed if they didn't let me in, I would keep pressing until the raw
sound ripped through the quiet ward like a buzz-saw and set the
loonies a'howlin.

After my third push on the button, the metal locks released from
the inside. I straightened and prepared myself. The door swung inward, to reveal Mrs. Huds' body shrouded in white.

She was stiff and starched from her nurse's cap to the white
stockings above her boat-sized, white leather shoes. Her disapproving mouth was drawn so far down at the corners, the lines along the
top of her upper lip were almost smoothed out.

"You!" Her head jutted forward on her short, fat neck. "How did
you get in?"

She looked over my head in the direction of the gates.

"Sorry," I said, "But, it's an emergency."

Her lips thinned out as her eyes lit on my face. "There-is-no-
such-thing-on-my-shift."

Behind her, a wail trembled down the hall.

"I need to see the doctor."

"Absolutely not!"

I stepped up to the bottom step, using my height to advantage.

She started to pull the door shut. "You will come back at regular..."

I shoved the door open wider, which pushed her back, creating a space for me to slip past. She made a quick grab for my shoulder, but I twisted sideways.

"Doctor Casbus won't mind," I hollered as I danced away from her down the hall.

"Freeze!" Her harsh tone nailed my feet to the floor.

Secure in her knowledge that she had me, she turned to the door. Her thick, white-stockinged calves bulged with muscles, as she pushed the heavy metal barrier shut. Turning back to me, her shoes squealed out a protest on the shiny waxed floors. I had the sudden urge to run but reconsidered. I knew she was the kind of nurse who would enjoy chasing someone down and jabbing a dull syringe into their ass cheek.

Huds yanked the bottom of her nurse's uniform down over her wide hips and let loose a loud "harrumph!" Straightening her shoulders and tucking her chin like an army marshal, she marched my way.

I backed up until I was across from her desk, but then, I found some courage and braced myself for what was coming next. Only, she walked right past me and moved into her alcove. Sitting at her desk, she proceeded to ignore my presence. I stepped forward cautiously and stood in my customary spot.

On the top of her desk, a silver lamp glowed over the pages of the open registration book. A skein of yarn and two knitting needles rested on the pages. One of the needles were pointing at a recent entry, and as I stared absently trying to think of what to do next, my mother's room number became clear. Who on earth would be visiting my mom? A name had been written down, but the yarn covered half the name. I could only see the first letters *McN...*

I tried to push the yarn out of the way, but Huds slammed her hand down onto the book with incredible speed.

I barely got out alive. "Sheez!" I said, clutching my hand to my belly.

The old battle axe squinted her blue, watery eyes with suspicion. I tried to ignore the skin tags standing at attention on her lids.

"Are you making a scarf?" Her mouth tightened. "Not that it's hard... to imagine you knitting for some loving grandchild..."

She never took her eyes from mine as her Clorox-dry hand slithered across the table, squeezed up the yarn and needles, and dropped both into a drawer out of sight.

I gulped and leaned forward trying to read the entry. She flipped the page.

"Seriously, lady. I just need to see the doctor."

"Doctor Casbus does not see patients at this time of night."

"I get that, but I'm not a patient..."

"What exactly would you term yourself as?"

I dropped my eyes to her desk. She had me there. I chewed on my lip and thought up a new approach. "Listen..."

"No. You stop talking." She flipped the page of the registration book and pointed a square-tipped finger at the first block on the page. "At eight a.m., I will inform Doctor Casbus you are here. He will decide whether he wishes to see you or not."

There was no way I was going to sit under her evil eye for the next three and a half hours. No damn way. I pushed my tongue against the roof of my mouth and made a loud "clop" sound and looked away as if she bored me.

The long hall was in night mode, only every other fluorescent tube lighting the way. One light was flickering, creating its own shadows as it flashed and died randomly.

This was my chance. It was now or never.

I stepped away from her desk and yelled down the hall, "Doctor Casbus!" My voice echoed back to us.

Huds slammed her fist on the desk. "You will shut..."

"Doctor Casbus!" I turned and started toward the inner asylum at a fast clip.

Huds jumped up and her chair skittered across the tiles.

"Doctor!" I ran faster. "Doctor—" I hoped my mother couldn't hear me.

"Doctor! Doctor!" A high-pitched woman's voice screeched from one of the rooms.

Suddenly, Casbus appeared from around the corner, standing directly in my path. I locked up my knees and dug in my biker boots to stop before hitting him.

He clutched for my shoulders, but I stopped just short of his reach.

"Ra-chel."

I tried not to grimace. The sound of his voice always stirred up mixed feelings. A combination of gratitude and disgust. I expect it was the role he played. He was both my mother's helper and her jailer.

Huds caught up to us, her enormous boobs heaving with the exertion of chasing me. "I tried to stop her..."

I scooted out of her reach, moving just slightly behind the doctor's tall, lanky form in his hanging white coat.

Skid marks from my boots created a black trail on the floor leading back to Huds's desk.

The doctor's monotone trolled out. "That's fine, Nurse Huds, I will take it from here."

Not one to give up easily, she lifted her chin and pushed her chest out. "I can escort her out immediately, if..."

"That will not be necessary." He looked down his sharp pinched nose at her. A moan filtered down the hall. "But do endeavor to calm the guests."

I listened carefully, trying to figure out if it was my mother's cry.

Casbus turned to me, blocking my view of the hallway. His Adam's apple stretched the papery skin of his throat into a point at the front of his neck. I quickly lifted my eyes to avoid looking at it.

The wire rim of his twisted glasses sat obediently upon his nose. The lenses were smudged foggy white, and I couldn't find his eyes behind them.

"Follow me, please."

His long strides made short work of the distance to his office. I followed as if leashed to him, but once at the threshold of his domain, I stopped.

I always paused here. He was used to it. He called it "avoidance dilly-dallying" because the counselling that happened behind his door was often difficult to face.

"Step inside," he commanded, and I obeyed.

Across the room, the leather couch lounged expectantly. I didn't take my eyes from it. Casbus shut the dark paneled door.

"You seem agitated, Ra-chel."

I could hear him moving, the starch in his white coat rasping loudly in the silent room.

"I am."

His voice was closer. "What has distressed you?"

A tug at the back of my neck and my jacket was sliding down my arms. My skin tingled.

"Things have been happening."

His hands landed on my shoulders with the hesitant brush of dying sparrow's wings.

I turned my head to the side and looked down at the blue veins snaking under his grey, liver-spotted skin.

He pulled his hand from my sight before asking, "What things?"

"Things..."

The wings were back, clasping my elbows, guiding me across the room. I took a few stiff steps. He moved passed me towards his chair, at which side, he stood waiting. I was restrained by the leftover sensation of his hands.

"Come, Ra-chel."

The couch *was* inviting. I did *want* to lie down on it. But only for a moment.

Casbus watched me come on until I was a few steps from him. Slowly, he lifted his stethoscope holding it out like he was bearing a cross at an exorcism.

"Lift your shirt, Ra-chel," he commanded. "I wish to check your heart."

Chapter 12: Sentinels and Watchmen

The grey stucco ceiling came into focus. I shifted, and the leather couch groaned out an embarrassing noise.

"Do you understand, Rachel?"

I swung my feet to the floor and sat up, then clutched at my head as the room suddenly spun.

When I raised my head and focused on the room, I found Casbus standing at the window. His hands were clenched behind his back.

Something about those hands...

He turned, his steel-grey hair blending into the window's metal inner frame. Outside, behind him, the colours of dawn were streaking across the sky.

On other visits, when I'd *come to* like this, I'd just answer "yes," and leave as soon as I could. But this time, I needed to truly understand what it was we had been discussing.

"Actually..." I shifted to clear the tight feeling in my chest. "If you could just explain what is happening, Doctor."

Casbus held his silent stare. When he stood like that, stock still, he looked like a chameleon on a branch, seconds before its thick, sticky tongue rocketed from its mouth and slapped some unsuspecting prey.

"Please."

He tucked his chin in until the grey skin folded under his jaw. "What you have been experiencing are typical reactions to the profundity of your psychological exploration."

I ran the sentence over in mind, trying to wring out its meaning. "So, our sessions are causing me to be crazy?"

"You have much childhood pain, and we are stirring it to the forefront." Casbus walked slowly to his desk, each step ending in a slight hesitation as if he would lean back instead of stepping forward. "Your mother was very cruel to you, and until we have discovered everything you have suffered, you will not heal."

"But..."

"Your mind is still withholding events, Ra-chel. Things have happened that you are not ready to accept." He put his hand on the back of his chair.

"So, that's why... everything... last night?"

"Precisely." He pulled the chair out and sat. Turning his attention to the stack of work on his desk, he lifted the corner of a paper, and appeared to look under it. "All is a result of your psychosis," he said to the paper.

He'd given his signal that our session was over, but I held up my hand for more time.

"So, let me get this straight." I licked my lips. "You're saying the voice on the telephone, the gruesome visions, whatever was in my apartment last night, was all just my imagination?"

He didn't look surprised as I ran through the list of events from the night before, so I figured I must have been sharing this stuff with him earlier.

"That is correct. You must not make the same mistake your mother has made. This has nothing to do with religion, and everything to do with science."

"Science?"

I wanted to believe him. I wanted to feel relieved that it was all in my head. But if it was, why had Lennox acted so afraid of me in the Albion? And what had he meant when he'd said to Angus, "If ye don't turn 'er, ye could end th' curse forever"? And where had the cassette tape come from?

"Did I tell you about the cassette tape?"

The Doctor's hatchet nose rose, "Cassette?"

A knock came at the door, and Casbus bid them to enter. I quickly finger-combed the back of my hair.

The door opened revealing my mother's male nurse filling the doorway with his bulk.

"Ahhh, Patrick."

Patrick was a big man, and he looked even bigger in his green, cotton scrubs. He'd shaved his head since I'd last seen him, and his dome shone a rich, earthy brown. He didn't acknowledge my presence as he handed Casbus a bottle of pills.

"Thank you." Casbus checked the contents and wrote something down on the paper in front of him, while Patrick stood at his side, waiting.

Looking at them beside each other, I was struck by the bizarre contrast between the two caregivers. Patrick's dark, shiny skin stretched tightly over his round forehead and was smooth on his fleshed-out cheeks. Casbus' features were boney and brittle, his white skin dry and papery over his scare-crow like frame. Patrick's shoulders and arms were bulging with weight room muscles, which he used to subdue patients. All Casbus' muscle was in his brain.

Casbus caught me staring at Patrick and tapped his pen on the desk, twice.

My eyes darted to his steamy glasses.

He tapped his fingers on the pill bottle's cap three times. His voice kicked in. "Rachel, I am prescribing this medication to you. Taking these pills will resolve your more recent symptoms."

Patrick looked at me and glanced away.

Casbus set the bottle on the edge of the stainless-steel desk and spoke to the nurse without taking his eyes off me.

"Can you ensure that Ra-chel gets home?"

"Yes, Sir."

Standing up, I brushed my sweaty palms down my thighs. "I was hoping to ... uh, see my mom?"

Casbus tightened and gave me that chameleon stare. "I don't think in your current state, a visit with the woman who has disabled your psyche is advisable."

"But ..." I took one step toward his desk, unable to keep the disappointment from my face.

He ignored my pleading and started sorting his papers. "Next time, you may see her."

Patrick held the door open and tried to catch my eye.

Sighing, I picked up the bottle of pills, turning the container in my fingers.

"Is it really this easy?" I asked.

Casbus ignored me.

"Fine!"

I grabbed my leather jacket and walked out past Patrick as if I didn't know him, but his long strides caught him up immediately.

Huds was nowhere in sight when we turned down the long hallway, which was just as well. I was too tired to deal with the old battle axe and whatever vengeance she had in store.

As soon as we were out of sight of Casbus, Patrick looked me over with his golden hawk eyes that never missed a beat.

"Gathering your report for my mother?" I quickened my pace.

"Why are you here?" he asked.

"No small talk for you, hmmm?"

An inmate banged a metal door from the inside as we passed, and Patrick paused to speak soothingly to the 'guest'. I didn't want to run into Huds alone, so I stopped, waiting for him to catch up at the exit.

"How is she?" I asked, as he gripped my elbow and ushered me out.

"She wants to see you."

"She told you that?"

"It doesn't matter, you heard the boss."

I paused on the concrete stairs and looked out over the gardens. The sun warmed the part in my hair, taking away the chill of the morning. Mule ear daisies drooped from the weight of the night's dew above the shorter flowers fading in the gardens. The daisies were the last bloomers in fall, and the bees made their sluggish way through the filtered sunlight to get to them.

I was always touched by the beauty of the Homeward gardens, but even more so this morning. The pills, if they worked like Casbus said they would, gave me a sense of hope.

"Do you think..." I turned and looked at Patrick's jaw as he looked out over my head. "Do you think, if I ever needed to, do you think Casbus would let me live here?"

He sniffed heavily, a consequence of his early years in the boxing ring.

"Patrick?"

He looked down at me as if I were an irritating, younger sister. "You can't be caged, Rachel. It's as simple as that."

"Well, duh," I tsked. "I don't want to live in a cage."

He raised his arm and waved at a black car parked at the far building lot. The sound of its engine starting carried easily to us in the morning quiet. The driver followed the one-way signs, taking the long way around. We walked down the stairs.

"Stick to your resolution, and you won't need this place anymore," Patrick stated.

I kept my mouth shut and my eyes down.

"You are sticking to your resolution?"

I avoided his seeking look as an image of Donald's plaid jacket flashed before my eyes.

"So far." I scuffed my boot against a piece of loose concrete.

A sense of unease invaded my newly found sense of calm. Had I been stupid enough to share any details about the American with Casbus?

"Seriously though, I would have been better off going home with someone last night, rather than staying in my apartment alone."

Patrick's dark brows drew together over his crooked nose. "Why, what happened?"

I wanted to tell him, but he'd just tell my mother, and she'd start praying for my soul. Instead, I kicked the loose chunk of concrete, and it skittered across the road.

Patrick accepted my stubborn silence. He held out his wide hand for my coat. I gave it.

"Turn."

I did and slipped my arms into my jacket, while he held it up for me.

"Is this how you hold my mother's straight jacket?" I shrugged away from his hands, pulling my coat the rest of the way up myself.

He clasped my upper arm and turned me back around. His big hands reached for my neck and for a second, I thought he might throttle me. But, he only straightened out my collar, making sure not to touch my skin. He never touched my skin, and that rejection alone was enough to make me want to seduce him.

"Stick to your resolution," he encouraged, frowning at my softening body language. "Six more days."

"Well it would help me to stay on track, if there was more than just a monetary reward."

I gave him a knowing waggle of the eyebrows.

His indignant stare was a total buzz-kill, but his hand was still on my collar. I was tempted to turn my head and lick his round knuckles, just to be naughty.

"There *will* be a reward. A reward of the *spirit*, a reward much greater than that of the flesh."

"Nothing like a little Bible talk to turn a girl on." I jammed the pills into my jacket pocket. "Seriously, you've been hanging around my mother too long."

He jerked on my collar, forcing me to look at him. "You have to trust! Trust your Momma! Trust yourself."

The words sounded vaguely familiar.

"Did my mother tell you to say that?" The black car pulled up at the bottom of the stairs. I ignored it. "Cause you and I both know she's crazy, right?"

He looked past me and gave a hand signal to the driver.

"Trust, Rachel."

"Who do you trust, Patrick?"

He took my elbow and walked me down to the car. Opening the door, he waited until I got in before carefully shutting it.

I rolled down the window, "You want me to follow this celibacy bullshit, but you won't even tell me why? Seven days can be a long time. You can build an earth in seven days, you know."

"You listen to your Momma. I'll listen to my grand-daddy Ebba, and we'll come out on the other side."

Ebba? I was sure this was the name on the cassette tape. It wasn't a name you'd likely hear twice. It was time to get some answers. I scrambled out of the other side of the car and turned to face Patrick over the roof.

"You tell me what's going on, or I'm going to start screaming."

The look on Patrick's face told me I'd hit the nail on the head. He didn't want Casbus coming down on him.

I opened my mouth and gave a squeak. His face clouded in anger, but he slapped his big hand down onto the roof of the cab, and the driver pulled away from us. Now, there was nothing between us but air and a few feet of asphalt.

With a quick look over his shoulder to make sure we were unobserved, he took my elbow and marched me in the direction of the cut fence. I swear I was getting sick of all the manhandling.

"Tell me about this Ebba," I pressed, yanking my arm from him and jogging a few steps to keep up to his long stride.

We rounded a bend, which placed the rhododendron bushes between us and the building. Finally, Patrick slowed his walk.

"Ebba..." he said, frowning. "Our families were connected a long time ago."

"What do you mean?"

"My ancestor... his name was Ebba, worked for one of your ancestors."

"No shit."

I shivered and wished we could walk on the other side of the lane where the sun was touching the grass.

"So, you and my mother were playing what... 'guess my genealogy' and our family trees intersected or something?"

He placed a finger to his lips. Ahead of us, a beautiful blue bird was splashing in a birdbath. The stone bowl was blackened inside by algae that had been touched by the frost, but the base was beautiful. It was covered in orange lichen that had grown up the sides like a papery plague. The bird bathed in the cold, brackish water, flapping its wings and splashing up drops that soared like crystal bubbles in the morning sun.

In a low whisper, Patrick continued. "Over 350 years ago, our families worked together to solve a problem. Only it was never solved."

I let out a snort of disbelief. "Three hundred and fifty years ago."

He eyed the bird, not seeming to care whether I believed him or not.

"Okay, I'll bite." I put my hand on my hip. "What was the problem they were trying to solve?"

He slid his glance my way and the sun cut behind his irises making them golden.

"You," he said.

A chill shivered the back of my knees. Before I could say another word, Patrick made a grunting noise and bolted past the birdfeeder to disappear behind the honeysuckle.

"What the..."

"What are you still doing on the grounds?"

I spun to face the heavy-jawed frown on Huds' face.

"I was just..."

The cab pulled up behind her, the bumper almost touching the back of her calves before she moved to the side.

"Just waiting for my ride!" I grinned and waved, then jumped into the car's back seat.

"Burn rubber, boss!" I ordered the cab driver.

The grin dried on my face like plaster, while the car pulled away from the old battle axe. When we were past her, I turned in the seat to look out the back window, worried about Patrick.

Huds was bent at the waist staring into the bushes where he had run through.

The Virginia Wilds: The Powhatan Alibi

When Scarlett first started to feed, she selected only those in the colony who would not be found or missed, settlers at the outskirts of the slow creeping civilization, men who had no family or neighbours, and trappers who were nomads. These were the first victims providing the sustenance Scarlett needed to prepare for the miraculous spark of life, William Cain, her husband, would place in her belly.

Scarlett left her victim's body scraps for the wild creatures to consume. Evidence was gulped by the black bear, ripped and shredded by the coyote, and pecked to pieces by the crows. Shred by sinewy shred, the She's heinous deeds were cleaned from the bone and ingested into the North American food chain.

When those unfortunate enough to be hunted by the She did not show up to buy their pound of sugar or flour at the fort's mercantile, when they did not arrive in port to trade pelts with the merchant ships on schedule, the good people of Jamestown pointed their suspicious thoughts to the only "other" they knew and wondered aloud if the Powhatan Indians were breaking their treaty for peace.

The colonists' misguided blame was fortunate for Scarlett, who could usually only feed for a limited number of years in one place before people became aware of the demon among them. That was the trouble with intelligent prey. They would only stand to be prey for so long, before they would become the predator.

This switch of roles had happened many times in the past, yet Scarlett had survived for centuries because she had thought long term. How could she not? She was an entity who could roam for eternity on the earth she shared with a population of beings whose lives were like short seasons next to her longevity. She was immortal, unless they caught her, a fate which had befallen many of her species over the centuries.

Scarlett mourned the memory of the thousands of her kind who had been burned and decapitated and spiked with stakes carved for death. After so many slaughters, the few who had escaped persecution had each come up with their own strategy to outwit their food source. Some had even learned to bend time, to forever exist in a period before enlightenment, before gunpowder, and organized government.

Some had disappeared without a trace. One such was Scarlett's true mate, Gräfen. He was a predator like herself, but not common. He was their King. None existed higher on the food chain than Lord Gräfen. Through breeding with him, Scarlett had kept her line pure.

Only now, time was running out. Scarlett could not find her mate, and she was not willing to outwait her luck.

Scarlett needed to have a child, for she had devised her own way to survive. She had become like the Cicada that spends nine-tenths of its life burrowed safely underground. After years in its larvae form, the Cicada nymph digs to the surface, sheds its husk and flies to the trees where it buzzes in the heat of summer, until it attracts a mate and continues its line. Only Scarlett didn't burrow into the earth. She burrowed in her own young. She became a parasitic suspension within her descendants.

She hid like a shadow in the souls of her offspring, biding her time, until the descendants of her victims forgot to fear her or died. After which, Scarlett waited another two or three generations, until the tales of her heinous acts of violence and ungodly feeding became folk lore—stories told to the gullible to scare them in the night.

While this beautiful and deadly creature waited, her family line grew and spread its tentacle-like branches into the larger population. Her daughters bred daughters, and granddaughters, and great-grand-daughters and so forth, until they too forgot the role they played in carrying evil close to their hearts.

Yes, it was a perfect plan for survival. But in order to prepare for a sleep of such lengthy duration, Scarlett had to build up her energy. Just as the great Canadian grizzly bear must stand in the cold rushing waters of the Athabasca gulping salmon, Scarlett had to cut the strays from the herd in Jamestown, filling her belly for the growing of her vessel, and the long hibernation ahead.

Chapter 13: Adam's Reach

O h, the pills were good.

My muscles relaxed, and I sank a little further into my saggy mattress. My mind was floating on clouds called "peaceful" and "safe", and when I came down a little, I wondered if the meds could finally bring me a normal life.

The future only held my thoughts for a second or two before they drifted to delicious things, like hot Highlanders with brandy-wine hair and emerald-green eyes.

Angus.

A flush warmed my cheeks, and I pressed my hand against my face.

Angus was different than any man I knew. Dangerous, sexy men were my regular cup of tea, for I liked to push the bar just for kicks. Angus wasn't like that. Oh, he was sexy, no doubt, and his foreign ways changed the game enough to excite me. I couldn't always tell what he was saying, or thinking, couldn't always predict what he would do. Maybe it wasn't just the accent, the cultural difference. Maybe it was that men like Angus didn't generally want women like me.

I released a big sigh and cuddled further into my blankets.

He had compared my eyes to a jar of Scottish honey "shining golden in the sun". It proved Angus had only seen my good side. What would he have called my eye colour if he'd seen the frightful things that bounced around in my mind? Scottish tar? Sheep shit?

I shook off the negative thoughts.

A shy ray of light shone into my eye through the open curtain above my bed. I was too comfortable to reach up and pull the curtain closed. Instead, I buried myself deeper in blankets and relived the way Angus had pulled me up onto his lap at the Albion! His hands had been strong and sure, no fumbling, no hesitation. I had so wanted to slip my hands under his shirt and caress the muscles I had seen straining against the cloth.

I floated sensuously for a few more seconds, wrapped in 'what could be' fantasies.

When would I see him next? I could call him.

Suddenly, I jarred fully awake as I realized I didn't even have his phone number.

"Argh!" I mumbled forlornly falling back onto my pillow.

It was just as well. I didn't know how to make it work with a man who was confident and handsome and normal. I was setting my sights way too high, and I'd just end up getting hurt.

I closed my eyes, allowing my mind to drift off again. A juicy scenario with Angus the Bull ran through my sleepy mind as I dozed in fits and starts. After a few muscle twitches jolted me awake and set my nerves on end, a nightmare sucked me down.

I WAS INSIDE A ROUND building, a wall of field stone curved without corners until it touched itself, like a snake eating its own tail. Cold seeped out of the porous grout lines between the floor's stones, leaching out a dampness that sucked the heat from my bare feet.

I stopped pacing to rub my hands up and down my bare arms. I blew air into my hands and was surprised to see a white mist form. No wonder the rough slate floor felt like ice. It was freezing. Lifting my foot, I placed it sole to shin in an effort to warm it against my leg.

I studied the chamber. The only light in the room was coming through two small windows at least twelve feet above the floor. And above that, the stone walls faded into black. I could not see the ceiling. I didn't know how high the roof was.

It struck me I might be in a silo, but, across the room was a fireplace, and a bed off to the side.

I searched but found no blankets, no sheets, and no wood to burn. The grate was clear of ash as if it had never held a fire.

"Damn!" I cursed in frustration.

At the same time, I spoke, I thought I heard someone call my name. I quickly scanned the room.

The wind blew down the chimney, causing the material of my light shift to flutter at the same time a man's voice whispered behind me, "Mah dahlin."

I spun, adrenaline spiking through my veins. The room was empty.

"Will you evah be able to forgive me?"

The agonized whisper had me turning again, and this time my eyes lit on the plank-wood door imbedded in the far wall. Sweat broke out along my back, and I began to shiver, my teeth chattering with cold and fear.

I ran to the door, stumbling on my long skirt, terrified someone would grab me before I got to it. Just as I reached for the iron ring the door flew open, banging my knuckles and almost knocking me backwards. I righted my balanced and stared in surprise.

Two men stood in the doorway. White swirls of thick mist curled around their woolen knickers and hand sewn shoes. Behind them a thick fog rolled across a grey countryside.

They were dim, blurred, and it wasn't until they lifted their heads that I saw who they were. Duncan and his side-kick, Colin.

Happy to see them, I stepped forward, a cry of welcome on my lips, but they ignored me. They knelt into the fog and lifted an unconscious man up from the ground. The thick mist swirled away from his back, revealing a shock of dark reddish-brown hair.

Angus.

"What's happened?" My voice was strained.

Angus' head was slumped down between his shoulders. His feet trailed uselessly behind him as they dragged him forward. I stepped aside to let them enter.

"It's awrite," Colin grunted as he struggled to heft his half of Angus' body. "His blood's too thick is all."

Angus groaned, and Duncan said something in Gaelic and somehow, I understood his words. He said something about my helping Angus.

I wanted to leave, run out the door while I had the chance, but I was afraid to be alone, so I followed them back into the place I had been trying to escape.

Colin and Duncan lowered Angus awkwardly to the bed, Colin half falling on top of the Highlander. The mattress ropes groaned under the Scotsmen's weight, but the coils held. When Angus was settled, the two men pulled their hats off their heads and stood looking down at their friend.

"What should we do?" I interrupted their moment, which looked suspiciously close to a last rites ceremony.

They avoided my eyes. "Only ye ken what tae dae, lass."

"I don't know anything." My voice was too high. "I don't know why I'm here."

Their faces were grim as they backed away from me, their hats crushed against their chests.

"Where are you going?" I called out. They kept moving away. "Don't leave me alone with..." I paused. With what? I cast a furtive look around the room.

When my back was turned the two men slipped out through the door. When I looked, they had disappeared into the grey mist.

I ran toward the doorway, intending to go after them. But, the heavy barrier slammed shut with an echo that rose up into the endless ceiling.

"No!" I stood wringing my hands.

A whisper in that voice broke the silence from behind me, "What name have you taken?"

In a panic, I rushed the last few feet to the door. I clutched the iron ring with half frozen fingers. It was so cold, it burnt my palm, but I clung stubbornly and pulled. The door was solid. I leaned back and dragged on the ring with all my might to no avail.

The man's voice spoke again, the Southern drawl seeming to float down from the darkened ceiling. "I could have saved you. If only you had stopped!"

"Colin! Duncan!" I pressed my cheek against the smooth wood and shouted their names. I hammered the weather wood, keeping up a racket so I wouldn't hear the voice speaking to me. I hammered until bruises coloured my hands. I screamed out my fear until my voice was a harsh rasp, but they didn't come back for me, and Angus never stirred.

I slumped to the floor in despair. Pulling my long skirt down over
my knees, I tucked it beneath my cold feet.

Angus lay sprawled where the men had placed him, his body
splayed out like a fallen soldier, not twenty feet from me.

I contemplated going to him, but I was afraid to leave the door.
Afraid to cross the room.

The cold slate caused a bone ache through my limbs and finally I
could stand it no longer. Pressing my back against the door, I slowly
pushed myself into a standing position. My knees were shaking as I
walked to the bed.

It was only 13 paces to Angus' side, but it felt like an eternity.
And then, finally, I stood beside the bed looking down on him.

His eyes were closed. His leg hung off the mattress, the edge of
his boot heel braced against the floor as if he had just flopped onto
his back from a standing position. A few buttons were missing on his
white shirt and it had fallen open to reveal a dark line of auburn hair
running up the centre of his belly from the waistband of his pants.
His ribs expanded in a slow steady rhythm as if he were just asleep.

I wanted to wake him. I wanted him to comfort me.

"Angus?"

What was wrong with him? His shirt was clean, unstained by
blood or dirt or any other signs that might explain the reason for his
unconscious state. There were no bruises around his face, no broken
angles to his bones. He appeared to be sleeping peacefully in a bed
much too small for his size.

At that moment his arm slipped to hang down from the mattress
with his thick fingers pointing at the stone floor. Beneath the roll of
his white sleeves, the muscles of his forearm showed.

I knew this pose. I knew this flesh.

Angus' arm was like Adam's in Michelangelo's Sistine Chapel
painting. The image had adorned the first pages of my mother's
Bible. Often when I was locked up and ordered to read the scriptures,

I would stare at the picture, memorizing the curves and dips of the muscular limbs. Angus' hand pointed to the floor just as Adam's hand was stretched out for God's touch in the painting.

It was this arm, this slab of muscle that took my eye and would not let go. The threatening roils in my stomach returned, and I recognized it for what it was. It was hunger. A deep aching, cavernous hunger that only someone who had felt starvation could know.

Now I wanted something else from Angus.

I knelt at his side as I had knelt by the little altar in my mother's closet. My hand alighted on his ribs as they rose with each breath. I leaned closer, my breast pressing against his arm until the fire of his flesh threatened to scorch my skin.

Desire uncoiled like a dragon's tongue unfurling within me.

"I have waited for this day," I whispered.

He groaned and thrashed his head as if he were in pain, and the movement touched me like a lover's caress.

Here was my want. Finally, after all these years, here was the cure.

"I can help you." I licked my mouth.

Angus was beyond answering, beyond making decisions. I would have to decide for him.

At his waist was a dagger sheathed in a leather belt. I scratched at the flap, and before I knew it, the knife filled my palm. I raised the blade, and the sharp edge flashed silver as it touched the light streaming from the window far above.

I could smell the musk of the animal sacrificed for the bone handle. I brought the knife to my face to better hear its bleating terror as its blood darkened the soil around its panicking hooves.

Then I lowered the bleating dagger further and delicately slit the soft skin on the inside of Angus' arm. Blood welled, filling the slice like a red globe that paused, shimmering for three heartbeats. It broke from his damaged flesh and flowed towards his hand, until finally, the liquid jewel hung quivering on the end of his finger.

My chin trembled in response.

The drop brimmed as its red trail slid to join it. I eagerly waited for it to grow too heavy to hold to his fingertip. At the second of its release, I swooped and caught it on my tongue.

THE SOUND OF THE LANDLORD'S children jumping on the floor above woke me. Groaning, I dragged my cotton-head from the pillow. Sunlight streamed through the window over my head, making me vow to never again fall asleep with the curtain open.

Judging by the strength of the sun, it was late in the morning. I should have felt refreshed, but I didn't. My joints hurt, my head was a stuffed drum, and my eyes burned.

I shuddered at how real my dream had seemed. If I thought about that now, I would surely go crazy.

Digging in the nightstand with one hand, I found the bottle of pills Casbus had prescribed. The small typed instructions blurred. My hand shook as I twisted the cap. Who cared anyways how many pills Casbus thought I should take? I was done with fear. The doctor had promised these would control my delusions. I figured I only needed one more to keep the 'crazy' at bay.

Popping the tablet under my tongue, I lay back down in the bed. It tasted bitter, but I hoped it would work faster if I let it dissolve under my tongue. Staring at the stained ceiling tiles, I imagined the pill's magic running down my throat with each swallow. A sleepy feeling of calm weighed on my lids.

When I was almost gone, I jerked awake, aware that if I fell asleep again the nightmare would suck me down.

I threw off the quilts and staggered out of bed.

Chapter 14: All Roads Lead to Rome

It's amazing what a little sunlight can do. My apartment looked much different than it had the night before. The structure was the same, but things which had seemed threatening in the night looked normal, now. Except for my bathroom which had never been normal. My kitchen was flanked by two doors. The one on the left led to a toilet and sink, and the one on the right led to a shower stall that jutted out into the landlord's side of the basement as if it were an afterthought. It was literally a steel cage hiding behind a door.

Hammering sounds on the other side of this door alerted me that the landlord was in his basement working. There was no roof over the shower stall, and sometimes when I showered, I got the creepiest feeling he was teetering on a stool, stealing looks at my naked body.

I decided to skip the shower. Quickly sponging off using the bathroom sink, I donned the same jeans I'd worn the night before to avoid creating unnecessary laundry. Grabbing a green off-shoulder shirt, I slipped on matching flats.

I needed a smoke, badly, but held to my rule of food first. After a few hurried mouthfuls of granola cereal, the kettle started to shriek.

The sound startled me. I quickly shut it off, noticing right away the hammering in the basement had stopped.

The landlord knew I was up.

All of a sudden, the air seemed hot and oppressive, sticking to the insides of my lungs and gumming up my thinking. It was an old feeling, pinned to the inside of my rib cage by another man. But the landlord could resurrect it, especially when he arrived unexpectedly to leer and try to convince me to consider sex-trade, rental options. I had to get outside before he trapped me in my apartment.

Taking my teacup, a smoke, and a lighter, I made a quick exit up the concrete steps and out into the sunny, fall day.

"It's about time, lassie," an impatient voice said, when my head crested street level.

I started, spilling hot tea on my hand.

Angus was sitting on the stone fence that separated my landlady's flowerbed from the lawn. He looked unbelievably handsome in a cream knit sweater that pulled across his pecs.

"Nae need tae be fearful." He stood and leisurely stretching out the kinks in his shoulders.

Instinctively, I stepped away from his size and took a good look at his shadow that was cutting across the flagstones. It was brown and textured, like an antique photo. My shadow beside his stood out as a brilliant red silhouette of my body. To Angus, both shadows would look black, because he, like everyone else, saw the shadow world in shades of grey.

I ran my glance up his body to his eyes, which seemed to be crinkling in amusement.

"How do you know where I ..." I tried to sound outraged, but I got caught up in the patch of reddish chest hairs peeking above the V-neck collar of his sweater, "...where I live?"

"Yer raven-haired friend thought ye might like company for breakfast," he grinned down at me.

Unbelievable! This was Lene's payback for the attention I'd taken for myself at the bar.

He turned his wrist and looked at his watch. "Though, it's too late for breakfast, now."

I said nothing.

Cold sober and on my landlord's doorstep, I was a different girl than the one Angus had met at the Albion. As my grandfather always said, you don't shit where you eat. To me that translated to any number of handy life mottos, like you don't court danger on your doorstep. As well, my impulses were reined in by the meds. This morning, I wouldn't be so quick to throw myself into a risky situation.

I set my teacup on the stone edging and leaned into my lighter flame to buy myself a moment to think.

Blowing the smoke out of the side of my mouth, I said, "Lene was wrong" in my best James Dean.

Angus put his boot up on the stone beside my teacup and leaned on his knee. "Hmm," he nodded at me, as if we shared a secret. "Sae that's how it is."

I gingerly lifted my teacup away from the steel-capped toe of his shit-kicker.

When I didn't answer, he continued, "Well, I'm here now. Might as well stay."

My chest rose my breath quickened. I didn't know the man from Adam, but I knew men. More men than I should have known. Even though Angus was being a little more forward than I liked, I was secretly happy he had found a way to reconnect with me.

Angus watched the thoughts cross my face. "That's settled, then."

Taking his foot from the half wall, he placed his hand on my back and guided me back down the cellar stairs.

Suddenly remembering my promise to Patrick, I stopped just inside the door. It didn't stop the big man. He turned sideways to get between me and the couch, making no effort to avoid brushing his chest against the front of my body, and watching my face as he did so. His closeness brought his scent to my face. He smelled of greens and nature, like cedar. I almost leaned in and sniffed him up.

He kept right on past me. I stood by the door, hands hanging at my sides, the smoke from my cigarette rising to heat my knuckles and watched him invade my private space.

My entire home was one big open room, entirely visible from the doorway, and I could imagine how it looked to him—a man of the world.

On the far left, my little white fridge, which was Mayberry old, had one of those rounded tops and a yank down handle on the front door. It could never hold enough food to feed a man like Angus. Hell, he probably ate steak for breakfast, lunch, and dinner in order to grow those muscles of his.

The guy was like a shiny new coin and it made everything around him look old and ratty. I was embarrassingly aware of the duct tape repairs on my vinyl kitchen chairs and the worn armrests on the grey couch that had been part of my meager inheritance from my grandmother. The more he looked around, the more uncomfortable I became.

"No gadgets?" Angus asked from the living room which was sectioned off from the bedroom by the couch.

"I'm sensitive to noise."

I wasn't about to tell him voices delivered messages to me through electronics, and after last night, apparently without electronics, too.

The cassette tape! How could I have forgotten about it until now? My eyes darted to the kitchen table, but it wasn't there.

"Hmm." Angus seemed to be thinking about something as he moved to my bookshelf and ran his fingers along the frayed cloth covers of my classic book collection. "Lots of books, though."

It wasn't a question, so I didn't answer.

Instead, I tipped my head trying to peer into the dark corners under the table, but I was too far away to be sure the cassette wasn't under there.

Angus nodded, as if I had spoken. He moved to the opposite side of my antique bed. The ornate wooden headboard was as high as Angus' shoulder. There was a crack traveling down the centre of the carved swirls, for the wood had been dried brittle by a century of use.

Had I put the tape in my night table? No, I had meant to bring it to Casbus as proof. Only, I didn't think I had found it.

Angus stared down at my jumbled sheets, and I forgot the cassette and blushed at his scrutiny.

While he studied my bed, I studied his handsome profile. His profile line flowed smoothly from his thick hairline over his intelligent forehead, and his fine, straight nose. His lips were full, his beard little more than a shadow covering the strong jut of his chin.

God, he was so sexy! I couldn't figure out why he was attracted to me. Or maybe he wasn't... I'd never seen a man so interested in furnishings before. Angus dragged his hand slowly across my pillow.

"Thinking of suffocating me?" I baited, wondering if he wasn't a serial killer after all.

"That's not what I was thinking about."

I could feel the heat of his gaze from across the room, and he knew it. He held my eyes long enough to make me squirm. Then he moved into the neutral space of the kitchen, which was two steps from the bed and pointed at my teacup

"If yer not gonna make me tea, I'll have tae drink yers," he smirked, revealing a dimple.

Serial killers don't have dimples, do they?

As I passed him, Angus took my teacup, his fingers brushing mine in the exchange. My blood simmered, but I kept moving. My typical pattern would be to throw myself into his arms with abandon, just to put an end to the sexual tension, so I didn't dare stop.

At the counter, I ran some water on my cigarette and left the butt steaming in the stained sink. Smoking in my apartment was becoming too common. I'd have to get tough on my rules. But, maybe not today.

Filling the dented kettle provided a chance to gather my wits. As I placed the kettle on the element, Angus stepped forward until he was standing behind me. He slipped his arm past my waist to turn on the stove element. I was trapped.

His deep voice warmed my ear. "Ah was sorely disappointed when ye ran off last night."

He wasn't touching me, but I could feel the heat radiating off his body and it was making my skin electric. If I turned my face to the side, our lips would meet. I closed my eyes and tried to resist.

His voice was seductively low. "Now's yer chance tae finish what ye started, lass."

Oh, how I wanted to, but his "owe-me" tone had to be dealt with.

I twisted my body to face him making sure not to touch him, anywhere. The oven handle pressed painfully into my tailbone.

"And what would that be, Highlander?"

"What." He considered my annoyed expression and grinned. "Suddenly braw?"

Putting my hand on his chest, I tried to move him back. He was as solid as stone, and like a fool I stopped pushing, just to feel his heart beating under my palm.

"Seems tae me, we were making progress." The deep purr of his accent rumbled along my nerves.

He looked down at my hand, then raised his head to raise an eyebrow at me. I didn't feel mocked. I was surprised as he was at my sudden softening.

He placed his warm, calloused hand over mine said, "Ye ur such a mishmash of sweet and sharp," his nostrils flared. "I cannae wait tae husk yer layers and see who's below."

I was desperately close to lifting my mouth to his.

"Might take me all week tae sift through ye."

Seven days with the Scottish bull? I almost swooned at the thought.

Seven...

Something about seven was important... Patrick!

I yanked my hand from his chest and immediately felt the loss.

"Keep your hands off my layers, if you please, Scotsman," I said, but not unkindly.

He barked out a laugh and stepped away, giving me room to scoot.

"Calm yerself, Kit." He picked up one of my granny's once-white, vinyl chairs and flipped it around with a twist of his wrist. Lowering his bulk into it, he crossed his arms over the back. "Tae kin a woman like yerself takes time, and time I have."

I put my hand on my hip and raised an eyebrow. "Oh, that's what you're after... understanding."

"I dae want tae ken ye a little better, before...."

"Bullshit." I squinted at him, suspicious. What guy had ever wanted to get to know me?

"An' why not?" His face threatened to break into a smile.

"Because there's not much to know," I lied.

He dropped his glance down my body and back up again. "Oh, there's more tae ye than meets the eye, lass."

He'd run for the hills if he really knew. "And why do you think that?"

"Ours is not a meeting of chance."

"Are you talking about fate, again? Is that your excuse for stalking me?"

"Do I have tae stalk ye?"

His eyelids dropped, hooding his eyes, but he was still grinning.

"Are ye runnin' from me?"

I was tongue-tied, unsure of what to say.

With his elbow on the back of the chair, he studied my anxious paralysis.

"Run if ye wish, but ye cannae get away from me, Kit." There was a second's pause, during which his smile slid away. "I cannae let ye."

The German Ocean: He Who Let Her

Out

Twelve years before William Cain planted his seed in the heaving, clutching beauty beneath him, Erland McNab paid for passage on a trade ship leaving the Swedish port of Stockholm. The ship was carrying timber and unfinished metals and was bound for Scotland. After almost a year of convalescence, Erland McNab was finally healthy enough to go home.

He was travel weary, having crossed the German Ocean and half of Sweden to fulfil his destiny, but he knew it could have been worse. Many of his ancestors had tracked her further: Muscovy, Wallashia, Bavaria. No place was too far, when the threat of death hung over the entire clan. Erland knew, had he not kept to the bargain his ancestors had made with The Fergus She centuries before, a harsh punishment would have befallen them all. Sweden was not so very far to go, and lucky for him, there had been many Scottish merchants who had provided shelter and food along the way.

At 23, it seemed as if Erland had spent half of his life waiting for the She to demand him at her side. Ever since his 16th year, the other lads his age had wed women, participated in clan raids, and secured their futures with crops or trade. Yet, all the while Erland, first born son of The McNab, had waited.

The wind snapped the sails above his head, pulling him into the present. The descending orb of the sun set the water to shimmering as if a thousand stars were dancing just below the surface.

Erland considered how like the ship he was. She was like the wind, compelling him to her, and in his rush to obey, he had left a wake behind him, just as the ship creamed the waters behind the stern.

The sun dropped beneath the line of the horizon, leaving behind an orange sky that fired the rippling waters. Erland shivered and drew his plaid close as he remembered the same glitter in the She's eyes. Before the She had risen behind them, those same eyes had been the soft brown colour of a hunted deer's shivering glance. But they had turned at the moment of her changing.

Chewing a dry piece of skin on his lip, the young Scott's attention wandered to when he had first arrived at the thatched-roof cottage in Sweden. The draw had been so strong he'd only had to follow it to find her. It called him across the ocean, through towns and villages, over hills, across rivers, and through it all, the thought of meeting her kept him in a state of excitement.

All through his short life, he had dreamed of the day they would meet. He had imagined the beautiful home and the fine woman he would find there. He had expected a powerful beauty. On the final day of his journey, he'd been disappointed to arrive at a peasant's hut, its sod roof crumbling dirt over the doorway.

Erland had needed to duck his head to get through the small opening. But once inside, his eyes had adjusted to the dim light, and he had spied the girl. She was tossing and mumbling on a filthy matt, feverish... unconscious. Her clothes had been no more than rags, and her body was unclean, its scent filling the cottage with a cloying stench that forced Erland to breathe through his mouth.

The squalor and her condition had shocked him, and he had suffered a moment of doubt. It wasn't her age, for he knew she had to be eighteen for the change to begin. It was her frailty. Boney knots pressed under the pale skin of her thin wrists.

He had paused there, his bulk filling most of the hut. Unsure of what to do, he continued to stand, looking down on her soot-smudged face surrounded by matted, black hair.

So shocked at the reality of the task before him, the young Scot failed to notice the old crone sitting in the shadowed corner of the hut until she rose from a twisted wooden chair. Her age was impossible to tell, but she was very old, her face scored by deep lines, her lips disappearing into a toothless mouth. Her lids pinched eyes the colour of steely flint that considered him warily.

"Death will be your reward if you don't take her," the old witch cackled. "Death to you and yours."

Erland tried not to stare at the humped back bulging beneath the old woman's rough woolen cape.

The crone thrust her gnarled fingers into the air between them.

Erland gulped against the dryness in his mouth, before dropping a few coins into the old woman's palm, as he was sure many men had done before him. The twisted fingers closed upon the coins, and the hand was pulled back beneath the cape. The hag gave him a heartless sneer and shuffled out. The wind slammed the stick door shut with a rattle.

He was alone with the girl, alone with the memory of the instructions the men of his clan had sent him off with.

"Woo her first," his father had said.

"If thae heart of thae host loves ye, then thae She won't harm ye when herself rises in yer arms, lad," Uncle Sheamus had promised.

"Put goose grease on yer dick, and thae fires of hell won't burn yer balls off," his younger brother had counselled, with all the somberness of a prophet.

But how does one woo an unconscious woman? Erland wondered, as he pushed at the girl with the toe of his shoe. She did not seem to feel his prodding, for her eyes remained closed. Erland decided he would do this thing quickly, and then, flee back to Scotland where he belonged.

The Scotsman slid the long ends of his plaid to the back of his belt and knelt, not bothered by the rough mat beneath the thick callouses on his knees. Carefully, he braced himself above the frail body and used his leg to push hers apart, for he loathed the idea of touching her soiled body with his hands. With a silent prayer that she was not infected with any disease that might kill him before he got to live his life, Erland brought to mind the prettiest girl in the clan. Holding that tantalizing image in his mind, he carried out his duty, while trying not to breathe through his nose.

It was almost a mercy when the She rose to take control of the girl's half-starved body. Erland felt new strength cause a shudder through the slight form beneath him. The eyes had opened, the pupils locked on his own. He was taken with the velvety chestnut of her irises, and the gentle soul he had a quick glimpse of before the dark centre bled ink and her eyes turned black.

The girl had struck him with unnatural strength, and he had fallen onto the dirt floor, his legs splayed out before her. Standing in her rags, her posture triumphant and proud, the She had raked her gaze from his face to his short hose. Her brazen stare shocked Erland who had never seen a woman act so boldly.

He had been warned that he would journey far to couple with this creature who held his clan to a debt. But nothing could have prepared him for the exquisite, yet terrifying night that had come.

Erland drew the sea air deep into his lungs and tried to halt the memories before the She could leap upon him in his mind. He was not ready to recall the rest, the blood, the pain, the journey to death's door, and his own timely resurrection.

The young Scot brushed his hard-skinned fingers against his neck, feeling the welts of scars poorly healed. The scars would be his 'proof' to the clan that he had paid the debt he had been born into. He had kept the McNab's word with The Fergus She.

The only duty left to him now was to find a woman and make a son and pass to him the promise that in a few more generations, his descendants would receive the call. Erland doubted he would be alive when the next McNab was beckoned by the She.

Erland looked up at the stars and thought about how life was just a cycle. Just like the sun would rise, a first-born son of the line Mc-Nab would be called upon. And when that time came, his descendant would have to answer. He would travel to wherever the She was and release the devil from the constraints of the body it was inhabiting, forever burying the true owner of the body in a tomb of her own flesh.

Such was the price of oaths.

Chapter 15: A Gentleman's Kiss

Angus hadn't taken his eyes from mine, and I was tumbling into a hopeful and foolish belief that maybe, this time I could have a real relationship. Then the kettle let out a half-hearted whistle of warning, busting through my fuzzy moment, and freeing me to turn the element off.

My back to Angus, I wrestled with conflicting emotions. What was I, twelve? I was acting like a groupie, hanging on his every word, melting away inside until I was a puddle of stupidity.

I could feel his eyes on my back, as I fumbled with the tea bags.

Red Rose tea, a man, a woman, and a little chitchat. It should have been a comfortable moment. Yet, like a virgin about to be sacrificed at the volcanos' edge, I could sense the precipice dangerously close to my feet.

Did I dump the tea and tell him to leave? I was no different than a humble village girl. When faced with the hot, mesmerizing lava below, a simple girl would forget about escaping back to the village. Gods were like that. They hooked you in. Made you think you had control until you were free falling into the flames.

Yet, the meds were making a huge difference. Instead of sabotaging myself by jumping right into the sack, I was making Angus work for it. Almost as if I was worth more than just sex, maybe even worthy of a relationship. Was I ready for a relationship? Sex I could do, and hell, I could do it well. But nursing "togetherness" outside of the bedroom? I didn't even know how to make conversation that wasn't flirty, teasing, or caustic.

Chewing on my fingernail, I decided I was medicated enough to try.

Picking up the pot and a cup, I turned to face him with false cheer. "Only in Canada".

To my surprise, he hadn't been looking at my ass. He was looking at his watch, which was a little insulting. He lifted his eyes and said, "What?"

"You know, only in Canada." I put the teapot down onto the 1930s, grey linoleum table. "Red Rose tea? The commercial?"

I poured a bit of steaming, rich liquid into my cup to check the colour.

"Is that why the wee rose?" He traced the red rose painted on my table top.

"There's a rose on the table because my granny liked roses."

Angus tipped his teacup and drained the cold tea from breakfast and held out his cup for a hot refill. After pouring, I sat opposite him, wedged in between the table and the fridge.

"An' what do ye like?" he asked.

I checked to see if he was mocking me, but he looked genuinely interested. I couldn't recall any man ever asking what I liked, at least not outside of the sheets. I didn't have an answer.

"Ye like reading," he said, as if it were a great secret.

I succumbed to flirting. "I like it when you trill your tongue like that on your 'r's."

His eyes darkened, and he rubbed his thumb across the tips of his fingers. "Do ye now, lass?"

A hot flush coursed through me. I put my head down and mentally slapped myself.

Drawing in a steadying breath and tucking my hair behind my ear, I told myself I could not do that again, not if I was going to attempt normal conversation.

"How long are you here for? In Canada?"

"How long do ye want me tae stay?"

That sounded dangerously like commitment, and I was seized by an impulse to run.

"Don't," I shook my head, patted my pockets for my smokes and not finding them, scratched at my hair. "Don't play with me, Angus."

"I get the impression ye like tae play, Kit."

I tapped my nails on the table. "I can't ..." I cleared my throat. "I can't flirt with you. I can't handle it."

He was burning me with those smoldering eyes, and my temper flared because I couldn't do anything about it.

"What do you want from me!"

"Ye'are a cannie one tae notice I have an underhanded purpose."

I raised my chin, readying myself. "Did Lene put you up to coming here?"

He looked earnest as he leaned forward, sliding his hand across the table towards me. I didn't pull away when he placed his hand over mine.

"I had fun last night, and I like ye." He gave my hand a little shake. "Is that sae hard tae kin?"

I pressed my lips together. He shook his head giving me a disapproving fatherly look.

After a few minutes of silence, he nodded, "Awrite. If ye cannae tell me what ye like, tell me what ye don't like."

"I ..."

Faint laugh lines crinkled at the corners of his eyes.

I shrugged, feeling painfully out of my league.

"It's awrite lass, I already ken what ye don't like."

"Oh yeah? What's that?"

"Ye don't like people getting close tae ye."

I pulled my hand from his. "Screw you."

Where were those damn smokes?

"Why do ye think that is, Kit?"

He was trying to tease me, but I saw a flicker of sadness cross his face, and I wished I had something stronger than tea to drink.

"I don't need another psychiatrist. One's enough, thank you very much."

The look he gave was more than I could take. My pride boiled up over the meds.

"I know what you like! You like to touch everything. You drag your greasy fingers all over my books and my furniture. Stop touching my stuff! Better yet, get out!"

He scowled and put down his cup with a bang. "Yer not makin' this easy."

"Making what easy?"

He sighed and rubbed his hand down his face. This was the part where he should have figured out I was more trouble than I was worth and got up and left. If I'd been thinking straight, I should have let the silence hang until it got unbearable and forced him to leave, but I couldn't cut him loose, not yet.

I scrambled for something to say, "What did Lennox mean, at the Albion, when he said he wouldn't go through with it?"

Angus adjusted his features into a neutral expression. "I don't recall."

"He was talking to you, standing by the wall when Lene was on the phone."

A tic jumped in Angus' jaw before he answered, easily, "Och, some bet he had with the boys."

"But this was about a woman. I heard him say so."

Angus laughed deep in his chest. "All bettin' 'tween men is about women, lass."

He was quick to come back to his good nature, his smile so warm and generous, he melted away my agitation. I was becoming hooked on that humorous sparkle in his eyes, and I didn't really want to be prickly. I offered a flag of truce.

I stuck out my hand for a shake. "My name's Rachel."

His teeth flashed as he gave a nod, closed my hand in his and said, "And sae it is."

Angus stood and pushed his chair out of the way with his boot. A cocky smile revealed his white teeth. Pulling on my hand, he drew me out from behind the table until I was standing in front of him.

He bent down and before I could say a word, he cupped my face with his hands and pulled me up to his mouth. I grabbed at his wrists, becoming steady once his lips covered mine.

His lips were soft and warm, and I leaned into the moment, holding still while we breathed together. Then he began to tentatively explore my mouth and a warmth tugged in my centre, promising to melt away my resistance.

The kiss became dangerously loving, caressing my scarred heart with promises of tenderness. He tilted his head to the side and deepened the urgency. I slipped my hands around his back, trying to press my body against his, but his hands held me captive, held me at arms length so the only sensation to concentrate on was his tongue delving deep into my mouth.

I took him and met him in a dance of passion, played out with our lips, our tongues, our breath. As my knees weakened, he drew back slightly to tease my resolve, kissing my passion into submission with softer caresses. In his arms, a sweet high flushed away the baser desire, and I relinquished my fire to his growing tenderness.

When he pulled away, I groaned with disappointment.

"Open yer eyes, lass."

My hazy focus found his face.

"Scottish honey," he whispered.

His thumb stroked my cheek.

I wanted his mouth back on mine, but I didn't know if I could control myself and stop when I needed to. My eyes darted nervously to the bed behind him. He followed my gaze.

Brushing the hair away from my eyes, he said, "Today, Rachel, I'm only going tae kiss ye."

I'd never had such a promise from a man.

"On your Scottish honour?" I probed, tilting my chin, suspiciously. "Even if I beg you for more?"

In a somber brogue, he vowed, "Ah swear it oan th' souls of mah dead ancestors, and by th' honour of th' McNab clan, I wulnae dae more than kiss ye thes day."

The gravity of his speech shivered along my skin.

"That's a bit much, but okay."

"Yer a saucy one, ye are."

A flutter of insecurity made me ask. "Yes, but do you want more?"

He locked down my joking with a smoldering look. "I want ye like nothing Ah've ever wanted in this world."

His eyes were burning like Northern lights, flickering between green and gold, and the hunger in his gaze spent my will. I slipped my arms around his neck and kissed him until my lips were bruised and raw, until a spin started up behind my eyelids, making me light and feathery. But he wasn't done. His hand cupped my jaw and he tilted me in a slight dip, nestling my head firmly in the crook of his arm. Held so, he worked me over, his mouth becoming more demanding, and I thought I would faint from the intensity.

The last chards of distrust I had been hoarding in my heart quivered and faded away under his attentive pursuit. With a soft moan, I gave in fully to his demands, allowing him full access to my being. He knew the moment of my surrender and marked it with a grunt of approval.

Chapter 16: Blood Makes the Line

A sharp hammering on the front door caused me to jolt out of Angus' arms as if I'd been zapped by an electric surge.

"Open up! I know you have a man in there!" A voice shouted.

"Omigod!" I fisted my hand against my mouth. "It's the landlord."

Dread dropped into the pit of my stomach like a stone.

Angus' confused look turned to something between determination and fury as he took in my reaction.

He crossed his arms and stood like a sentinel in the centre of my apartment. "Open the door," he told me, his voice as cold as a Canadian winter.

I hesitated, sure I'd get the boot this time, but Angus' grim nod spurred me forward. I opened the door a crack.

My landlord stood outside in his typical handyman jeans and plaid jacket. The skin on his face was purple and blotchy, maybe from the fall weather, maybe from anger. He was literally vibrating with outrage. If my home hadn't been on the line, I might have laughed, for his nose was quivering like a rat.

"I know you've got a man in there," he accused, pushing up the side of his grey toque.

I slouched to take up the two-inch difference between us, trying to make myself appear less of an Amazon.

"I can explain..." I tried to think of a quick lie, a reason why I'd broken the house rules.

He pushed his chest out.

"Rachel." Angus spoke impatiently behind me.

Caught between the two of them, I stepped back, opening the door wider until the landlord was standing directly in Angus' line of view.

The quivering stopped when he looked past my head at Angus filling the space behind me. He pulled his toque lower over his brows and set his jaw.

"What's the problem?" Angus asked. He was speaking slowly, enunciating without his accent.

The landlord stepped forward. I stepped back, bumping into Angus who gently moved me to the side, making room for the landlord to enter.

Keeping a wary eye on Angus, he pulled off his work glove and shook his finger at me. "You know the rules! You're not to have a man in this apartment."

I shrunk back as a spray of spit flew from the man's mouth.

"That's archaic, and very probably, illegal." Angus said. He stepped closer. "She pays her way."

I did a mental check, trying to remember if I had paid the last month's rent.

"You," the landlord turned to him, "have nothing to say about this."

He turned back to me, "And you... Is he going to give you a home when you lose this one? Is he?"

I avoided Angus' eyes. "No one needs to give me a home."

"Well you have one here, missy, and you're throwing it away, for what?"

I thought about being back on the street. The landlord looked Angus up and down, scathingly.

"Is it worth a quick screw with this Neanderthal?" He asked, piercing me with an ugly glance and thumbing at Angus.

Angus grabbed his hand, twisting it to the left. The landlord squealed like a pig and dropped down on one knee.

"What are you doing?" I cried out.

"Apologize to the lady," Angus demanded, never taking his eyes from the landlord moaning at his feet.

"Stop it!"

"I'll set the police on you..."

Angus gave another twist and the landlord squawked, grabbing his elbow with his other hand.

"Apologize."

I grabbed Angus' arm. He felt like banded steel. I couldn't make him stop. I was invisible to them both, unable to control the situation. Panic rose to clench at my throat. I stepped back, my hand at my neck.

"I apologize," the landlord sputtered. "I'm sorry. Damn you!"

Angus threw the man's hand away from him, and the landlord fell forward onto the rug near my feet.

I stood speechless, my eyes filling with tears.

You'll pay for this." The landlord scrambled up and staggered to the door. "And you, missy..." His eyes were bloodshot. "You better start packin.'"

A mental numbness spread through me like a frosty mold. I'd just lost the only place I could call home, and I didn't have first and last month's rent for another. A tear cut loose from my lashes and dropped through the air to the rug as I realized what I must do.

The landlord banged out the door.

"Wait!" I rushed out the door after him, catching the back of his jacket as he reached the top stair.

"Please," I insisted.

I glanced back over my shoulder, but Angus hadn't come out of my apartment. "Please, we can talk..."

He turned.

I looked away from his triumphant sneer and whispered, "Later."

A hungry look darkened the landlord's eyes and everything good and sweet unveiled by Angus dried up and hardened like obsidian.

"Get rid of him," the landlord ordered.

I resisted the impulse to tell him to go to hell, wiped the last tear from my eye. I nodded.

The landlord dug in his chest pocket with his uninjured hand and pulled out the cassette tape that had been on my kitchen table the night before. He held it out to me, and I could see there was no ribbon streaming from it.

"I fixed it for you."

He fixed it? Sometime between last night and now, he'd been in my apartment. Either when I was at the Homeward, or when I'd been sleeping.

"Thanks." I bit the word out and reached to take it from his grasp.

He trapped my hand with his short stubby fingers. "Later." His eyes glittered like mica.

I turned to hide my disgust. The cold wind whipped away the last of my warmth as I stared down at the open door to my apartment.

The beautiful moment I'd just shared with Angus was ruined forever. I had to take care of myself. There was no one else to help me. Gulping down my nausea, I took the steps down, one at a time and each concrete block was a marker for each brick in the emotional wall I resurrected inside, hardening myself against love, against trust, against the promise of what I thought Angus was going to be.

I gently closed the door before looking at him.

Angus stood glowering beside the couch.

"Ye should not have gone out with him. I had it under control."

I raised my eyes and gave him the ice look. "You don't tell me what to do!" I let my rage loose to flare hot and destructive. "You do not control my life!"

"What did ye promise him?"

"Anything," I spit the word at him. "Anything that will allow me to stay here."

His face was red, and a vein pulsed at his temple. "Is that all yoo're worth?"

"How dare you!" I shouted. "You just screwed up my life, and you expect me to leave it that way?"

"Ye don't have a life, Rachel."

"I did until I met you."

I didn't know, then, how true these words would become.

I pointed at the door. "Get out!"

I was shaking with anger, not sure what I would do if he wouldn't leave, when I suddenly choked on my spit. I coughed into my hand, but my mouth kept filling with liquid. Hacking, I coughed out a spray of red between my fingers.

Angus' face reflected my alarm. I wiped my chin with my hand. It came away slicked with blood.

"Are ye a-right, lass?" He stepped forward, opening his arms to me.

I side-stepped him, moving quickly to the kitchen sink, my hand cupped beneath my chin as the tinny taste pooled under my tongue. Over the sink, I opened my mouth and watched the slick red drops fall.

Angus had moved up beside me.

I turned my back on him and tried to spit the blood out to clear my mouth enough to speak, but it kept coming.

"Don't be alarmed lass, I kin what's happening," he said from behind me.

I unravelled a handful of paper towel and dabbed the inside of my mouth to figure out where the blood was coming from.

His hand on my back was all I could take. Hot tears fell to mix with the blood coagulating in the bottom of my stained metal sink.

"Yoo're going tae be a-right."

I was bleeding from my mouth. How was that alright?

"This is natural fur ye."

I spit into the sink. "What?" My voice was slurred. "What does that even mean?"

I put the paper towel over my mouth and turned to look at him.

"This is part of yoo're journey, set from the day ye were born."

What is?" I mumbled into the wad.

He held his hands out. "I don't kin why ye weren't told."

I stamped my foot. "Told what!"

He took my hand in his, even though it was smeared with dried blood. "Told about us. About what we have tae dae."

Angus was talking crazy and if my mouth wasn't filling up again, I would have laughed out loud, because the irony was too much. The one man I had found, the one man I could have loved... turns out he's crazier than me.

I shook my head slowly, unable to believe it.

"Kit, don't..."

Angus tried to hold onto my hand, but I pulled it away and pointed at the door.

He looked troubled. "Destiny, Kit."

I took the towel from my face. "Bullshit."

Blood trickled out of the corner of my mouth and ran down my chin.

"Please leave," I spoke through the gore.

He didn't move.

I turned and gagged into the sink.

"When yoo're ready tae hear the truth, I'll come back," he said, softly.

The door shut behind him, held back my tears, and drooled blood into the sink.

ONCE THE BLEEDING SLOWED, I found its source. Above my eye teeth were slits like shark gills oozing a mixture of blood and water. Had Angus passed on some fast-acting venereal disease through his kiss?

I patted my gums until the leeching stopped, washed my face, and cleaned the sink. Turning, I took in my empty apartment—barren without Angus in it.

Blinking my eyes rapidly, I drew out my old friend, anger, to kill the hurt. It was like lancing a boil. Once you see the pus, you forget about the cut.

I looked for something to take my rage out on. The cassette tape was on the counter. I screamed and swiped it with my hand. It ricocheted off the wall and rattled like old bones as it fell behind the fridge.

Chapter 17: Lies Beneath the Leaves

My rage was still loose, whipping up all kinds of self-destructive impulses, including throwing the teapot across the room. But, I showed rare restraint by carefully carrying the teapot to the sink. The tea bags flopped wetly, breaking open and spilling mushy leaves into the drain as I poured out the still-warm tea.

In a daze, I watched the amber liquid trickle and pool in the gouges and dents of the stainless-steel sink. The colour of the tea against the steel reminded me of Angus' hair in the morning sun.

If the landlord had minded his own business, I would have been running my hands through Angus' hair. I would have been happy. I wouldn't be worried about losing my place. I wouldn't be contemplating letting the creep touch me.

My anger dwindled with the tea, replaced by a heavy ache of loss and regret. I shouldn't have broken the rules. When I break the rules, I get broken. I knew that.

Some part of me wondered if it wasn't just as well things turned out bad. Something was off about Angus. I mean, everything was good, but he knew things he shouldn't know. He showed up where he shouldn't be. But he was so damn sexy, I kept ignoring my instincts. Even knowing something was wrong, maybe even dangerous after that little episode with the landlord, my lips weren't about to forget his kiss anytime soon.

Hot tears washed my eyes, and I swiped at them with the back of my hand. The reality was, Angus wasn't going to take care of me. He didn't offer, even when the landlord asked if he would. I had to take care of myself.

I walked to the bed-side table and grabbed another of Casbus' specials. Placing it under my tongue, I waited to swallow until the pill was dissolved.

Outside my window, the landlord's Firebird roared to life. I knelt on the bed and cautiously pulled up the corner of the curtain to watch the car back out of the lane with relief.

The landlord was gone, for the time-being.

I flopped down onto my bed and let out a loud sigh. I needed to get good and drunk before I could face his upcoming visit. That way I'd be unaware of whatever he did. That way I could stand it. Maybe.

The pill tasted bitter. I got up and grabbed a glass, Just as I was about to turn on the tap I noticed the fine tea leaves had settled into recognizable shapes in the bottom of the sink. I didn't know what I was looking at, but I knew it was not random.

I'd had some experience with this sort of thing before. When my mom would get too fanatical, I used to escape to my friend's house, and her step-mother would read my tea leaves. There is a delicious sense of justice in having your future told, after being Bible whipped with the Old Testament.

With a quick glance over my shoulder to dispel the imaginary baleful and disapproving glance of my absent mother, I examined the sink.

The first shape was round with four lines coming up from the top. Each line was slightly tapered, and then, spread out. It looked like a puffer fish or a broken tennis racket, though neither had anything to do with my life. The X was there. It was always there. It was the warning to stop, and it was expected in a derailed life like mine. I ignored it.

I was looking for something new, something hopeful. Maybe not quite a heart, but some guidance about Angus, about who he was, about whether I could trust him.

In the random sludge, a strange shape, almost like a bouncing ball trail with a quick directional change caught my eye. I had never seen this one before. Using the tip of a knife, I separated the intersecting arch points. The broken symbol had no meaning I knew of, so I carefully joined the points back together before separating another spot.

"Just like the dinosaur's skeleton is in the tar pit, the message is in the leaves," I whispered.

Leaking out the last rivulets of clear amber liquid was the shape of an arch. I had never read the arch, but I guessed my friend's stepmother had. With the symbol separated from the clump, it was simple to see the natural division in what was left.

I grabbed a notepad and pencil and carefully sketched out the symbols. When I was sure the rest was random nonsense, I twisted on the tap and watched while the water spattered out and washed away the mess.

Sitting at the table, I studied my notes. Each symbol had to be read together because the reading was for me. But three of the symbols were tied together and had to be parted, which could mean the reading had another connection. I was going to need help making sense of it.

The phone's shrill ring cut through my thoughts, and I jumped.

"Judas!"

I grabbed my pencil before it rolled off the table and made my way to the phone.

Lifting the beige handset on the third ring, I answered. "Hello?"

"Have you checked the children?" A fake male voice said.

I rolled my eyes. My most irritating friend, and the last thing I needed...

"Magda."

"Whatcha doin?" She asked in her singsong way.

My initial irritation slipped away, as I confessed I'd been thinking about her step-mom and how she could help translate the meaning behind the tea leaves.

"Is Jean around?"

"Yes..." A soft noise shuffled in the background. "But first, I want you to listen to this!"

The phone line launched a song into my ear that was definitely not Magda's typical heavy metal listening. It sounded more like a rock-a-billy, love ballad and at this moment, love was the last thing I wanted to think about.

"Magda!" I hollered into the mouthpiece.

The serenade continued.

"Magda!"

Just as I was about to hang up, she came back on the phone. "Well?"

I sighed in exasperation, "Smooth..." and tried to get her back on point. "Listen..."

"It's Robert Plant!" She squeaked excitedly. "I swear, he's back and this is his new song, "Sea of Love". I can't get enough of it! It's just perfect for shadow boxing."

The "pffft pffft" sounds of her punching the air came over the phone. If she had her gloves on, that meant she probably was no longer holding the phone.

I put two fingers in my mouth and whistled until she answered.

"Magda! Listen, I need your help reading my tea leaves. There might be a serious message here, and I need to know what."

She hummed a few bars, asked what I'd seen, then kept on humming.

"The arch. I saw the arch in my leaves."

"Annnnd?" She drew out the word.

"And the three."

"The three. Hmmmmm. Annnnnd?"

"It's too confusing to explain over the phone!"

"It's not confusing at all. I already have your reading figured out."

Before I could enlighten her on the symbols I hadn't shared, she smacked her lips and said, "The reading is this... you must stop the threesomes because it's making me over-emotional."

I started to laugh. I couldn't help it. I was stressed, exhausted, and pretty much heartbroken. I laughed way too long, while Magda hummed her new favourite song and sucked loudly on her cigarette.

I coughed to a stop. "You're such an ass."

"Jean says she'll give me a ride over to your place, today."

I listened to the line crackle in the silence, while I tried to decide if I could handle Magda right now.

"I can read the leaves for you."

Come to think of it, her being at my place would be a good way to keep the landlord away.

"Listen, there's something else you need to know about the tea leaves. I shared the tea with a man."

The scrape of a needle scratching across a record killed Robert Plant's voice.

"What man?"

"Just some guy, but that's not the point. I ..."

"Did you screw him? Did he have a big wang?"

"Magda, for god's sakes."

"Tell me everryyything!"

"There's nothing to tell. That's why I'm reading tea leaves."

"You didn't jump in the sack with him? What's up with that?"

I didn't take the bait, concentrating instead on the click I heard come over the phone line. My eyelid twitched.

"Sooooo, let me come over. I've got some new moves I want to try on you."

Magda was a combat nut, and she loved pitting her karate moves against my street fighting skills. She had yet to take me down. I usually enjoyed the challenge, but there was no way I was going to engage in a wrestling match with her. Not tonight, nor anytime soon in the next week.

"We can hit the bar instead."

"You can introduce me to this mystery man, and I'll help you get him between your legs."

I heard that weird shuffle noise in the background, again.

"Magda, someone's listening in on our conversation."

There was total silence followed by a click.

"It was just my loser brother."

"You don't have a brother."

"That's why he's a loser."

I laughed, but I was a little creeped out.

"We can work on your tea reading when I get there," she promised. "And I'll bring my Led Zeppelin albums."

"You know I don't have anything to play them on."

"Who said anything about playing them? We can just look at the covers."

She gave a dreamy sigh, and I made a vow to get drunk. Suddenly, I remembered the cassette. "Wait!" I yelled into the handset. "Bring your ghetto blaster."

"What for?"

"I've got something I need to play."

Chapter 18: Ancient Readings

While I waited for Magda to show up, I kept one ear on the driveway hoping the landlord wouldn't arrive first. Every time a car drove past on the road, my hands would start to sweat, and I'd fantasize about cutting the landlord's balls off.

Thanks to my treatments with Casbus, I could spot the crippling worry and use some strategies to put the landlord and Angus out of my mind.

For tonight my plan was to listen to the cassette tape and jot down what it said. I was going to figure out the tea leaf reading with Magda's help. And, after that? I was going to prove to Angus, and myself, and anyone else who cared that I damn well did have a life.

The plan set, I took advantage of the landlord being away by taking a quick shower. Standing in front of my closet door mirror, I squeezed my damp body into an acid washed miniskirt. I turned left and right in front of the mirror. My legs did look like they went on forever, and tonight I was going to use that to my advantage. I pulled a sheer black crop top over a red bra, and back combed my hair into a totally awesome do. Magda arrived just as I was applying the last swipe of smoky shadow to my lids.

I opened the door. With my backcombed hair on top, and my red pumps on the bottom, I was cresting over six feet in height. I was giving off a serious vibe that announced I was ready... for anything.

Magda leaned back, slid her John Lennon sunglasses down her nose, and announced, "Radical!"

I laughed but was secretly pleased by her compliment.

As I held the door open for her to maneuver through, I gazed over her head. I could just see a hand waving from the station wagon, but before I could wave back, the car pulled away.

"Hey, isn't your step-mom coming in?"

"What for?" Magda smirked, putting the ghetto blaster and her military green canvas bag on my coffee table. She dug in her jean jacket pocket and held up a little, brown vial between her finger and her thumb. "She'd just be a bummer at the party."

"Deadly!" I grinned back, shut the door and locked it.

Two burned knives later, I was hacking away, trying to clear what felt like a hairball in my throat, but oh, life was so much funnier.

"I'm surprised at you." Magda turned sideways in the living room chair to hang her feet off the side.

The back of my head was resting against the couch. The ceiling was way too interesting at this moment to answer Magda. She kept talking anyway.

"Normally, you'd be all pissy."

"What do you mean?"

She raised her voice in an imitation of a frightened little girl and waved her hands around. "Oh, the landlord."

"Yeah, well, things change." I sounded as if I were in complete control of the situation.

"Really? What's changed? Did you finally spread your legs for the old creep?"

She was killing my high. I pushed myself up into a sitting position, not caring that my miniskirt was almost around my waist.

"How long have we known each other, Magda?" My voice droned out in the robotic tone I reserved for bullies and my mother.

"Long enough for you to have smoked 400 cigs I've paid for!"

Her answer made me forget where I was going with my question, so I ignored her and turned my attention to the cigarette pack Magda had tossed onto the coffee table. I could hear her complaining. I didn't answer. I ran my fingertips over the tinfoil slip protecting the filters. The rough feel of the tin paper drew me in, the crackling a mesmerizing reaction to my touch.

"Rachel!"

"What?" I put the cigarette pack down and gawked my eyes.

"You're such a space cadet!" She waved her hand in the air. A bubble of stoned laughter slipped past her lips.

I was still confused, "What?"

Magda imitated me, "What?"

The tickling in my cheeks pulled my mouth up into a smile, and I cracked up.

She slurred out some unintelligible line followed by blurts of stoned laughter.

"Stop it!" I slapped the couch cushion beside me in mock outrage. At the impact, a cloud of dust blew up from the old cushions to whiten the air.

I barked out a shocked laugh. Magda slapped her forehead with her hand and pointed at my couch.

"Time to dust!" she shrieked.

"You think?" I leaned back, and belly laughed. The idea was just too funny. Who gave a shit if there was dust when you're going nuts! A cramp started in my stomach muscles.

"Stop!" I begged and pushed the bubbling urge down, while I gasped for air.

Remembering my gums were unstable sobered me instantly. A gentle probing with a tissue showed no bleeding. I hid my relief from Magda who was slowly calming, shaking her head and moaning out some call on mercy.

"Okay, okay." I finally remembered our purpose. "So, listen, Magda, I want your help with this tea leaf thing."

I retrieved my notepad and shoved it into her hands. She took hold of it but gave a stubborn look.

"What were you wiping at your teeth for?"

"Gingivitis. Now pay attention."

I tapped the paper with my red fingernail, trying to draw her eyes to the symbols and lines I had jotted down.

She squinted at my face as if trying to see past my closed lips into my mouth.

"Magda, please."

"Fine!"

Her delicate hands shook out the pad making the pages fan with a whoosh. She blinked a few times, comically drawing the pad closer to her nose and pushing it out away from her face, as if she couldn't read my drawings.

"C'mon!" I went back to my spot on the couch, fighting the urge to giggle. "Only you can tell my future."

She gave a sly look. "If you only knew."

"Knew what?"

She held the weird secretive stare until I sat up straighter and frowned. Then she dropped her glance, shrugged and said, "Knew how to read your own damn tea leaves."

She tugged off her jean jacket revealing a big blue eye on her Cheap Trick "All Shook Up" World Tour T-shirt. Leaning forward with her elbows on her knees, she took a closer look at my drawings.

I couldn't quit glancing at the eye on her shirt, while I waited for her to scan the pages.

She bit the end of the pencil, then spoke around it. "On the phone you said you shared the tea with a man, right?"

"Right."

"That means everything I read in the symbols has to be taken in the context of that sharing." She paused. "Understand?"

"Maybe." The drugs were interfering with my ability to think clearly.

Magda looked back at my notes. "This symbol is interesting."

"Which one?"

She held up the paper and aimed the pencil's point at one of the tea leaf sketches.

"Oh, that. Washroom for men, right?"

She sucked in her cheeks. "It's more than a shit-house sign. It's Mars."

"Tell me more, Professor know-it-all."

She shook her head. "I don't know how you get through life. Listen. The signs come from ... never mind... basically, the "washroom" sign represents Mars, iron, and men."

I was already getting bored and started picking at my fingernail. "That's what I said."

"Okay. So, this sign is used now for the men's room, but at one time it represented other things... like.... like uh..."

She seemed to be debating whether to share or not.

"Like what?"

"Like biennial plants."

I chuckled. "Waiting here for something relevant."

"Everything could be relevant... that's the point."

I rolled my eyes and sighed. "Okay fine, what's a biennial plant?"

"A plant that flowers once every two years."

"So, something you don't want in your garden, right? Cause what's the point?"

"Maybe," she leaned back in her chair. "So, this, what you say you found in your tea leaves..." She waved the paper at me. "Let's say its a typical male sign with a circle and arrow."

I nodded. "Let's say that."

I started to laugh at the seriousness of it all.

"But!" She interrupted me. "Why is the arrow turned backwards? That's my first question."

"Right," I giggled, again.

I tried to put my thinking cap on. "Maybe it's not really talking about a man?"

"No, it's too detailed and specific. Do you know how hard it is to create a symbol like this with tea leaves?" She raised her brows.

I started to shake my head, no, but she continued her little rant. "We have to respect that."

"Ohhhh kay." I reached for another smoke. "Respecting the tea leaves, here."

She tapped the yellow pencil against her teeth. "It's a male symbol." Tap, tap. "But maybe the man doesn't know he's a man."

"Like, omigod! Who couldn't know?" I raised my hands in the air. "I can tell if someone's a man from 20 feet away."

"Is he a man?"

I frowned at her. "Who?"

"Duh!" She tilted her head, her chestnut hair falling like a curtain to the side. "The guy who shared the tea!"

I closed my eyes and let myself float back to that kiss. "God, he is undeniably a man."

I lit the smoke and blew out a fountain of grey into the air before me, thinking of Angus' fine body.

"Oh, oh, somebody's got it bad," she mumbled, while she scribbled on the page. "Is this serious? Is this something I should know about?"

"Don't hold your breath. I think it's over." My high started to drop out at the bottom.

"That's a surprise."

I slipped on a fake smile, trying not to be a buzz kill. "So, the arrow points in..." I encouraged.

Magda was rude, but she was easy to redirect.

She scratched at the back of her head. "Maybe he has an inverted penis."

I burst out into stoned laugher, choking on my smoke.

"How would that even work?" Magda was making all these lewd hand gestures.

"Stop, please..." I begged her, while tears ran down my face. I didn't want my make-up ruined.

"Well does he have an inverted penis?" she asked.

"No," I shook my head. "I don't know. I didn't look."

"What's wrong with you? You always look."

I wasn't sure how much I wanted to share with Magda.

"He's... different."

"Diff-her-ant?" She flopped her hand in a weak wristed flap. "Or different?" Her golden-hazel eyes dominated her heart shaped face as she waited eagerly for my answer.

"Seriously." I rolled my eyes but couldn't help a smile. "Just... not my regular type."

She nodded and marked something down on the notepad. "Okay, so maybe that's the backwards arrow. He's a man, but not your regular man."

I accepted her theory.

She looked at the markings I had written on the paper and asked, "So, what's with the thistle?"

"What thistle?"

She held up the pad and pointed to what I had thought was a puffer fish.

"That's... is a thistle... what d'ya know."

"Hmmm..." She was really getting into this. "So, thistles are plants, prickly, purple flower, feed the Goldfinch, symbol of Scotland."

"Ohhhh."

How could I have not connected to the Fergus Highland Games sign posted by the local high school? The one that had the big thistle on it.

"Scottish!" I slapped my thigh "He's from Scotland!"

My heart started an excited pattering in my chest. "This reading *is* about him!"

Magda rolled her eyes. "Well, I'd say it's pretty straightforward."

"The reading?" I leaned toward her, excited to hear what she thought.

"Sure. He's a Scottish man who is not your typical man. The arch in your leaves brings you together, and the Ram symbol, the V stands for fire, cleansing, or rebirth. He's going to transform you, Rachel. In ways you can't imagine."

She threw the notepad down onto the table like she was making a touchdown with a football and hollered, "Humma!"

A guffaw forced its way through my lips, buzzing out like a raspberry. At the ridiculous sound, I succumbed to hysterical giggles.

Magda laughed with me.

Wiping the tears from my eyes, I let out a happy sigh.

"Okay, what about the three?" I asked when she'd calmed down.

"Isn't it obvious?" she said. "The transformation is pregnancy. You're going to give birth."

"What?" I sat up straight and pulled my skirt down. "No way!"

"Well then, stop. That's why you have the X warning. Stop now while you're ahead. Unless you want to be transformed into a big, fat preggo."

The image was too much, and I burst into another fit of giggles.

"Let's have some moosack!" Magda rifled through her bag.

"Wait! Wait! I want you to play something else."

I hurried to the fridge and looked behind it for the cassette tape I'd chucked. It wasn't visible, so I tried to muscle the fridge away from the wall.

Magda was babbling on about wanting to pay some top ten Much Music runaway hit, while I stared at the humming motor, a little worried about the wires and metal tubes at the back of the fridge.

It was old, and I wasn't sure what kind of safety rules they'd had back when they made this model.

I squeezed behind the fridge, bending my knees and lowering myself down enough to reach under it. I was wiggling and grunting so I didn't hear Magda approach.

"Be careful you don't get electrocuted," she warned, in a soft, low voice.

A spider skittered along the wall.

I couldn't get any lower from this angle, so I cautiously pushed out from behind the fridge. Magda was standing too close to me. "What did you say?"

She looked a little calculating, but then, her face cleared. "Be careful back there."

I hoped the hash wasn't making me paranoid.

"What are you looking for anyway?" She craned her neck trying to see behind me.

This time I squatted first and slipped my upper body between the wall and the fridge. "It's a tape."

"What kind of tape? And why's it back there?"

I mumbled, "Long story."

I shoved my fingers under the metal edge of the fridge. I could feel soft mounds of dust and something crunchy like an old cracker. My fingers banged a solid object that slid ahead of them.

"Oh," I forced my hand under the rusty edge, the metal pushing the skin back on my knuckles.

"Waiting here..." Magda droned.

"Just a minute, I've almost got it." My legs began to cramp, and I shifted to relieve them. "Hand me a comb."

She passed one of the knives we'd burned the hash on. "Great idea," I said, sarcastically. "Haven't you heard the toaster rule?"

Careful not to touch the knife to any of the wires in the back, I slid it under the fridge, hit something and heard a plastic rattle. A few more swipes with the knife, and the tape launched out to skitter across the kitchen floor followed by a number of dust balls and a lost paper clip.

"I got it!" Magda yelled.

We sat down opposite each other, the ghetto blaster on the short coffee table between us. It was past dark, almost time to go out to the bar. I wanted to listen to the tape before we left, not after we came home, not before going to sleep.

My heart was thudding as Magda placed the cassette in the door and shut it.

"Rewind?" She asked, her finger on the button.

Who knew what was up with the tape now that my dick-head landlord had "fixed" it.

"I have no idea."

"I'm so sure."

I gave her the finger.

"Okay, let's just play it."

She pushed down the button, it clicked, the tape wheels started turning, and static poured from the round black speakers.

I leaned forward, listening intently.

"Did you..." she started.

"Quiet!" I raised my hand.

"What are we listening for?" she went on.

I was listening for a name. The same name Patrick had used at the Homeward—Ebba. Only, all I could hear was static.

"Turn it over."

She stopped the tape, ejected, and flipped it. Putting it back in, she pressed play.

A voice I immediately recognized came out of the speakers.

"These are delusions, Ra-chel, delusions caused by your fears. Fears of being alone and abandoned, fears your mother has planted deep within your psyche."

It was Doctor Casbus speaking with his hesitant, two steps forward, one step back praying mantis rhythm. My hand crept to my chest.

The voice continued. "You operate on fear, but I can purge you of it. I can eradicate the need to be afraid. I can leech out the terror."

"Who is that?" Magda asked, her eyebrows raised so high they wrinkled her forehead.

"It's nothing, shut it off."

Magda did her 'What you talkin bout Willis?' face.

"Look here...." The voice was compelling. "Look here and release your fear. Allow yourself to let go..."

The wheels turned the static over with rhythmic squeaks.

"Did you let someone hypnotize you?"

I met Magda's wide-eye stare and jumped up, trying to shut off the machine before it could release anymore ammunition for Magda's judgement.

But Magda leapt up, all arms and legs, blocking my way. She belly-bumped me backwards, laughing as if it were all a game.

I tucked my head and tackled her, but she got her short legs grounded and stopped our momentum. We wrestled while she screeched with excitement. She twisted to the side, trying to get me off balance and flip me over her hip. I dropped further, wrapping my arms around the back of her legs and lifting her into the air. Staggering under her weight, I arched, holding her on my torso and reached back for the off button.

"Why doctor..." A different voice lathered the speakers with Southern sugar. "It has been a dog's age since you last called upon me."

The voice of my other locked up my knees and we went down, Magda falling hard to the side, half on the couch. It didn't stop her. She loved trying her training moves against my superior size. Her leg kicked up as I gained my knees and started to rise. I tripped over the foot she hooked on my ankle.

Casbus' voice continued, *"I am at your service."*

I went down, my hand poised to slam the stop button on my way, but my palm missed the ghetto blaster and slapped painfully against the coffee table.

"I trust, sir, you are keeping your word and keeping that woman under control?"

Woman?

We both lay still, panting, our silence a shared pact to stop.

The wheels turned, squeak, squeak, squeak.

I scrambled up onto my knees, a second ago ready to end that Southern babbler if I had to rip the tape out with my teeth, but the voice said, *"Our mother,"* and laughed, a sharp tinkling sound like pieces of glass striking a tiled floor.

"What is this?" Magda slipped up onto the couch without taking her eyes from the ghetto blaster.

"Sh!" I leaned closer to the black speaker to catch every word.

"Shhe iss ssecure, Mistress." Casbus' voice had changed.

Magda snorted. "Mistress? Is this Elvira?"

"Shut the hell up, Magda!" I cranked the volume, but the static only got louder, and I could barely hear the conversation.

Magda stomped off to the kitchen, obviously offended.

The Southern voice, my 'alter' voice, continued. "And have you ensured, Doctor, that we are safe from vigilant action against our person?"

"Pleasse be ssatissfied that you are ssafe, Misstresss."

I listened to the choppy sparks of static interference until I thought the recording was over. Into our tense silence, she spoke again.

"Come then."

A strange sob.

"Come, get that which you need to continue serving me, faithful Casbus."

A garbled cry burst through the static causing my muscles to tighten.

"What's happening?" Magda was unexpectedly at my shoulder.

"Ahh!" I shrieked and jerked to the side. "Magda!"

"It's not my fault you're such a bundle of nerves."

I sat up from the floor and slammed the stop button.

"Who was that creepo?" She asked, standing with her hands on her hips, frowning.

I pulled the tape out and flipped it over to look at both sides. It had to be the same tape. It was black, and the white letters were faded, but what the hell? Who had made this recording?

"I don't..." I started to say, but I did know and maybe it was time to confide in someone.

I let out a sigh and stood up.

"I think I know who it was."

I dug deep for the courage to tell her.

Her nose wrinkled. "Why do you hang out with such weirdos?"

I gently closed my mouth and dulled my eyes.

Magda stepped past me and grabbed her canvas bag. "I'm going to get ready."

She stomped off a second time, slamming the bathroom door behind her. Her judgement didn't mean shit. She was just pissed because, once again, she couldn't kick my ass.

Yeah, it was just as well. Her little snit fit just saved me from doing something really stupid, like confiding in a 'friend'.

I put the tape back in the machine. Rewinding it, I pressed stop at the part I wanted to hear again. With a clack, the play button went down under my finger.

"...iss ssecure."

Stop. Rewind. Wishing I'd been smart enough to pay attention to the tape's tack number when I'd heard my "other" speaking, I watched it scrolled backwards. 0067... 0054 Stop! I hit play again.

"...you are keeping your word? Are you keeping that woman under control?"

This was it. I listened, my body tense, my ears straining.

"Our mother," the voice said, and she released a cruel and cold laugh.

"Shhe iss ssecure, Mistress."

Stop.

The recording chased the last of my high away. My mouth felt like it was growing shit hairs. I wiped the corners where spit was pooling.

Why would Casbus have a conversation like that with my alternate personality? Is that what he did when I lost time? Join my split personality in a plot against my mother?

I thought about lying on his couch, trusting him. I thought about all the time on his couch during which I didn't know what happened, because I couldn't remember the session afterwards. Was that how he "leeched" my fears, by calling my split personality "Mistress"?

"No. No. No." I was mumbling the word, over and over, my head shaking from side to side. I didn't know what to do. Who could I tell?

My stomach threatened to empty itself. I put my hands over my mouth, pressing my lips into my teeth.

"What's happening?" I whispered through my fingers.

So many things had happened over the last few days. And I felt like I was twisting one of those metal puzzles after trying to separate the two pieces for hours, and it all comes apart in your hands. I knew connections were there, and in one twist, the right way, it would all become clear. I just didn't know which way to turn the metal shapes.

My lungs were aching, and I realized I had been breathing too fast, too hard. I switch to inhale in through my nose, but my heart kept pounding. Black flickered at the edges of my eyes. I rocked forward, trying to slow down my breathing.

My mouth was dry. I could barely swallow. I regretted smoking the hash. I regretted taking the pills. I needed to be sharp, alert, aware. This was all too much... things were...

My panic was coming hard and fast, my lungs pumping in response. Nausea roiled over me, my lashes flickered in a pre-seizure warning. I clawed at my throat as I wheezed for air.

"Whoa, whoa," Magda had me by the arm, dragging me to my feet. "Don't go having a bad trip on me."

She slapped my face, startling me out of the downward spiral.

She lifted her hand again, but I grabbed her wrist.

My brain was foggy.

"Maybe we did too much," she suggested and slowly twisted her wrist out of my grip.

"Here," Magda pried the cassette out of my other hand. "Let's just put this away for now."

She dug up her purse, grabbed mine, and brought me my red high heels. "Put these on. You'll feel better."

Numb, inside and out, I obeyed like an automaton. She counted out the bus fare.

Once we were sure I could walk, she gave me a brilliant smile. "Let's not let this go to waste. We're having a good time. Everything is about the good times."

"The good times," I repeated through numb lips.

"Time to pahr-tay!"

I followed her out into the street, because I didn't know what else to do.

Chapter 19: The Lion's Crouch

The minute the bouncers opened the doors to the King Eddie, the fast beat of hard rock shook the air inside of my lungs, dancing the band's rhythm in my chest.

An angry looking bouncer in black gave us a nod, approving our slut-wear. I knew we looked hot when he waived the age check and the cover charge. The owner liked women like us. We were good for business.

The flashing lights and pounding music were assaulting to my raw nerves. The bar was packed with people pressing in to watch Helix onstage rocking the joint with some seriously tight heavy metal. The dance floor barely had squeeze room.

Magda grabbed my hand, forcing us through the crowd, our bodies all jammed together, wriggling and leaping to the tune of "Rock You". The press of the dancers created a comforting herd-like feeling of safety.

Magda shouted out the lyrics at the top of her lungs, spelling out the chorus with the rest of the crowd. She dropped her head and head-banged the beat. I watched her hair whip under the flashing lights.

Releasing a deep sigh, I let go and let the music take me.

For hours, we danced and yelled, and I punched the air and the music became my incubator, a tight, rattling bubble of external stimuli.

A bead of sweat cut loose from my hairline, just as the lead singer jumped into the air and did the splits. The stage lights flashed, blinding me.

Abruptly, my mood changed, and I knew I had to get out of the crowd.

"I'm going for a drink!" I yelled at Magda, but she couldn't hear a word. She couldn't see me through her thrashing hair. She was really rockin' out. I left her.

Getting through the crowd was a little tricky with my "no touchy the stuffy" policy, but it was made easier by the medicated mood I was coasting in. My height also gave me an advantage. I could see over most people's heads, which helped me find openings through the frenzied dancers.

I was really enjoying myself. I had found an even keel between the pills, the hash, and several hard liquor shots, thanks to Magda and her generosity.

I broke out of the dance floor and into the cooler air. It was an instant relief. But then, my retreat was cut off by some guy who gyrated in front of me, trying to get me back into the dance area I'd just left.

Leaning his lithe body back, he pushed his hips forward, and motioned me closer with his hands in some sort of limbo cha-cha move.

I brushed him away with a wave, but he still didn't step aside, so I dropped the smile, and took a threatening step towards him. Dude was smart and cha-cha'd out of my path.

Ahead was the mass of bar goers I called the people watchers. They were wrapped in leather, jeans and zippered dresses in black and blue and cream, glittering with silver and gold, the plumage of the 80s, hard rock crowd. I blended right in with my long bare legs, provocative clothes, and wild, uncontrollable hair.

Behind the watchers, multi-coloured biker bandanas created a rainbow pattern along the dingy, concrete block wall. This was the tougher crowd. They didn't dance. They watched too, but with a different intention—opportunity. Walking past them was like walking a gauntlet of threat. The men saw me as a potential conquest, and their women viewed me as competition. It wouldn't take much to get into a confrontation, and I often had, just for the fun of it.

Tonight, though, I wasn't seething with rage or angst, or looking for some sort of proof I was still attractive. I was just here, trying to stay suspended in the moment, with no thoughts of the past or the future. This was a new feeling for me, a new state of being I hadn't been able to hold before, and I was grateful to be experiencing it. Perhaps this was the reward my mother's nurse, Patrick, had been promising.

I moved into the hall that led to the washrooms. The music was quieter here, where the lounge lizards made deals, passing goods and money back and forth.

"Hey baby, come have a smoke." One of the sleazier dealers held out a hand welcoming me to join his little group. A half-finished cigarette smoldered in his fingers.

"Get bent." I clipped it up with my nails, pacified him with a promising wink, and kept going.

Keeping eyes averted, I slipped past a group hunched in a tight circle, making illegal deals. I had enough trouble. I didn't need to witness anyone else's.

Ahead, a couple of smiling gents saw me coming. They kindly held open the men's door.

After taking a deep drag on the smoke, I flicked it at their legs, laughing when they danced away from the sparks. I ignored their outraged comments and slipped into the women's restroom.

There was a hall between the entrance and the actual wash-room—twenty feet of soothing isolation. The grey painted concrete blocks rose up on either side of me, creating a silent, cozy tunnel that cut me off from the noise and lights and social atmosphere of the rest of the bar.

I wanted to stay, but I had to piss, so I entered the open area, and paused under the oversized iridescent bulbs dangling from the ceiling on ten-foot black cords. Their light barely touched the twist-ed washroom stalls at the back where light was absorbed by the gun-metal grey paint.

Realizing I'd been holding my breath, I exhaled the last of the smoke from deep in my lungs. Through the cloud I noticed a move-ment against the far wall. I walked to it, interested.

Around the corner of the last stall, a male biker in jeans and a black leather vest was shoving a woman up against the cold bricks. Their hands gripped and pulled at each other's clothing with an ur-gency that advertised their disregard for public decency.

His biker belt was undone, and it hung like a decapitated snake on his hips, flipping and flopping with the movements of his thrusts. His jeans slipped, exposing his ass crack. Her arms wrapped around his back, and I watched her slender fingers delve deep into the black hairs that created a V over his tailbone.

I questioned whether I was seeing reality or just a vision brought on by the return of my 'crazy'. Then sound synced up with their movements, her moans rising as their hips picked up the beat of his grunts. His white buttocks tightened and dimpled as he rammed against her, causing her head to bang against the wall.

I was drawn forward by a desire to join them... Join them, separate them, and then corrupt them.

These were not my dark suggestions running hot thrills down into my belly. These thoughts belonged to the part of me who spoke to Casbus as if he were a servant.

I held steady and judged them for intruding on the washroom.

But maybe I was the intruder. Who was I to judge them? I would soon be bent over for a grunting landlord.

At the thought of the landlord, my anger sparked up, warming me from the inside. I bit my lip as deviant thoughts slipped over my mind like slick oil, blackening my intentions.

A desire to sniff them quickened. Ever so quietly, I slunk forward until I was a foot away. The woman's eyes opened. Then, her pupils widened with shock, as she gradually focused on my deviant expression. Her fingers fluttered at the ends of her hands like falling birds.

I took another step closer. Now I could smell them.

She screeched, tugged on his vest in a new way. He ignored her. Too caught up in his crescendo of lust, he kept driving with vigor, lifting her up above his shoulder where she had to meet my hungry gaze. She slapped at him with her feeble hands, and I wanted to slap him, too.

My mouth started to water.

"Stop, stop!" she was hitting his shoulder now.

Heat licked the back of my eyeballs, and I released a low growl. Unable to resist, I struck the heel of my hand against the base of his bandana. She cried out, twisting her head to the side to avoid impact, and his forehead nailed the concrete bricks with a hollow sound.

He jerked his body around, spinning away from the woman to leave her standing exposed. Her breasts nestled like oversized, glistening lychee fruit in her open shirt. He was glistening too, wet and hard and pointing at me like a dowsing stick.

"She was watching us!" the woman screeched, her voice in the octave range that made me hostile.

"Cool it," he snarled at her.

Shoving himself into his pants, he advanced on me.

Instead of the Southern accent I expected, a growl reverberated behind my words.

"No. You cool it, douche," I warned, holding my ground.

I felt the muscles in my face moved of their own accord, my skin tightening here and loosening there, as if under a sculptor's press.

The biker halted in mid stride. His eyebrows rose, his mouth dropped open as if the ligaments in his jaw had been cut. Alarm slicked his face with a sheen of sweat.

His woman cried out and covered her face with her hands.

I basked in their fear, welcoming it into my universe as the rousing ambiance it was. Stepping forward, growling and contorting, I approached.

He threw up his hands to fend me off and quickly backed up until the corner where the walls met stopped him.

"I'm outta here," he said to the woman, never taking his eyes from mine. He slid along the bricks, his hand clutching blindly for the door that was still many steps ahead.

I watched his movements with pleasure, enjoying the jittering of his knees which seemed to lock up when he needed them most.

As the door swung closed, I swung my lowered head to the woman.

Growing horror slid down her features as it became clear to her I now had only one target. She turned her cheek to the cool wall, mumbling in terror.

Something about her helplessness made me stop. She was really afraid. Immobilized by her terror. It thrilled me and alarmed me, all at the same time.

I blocked out the trembling excitement, pressing against the growing threat.

When I did not pounce on her, her posture changed, alerting me to her intended escape. She chanced a glance at me through the side of her eye, clutched her shirt together in quaking hands and took a few slow steps towards the exit. Whimpering sobs kept escaping her quivering mouth.

I didn't have enough control, yet, to let her know she was free to go, but I had enough control not to stop her.

She rushed out.

At her exit, a shadow of disappointment dulled my excited state, followed by an unexpected flick cast through my guts as if a whip had been cracked in the recesses of my bowels. I clutched my stomach in surprise.

"You're really hardcore," a soft voice spoke behind me.

I was careful not to turn around completely and reveal my face. Instead, I turned until my peripheral vision picked up a petite blonde in baby blue standing by the smoky mirrors.

If I hadn't been on the meds, I would have known she was in the room before she spoke. Hell, if I hadn't been on the meds, she might have been a liability, a witness to what I would have done to the biker and his hairy ass.

Or maybe the meds allowed it to go this far... further than I'd ever allowed before.

"I didn't have the guts to tell them to leave," she timidly confessed.

I kept my face turned away. "They're total losers."

My voice wasn't quite right.

I cleared my throat and slipped into a washroom stall before she could approach me. Pulling up my short jean skirt, I sat down and tried to see my face in the toilet paper holder. The reflection was distorted, blowing my skull out around my eyes and jaw. The blurred image didn't divulge the reason for the biker's reaction to me, so I stopped looking.

"My name's Karen," the voice said, and I wanted to rip her throat out.

"Whoa," I whispered, pressing back, seeking myself.

The silence dragged on. She needed to leave.

I couldn't trust my own voice, so I used Deniro's. "You talkin' to me?"

She laughed, "Yeah, I'm waiting to buy you a drink."

I nodded at the inside of the washroom stall. "Rye and Coke. I'll meet you at the bar."

Finally, her heels clattered their way down the concrete hall. I waited for the air pressure in the room to signal the door had opened and shut. The hairs on the back of my neck felt the change. I opened the stall door and hurried out to do a quick check in the mirror.

There was no time for whispered prayers before I faced my reflection. Besides, I wanted to catch whatever they had seen.

My eyes shone like luminescent amber, Angus' honey grown hard and brittle, and lit from something not of this world. My nostrils seemed winged at the base of my nose as if a bloodless slice had released them from connecting to my face. And below, my mouth was swollen, my lips curling up and away from my teeth. My skin was pulsing with vibrant blood flow. I wasn't sure, but my jaw seemed longer. I ran my hand along my jaw bone, feeling the strange juts under my gums through the flesh of my cheek.

This was new. This was a physical reaction to letting "her" have a little more control. And on the inside, the lust I'd felt watching him pound the woman while she stared fearfully into my eyes had been hotter than the yearning I had felt in Angus' arms. The rush of slamming his head against the wall had been a better high than the hash oil. The anticipation of him attacking me had spiked more physically exhilaration than I'd ever known.

This was dangerous.

This was the lion's crouch before the spring. And, I liked it.

Chapter 20: Like Flies on Honey

Sometimes, cowards collect their courage and get you later. I was feeling reckless, and I hoped the biker man with his hairy ass was waiting to pounce on me. Full of delicious expectation, I left the washroom.

As I passed through the crowd, my shoulder blades tingled, alert for an attack from behind.

At the polished wooden bar, Karen was standing up on the brass foot rail, shouting over the noise ordering me a drink. Last call had been announced while I was in the can, and the King Eddie always cut off the booze at curfew.

Magda bounced up to us, raising a sharp eyebrow at me taking a drink from Karen's delicate fingers.

"Might as well make it a party." I toasted her and made the introductions.

There was an awkward pause, and I was reminded of Magda's possessive tendencies. Instead of trying to rescue Karen from Magda's petulant stare down, I relished the tension it created.

But Karen didn't rise to Magda's challenge, and I got bored. I searched over their heads for a new distraction. That's when I saw Lene.

"Hey." Lene barely looked at me as she breezed by with Duncan in tow. Her black hair reflected the blue stage lights like raven wings under moonlight.

"Where's Reg?" I asked loud enough for Duncan to hear.

Lene gave me a soulless smile. "Who's Reg?"

I didn't let her response convince me they were over. He was probably traveling or working late at his office, completely oblivious to the fact she was here with Duncan.

The sight of Colin coming up behind Duncan jacked up my sense of excitement. Where there are two Scotsmen, there could be three. I scanned the crowd looking for the Highlander.

Sure enough, he was leaning against the half wall that separated the dancers from the bar, staring right at me. One side of his mouth quirked up when our eyes met. He raised his beer in a salute but made no move to come forward.

Good bloody job, because even though a flush of expectation was washing over me at the sight of him, my pride was demanding I hold onto being pissed. His heroic actions had come close to getting me evicted. I should be mad at him, big time, only I wasn't.

After the washroom run in with the rutting couple, I was looking at things in a new light. The way Angus had twisted the landlord's wrist had me licking my lips. If I'd been in this state, I would have taken advantage of the landlord being on his knees. I would have made him beg and pay. I would have told Angus to twist...

Colin appeared at my elbow.

"When did you get here?" I asked him, wondering if Angus had been watching me dance.

"We four caem t'gether. Lene's showin' us th' town," he piped.

From across the way, Angus kept his eyes on me as he took another drink of his beer. Strangely, he still wasn't making any move to come forward. What was it he had said right before he left my apartment? Let him know when I was ready to talk?

I tilted my head slightly to the side and cocked an eyebrow. He raised his chin. I gave the man a cool nod.

He pushed off the wall and started our way.

Karen was at my shoulder sipping a Shirley Temple through a thin straw. "Who's that?"

"Oh," I kept my eyes on Angus, letting him know I was talking about him, "Some egotistical Scottish bastard."

"Maybe so, but he's gorgeous."

As he walked, he finger-combed his bangs back out of his eyes. The movement parted his brown, leather jacket, revealing a forest green shirt clinging to his pecs. Shamelessly, I dropped my glance to the faded wrinkles at the front of his tight, blue jeans. The bulge behind the zipper proved Magda's theory about inversion wrong.

I elbowed Magda, "That's the guy who shared the tea."

The three of us girls stood side-by-side and had inspired, naughty thoughts about Angus as he walked our way.

Angus stirred many good feelings in me, but tonight they came with dark and scary ideas. My 'alter' was getting way too predatory. I battled her back, and with her dissolving into my bloodstream, my courage to face Angus slipped away. I bit my lip, wondering if I too should slip away.

Karen grabbed my arm and the rye in my glass crested up like a wave to splash over my hand.

"Introduce me," she begged, never taking her eyes from his self-assured approach.

I cursed, switching the glass to my other hand and looked around for someone to wipe the spill on.

"Och!" Angus grabbed my wrist, "Don't waste it."

Everyone around us faded into the background as he brought my hand to his lips. He grinned at the wide-eyed look on my face and made a move to suck my fingers clean.

"Whoa!" I pulled away from his grip, covering my reaction with a shaky laugh, "I don't think so, big guy."

Karen stepped in front of me. "I'm Karen." She thrust out a petite hand.

Angus wrapped his thick fingers right up to her wrist and gave her hand a little shake, all the while piercing me with his smoldering eyes over her head. He was oozing male sexuality, and I couldn't find any words in my dry mouth.

"We need tae talk, Rachel," he said. "Alone."

"Alone," I whispered like a love-struck idiot.

Oh, it was clear there was no way I could be alone with him. Not when I was swinging between sadistic sexpot and ... another kind of sexpot.

"Yeah, well, I don't have time to talk to you," I scrambled for a reason, "because I'm busy having a life."

Take that!

"I shouldn't have said what I did."

He did look regretful.

"Which part? Hmm?" I put my hands on my hips and narrowed my eyes at him. He didn't expand on his apology, so I continued.

"The part that got me kicked out, or the part where I'm a loser with no life, or the really scary, stalker words about me being your destiny since you were born?"

"Stalker?" Karen stepped out from between us. Angus stepped in to face me, his body language tense.

"Ye still have nae idea what's going on, dae ye?"

"Why don't you tell me if you're so all-knowledgeable," I said in a snarky tone, feeling much more in my element. "Start with how you seem to know everything about my name, my age, my address, my ..." I cut my eyes at Karen. "...bleeding."

Karen's head pivoted back and forth between us.

"Well if ye picked yer friends better, maybe I wouldn't ken all yer secrets."

My mouth dropped open in outrage. I turned and gave Lene an accusing look.

Magda gave me a pinch, and I looked down at her. She held her hands in front of her belly and arched out the shape of a pregnant gut.

I rolled my eyes. Clearly, I was surrounded by idiots!

Karen took advantage of the pause to pounce. Getting to know Angus, she drilled him about his life. I eavesdropped to learn all the details I hadn't asked him about. It was embarrassing to acknowledge my selfishness and how totally lacking my conversation skills were.

Karen discovered he was unmarried and involved in the family business, which was some sort of Scottish land holding. He told her he was here in Canada on this family business, which could take another week or so. He came from a big family. Hell, she even found out Duncan and Colin and Lennox were his cousins. They were all close, but he was his father's only son, hence the family pressure.

Wow. Fifteen minutes and she found out all that. And, "all that" made Angus less threatening somehow. He had real problems and responsibilities.

I was still digesting his life story when the first chords of the slow song "Make Me do Anything You Want" rang out. Beers and glasses were set down as people paired up for the last dance of the night. The band, Helix, was working hard to ensure no one went home alone.

I watched Lene and Duncan make their way to the dance floor, holding back a wistful look from my face. I liked the slow songs but could rarely find anyone tall enough to dance with. What a stupid move, driving away the only potential guy taller than me.

Karen was still jabbering away at Angus, but he ignored her. Stepping into my view, he held his hand out. "Will ye dae me the honour, Kit?"

I'd never met a man who could disarm me so easily.

Patrick was in my head, telling me to say "no". I chewed at my lip and tried not to look too tempted.

"Dance with me." Angus gave me a meaningful look as if he had a good reason for me to say "yes".

Karen had the nerve to say, "I'll dance with you".

Unexpected jealously quaked through me, and I glared at the little man-stealer with malicious intent. Angus was watching too, his thoughts veiled behind a neutral expression, but his muscles were tense.

I handed my drink to Karen, almost dropping it on her feet when she didn't take it. As she fumbled to steady my glass, I brushed by her. Three steps toward the dance floor, I turned and gave Angus a sultry look, "Are you coming?"

His long stride caught up to me by the time I stepped out onto the dance floor. He gripped my arm from behind and spun me to face his "no more bullshit" expression. The move caused his bangs to slip down and brush his cheekbones, and I wanted to thrust my hand into his hair and yank his lips down to mine.

He tilted his head to the side.

"Yoo're a handful, ye are."

"You have no idea." I tilted my nose into the air.

Angus shook his head and pulled me into his arms. The warmth of his body touching mine sparked my senses into a living current. I could feel every inch of him and it purged every defiant, bitter, rebellious urge from my being.

I leaned into his embrace with complete abandon. He was so tall, I could actually put my head against his shoulder, and I did. It made me feel small and sweet, like Karen must feel with every man.

As one, we moved in rhythm to the song. His hand pressed my hair down away from his face, and he put his lips against the top of my head. His breath was hot on my scalp as he whispered some Scottish saying into my hair.

I didn't ask him to translate. I could tell by his tone he was still exasperated with me, but I could tell by the feel of his body he wanted me.

It would not be easy with Angus. If I didn't drive him away, today, it would be the nightmares, or my Southern Belle 'alter' who would scare him off. Or maybe Angus would drive me away, for I hadn't forgotten his erratic behaviour in my apartment. It was pretty much a sure thing my time with Angus would be short. The question was, what was I going to do with that time?

The music, the room, and all the people began to fade into the background. I brushed the question aside. Que sera, sera.

With Angus' hot body pressed along mine, it didn't take much to get right back where I'd been when he'd been kissing me into submission in my apartment. I stumbled a bit on my heels just thinking about it. He tightened his arms around me. More than his looks, his body, and the way his mouth had felt on mine, his unexpected chivalry thrilled me to the quick.

His promise to kiss me and nothing else had been a vow right out of a fairy tale. The trust his vow created was a new sweetener in the nectar of love—one I hadn't much sampled.

I pulled away, leaning against his arms to look up into his face. "Seems to me, you made a promise, but didn't keep it."

"Which promise was that, Kit?"

He looked so serious, I almost giggled.

"You know." I batted my eyelashes.

"Nae," he frowned, catching on that I was playing him. "I don't ken, but yer obviously going tae tell me."

I smiled and pressed my lips against his ear. "You owe me some kisses," I whispered.

He stopped dancing and looked down at me. "Yoo've got a nerve, ye do."

"Are you saying you won't kiss me?"

"I'm saying ye had yer chance, and ye chose tae kick me out. Yer loss, lass."

No man turns me down and goes home alone.

"What if I let you have free reign?" I tossed my hair out of my eyes and stepped back.

His hands unlocked from behind my back and slid down to the sides of my hips. "Let me what?"

"Do anything you want."

"Yer not likely tae go along with what I have in mind." He laughed deep in his chest.

I ran my hand down his side, feeling the muscles bunching at the top of his hip. "And what exactly do you have in mind, big man?"

He stiffened, slightly. "We cannae talk here."

I tried to hold in my laugh. "You're kinky?"

"Nae!" He hooked his finger into the waistband of my jean skirt and gave me a little tug forward.

I laughed with delight at his uptight frown and wrapped my arms around his neck. Pressing against him, my body expressed the freedoms he could experience with me.

"A promise is a promise." I pouted. "I thought you were a man who kept his word."

"Poor, wee lass."

"Well, what are you going to do about it?"

His laugh was deep and dangerous.

"Sorry, but times up fur yer mouth." His smile dropped. "That ship has sailed."

Before I could protest further, he buried his hand in my hair and placed his lips against my ear "We have tae move tae the next part of yer body for tomorrah."

I slid my cheek along his, drawing our mouths closer until I could feel the heat of his breath on my lips.

"Maybe for the sake of my next body part, I'll forgive you for the trouble you caused with my landlord."

"Let me earn yer forgiveness, Rachel."

I pulled back to see if he was mocking me and fell into the dark depths of his eyes.

He placed his hands on either side of my face.

"Let me drag yoo're forgiveness from ye, kickin' and screamin' and beggin' fur more."

And then his lips were on mine and his body was pressed along my length. The room spun as my knees grew weak, and my will slipped away in a warm rush.

His mouth burned its way to the soft dip where my neck and shoulder met. My skin was alive under the soft brush of his lips and the prickle of his whiskers.

Like an idiot, I blurted, "My friend Magda's staying over night at my place. I'll have to get rid of her, if we want to be alone."

"Hmm." He raised his head, looking over me at the crowd where we'd left the girls standing. "There's no getting rid of Magda."

The comment struck me as strange.

"You know her?"

With a "Shhhhh," his firm hand tucked my head against his neck. His skin was warm, his scent rolling over my senses, distracting me from the question.

Unexpectedly, an overwhelming desire to mark him shot through my instincts. Instead of closing the feeling down, I opened my mouth and gently bit down on the skin of his neck. He gasped and froze, his arms crushing me in an iron hold.

We stood, motionless.

He tasted like aftershave and salt. I swirled my tongue against the skin trapped inside of my teeth, and Angus groaned deep in his throat. He slid his hand up my side until his thumb was resting just below the curve of my breast.

"Stop," he warned, giving my rib cage a squeeze.

I increased the pressure of my bite and felt his lower back muscles ripple under my hand.

"Stop. Now," he managed to say.

I released his skin, pleased at the little indents my teeth had left on his neck.

"Why should I?" I teased, sliding my chin up over his jaw line and rubbing my nose against his.

"Because it's not time, lass," his voice cracked, and I was surprised to see his lip tremble on the words. "And this is damn well not the place."

Helix was dragging out the last song by reworking the chorus. I was thankful for the extra time under the blue and yellow stage lights, but I wanted more. Now.

I pressed my hips against his and swayed with a rhythm as old as time.

He was a hard wall of trembling muscle. "It's not time... not yet," Angus repeated.

Puzzled by his change, I peered up at him from under my drawn brows.

"What time *is* it Mr. Wolf?"

"We have time, Lass, don't wish yer life away."

Once again, Angus had put the brakes on, and though it stung that he could resist me, it also relieved me from having to fight myself to stick to my resolution.

The song ended.

I began to step away from Angus' embrace, but he didn't unwrap his arms. He was unaware of the other couples separating and leaving. I nestled back into his arms, and my heart grew sweeter with every stolen second.

Karen's soft voice killed my moment. "Here's your drink."

Angus released me, and reluctantly, I stepped back.

"Thanks," I said, sarcastically, looking down my nose at her.

I practically snatched my glass from her fingers, not caring if I sliced off some skin with my nails. She didn't look my way, too intent on tilting her adoring eyes up at Angus. He smiled at her.

I turned my back on them and looked for Magda. The dance floor was still emptying, except for the technicians who were breaking down the band's equipment. From the bar area, Duncan and Lene approached, holding hands. Magda and Colin were trailing behind, absorbed in an animated discussion.

"The bar is closing," Karen stated.

"Your grasp of the obvious is astounding." I tossed off my rye.

Magda gave a snort of approval and suggested, "Let's go to Rachel's place."

"That's a really bad idea," I snapped at her, wondering how I'd get Angus alone if everyone was there.

"Och! I think a quiet place tae ken each other better is a grand idea," Colin chirped, giving Magda the eye.

"Och, Rachel, lighten up." Magda rolled out the "r" in a pretty darn good imitation of the Highlander boys.

Colin just about tripped over his feet trying to get to her side. I wanted to give him a good push, so he'd knock some sense into the airhead. As if I wanted Karen at my place. Duh!

Lene adjusted her spaghetti strap, jiggling her boob like a lure on a line. "That's a no go. Rachel doesn't let anyone into her little sanctuary."

"That's just as well. It's a braw cave, it is," Angus winked at Duncan.

Duncan looked at Angus with surprise and asked, "When did ye get into her cave?"

A few high school snickers erupted.

"Somebody save me," I whispered in misery, looking around for an escape route.

"Well, I'm hungry," Magda said, selfish as always.

Colin pushed up his plaid hat, exposing his whitish eyebrows. "Me too!" he grinned at her.

"Settled then." Angus put out his elbow, and Karen rushed in to grab it. He gave me an apologetic look over her head, but I could see the amusement glittering in his eyes.

I gave him the once-over, letting him know I wasn't impressed.

Chapter 21: Cathouse Competition

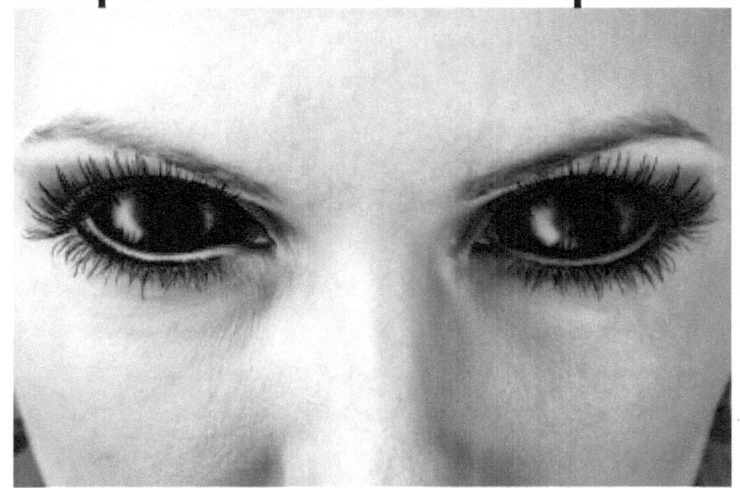

At the restaurant, we were seated in one of those large circle booths with a high leather back. Usually, my weak bladder dictated my seating choice, but Magda grabbed my hand and pulled me in beside her. Karen slipped into the booth behind me, leaving Angus to follow her in.

The steakhouse served up one meal and it was meat. The men seemed very happy about it. It didn't matter to me, because I was too worked up to eat. All I could think about was how to get Angus to return to my apartment to use up his days' worth of kissing. Like Cinderella-of-the-lips, I was ready to get what was mine before midnight.

Trouble was, Karen was separating me from my Scottish bull, and I wasn't impressed.

As I glared at the back of her head, she had the nerve to slide the table candle my way, so she could lean her elbow on the table and face Angus.

I leaned back towards Magda. "I'm going to call that bitch out."

She didn't even break eye contact with Colin to say, "Oh yeah? And who would that impress?"

Angus was looking up at the waitress, who stood mesmerized with her pen caught between her braces-straightened teeth. When he spoke, the muscles in his jaw moved under his skin, and I started to get worked up about his anatomy, again.

I stopped watching, but in seconds my eyes were drawn back. Watching him interacting with the other women was hypnotic, in a hazardous sort of way. I waxed between glazing off for him and foaming at the mouth about her. I wished I had bitten him harder, branding his neck so everyone could see.

My mouth filled with the taste of blood. Not again! I took a quick drink of water and wondered if I should dab my gums with the cloth napkin. But the taste was gone and a quick touch to my gums cleared up my concern. I went back to fantasizing about Angus.

Magda poked me in the ribs, and harped in my ear, "Why don't you just whip out a dildo and get it over with?"

I darted a look around the table, but the others were deep in conversation, and Colin was asking a question about the menu.

I giggled. "Was I that obvious?"

Magda widened her eyes in mock shock and shook her head at me.

I chuckled. My eyes returned to Angus' face. He was staring at the waitress. I followed his gaze, suspicious she had opened another button on her blouse. She said something, and he laughed deep and low in his chest, his white teeth flashing her a dimpled smile. The same smile he had used on me.

Jealously twisted my insides like an iron awl.

He hadn't paid me any attention since we had sat down. The more I thought about it, he hadn't looked much at me since we had left the dance floor.

I lowered my head and stared at my lap.

Was it over already? Did my loser time limit with men hold true even when we didn't get down and dirty?

His attentions for the waitress did not go unnoticed by Karen, either. She latched onto his arm and snuggled up against his shoulder.

I considered touching the candle flame to Karen's hair. That would distract her from my territory and remove those lovely tresses that framed her thieving eyes. Sliding the candle closer caused the hot wax to spill over the sides of the glass bowl and burn my finger.

The pain felt good.

"Well, we don't really have a daily special..." the waitress leaned over Angus' menu. Her breasts hung heavy inside her blouse, pulling the front down to expose more cleavage. "But I'm sure I could come up with something..."

I dipped my long fingernail into the hot melted wax of the candle, enjoying the sharp burn under my nail. The wax dried, tightening around my fingertip. I dipped it again pretending it was the waitress' skin I was poking holes in.

Karen reached over Angus' arm and picked up the menu, almost slicing the waitress' nipples off with it. "We can order directly from the menu," she piped. "Then we'll know exactly what we're getting."

The two women were locked in a stare down. Angus was mesmerized by the cleavage that passed by his face when the waitress stood up. I was intently tracking Karen's hand as it slipped down Angus' thigh.

Oh no... do not touch his thigh...

I glared at Karen's hand, focusing until each follicle on the back of her knuckles became distinct. I fantasized about burning that skin with the candle flame. I imagined the follicles releasing each fine strand of hair with no more sound than an underwater coral worm spitting out filtered ocean dust.

My arm twitched, yearning to act, but was stayed by the waitress' next comment.

"I get off at three."

You hussy!

"Oh, too bad." Karen smiled sweetly. "We won't be here, then."

We?

Her hand squeezed Angus' leg again, those clasping lady-like fingers pressing in on my meat, my muscle. I felt my facial muscles flicker as viciousness climbed my spine like a metal spider.

"What'll it be, Kit?"

Startled by his voice, I met Angus' eyes. His smile slid.

A clock was ticking out the seconds in the silence that had fallen around the table.

Six eyes were trained my way. A trickle of sweat ran down my temple.

"Uhem," I cleared my throat loudly, and the waitress blinked three times. I tried to adjust my face into a less threatening expression.

"I'll rememb..." I shook my head and started over. "I'll have a tea and my own bill, please."

She scribbled on her pad. The scratching pen deafened me.

I imagined she wrote, "Civilized response from savage responder" and that made me angrier.

"Ye need some meat on yer bones, lass. Why don't I order ye a steak?" His brows were drawn, but his voice was steady.

Duncan added, "She daesnae hae enough room inside her fur a rheumatic pain".

"I like my bones just fine, Highlander."

I turned my attention to Karen. "How do you like yours?"

She pasted a sugary smile on her pale face. "You really are too skinny. I'd be worried if I was your mother."

My mouth tightened in outrage, but Karen had already turned away to place her order. Somewhere deep inside me, a pressure built and then popped, and that's when I knew Dr. Casbus' pills were no longer working.

"I'll have the Beef Stroganoff," Karen twittered, happily.

Magda put a restraining hand on my shoulder. "Just ignore the bimbette," she said loud enough for half the table to hear.

I couldn't.

Every abnormal cell in my body was commanding me to scratch her eyes out and eat them.

How dare she talk about my mother?

My mother who didn't give a shit if I was fat or skinny. Hell, my mother was the reason I could go for days without eating.

Anger ran wild in my head, sprinkled with "suggestions" of what I could do to make Karen pay.

Then, much to my horror, my other stepped up to bat.

Why, she has no manners at all.

"Oh, no. No-no!"

Chapter 22: Ravine Runaway

I pinched my lips together, and desperately tried to find a way to get out of the booth without opening my mouth again. I was trapped by the others on both sides.

My throat felt like sandpaper. I grasped my glass of water, but my shaking hand sloshed the cold liquid down my shirt. It shocked me into motion.

"I want out!" I stood quickly, and my thighs caught on the underside of the table.

"Watch it!" Colin yelped as I set all their drinks rocking.

Angus put his hand on the table and pushed his way out of the booth. I wasn't waiting for numb nuts to get a clue and move. I put my hand on her baby blue cashmere sweater and gave her a good shove.

"What are you doing?" Karen's shrill question tumbled out into the aisle with her.

"When a girl's gotta go..." Magda joked.

I darted passed Angus without a glance.

As I ran across the restaurant, the tables blurred. I couldn't seem to escape my compulsions. They encouraged me to return to Karen and stab her with her fork. The restaurant was huge, and I took two wrong turns. Suddenly, a hand snaked out of a booth and pulled me in.

I fell forward onto my knees on the leather seat and ended up face to face with Lennox, the blond Scotsman from the Albion. He had me by the wrist and was holding up a finger to his lips.

"Nae a wurd," he warned in his heavy Scottish brogue. "I need tae tell ye what's happenin' tae ye. Ye deserve tae ken."

Clear beads of sweat shone on his upper lip. His eyes begged me to agree.

I weighed the situation.

If I left with him, I wouldn't have to watch Karen touch Angus. I wouldn't have to bear witness to Angus ogling the waitress' boobs.

If I left, I'd reduce the chances my 'alter' would take over in front of my new-found drinking buddies and gut Karen with a spoon.

And best of all, a big, blond Highlander had wrapped his hand around my wrist and yanked me to my knees. And he smelled like a man.

"Get me out of here," I whispered, and was startled to feel hot tears rise after the words.

He nodded, pulled me out the other side of the booth, and we rushed passed surprised late-night diners.

OUTSIDE, IT WAS A MOONLESS night. The streetlights made pools of yellow on the dark sidewalk, which shone wetly from an earlier rain.

"Thes way," Lennox sped left, yanking me along by my wrist.

I couldn't keep up in my high heels.

"Wait! Wait! Wait!" I dragged on him.

He stopped. He was frowning and cast worried glances back to the restaurant entrance. I pulled my red pumps off. Lennox grabbed the shoes, and together, we ran.

His boots hammered the concrete creating sharp blows that echoed off the buildings around us. My hair flew back from my neck, baring my flesh to the cool air. The wind we created cut through my sheer shirt and chilled my skin.

Yet, it was thrilling and naughty to be ditching my friends and running off with a stranger. Closing my eyes for the added thrill, I ran blindly behind Lennox's lead. I sucked cool air into my lungs, trying to drink in the night. This was what I needed. This was freedom.

"Oomph!"

Lennox stopped, and I crashed into his back, hurting my toe on the heel of his boot.

"Quiet!"

He pushed me up against a building. We flattened ourselves along the stippled wall like criminals hiding from the police. The wall was cold against my arms, but the bottoms of my feet were burning from running on the concrete. I embraced the pain.

We were both wheezing for air. Lennox cautiously looked around the corner of the building to check the way we had come. I took advantage of the streetlight above to check him out.

He was slimmer than Angus, but he was still ripped. His white t-shirt clung to his muscles, especially at the top of his spine where sweat had slicked the material to his skin. I remembered his offer at the bar to "scratch my itch".

Was this why I was here? Was this what he wanted?

I scratched the side of his tan camouflage pants.

"Anything more interesting over there?" I whispered.

He twisted back to me, fear raw on his face. My ardour slipped.

"What's the deal?" I asked, feeling wary.

"Yoo'll kin soon enough."

He snuck another look back at the restaurant. "Damn it tae hell!"

"What?"

He dropped my shoes, grabbed my shoulders and spun me roughly. "Run!"

We rushed behind the building, but I stopped at an impassible mass of brush. Lennox didn't hesitate. He just shoved me through the branches that scratched at my face. My bare feet caught on roots, but he kept pushing until we burst through the bush on the other side.

"Stop!"

I tried to push him away, then clutched at him for support, when I realized we were tottering at the top of a treed ravine. The sides were steeply sloped, and it was well over fifty feet to the bottom of the dark pit. A dizzy feeling looped around my head.

Lennox untangled my hand from his arm and tried to push me down the gravel slope.

"Hey!" I protested and knocked his hand away from my shoulder. "I'm in bare feet, hoser!"

He got another grip on my wrist and jumped down the side of the embankment. The weight of his body jerked me down after him. A bolt of pain shot up my arm leaving numbness in its wake. I half slid, and half fell until Lennox caught me.

"Let me go!" I screeched and struck at his neck.

"Listen tae me!" He grabbed my hands and pinned my wrists together. With his right hand, he brushed my wild hair back from my face, clutching a handful to hold me still. "Listen. Ye don't ken it yet, but ye need tae run like yer life is in danger."

"Are you juiced?" I yanked my arms down, trying to pull free of his hold. "Angus will..."

"Angus!" His mouth pulled down at the corners. "Angus is no yer friend."

I searched his eyes for the truth.

"Angus has one job an' that's tae ruin yer life, lass."

The sound of branches breaking above us at the ravine's edge drew his startled gaze upward.

He grimaced and returned his glance to me. His eyes were wide, the whites showing around the edges. "Ye hae tae trust me."

"Forget it!"

Lennox licked his lips, took another look up at the ravine's edge and then smoothed my hair against the side of my head gently. He gave me a resigned smile, released my wrists, and ran down the side of the ravine. The blackness swallowed him up, leaving only the sound of falling gravel and sand behind.

Another branch cracked above, and I spun to look up, a gasp escaping my lips. I didn't know what was up there but according to Lennox, I was in danger.

The hair stood up at the base of my skull, as alarm coursed through my body.

Earlier, I had crushed my alternate personality, driving her down where she couldn't influence my interactions with Angus. She was nasty, courageous, dangerous.

I needed her now.

Releasing the inner lock I had on my other, I spun and leapt into the air.

It seemed I fell forever. But then, she took hold and under her command, I bent my left knee to match the angle of the slope just before my feet sunk into the sandy gravel. The momentum carried me, and I slid through the loose soil like a surfer on a wave.

The gravel tumbling from my slide hadn't stopped rolling down the ravine, before I leapt again. Falling through the darkness, my feet struck the side and slid for a second time. On the third jump, I spread my arms in the air like wings to steady myself. The grit buried my feet, wrapping my skin with the left-over warmth of the day's sun.

I halted, alert, listening for the sound of Lennox's boots. His thuds were softer, more muffled. He had reached the bottom where the trees dropped their leaves to cushion the black, damp earth.

A shift twitched beneath my breastbone. I did not look behind to see who pursued me but lifted my nose to smell the air ahead.

Forest moss, snail trails and the scent of a man's sweat as he flees in fear swirled into my sinuses. I released a hot breath and it pooled into pillowing white frost before me.

It seemed I was no longer steeped in the black ink of a woodland night. I could see shades of grey speckling the dark spaces ahead. Each shape was an object within the forest. Blades were grass, octagons rocks.

I squinted at the bottom of the ravine, trying to see Lennox. Below, between the pillars that were tree trunks, a rectangle of white flashed.

The expectation of having him drew me into action. I leapt the last twenty feet to the bottom, angling my jumps to cut off the distance between us.

I was on his trail. I burst into a run, bounding over bushes and swerving between tree trunks. My skirt bunched up at the top of my thighs as my long legs stretched out for speed.

Lennox's gasps for air filled my ears as I passed him, my soft soles never touching the dry branches he snapped with his clumsy flight. I wrapped a smooth tree trunk with my arm, spinning my body around and slamming into his front like a juggernaut.

He launched backwards into the air, flailing his limbs as he thudded to the ground.

I landed on him before he stopped moving. My calves were bunched beneath my thighs, my bare knees almost touching my shoulders as I squatted above his still form.

I clawed my hands into the cool soil at either side of his head.

Lennox's eyes were closed. A low groan slipped from his lips.

Yearning radiated through me at the sound. I leaned over his torso, my breasts growing full and heavy as they hung above his overheated body.

"I'm itchyyy," the words rasped in my throat.

He groaned again, unable to find his way from wherever his jostled brain had taken him.

The night, the flesh, the strength coursing through my body urged me to follow my darker instincts.

I pressed my nose into the hollow of his throat, desiring to chew on his heart. It called to me with its racing beat, reminding me of the rhythmic dance our organs had shared in the Albion.

My back arched as if the Goddess Diana drew her arrow on my spinal cord. Facing the blanket of stars that pinpricked the night sky, I became alert in a way I had never been before. I was intoxicated by the scent of his sweat mixing with the dust of ancient crustaceans ground into the ravine's gravely mix. A heady purr escaped my lips.

Chasing him had aroused me, and I ached to finish the game that thrummed between my thighs. I leaned in over his body. His face looked like spilt cream against the dark soil.

"Wake up, Lennox," I ordered, as if he could rise from unconsciousness at my command. "Wake and amuse me."

His hand twitched in the dirt, the fingers clenching over his open palm. A hard coil of awareness tightened his stomach muscles under me. His eyelids fluttered open.

I grinned knowingly as his glance scurried around my face and jittered to scan the dark treetops above my head.

"Whaur ur they?"

He grunted out the last word as the pain from my tackle reached his awareness.

I leaned forward, my chest above his mouth, and pretended to look back the way we had come.

"Nobody there," I whispered.

I slinked down his chest, the buttons of his jean jacket catching like claws on my blouse.

"Please me, Lennox," I begged.

Dragging my tongue along his throat, I flicked his jaw line with the end. He released a shuddering groan, which might have been fear or passion. It mattered not.

"We have tae gie out ay here."

A familiar pressure rose in me at his rejection. My alter's sulky voice cast its rich velvet over the silence of the night.

"A gentleman would nevah make a lady beg."

Lennox's nostrils flared. He grabbed my hips and almost threw me off, but I locked my thighs and clutched his chin, my red nails pressing shadowy dents into his skin. I forced him to meet my eyes.

His pupils, wide with terror, dulled to a vacant stare beneath my steady gaze.

He was mine. I knew it as surely as I knew a rabbit was watching from beneath a pine tree ten feet from my right. He was mine, and he would do anything I asked him to do.

His surrendered state filled me with a savage need to test his willingness. I drove my mouth down, crushing his lips against his teeth. He pressed up into the kiss until the tang of his blood greased the end of my snaking tongue.

Chapter 23: Séance with Mr. Spiritoe

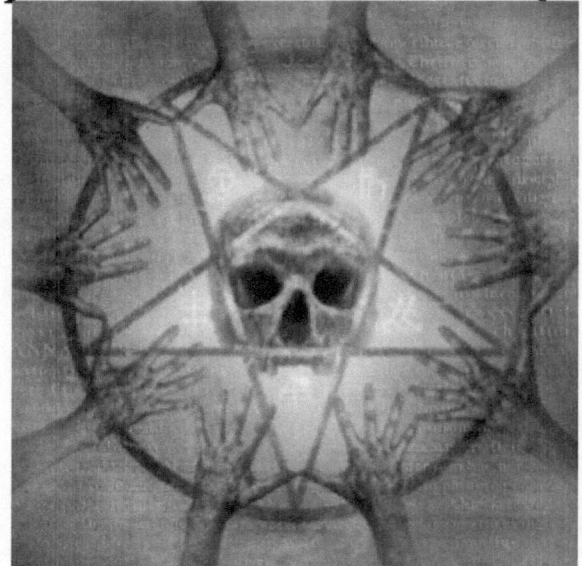

With a gasp, I bolted upright in bed. A few moments of blurry-eyed blinking in the dark helped me recognize my surroundings.

"Jesus!" I gasped with relief. I was safe at home, in my bed, in my apartment, alone.

My bra was suctioned to my skin with sweat and I pulled it away to let the air circulate underneath. I started to take it off altogether, when a faint noise from the direction of the couch stopped me. A sleepy mumble followed.

"Who's there?" I whispered, clutching the sheets to my chest.

"God, Rachel," a bored voice carried from across the dark room, "It's five-thirty in the morning."

Magda.

"What are you doing here?"

"Hello? Sleepover?'

"Right."

The flick of a Bic lighter scratched, spitting out a spark that gave birth to a flame. It lit Magda's face, casting strange shadows around her eyes, and giving her a sinister look.

I watched, wishfully, as the flame caught the end of the cigarette dangling loosely from her lips.

The tobacco curled away in bright agony.

"Do you have to smoke?" I asked.

"It's not my problem..." she took a drag, making the red ember glow, "if you choose to make stupid rules for your habits".

I rubbed my arm.

She blew the smoke out noisily, and I drew in a deep breath trying to capture some of the second-hand glory.

"So, why did you leave me at the restaurant, last night, hm?"

I tensed as the night's events tumbled into the forefront of my mind. I hadn't meant to leave her. Hell, I hadn't even thought about her. I had needed to get out of the restaurant, so, yeah, I'd run....

Like a linear film, the night played out in my mind's eye until I recalled the chasing, the capture, Lennox.

I yanked off the covers and leapt out of bed.

"Rachel!"

"Give me a minute to piss, will ya?"

Slamming the bathroom door behind me, I leaned against it and clutched my hair with my hands. The wooden door was cool against my back, for I was only wearing my red bra and panties. At least I still had on my underwear.

I replayed the memories again. The kiss, a brutal joining of our lips, and then my memories stopped at a black wall. I needed to figure out what had happened with Lennox afterwards.

Flicking on the light, I turned to the mirror and faced myself. I ran my glance up and down my body, searching for clues, for signs of Lennox, and what might have become of him.

There were dirt and grass stains on my knees. Scratches were slashed up and down my shins, marks from being pushed through the bush at the top of the ravine, and the run through the forest.

When had I ever run like that, immune to pain, moving so fast it was like flying? Not since I'd been a wild child, racing the wind to escape my life. And in my bare feet? I hadn't felt much at the time, but now my feet were sore. I lifted my right foot and checked the bottom. It was coated with a dirty stain along the sole. A slice in the skin of my heel yawned open bloodlessly, as I inspected it.

I met my eyes in the mirror, then looked away. A woman knows when she's had sex.

"Damn it!"

It was only the second day after my birthday, and I'd already broken my promise to Patrick. If he was right, I'd just ruined my chances at getting better, anytime soon.

A bang against the door made me jump. "Are you still pissin'?"

"I'll be out in a minute!" I barked.

I stared at the mascara smudges darkening my eyes. Tear streaks made tracks along the dust on my cheeks. I touched my lip where it was swollen and red above a raw spot on my chin. My fingernail was broken in a jagged line and filled with black earth. I absently dug it out with my other nail.

It wasn't as bad as I had thought it might be. Hell, I didn't look any worse than the night I'd spent with the carny at the Erin Fall Fair. Maybe that's all it had been, just one more night with one more carny. Maybe Lennox was stretched out on his bed, alive and well.

But just in case, I couldn't let Magda get a good look at me or she'd start to guess.

I turned on the sink tap and stripped off my panties and my bra. A dark, rusty stain ran along the inside of the bra's cup. It could be blood.

"Oh, God," I whispered.

I checked my breast, and my neck, and the inside of my nostrils and my gums to see if I had been the one bleeding. I had a few scratches on my shoulders, but nothing that would have left the amount of blood needed to soak through a padded bra. I would need the blouse I had been wearing to know how much blood had actually been spilled.

I thought back to Lennox lying still on the ground beneath me. Had he been injured? I tried to recall but couldn't remember anything past the first kiss.

With shaking hands, I rinsed out a washcloth and washed off as much of the dirt and semen as I could, grabbed my Madonna "Like a Virgin" nightie off the door and put that on.

When I came out, Magda was back on my couch. She hadn't flipped on any lights. The red eye of her cigarette winked at me.

I stumbled through the dark to my bed.

"So?" She was determined to get her explanation. "Why'd ya ditch me?"

I sat up against my pillows, tucking the blankets around my waist and released a loud sigh. "I didn't feel like sticking around."

"Seriously!" She scathed and sucked on her cigarette.

"Listen." She wasn't going to shut up until I apologized. "I didn't feel like watching Karen and Angus get it on, alright?"

There was a long silence while I waited for her highness to lay off

"Well," she said, "I brought your jacket home."

I barely squeezed a "Thanks" from between my tight lips.

"And your shoes."

I released a long breath. So, it was her at the top of the ravine? She was who Lennox was afraid of?

I heard the cardboard lid of the cigarette pack whisper open and Magda's nails scratching out another smoke. She used the butt to light the new one.

"Chain smoking? Seriously?"

She ignored my complaint.

I grumbled, "Give me one, then."

She threw the lit cigarette at me. I watched the red tip tumble through the air and caught it before it landed on my quilts. Sparks flew off the end and burned the soft skin between my fingers.

"Jesus, you're a dipshit, sometimes." I sucked on my finger.

She laughed.

My nic-fit dissolved with the incoming smoke, relaxing my neck and shoulders. The empty pit in my stomach closed up nicely.

"Don't give up on Angus just yet, Rachel."

"Oh," I sneered into the darkness. "I don't want him now that he's been in the cashmere folds, thank you very much."

"He didn't go home with her, hoser." The squeaky springs of my old couch protested as Magda shifted around. "We were too busy looking for your sorry ass."

"What?" I blew out a stream of smoke and picked a piece of tobacco off my lip.

"What d'ya think? You went to the can, leaving behind your jacket, and you never came back."

A smile plucked at the tops of my cheeks. "He was worried?"

Maybe there was hope for Angus and me, yet. Unless word got out about my ravine encounter.

She didn't say another word, and I took it as a yes. I finished my smoke in silence, dropping the butt into the glass of water beside my bed. Then, fluffing my pillow, I prepared to lie back down.

"Not so fast Sleeping Beauty," Magda was up, padding across the kitchen to the light switch.

"Ughn," I groaned when the florescent square lit up.

"I called Jean last night." Magda rummaged in her bag on the kitchen chair.

"What for?" I sat up.

Magda pulled out a piece of paper and carried it over to my bed. She sat cross legged on the bottom. "Well, duh, you were missing. I asked her to have an impromptu séance with Mr. Spiritoe."

I laughed. "Are you legit?"

Mr. Spiritoe was Magda's family ghost. I generally didn't believe of their encounter stories with Mr. Spiritoe, but it always made for good entertainment.

Magda was looking at me with barely contained excitement.

"Alright, fine, I'll bite. What did Mr. Spiritoe say?"

"You might want to stay calm for this," she warned, before ceremoniously unrolling a white sheet of paper.

"What *is* that, your scroll?"

"Here ye, Here ye!" She laughed at her own joke.

I rolled my eyes and leaned back against the pillow. "That's mental. Forget the paper, just say it. But say it quietly in case the landlord thinks we're having a party and decides to come down for a cluster f-."

She interrupted me. "Fine! This was all I could find to take notes on, but if you don't want the details..." She rolled up the paper with a vengeance.

She held her deadpan expression.

I waited her out.

"Mr. Spiritoe says your new man is the cure to what ails you."

Which one?

"Really."

"There are more particulars here." She flicked her lighter and waved the roll of paper around in front of the flame. "If you care to know them."

I sighed. "Fine. Read from your scroll, Magda."

She slowly unrolled the paper. She really did resemble a full-sized Tinkerbell, with her big eyes and heart-shaped face.

"As you know, Mr. Spiritoe does not speak in full or grammatically correct sentences."

"Got it."

"Mr. Spiritoe, under the guidance of ma mère, said the following when asked about your new man, 'Reactant A Reactant B Organic catalyst cross-coupling'".

"Cross-coupling?" I laughed. "So... we're going to have sex?"

"Pretty much."

That made me feel warm and fuzzy.

"And he's my orgasmic capitalist? I can see that." I grinned.

"Get it straight, Rachel. Organic catalyst."

I looked up to the left. "Umm, that means nothing to me."

Magda stabbed the air with her finger. "Exactly! Welcome to the world of Mr. Spiritoe."

"Oh Lord." I waited but she didn't continue.

"C'mon!" I urged, thinking of the wasted sleeping time. "What else?"

"Mr. Spiritoe, under the guidance of ma mère, said the following when asked if you would have a lasting relationship with this new man: 'Transformation Transoceanic Transitional'".

I chewed on the words for a few moments. "What the hell does that mean?"

"That's what Jean asked." She consulted the scroll again. "Mr. Spiritoe said, "Cross your T's for sacrifice."

"Sacrifice?" The image of Christ strung out beneath the Pope's hand in *The Mercury* picture came to mind. I frowned.

"That was all Mr. Spiritoe would surrender." Magda's tone was lofty. "But note there are four T's in Transformation, Transoceanic, and Transitional."

"Actually, there are five."

"Who's counting," she snapped.

"So, five sacrifices have to be made for me to get an orgasmic catalytic reaction?" I reached for another of her smokes and lit up. "Sounds worth it."

"Mr. Spiritoe said 'crossed t's', so if we put caps on Transformation, Trans..."

"Yeah, yeah. I get it. Two crossed t's, two sacrifices."

"Takes two to tango," she sing-songed.

I was having this conversation with bravado, but inside I was feeling shaky. I didn't like the idea of sacrifices. "Did your mom translate this for me? As in, what the hell does all that mean?"

"Step-mom," Magda tossed the scroll across my apartment, and dug out another cigarette. "She's worried."

"Ye-ah! You told her about me taking off!"

"Why do you think she was talking to Spiritoe? I thought he might be able to tell us where you were." She lit up and took a deep drag.

I let the silence hang, hoping she'd go back to the couch, but she had more to say.

"Mr. Spiritoe is weird, but he's usually not so ... specific... scientific... rhythmic."

"Unlike you."

She snipped a hangnail off with her teeth. "What I find weird is that, all of a sudden, you want to hear what Mr. Spiritoe has to say."

She raised her eyes and caught my worried look before I could clear my expression. I just shrugged. I didn't owe anyone any explanations.

The silence dragged on while Magda stared at me, and I became uncomfortable.

"So!" She tilted her head to the side. "Did you leave the restaurant with anyone?"

I frowned. "Did you?"

"I already told you. We were looking for you."

"Karen?"

"No, Angus sent her home in a cab."

I couldn't hold back my smile. "Looks good on her."

Magda raised her eyebrows, still waiting.

I looked away first.

"So, I came home."

"We came here. You didn't answer the door."

"Maybe I was sleeping."

"Maybe the landlord let us in."

My nostrils flared. "You didn't."

"You could have been dead!" She threw up her hand. "We had to check."

I shook my head imaging Angus, Colin, Duncan, and Lene all crowded into my apartment. "You didn't go through my stuff..." My eyes darted to the ceiling tile where Donald's jacket was hidden.

"No, we didn't go through your stuff. Angus and Colin stayed back down the street. I'm the only one who came in. Angus seemed to think the landlord wouldn't like seeing him."

I wasn't used to having people watch out for me. I liked being able to do what I wanted, when I wanted, without having to explain myself.

"You had no right..."

Magda clicked her tongue. "Maybe if you'd pull your head out of your ass, you'd realize some people actually care about you."

She got off my bed, stomped across the kitchen to turn out the light and went back to her covers on the couch.

I didn't need their help or their so called 'care' excuses for breaking into my place. I knew what happened when I let people *care* about me. Then what? Who always ended up getting hurt?

I dug down into my quilts and tried to justify my anger, but it didn't hold. Magda had a right to be worried.

Whatever.

I stopped thinking about it and instead, I tried to puzzle out the words transformation, transoceanic, and transitional. But like counting sheep, the monotony of going over and over an unsolvable puzzle finally put me to sleep.

Chapter 24: Harvest Preparations

An hour or so later, I awoke with a start. I must have cried out because Magda immediately asked me what the hell I was doing waking her up again.

"I had a nightmare." I rubbed my eyes.

Magda was a dream junky and loved to hear about my night terrors. She changed her tone and asked, "Was Lennox in it?"

"Why would you..." I stopped myself and changed tactics. "Who's Lennox?"

"Nobody." I waited for more. "Just when you didn't come back, we went over to the guys' place before we came here. Their friend, Lennox, wasn't there. Duncan thought maybe you were with him.

"Why would I be with someone I don't know?"

"Settle, it was a random question."

I rubbed my eyes and tried to relax. God, my mouth tasted like crap. I pushed aside the curtain. Sure enough, it was light out.

Magda stood up and pulled on a sweatshirt

"I'll cook up some grindage, while you tell me about your nightmare," she offered, going to my fridge.

"Okay, but put the kettle on first."

I wasn't sure how to start the telling. My dreams were multi-sensual, my imagination fed me smells—some of my dreams were only made of scents. Others were a kaleidoscope of images, some a symphony of voices and accents. It was hard to weed through and find the 'story' in the dream.

As if she could read my mind, Magda encouraged, "Start with the strongest image".

I thought of the first picture I'd seen in my dream. I held to that until it became clear. Finally, I could almost smell the dew on the grass, and then I was there.

"I was standing in this green field... that went on forever... hill after hill, divided by stone fences. The sun was shining but it wasn't hot, just... nice."

"That's sounds real scary." Magda had found the eggs and was digging in the crisper for veggies.

"What else did you see?" she prompted over her shoulder.

"To my right, there were these ramps or whatever... you know, like wooden stalls for loading cattle. And uh... men."

"Oh goodie. Some men. What did they look like?"

I waited until she stopped yanking the frying pan out of my crowded cupboard.

"Like, you know, the actor in the movie *Highlander*. Men in plaid shawls draped over white shirts."

"This is getting interesting." Magda hacked up phlegm. "Can you answer the burning question?"

"What burning question?"

"What was under their kilts?"

I barked out a laugh. "I don't need to have those kinds of dreams."

"Are you saying you're getting some?" She leered at me, as if she was joking, but I was pretty sure she was still trying to dig up info about last night.

I stopped smiling. "I think the burning question here, Magda, is why I do have so many nightmares?"

"Be-cause you're nuts?" She pretended it was a wild guess, but it hurt.

Silence hung between us.

She shrugged, "I still love ya. Now keep talkin'"

Why was I so hurt? I knew I was nuts.

"Alright." I took myself back into the nightmare. "The men were bringing up these big, brown, hairy cows with really wide horns. And I could see these hands on a sword, but I couldn't see who was holding it. The sword swiped at a cow... and the blade... it slipped into the cow's throat... like it was made out of hairy butter." I shuddered at the memory.

Magda beat the eggs harder.

My voice dropped to a whisper, as I recounted the unpleasant scene.

"The cow went down on its knees on the grass. It was making these horrible bubbling, gurgling sounds."

"Then what?"

My heart was pounding like a hammer. "I just watched until the cow bled out and died."

Magda bellowed out a tortured moo and burst out laughing.

"SHHhhhh. Quiet! I don't want the landlord to hear us."

We listened for sounds the landlord might be getting up, but no creaking came from upstairs.

"Seriously, Magda, it was gross. It was ... cruel. But it gets worse. In my dream, I looked down, and saw I was the one holding the sword. I was doing the killing. Only I wasn't shocked or upset, I was happy. No, better than happy. I felt... high."

I had really felt orgasmic, but some things you don't share with friends.

The pan sizzled as Magda poured in the eggs. I wiped a sheen of sweat off my forehead with a corner of the quilt.

She chopped at the onions and pepper.

The sick feeling from the nightmare had come back, and I wasn't sure I should tell her the rest.

"So, why were you killing them?"

"I ... I don't know."

"Maybe you were a butcher?"

"No. I was wearing a dress. Like ... like a princess dress in yellow silk. The front was covered in blood. And it had this... low neckline, and my boobs were almost popping out because the weight of the blood was dragging the hem down."

"Sounds seriously sexy," Magda said in an Elvira impersonation.

"It wasn't sexy! Listen, my hands were on the sword, but my eyes were on my ..."

"Boobs!"

"No, my dress!" Normally at this point, she would have pulled a laugh from me, but she didn't know what happened next.

"This is serious. Listen. I swung the sword again and watched the blood spray all over my skirt. But there was no moo this time, so I looked up, and I saw..." A gag tugged at my tongue. "I saw... I'd cut Angus' throat."

"Holy shit!"

Finally, a reaction.

"Horrible, eh?" I peered at her, dread making me want to plug my ears against whatever judgement she came up with.

"You've got it bad."

"What?"

"You, you're totally hooked on Angus." She turned to sprinkle grated cheese on the omelet and returned the lid to the pan.

"That's such bullshit!" I got out of bed and moved to the cupboard to get plates.

"Mouldy mildew, mother of mouthmuck, dangle and strangle and death!"

It was never a good sign when Magda quoted *The Dark Crystal* movie.

"What happened to you?"

I looked at her, my arms in the cupboard. She was staring at the scratches on my legs.

"Oh," I pulled the plates out and lowered my heels to the floor. "I fell into a bush."

She tilted her head to the side and scowled at my thighs. With one hand, I tried to tug the nightie down.

"Are you sure someone didn't fall into your bush?"

A memory of grinding myself against Lennox burst into my consciousness, and my face lit up with shame.

I put the plates down on the table, making sure not to slam them and changed the subject.

"My nightmare is not about me wanting Angus, I dreamt about him last night, too."

Time ticked while I waited for her to be redirected.

"Aha! Point proven. Two nights in a row." Magda carried the frying pan over and cut the omelet in half. "There's no toast. Your bread was moldy."

"Magda," I sat and stared woefully at the food. "I'm cutting him in my dreams."

"Of course, you are." She put the pan on the stove and came back. "It's exactly how you would love someone. Punish him for making you fall in love—for making you vulnerable."

Doubt froze me. Was I really so pathetic?

Magda sat down, stabbed at her omelet, and stuffed a forkful in her mouth.

"I wuv yoo," She mocked in a Dracula voice, slicing at the air with her butter knife and giggling around the egg.

Maybe Magda wasn't so far off. I had cut Lennox's lips with my teeth and it had been a major turn on.

The kettle started to whistle giving me an excuse to escape her scrutiny.

"Let me ask you this..." Magda talked with her mouth full. "Do you want him?"

I took my time putting the teabags in the teapot, remembering the way Angus had held me while he'd kissed me, right here in my apartment. Could it have been only yesterday?

Last night, when we had been dancing, I had been heady at his closeness. With my arms around his neck and my body lined up against his, it was like slipping two pieces of a puzzle together. We fit perfectly into each other's dips and curves. And when he held me in his arms, it felt natural, like there was no other place I should ever be. There was no doubt I wanted him.

Did Angus want me? There was no denying the bulge in his pants when we danced together. No avoiding it either. He seemed to seek me out, but then, he would pull away, making excuses about timing. And him laughing up at the waitress and giving his attention to Karen at the restaurant were not the best moves for a guy looking to score.

I poured the hot water into the teapot while Magda was strangely silent behind me. Lennox had said Angus wasn't my friend. He'd been wanting to tell me something. But every guy who wants in my pants tries to oust his buddies with bullshit. It was Lesson number one from Woman Manipulation Class.

It had worked for him, too. He had gotten into my panties. Or I had ripped them off for him. Only, being with Lennox hadn't purged my need for Angus. I couldn't remember the whole night, but I knew how I felt now. I wasn't as wound up but thinking of Angus was reigniting my heat. I didn't just need a quick fix, I needed the man himself.

Magda was putting her fork down when I turned back to the table.

"Holy shit," I exclaimed, seeing her empty plate.

She was eyeing my food, and I wasn't hungry anyway, so I offered it to her. Just before she stuffed in the first forkful, she stopped and asked, "Did your doctor say you were underweight?"

Before I could answer, she laughed and corrected herself. "Oh no, that was Angus."

I frowned, thinking back to the restaurant and the steak conversation. "He didn't exactly say that."

I sat down beside her and sipped the tea, burning my tongue.

"Speaking of your doctorrr..." Magda dragged out the word until I filled in the name.

"Casbus."

"Right." She gulped a mouthful of tea. "So, this cassette tape..."

"What cassette tape?"

"The cassette we played yesterday on my ghetto blaster?"

I shrugged.

"The one that's in my bag?" she tried again, but I just opened my eyes wider.

"Did you hit your head last night?" She started digging through my knotty hair.

I slapped her arm away. "Get off!" But I couldn't help running my fingers over my scalp to check for bumps.

She let the subject go, stood up and rubbed her belly, "Mmmm mmm! You don't know what you missed."

She grabbed her bag and dug inside of it, pulling items out and making a mess all over the table and chair. When it was empty, she turned the bag upside down and gave it a shake.

"What are you looking for?" I asked.

She stuck her hand inside, again.

"Chill out, Magda, I have shampoo and stuff if you need it."

"You're not fooling anyone," she gave me a dirty look.

"What?" I laughed.

She repacked the bag and slung it over her shoulder. "I cooked, you do dishes."

She disappeared into my washroom, reappearing with her hair brushed and her clothes changed ten minutes later.

"Oh yeah, I promised Colin we'd go over to his place today."

I looked up from my teacup in shock. "You promised what?"

"We'll go over, watch movies all afternoon, and then leave."

"Well... I work tomorrow."

I was annoyed she would volunteer me for another visit with the Scotsmen, even if this was my way back to Angus.

"Sooooooo?"

"So, maybe I need a break from the haggis eaters!"

She put her hands on her hips. "Isn't it you who always says, 'might as well make it a party?'"

"I never say that."

She pursed her lips at me until I couldn't stand her hard scrutiny any more.

"Fine! We'll go!"

"So, hurry up, already."

WHILE BRUSHING MY TEETH, I remembered I had left my bra and undies in the washroom earlier that night. A quick glance around proved they were gone.

"Where's my bra?"

Magda was fiddling with something by the front door. "I put it in the sink to soak. Looks like you got blood on it or something."

Alarm pricked over my scalp. Had she had checked the crotch of my panties, too?

She turned and looked directly at me. "Did someone hurt you last night?"

I cut my eyes to the side and resisted the urge to cover my body with my arms.

"Of course not."

"Did you hurt someone else?"

"Jesus, Magda! Who would I hurt?"

She let that question hang in the air for a good minute. They she grabbed the door nob and turned it.

"I'm going out to buy smokes. Be ready when I get back."

Chapter 25: The Price of Eggs

I didn't get ready right away. As soon as Magda was out the door, I put a new plan into action. I hadn't told her everything about my dream. She didn't know about my ancestor's diary. I hadn't thought of it, but the nightmare had triggered a memory of my great-great-grandfather's journal. He had been a boring and long-winded writer. He wrote shit I had never been interested in. Mom used to read to me from the tea-coloured pages of his old journal, because it always put me asleep.

But now, thanks to his desire to record his life's details, including a strange, hairy herd of cows, a neighbour had shipped into the area, I finally had some dots to connect. I just needed Magda to stay away long enough for me to do it.

I put on an oven mitt then dragged a kitchen chair under my secret ceiling tile. Reaching up, I carefully pushed the tile forward, but it snagged on Donald's coat.

"Damn!"

After my actions with Lennox, Donald's coat was looking like a liability, and with the landlord letting Magda into my apartment, it was time to clean house. With the oven mitt, I pulled the Muskoka jacket down, letting it fall to the floor.

Reaching up into the dark space above my head, my hand slipped over my mother's diaries, a stack of pink and blue Hillary notebooks tied together with twine. I balanced on my toes until my grasping fingers found the fragile edges of the leather-bound journal. I carefully pulled it out, stepped down to gingerly lay it on the bed and replaced the ceiling tile.

Before I could read anything, Donald's jacket had to be disposed of. It was lying on the floor looking way too much like an upper torso with splayed arms. I picked it up and held it close to my nose. Giving it a sniff, I hoped to trigger some clue as to how I'd ended up with it in the first place. Even with his barbeque meat scent in my nostrils, my mind stayed locked down with no revealing images playing to tell the story.

No matter—the coat was on its way out.

Carrying the chair against my hip, I banged my way into the metal shower stall. The ceiling was open above it. Climbing onto the chair, I cautiously raised my head into the three feet of open space between the upper floor joists and the top of the shower stall.

On the other side of the basement, a single light bulb hung above the landlord's white washing tub. Its harsh light cast enough rays to show me the piles of laundry lying on the rough concrete floor, sorted by colour. The landlord's work clothes pile was easy to see. Jeans, plaid jackets and brown workpants. Perfect.

If the landlady had been down here doing the wash, she was nowhere to be seen now.

I stood tall to keep my armpit from getting scratched on the metal and slipped Donald's coat over the top of the shower stall. Swing-

ing my arm back, the weight threatened to pop my elbow as I swung
the jacket forward, pointing it toward the piles of laundry. Back and
forth, I swung it, until the weight had enough momentum to fly
through the air and land in the pile of dark work clothes, where it
would best blend in.

At least that was the plan.

Footsteps sounded from the landlord's basement stairs. I quickly
released the jacket. It flew, all empty sleeves and plaid plumage, and
landed just short of the pile of jeans and work shirts.

"Shit."

I dropped down into a squat on the chair and stripped the oven
mitt off my hand. Hidden inside the shower stall, I listened.

A humming started up in a woman's voice. It was the landlady. I
crossed my fingers, hoping she wouldn't notice anything out of the
ordinary.

Her slippers dragged across the floor with a gritty sound. The
metal clang of the washing machine lid opening rang out. The plastic
cup scratched the dry laundry soap inside the box. Zippers and buttons screeched on the metal drum as they were pushed in. The click-
ing of the dial, the slamming of the lid, and the trickle of water filling
the machine, followed each other.

Then those retreating slippers, sliding on their way back to the
stairs. I waited till she closed the door to the basement. Inching my
way up the stall, I carefully balanced on the chair and cautiously
peered over the top.

The pile of work clothes was gone and so was Donald's jacket. I
smiled, feeling clever.

The walk to the store should take Magda about thirty minutes,
so I had about fifteen left before she returned and demanded I leave
with her.

Carrying the chair with me, I hurried back to the bed and picked
up my ancestor's journal in shaking hands. The penmanship swirled

across the tea-coloured pages, fading away to grey shadows in some sentences. Why on earth my great-great-grandfather had written in pencil was beyond me, for it hadn't stood the test of time. Half the words could barely be read and what use was that?

I moved closer to the window above my bed and held the journal up towards the sun. I scanned past weather reports, the price of eggs, and the birth of family members. About three quarters of the way through the journal, I found the part I remembered from Mom's readings.

> A new family purchased Lot 7 Concession 12 from my brother, Maurice. Scottish brothers by the name of Mc-Nab. Winona was sorry to hear they didn't bring any wives or children. West Garafraxa can be a lonely place for a woman like Winona.

I skipped past more gibberish about quilting bees and the cost of flour. I thought I heard a noise by the front door, lifted my head, and listened for Magda. Satisfied she wasn't back yet, I turned a few more pages, scanning the faded penmanship for the name McNab.

> Maurice asked me to have the McNabs over for dinner in order to complete the sale of the land with paper signing. Winona's baking an apple pie using last year's apple preserves.

A few pages after, I almost missed an entry because Gramps didn't write their name.

> Found the Scotsmen's manners a bit off-putting. The elder brother took a shine to Winona, showing her undue attention that embarrassed us all. I have forbidden her to

speak to him again. Maurice will have to complete his transaction without my assistance.

I spun some more pages, accidently ripping one and saying "sorry" out loud. Close to the back of the journal, I found the last entry with Angus' last name in it.

> The McNab was here. Winona has disobeyed me. I cannot bring myself to speak to her. Together, we will seek Reverend Clyde's guidance after service on Sunday.

I held the closed journal on my lap. I wanted to read more about Winona and how things ended, but I was out of time and out of journals. I only had the one book, and the final entry in it talked about Parry Sound blueberries coming in on the train.

I thought back to Angus' comments after my landlord had left, yesterday. He'd said, "What ye and I have... it's bigger than us... it's older than us."

And again, back at the bar, I overheard Angus saying to Lennox, "Listen to me cousin. We are here tae do a job. If ye cannae handle that, ye have tae return home."

Had Winona's McNab been 'there' to do a job, too?

Karen had found out from Angus that his family was in the land buying business, so the McNabs in my grandfather's journal were probably legit buyers.

I chewed on my fingernail, peeling a sliver off with my teeth.

Patrick had said his and my ancestors had intersected hundreds of years ago. Maybe the McNabs had crossed my ancestor's path too. Maybe there was more to this fate bullshit... Just as Angus had been claiming all along.

Angus had told me when I was ready to hear the rest, I only had to ask him.

Well, I was ready.

It had been more than thirty minutes since Magda left. I quickly returned the journal to the ceiling nook and replaced the chair.

I stripped off my nightie on the way to the shower stall, dropping it on the kitchen floor. In the shower, I soaped my legs until the bubbles stood up like clear caviar on my tanned skin. Turning my back to keep the hot spray of water behind me, I rested my foot on the shower stall at hip level. I checked the scratches for thorns or signs of infection. Concentrating on my skin helped me avoid the racing thoughts that threatened to engulf me.

Every time I saw Angus, we took things a little farther. If I went with Magda today, there was a good chance I'd end up pinned against a wall, a table, or the floor by Angus. Based on my track record, it would be hard to resist him, but resist him I should until I puzzled out this McNab mystery.

Maybe I shouldn't go.

With enough persuasion, the Highlander would be able to take me any way he wanted. Weak woman that I was, I imagined all the ways as my hand made soapy circles on my other leg.

Rapidly, the skin on my neck tightened—a signal my bastard landlord was on the other side, counting the seconds to when he could safely try to peek at my naked body over the top of the open shower stall.

Dropping my leg, I quickly searched the open ceiling above. No leering face peered down from the cobweb-laced rafters of the upper floor. I could try to prove it once and for all, by grabbing the edges of the flimsy walls and pulling myself up high enough to look over. However, I doubted the unsupported walls of the steel stall would hold my weight. Without a chair to stand on, I'd probably end up wet and slippery, splayed out on his floor in all my unclothed glory.

"I know you're there," I confessed into the steam.

"What?" Magda yelled from inside my apartment.

"I know you watch me, you sick freak!"

My ears felt alive as I listened for any sound that would confirm
my suspicions. As usual, there was no response.

The shower spray started to cool off as the hot water tank emptied. I quickly rinsed and shut the tap off before the water became
icy. Opening the stall door just enough to reach into the kitchen and
grab my towel, I wrapped it around myself, and stepped out.

Ignoring Magda, who sat by the front door, I moved to my closet
and started shuffling clothes about.

"What were you saying in the shower?" Magda asked.

Relieved the heat was off me for a while, I threw the landlord to
the dogs.

"Freak boy."

I shimmied into my black, skinny jeans and a red tube top.

Making my way to the dresser, I picked up my childhood jewelry
box, a gift from my mother. After reading Grandpa Courdrey's journal, a little sentimental feeling tugged at my heart. I flipped the jewelry box over in my hand and twisted the rusty, metal wing.

The inside mechanics scratched in response. Putting it down, I
unclasped the top, releasing the plastic ballerina to pop up in her
one-legged stance. The little dancer's paint had long since faded from
her tutu, transforming her into a plastic chameleon that blended
into her clothes until I couldn't tell where she began and where her
clothes ended.

"If the landlord is being such a freak, you should move," Magda
suggested.

The clinking of the metallic tune soothed my rare moment of
homesickness.

"Where would I go?"

"Alright, fine. Stay, but at least screw the guy and save some rent
money."

In the box, my cheap second-hand necklaces, scored from dusty
shops on Wyndham Street lay twisted together. I pulled two apart.

The fine chain with the silver cross was the first to let go. I usually didn't wear it because of how my body reacted to the religious symbol. But it was pretty, in a simple way, and there was always the possibility the pearl in the centre of the cross was real.

Today, the way the chain had released itself from the knot seemed like an omen. I rubbed my thumb over the pearl, holding the cross in my palm and waited for my body to respond. The only rumble was hunger for a missed breakfast. I took it as a sign I was getting better, with or without Casbus' drugs and Patrick's celibacy.

I draped the chain over my head and let the cross swing down onto my chest. The comforting weight of it felt good.

Next, I untangled the golden, angel pendant. The fat cupid looked up at me as if blaming me for his broken wing. The edge was sharp, usually too sharp to wear safely, but I considered it a good thing to have in case I needed a weapon.

Magda was still rattling on about the landlord.

"You're always opening your legs. Might as well get something out of it," she mumbled.

The jewelry box tune twanged to a stop with a metallic echo.

I steadied my voice before I answered her. "I sleep around, Magda, but I always choose who I sleep with."

I turned, and we locked eyes. I had never pulled "street" moves on her before. Never had to because she always backed down first. But this time, her face didn't soften, and she didn't hide her insult behind a giggle. I could feel the 'crazy' hoping Magda would push me farther. Carefully, laying the rest of the chains down on the dresser, I gave Magda my full attention.

"You got that?" I tipped my head slightly to one side and narrowed my eyes at her.

She held my gaze, her chin thrust out, stubbornly.

The blood picked up speed in my veins, making me wild with beats.

I took a step toward her. She dropped her glance. The malicious excitement coursing through my veins was over-the-top. My dark side wanted to have a go. It took all my willpower not strike her in the face.

I turned my back on her again and filled my chest with air. I tracked her movements with my hearing but kept my hands busy shaking out an intricately-linked chain with a grey stone wrapped in metal wire at the end. With its release, my longest necklace, the chain ending in a hammered piece of copper, fell free from the knot.

Cheap stuff, but I liked to imagine the pendants had been chipped and shaped by cave dwelling forefathers. When I touched them, visions of line drawn antelopes leaped in jerking stop-motion bounds through my mind. I dropped these two onto my chest as well, and immediately calmed as the raw chunks of nature tangled on my breasts.

Looking up quickly, I caught Magda watching me, her expression laced with loathing. I blinked and looked at her again. The line between her eyebrows was gone, the twisted mouth relaxed. Maybe I was seeing things.

"Are we going or what?" she asked.

I picked out my curly hair, scrunched some baby oil into it to keep the frizz down, grabbed a shriveled apple from the kitchen counter, took three huge bites and chewed it all at once. Pausing by my night table, I pondered taking a pill.

I had been doing great until the timeline thoughts played in my head, and I didn't want Magda to know I was on anything. She had already thrown enough "dirt" at me this morning. Not to mention, Casbus was now on my "do not trust" list, until I could figure out what the hell was going on in that cassette tape recording.

"Today, sometime?"

I walked away from the night table empty handed and followed Magda out into the sunshine.

Chapter 26: Shadow Watcher

During the thirty-minute trip, I planned the questions I would ask to find out more about the McNabs and their purpose. There were too many coincidences, and it was time for me to get some answers.

In no time, we were standing in front of a cheap war-time house in the "Ward" section of Guelph.

Magda rapped on the door.

The bare-dirt yard broken up by a few patches of dead grass stood out in contrast to the well-manicured Italian yards on the street, gardens full of frost-touched tomato plants, colourful mums, and purple kale. Every other yard and house looked lovingly cared for, while this one looked like shit, with drooping eaves, missing shingles, and paint peeling forlornly from the white-trimmed windows.

That would be my first question, whether this lot belonged to the "land-purchasing" Scotsmen of my ancestor's journal.

The door opened, but instead of it being Angus, Colin stood there with a welcoming smile on his face. This was the first time I'd actually seen him without his hat. He was bald. Just as he'd been in my silo nightmare when he'd backed away from me with his hat in his hand. Bald as an egg.

With a sense of wonder, I acknowledged I had dreamt something I hadn't known.

"Welcome tae our wee hame, ladies." The short Scotsman bowed low and kept his head down as Magda slipped past him and entered the house.

I stayed where I was, standing halfway across the front lawn where the sun arched over the roof to kiss the ground in front of me.

"Actually, Colin," I called to him. "Can you come here?"

He lifted his head like a startled terrier.

Magda's head reappeared in the doorway, her brows drawn together.

I tried a disarming smile.

"Just for a second."

They looked at each other, and I was sure a silent message passed between them. But, he returned my smile with a tight grin and moved with a stiff-need gait down the concrete steps.

His shadow stretched out in front of him, as if bowing to me in supplication. I kept my eyes on it as he approached, watching for any change in colour or texture that might tell me a bit about him.

It wasn't normal. It wasn't black. It had the same vintage brown quality to it that Angus' did.

Perhaps it was their family shadow colour, or perhaps it was the Scottish version. Whichever, it was consistent with all of the McNabs. Even the halo around Duncan's head from that first night in the Albion had been a faded brown colour.

Though his shadow was lying at my feet, Colin still hadn't reached me. He was dragging it out, but I had what I needed.

"You smell that?" I asked him.

"Smell what?"

I shrugged and walked passed him on my way to the door.

He shifted sideways to get out of my way. Why was Colin acting so fearful? And why did a spike in my belly approve of his behaviour?

"Smells like bullshit," I mumbled.

THE INSIDE OF THE HOUSE was just as drab as the yard. There was a wooden table, a faded couch, and a square television, all surrounded by blank walls. There were no books, paintings, pictures, trophies—nothing to give me a clue about the people who were staying in this house.

Colin followed me in, picked up his wallet from the table, and shoved it into the pocket of his brown cords.

"Whose place is this?" I asked.

He hesitated before answering, giving me that look people get once they start catching on to my odd behaviour

I softened my features and tried to look interested.

"Och." He shrugged. "We're just renting fur now."

"Looks pretty temporary," I noted, remembering what Angus had told Karen about staying for a few weeks.

Magda was listening carefully to his answers.

"Well, ye ne'er can tell," he winked at Magda, and was rewarded with her lovely smile in return.

Magda interjected, "Have you heard from your friend, Lennox?"

She watched me while Colin answered.

"Nae." He looked at Magda and then followed her glance to my face. "Not a word."

I coughed into my hand and pushed my fingertips into the front pockets of my jeans.

I wasn't surprised they hadn't heard from Lennox. He had appeared pretty irrational about Angus' motives. Cousins or not, there didn't seem to be any love lost between the two. Or maybe he was still lying in the ravine.

I pushed that thought away.

"Where's Angus?"

Colin nodded to one of the doors branching off the living room, "He ain't up yet."

"Wow." Magda looked at her watch. "I thought we were bad."

She smirked at me.

"Och, Angus ne'er sleeps in. He's just no feelin' well."

Colin lifted car keys from a hook by the fridge.

"What's wrong with him?" I asked.

"His blood gets thick, is all." Colin slipped his arm through Magda's and steered her to the door.

They didn't see me react.

'Thick blood' was what Colin had said in my dream when he and Duncan had dragged an unconscious Angus onto the rope-framed bed.

"As a matter o' fact, I wonder if ye can stay with him while Magda and I git some videos?" He plunked his plaid hat on his head and didn't wait for an answer.

The door shut, and I was alone.

Chapter 27: The True Self Revealed

My skin was still crawling from Colin's reference to Angus' thick blood.

Something was going on, but I couldn't pin it down.

I tapped my fingers against my lips. Should I wake Angus up and demand answers to my questions, or just wait until he got up himself?

The other option was to bolt. But if I left, what about Magda? I didn't know which Jumbo Video they had gone to, and I had no way to contact her. She'd be so pissed I'd dumped her a second time, she might call the wrath of Mr. Spiritoe down onto my head.

Besides, it was time for that talk Angus had promised. This was my chance to be alone with him and to ask him about what I'd read in my ancestor's diary.

My anxious thinking was cut short by a low groan.

I craned my neck to look down the dark hallway.

"Hello?" My voice trembled on the word.

A whimper, low and sad, compelled me to move cautiously across the living room floor.

Suddenly, a creaky floor board squealed under my weight, warning of my advance. I froze in my tracks.

"I'm coming down, now."

A clock on the wall ticked away the seconds. No one answered. Cracking out my neck, I pushed my shoulders back and walked the last few steps to the first doorway.

The room was dark inside. I searched for a light switch on the outside wall. There wasn't one. My heart in my throat, I stepped in through the doorframe.

On the other side of the room, a few splinters of sun squeezed between long, thick curtains covering a window. In the centre of the room, someone was lying under a white sheet on the bed.

"Angus?" I whispered.

The sound of a furnace turning on somewhere in the house was followed by the low rush of hot air pushing through the vents.

I didn't take my eyes from the bed as I slid my hand along the wall beside me, searching for a light switch.

"Highlander."

I gave up scratching at the empty wall and accepted I had to cross to the window. Scanning the gloom at the corners of the room, I hurried to the window and clasped the curtain. That familiar feeling of foreboding attacked my stomach, and I cursed the horror movies that had put it there. I yanked the curtain to the side.

Piercing shards of sunlight drove like sand pellets into my eyes. My pupils were slow to adjust to the light and my eyes filled with tears.

I turned to the bed. The sunlight infused the room. It should have chased the tingles of fear away but laid out before me was a morgue scene. A white sheet covered a sleeper from head to toe, hiding the body's identity.

Whoever it was, was tall...as long as the bed...as long as Angus.

I took a step closer trying to see through the crisp white material, but the dips and peaks of the form beneath the cloth revealed nothing.

Passing by the shape of the body under the sheets, I moved to where the head should be and watched as the sheet lifted above a breath.

Relief tingled down my arms. I released a nervous sigh. My returning courage encouraged me to reveal the sleeper's face. Pinching the material with my fingernail, I slowly pulled the sheet down.

Wavy, brandy-wine coloured hair was the first give-away. But just to be sure, I pulled the sheet all the way to his waist. He was naked, his pecs full and round under a swath of curly, chest hairs. The lower half of his face was covered with a ginger shadow of whiskers. His eyes were closed, the thick dark lashes lying against his skin like shadowy feathers. As I memorized his face, he moaned again, shattering the illusion of serenity.

Now, I noticed the frown lines between his eyes, the sweat curling the hair at his temples. I thought he was having a nightmare, so I lay my hand on his shoulder intending to shake him. But even before I touched his skin, I could feel the heat coming off. The man was sweltering with fever.

I pressed my palm to the side of his face, then touched his forehead.

"Omigod, Angus," I blurted.

He was sick. I looked around the room, not sure what to do. A rare memory of kindness, of how my mom had sponge-washed me when I'd had the flu as a child, arose.

I hurried down the hall to find the bathroom and wet a cloth. When I got back, Angus' face and neck were covered in a sheen of sweat. With a fever that hot, the washcloth should have shocked him awake, but he only stirred and mumbled a few broken sentences as I wiped his brow. I drew the cloth along his arm, which was incredibly heavy, the muscles twisting under my wet fingers.

The evaporation of the water on his body normally would have cooled his skin, but he was just as hot to my touch after he air dried.

Wiping the cloth over his wide chest again, this time I noticed the curly hairs spring up behind my hand like an army coming to attention.

I slid the cloth down over each mound of stomach muscle hidden beneath a warm layer of flesh. Angus wasn't just cut. He was prime—marbled and muscled to survive.

These genetics had thrived under furs, carried his ancestors over mountains, released arrows, swung iron, and clubbed with rocks.

The cloth slipped past his navel. Just beyond, a lush edge of dark hair waited beneath the sheet.

I stilled my hand and closed my eyes.

"Don't get all weird on me," I said, then shook my head, reminding myself he was unwell.

On the next swipe of the cloth across his stomach, I was surprised to feel his skin beneath my hand. The cloth was gone. Then forgotten, as I explored his rib cage, pressing my fingers gently into the dips between his ribs. An intimate visual of his corpuscles smoked my senses, causing me to gasp aloud in delight.

Angus moved for the first time, tossing his head from left to right and settling again. The stirring broke up the bizarre images in my mind, but only for a second before I was drawn back to his solid working muscle, which seduced my thoughts with brawny bits.

The odd lusting wove in and out of my perception—a push and pull between my concern for Angus, and my alternate personality's preoccupation with flesh. Such bizarre thoughts belonged to her, not me, and I was positive it was Angus' vulnerability that was triggering them.

Finally, I understood what my 'alter' was. She was a huntress. That much I had worked out, after leaping through the ravine during the night. I hadn't been following Lennox. I'd been hunting him. I had chased him, overtaken him, and ultimately, the She had brought him down like the antelope he was to her.

According to Casbus, my mind had created her to protect me from men. But with men like Angus, I didn't need protecting. I wanted to be with him, as an equal, as a lover. Just me. So, I needed Angus to be too healthy and capable to tempt her.

My 'alter' wasn't going to steal my time with the Scotsman. This one was mine.

"I want you to wake up, Angus."

Despite my stern tone, his eyes remained closed.

My 'alter' thrilled when his nostrils flared with another shuddering breath.

Squeezing his shoulder, I gave him a little shake, fighting the urge to press my fingers into the cords of his muscles.

He didn't respond. I shook him again, hard enough to make his head move from side to side.

"You *must* wake up!"

His eyes remained closed, and alarm skittered over my nerves. He seemed defenceless, lying with his hair falling back from his forehead. His mouth so soft...he seemed completely unaware.

His oblivion was tantalizing.

"No, something's wrong," I said out loud.

But those lips...I wanted to set his skin tingling before he knew I was there. And, I wanted to savour his startled response when he awoke, trapped beneath my mouth.

The silky strands of his hair slid softly between my fingers. I could do anything to him, and he would never know. I leaned over his face, my hair swinging down to brush his lashes. That's when I saw the little indent in his chin beneath his whiskers. Pressing my finger against this dimple in his flesh, I pulled down. His bottom lip pulled away from the top, opening his mouth ever so slightly.

A sultry "Oh" escaped me as I sighed, heady with the prospects of what I could do.

I lowered my mouth to his lips—thick, supple velvet. He did not respond. There was no change in his position, no resistance to, or acceptance of my kiss.

My excitement rose, and I kissed him in earnest, turning my head to the side and molding my mouth to his.

A slight brush of movement stilled me. I tracked it to the air flexing slightly as the vein in his neck throbbed with an increase in blood pressure.

Angus released a moan, but unlike the tortured sounds of his fever, this one was a provocative expression of need. His wide hand clutched the back of my head. Holding me to his mouth, he pressed back.

I slipped my hand to the centre of his chest, my fingers spreading possessively over his heart.

Like a drowning man, Angus sucked air in through his nostrils as he consumed me, and I was the one left moaning.

I felt my 'alter' retreating, leaving me with a man, not merely a bundle of bone and blood for her fixation.

The intensity of his kiss turned soft, and the pressure of his hand lightened, allowing me to pull back and consider his eyes. I had expected soft, sleepy desire, but was met with a hard and cold gaze—emeralds glittering from within as if fueled by ice.

"Angus?"

His hand slipped down over my shoulder.

"Take off yer clothes." He held me with his forceful stare. "I want tae see ye."

I blinked and straightened. His hand slipped away. Standing by the bed, I frowned at him.

He pressed his mouth into a hard line, and his green eyes swept my upper body. "Now."

I winced at his scrutiny, which no longer felt sexy.

"Off!"

"How dare you order me!"

"This is what ye want, isnae?"

I stood there as he looked at me as so many men had.

The beauty of the moment dulled into dark shades of disappointment, then grey shades of submission. A familiar numbness slackened the muscles around my mouth and shallowed my breathing.

"Now."

My chest was heavy as I grasped the red heel of my pump and pulled it from my foot. The shoe hit the floor with a sharp clatter.

Angus pushed himself up the mattress until he was half sitting against the headboard. The position bunched his stomach muscles into hard mounds beneath his pecs, testimony to his brute strength, and below...

He might not be sweet talking me, but he wanted me. That much was obvious.

"That a girl." His tone was approving, and a willingness to please him quickened.

I grasped the other heel, triggering a memory of Lennox from the night before. I tossed the memory with the shoe.

Placing my hand over my tight stomach, I felt a tremor shivering beneath my skin. It wasn't quite the hollow echo I was used to. It was more like the expectant quaking of a nervous dog waiting for praise.

I hooked my finger in the elastic material of my tube top and slowly pulled it down. My breasts strained at the top of the restraining material and then slipped free. His eyes gleamed like glass as he watched.

The tube top pressed beneath my breasts like a whore's corset, and I left it there for it was the perfect complement for my whore's heart.

Angus reached out his hand.

"Come tae me, Rachel."

My blood was sluggish, my thoughts foggy and listless, a textbook state to experience the heightened sensations of what he would do to me. Yet, still, I resisted.

This wasn't how I wanted it to be. Not with him.

I delayed obeying by twisting the metal button of my jeans and pressing it out through the button hole.

Angus laid his arm down along his torso, his hand resting on the white sheet above his crotch. His fingers moved as he watched me.

Each tooth of the zipper released with a distinct click like the countdown of a timer. I peeled off my tight jeans.

My skin was indented by the seams, which left a flesh railroad track leading down into my patch of blonde curls.

Angus' cheeks flushed a deep red. He growled with impatience. "Come!"

I lifted my knee to the mattress.

He clutched me with his left hand and yanked the sheet to the side with his right. From under the trailing material, the perfect form of his leg was revealed.

It called to her, my 'alter', inviting her to join us.

Gluteus, femoris, sartorius... the poetry of the human thigh. She invaded my mind with her thoughts.

I had wanted to make love with Angus, but his dominating behaviour had taken my healthy desire and twisted it into remnants of my traumatic history.

Now, with her here, I wanted to knead his thigh until my fingers slipped between the sinewy bands. I wanted to explore the density of bone below.

"Saphenous," the Southern accent slithered out.

I bit my lip to stop her words, but I was weak. I was in a state that succumbed to the will of the strong. I was the perfect vessel into which she spilled.

"Gracilis."

The word was silky, spinning my submission into a web of meaty menace.

Angus' eyes flickered with fear.

I climbed onto him like a cat, holding myself just above his hips. The big man kept his eyes on my face, his hand tentatively cupping the curve of my breast where it met my chest.

Excitement broke upon me like a cutting wave, washing away the detachment. I became the cold, hard glittering light I had seen in Angus' green eyes.

The scent of his skin and hair further aroused my attention. I tilted my head and drew in the odours. The dust under the bed, the thirty-year-old varnish on the hardwood floor, even the sparking iron scent of the sunlight streaming through the window filled my sinuses.

"Femoris," she forced the word out into the air between us.

His eyes widened, and his hand dropped. The air cooled the spot where he had touched.

My spine straightened as my chest expanded with her presence. Blood coursed my body, infusing it with adrenaline.

"*McNab*," she said the word like a victory speech.

Angus shuddered and raised his forearm over his eyes.

Beneath me, the end of the sheet still clung to his hips like a Grecian cloth. His arousal pushed against the material with the impudence of a land-claiming flag. Seconds ticked by.

"Get on with it," he said.

Angus had what he needed, so he could hide beneath his arm if he wanted.

Leaning my body forward, she bit the fine veins showing through the inside of his pale wrist. He tensed, but he didn't push me from him.

Pulling back, she looked with satisfaction at the small indents in his skin.

My mouth opened to release her next words. "Now Rachel, you *must* realize, your love for this man is a fool's game."

A cold wash of shock chilled the base of my skull, for never in my entire life, had my 'alter' addressed me through my own mouth.

Angus dropped his arm to stare at me, a grimace distorting his good looks. His disgust was enough to fire me into action. I mentally grabbed my alter and tried to drag her down, back down where she was harmless and helpless.

A loud crash came from the front of the house, and I thought it was my mind putting in the background noises to my battle with my "other". But the sound of boots running down the hall alerted me to the reality of the moment.

Not knowing who or what was coming, I cried out, and slipped from Angus to stand by the side of the bed. Facing the open doorway of the bedroom, I crossed my arms over my naked body.

Chapter 28: Cain Lives In Us All

"Rachel!" With shock, I recognized Lennox's voice. "Rachel!"
"Bloudy hell!" Angus roared from behind me.

I shrieked in surprise as his arms wrapped my waist, and he lifted me backwards onto the bed. Climbing over me, he tossed the sheet over my hips, before vaulting from the mattress.

He staggered when his feet hit the floor, but his voice boomed with outrage as he yelled, "Lennox McNab, by all the Saints!"

Lennox burst into the room, sliding to a stop when he saw me in Angus' bed. He ignored Angus who was standing like a naked, demi-god guardian between us, crouching with his arms out to his sides, his hands gripping the air. His thighs and buttocks strained with brute strength as he bent his knees.

Lennox locked eyes with me over Angus' shoulder. "Rachel, is it ye lass, or t'other?"

I opened my mouth gaping like a fish, but I couldn't speak.

Lennox's face was scratched, his eyes and lips swollen, and his bottom lip shone with fresh blood. His neck was covered in bruises in the shape of human bite marks. Like my bra from the night before, his t-shirt was stained a dark rust colour around the collar.

"You get the hell out!" Angus took a threatening step toward him, and I pulled the sheet up higher.

That seemed to answer Lennox's question.

"Rachel, don't dae it. Dorn't lit heem release 'er!"

His accent was so thick; I couldn't understand what he was saying.

With a roar, Angus rushed him, and they went down like two bulls writhing madly to pin the other. The dull thud of flesh on flesh was followed by a sharp crack of bone as they swung and struck.

I squeezed my eyes shut, but my 'alter' opened them to watch with delight as Angus beat Lennox down, strike after strike, until Lennox was no longer moving. I screamed at him to stop.

And he did stop, his head hanging down, his sides heaving from exertion. Angus staggered up from his knees where he'd been straddling Lennox, his cousin's blood dripping from his knuckles.

I covered my mouth with my hand, my chest heaving at the sight of Lennox's still form splayed out on the floor.

Angus stumbled to the side. His erection was flaccid.

"Is he..." I didn't dare speak the word out loud.

Angus turned his savage face my way, looking at me with a madman's determination.

"Lower the sheet." His voice was dead, lifeless.

"Angus..." My lips trembled, and I blinked away the tears to clear my vision. A sob shuddered from my mouth.

His thigh muscles rippled with each step as he walked up to the bed and yanked the sheet from my hands. I screamed as it tore one of my fingernails to the quick.

"Angus, please." I covered my breasts with my arms.

He didn't see me. He didn't hear me. He turned away to lay the sheet over Lennox's body, covering up his face.

"He's dead?"

Angus whipped his head around, his narrowed eyes as dull and empty as clay.

I skittered sideways to get off the bed, but he moved faster. Landing on the mattress, his weight bounced me into the air where he grabbed at my limbs. I twisted, landing on my stomach, but before I could scramble away, his hand gripped my ankle like a steel shackle.

I pushed at the bed with my other foot, clawing my way off, but Angus yanked me back, so hard, pin pricks of pain radiated along my leg.

"Stop!"

He flipped me onto my back, gripping my body cruelly to drag me under him, and pinned my legs with the weight of his thighs.

"Bastard!" I clawed at his face.

He tried to catch my hands, but I flailed like a madwoman to keep them out of his reach. He dropped his body on top of mine, his mass brutally crushing the air from my lungs.

His thick fingers wrapped my wrists so tightly, my skin burned as he pinned my hands to the mattress on either side of my head.

Gasping for air, I lay helpless under his enormous body. The wind whistled in his throat, his breath blowing the fine hairs at my hairline.

"Let me go!" I writhed beneath him.

"Rachel!"

I gave another twist, but he wrapped my legs with his thighs that were like bands of iron.

"Rachel," he moaned, and the plaintive tone in his voice stalled my fight.

I could feel his heart pounding against my chest. Shivering, despite the warmth of his body weighing me down, my teeth chattered with tension.

"Let me dae what needs tae be done."

Angus sought my eyes, so I let him see them. I searched for a sign of the man I had trusted, the man I had been willing to trust, but Angus closed his lids before I could find him.

He brought his face closer, pressing his forehead against mine, and this time his bangs brushed my eyes. I closed them, and he kissed my eyelids tenderly.

"What..." I bit back a sob. "What has to be done?"

But I already knew, for he was rubbing himself against me, and I could feel his flesh growing between my legs.

"I'm sae sorry, lass."

"No!" The word screamed from my bottomless memories.

A useless word.

A word that stopped no one.

I tried to bring my thighs together, but he forced his knee between my legs.

"Shhhhhh," he whispered, kissing my lips, and I sobbed the word "why" into his mouth.

"I wanted tae tell ye. Tae explain... I thought if ye knew, it would be easier."

I wanted to say, "rape is *never* easy," but my mind betrayed me and slipped me down into that safe place inside, and she rose up in my stead.

"Look at me, lass," he pleaded. "Tell me ye understand."

My other flickered my eyelashes open like lifting a curtain before a performance.

His eyes were glistening. "Remember what I said tae ye about destiny? Our destiny?"

She nodded my head, and I felt her delight in pretending to be me.

"This..." he squeezed his eyes closed, cleared his throat and said, "This is our destiny."

Hot tears filled in the back of my throat, and she swallowed my excess.

He opened his lashes, the pain pooling in the green depths. "From the time we were born, ye and me'self, we were headed here, tae this moment."

Couldn't he hear the doubt in his own voice?

"We have tae dae this."

I remembered the moment in my apartment when I thought he might be a stalker.

"Please lass, don't make it harder."

Keeping his sorrowful eyes on mine, he softened his grip on my left wrist. She let my hand lie limp, but inside she bunched up with tension.

Angus let go completely and slid his hand down my side, his warm palm heating my waist.

I didn't want his hands on me. Not those hands that had beaten Lennox to death. But I had chosen to leave this scene, and She had chosen to be present.

He nuzzled the side of my neck, breathing in my scent. "Ah've known about ye all my life."

He lifted his head and the sadness shifted. "Yoo're more beautiful than I had ever hoped."

She snickered inside, but I felt her jealousy prick.

"I need ye, Rachel, and we need us." He kissed the end of my nose. "We can't be complete if we are apart."

She smoked my eyes, and Angus responded, kissing me-who-wasn't-me, while she held still beneath his seeking. His mouth was gentle as he explored my lips, then increasing in intensity when I didn't fight back.

She flicked the tip of my tongue against lip. I silently cursed her for her betrayal.

Angus, encouraged, cherished my mouth with all the talent he'd shown before. His other hand slipped between us. Every touch I had hoped for came true as he gently traced my curves, and expertly enticed the dips of my body. I tried to resist him. I truly did. But my body was no longer mine, alone.

He was drawing sensation from me, like a humming bird draws nectar from a flower. He touched me as if he had known me a thousand times, and knew every secret of my body, every desire of my mind. He was well practiced at rhythm, pressure, and stroke.

She wasn't held back by morals, or emotions, or any of those rules that would have stopped my impatient flames of yearning with the cold chill of judgement.

She led my body into betrayal and then, suddenly, she fell away, and it was only me there beneath his warm skin, arching against his hand.

My soul, which had previously cringed from his fierceness and violence, sold itself to desire and welcomed him in.

Chapter 29: It is Not the Heart, but the Flow

I was a magnet, and Angus was my lodestone.

His draw caused me to flicker with my 'alter', changing places with her randomly as we vied to dance with him. When she took over, my awareness would fade out, and when I came back to the moment, I'd find myself wrapped in a new position with Angus' limbs.

His intoxicating man-scent glided over my senses, as I slid my body up his belly, my eyes locked onto the dock within his collarbone. His chest hairs tickled my chin, bending like a hundred little fingers egging me on to that pulsating beat in his neck.

I tested his skin with my tongue, tapping the wet tip against him like a gecko licks at its eyes. Stretching my mouth wide, I latched onto that vibrant throb beneath his jaw. My gums pulsed above my teeth, and I gulped back the warm blood that flowed from the slits I knew were there.

Angus' heavy hand slapped the back of my neck, and I thought he would rip me off by the scruff. He was rougher with my 'alter', but at my shriek of surprise, his touch became gentle, and he stroked my hair.

"That's it, Kit."

A thought of Lennox cooling on the floor tried to invade my thoughts. I sat up on him, tempted to look where Lennox was lying.

Angus tugged the chains around my neck, drawing my attention back to him. He untangled my medallions to release my cross from the others. The chain draped like a bridge between us as he inspected it closely, rubbing the centre pearl in small circles with his thumb. The way he held it out, tilted to the side, made it look like the X from my tea leaf reading.

Angus yanked on the cross, snapping the links painfully against the skin of my neck.

"Hey!" I slapped at him, but he grabbed my wrist, holding it away from his body.

"Be still."

I obeyed, as he slowly brought the cross to his mouth, closed his eyes and pressed a reverent kiss into it. His low voice spoke some Scottish words I could not understand. Then my cross was flying across the room, the chain hitting the wall with a tinny rattle.

He sat up and grasped my hips.

"Hang on tight, Lass," he said, and then he made me forget... everything.

THE SOUND OF OUR SKIN slapping sharply against the sweat on our bodies was vulgar in a room where a man lay dead. We didn't care. Human decency was absent.

We were too far gone, as we tried to linger in that sweet moment of nothingness, that pause on the edge of infinity. Our mingled cry tumbled us into a blinding flash of exquisite pleasure. His member jerked and spat like a cobra into my womb, and from our combined juices there was a birthing, a writhing, an evil uprising.

It was at that moment, I realized I must save myself.

I tried to twist from him, but he held me in place. My alternate personality blossomed, her dark essence crawling like a subterranean creature into the marrow of my bones, spooking my soul into flight. Free will powdered and dusted in the air. Cloying, it clogged our lungs, and still, the echo of our orgasmic cry hung suspended between us.

She jammed my elbow into his clavicle, driving him down onto his back. Crouching on the Highlander's pelvis like a gargoyle about to ride him to hell, she threw back my head and laughed like a fiend.

Every nightmare I had ever had, played out in my mind in a speeding collage of horror, and it all happened in an eternal second. And suddenly, it was over. Time congealed back to the present to find me terrified, cowering within myself as a whipped child cowers in a corner, as my madness matured into a powerful puppeteer of my body.

A single tear fell from my eye, swinging forward in a sickle arc as if blessing the Highlander's brow. A shattering scream cut from my throat. My spine arched backwards in a crippling spasm until my hair dusted the bottoms of my feet.

Then she lashed my head forward, burying my teeth into Angus' neck. The sharp spurt of his blood hit the roof of my mouth.

That brutal god-like strength that had beaten a man to death could not save his own life, for now he gave no fight.

Passively, he gave only of himself, never lifting a hand against me.

Sucking and gulping and swallowing like a feral beast, I rolled the glory of his crimson warmth into my throat and growled for more.

Chapter 30: Life is a Feeble Gamble

It might have been minutes, or hours, during which I had shuddered through a thousand orgasmic-organ restarts before his pumping liquids slowed. She swallowed the last drop of tin-flavoured blood and sighed like a sated lover against his rapidly cooling skin.

As I lay upon his chest, dazed with fulfilment. The feeble tapping that was Angus' heart drummed out a weedy attempt to hold onto his life.

Through my sleepy lids, I spied the silver cross huddled in the corner, glistening with an aura of goodness that could not help me now, for I had tasted the gift of sin, and it was unforgettable.

Light beams streaked in from the window, shot by the sun setting in a cloud of billowing red. I stared at the skyline until Angus' heart set in his chest.

He started to convulse.

His quaking torso tried to throw me off.

I held on, enjoying the ride.

Then, he stilled.

And cooled.

And finally, a cold shock of reality jolted me to my senses.

Angus needed an ambulance.

With the return of my reason came the realization that I did not have control of my limbs. I commanded my body to move with silent orders. But it ignored me. I tried to lift my head, but my attempt failed as I thrashed only in my mind. I strained to slide off Angus' body, but it was as if my arms were welded to his skin.

Again, and again, I tried to tense and flex, reach and bend. The effort I was putting into moving my body should have ripped a groan from my throat. Instead, my lips curved into a smile that silently mocked my hopeless efforts.

That's when I knew I had slipped into that place I had fought to stay out of all my life. Before Angus, I had been in control, and my 'alter' had been the "other". Now she seemed to be the governor of my flesh.

He's going to die, you bitch. Let me out! I shouted, but the words were only thoughts.

She answered me with my mouth, "Oh fiddle dee dee. Why do you worry your pretty little head, so?"

Her response was light and airy, full of a carelessness that can only belong to someone without a conscience.

She rose to sit on Angus' bed and stretched like a cat.

I experienced her actions as feathery little whispers of the graceful movements she was putting my body through.

My mind grappled with reality as she continued speaking.

"You cannot help him, for if you dial zero on that silly contraption, you will only bring the law down onto your own head," she drawled into the silent bedroom.

Her words were slow and soft, delivered in a porch swing cadence.

I was so intrigued by the sound of her voice, I could barely concentrate on her meaning.

Pointing my toes, she touched the floor with my foot as if dipping it into a hot bath. Finding it held, she stood and delicately moved aside the bed clothes until she located my jeans. Holding them up for inspection, she looked at the inside-out legs with disdain.

"And then, we will both lose our freedom," she continued with finality, as she pulled on the jeans. "Is that what you want?"

Freedom? I shook myself out of the numbing shock and tried to understand her point.

She turned and pointed at Angus, her movements fluid and graceful like a silk scarf in a gentle breeze.

"You have taken this man's life. You will pay for it. They will make you pay."

I cringed as my mind conjured images of the Guelph Correctional inmates in their orange jumpsuits, raking the leaves away from the community park. She read my thoughts. A tinkling chorus of high-pitched notes chimed from my vocal cords.

"Don't you worry your little head about him. He served his purpose. We both hold our own survival in high regard, Rachel," she said. "I will always keep us safe."

She bent over Angus' body until my breasts brushed his arm. "My survival is the main reason Mr. McNab, here, needs to live."

She yanked one of my necklaces from my neck. It was the cupid with the broken wing. Using the sharp edge, she opened up a vein on the inside of my arm. I cried out at the jab, feeling it the same as she did. But she enjoyed the pain, languishing in the fleshy slice with dark pleasure.

As I cursed her from within, she gripped Angus' jaw, her nails digging into his flesh as she roughly opened his mouth. She held my arm over Angus' lips and fed him my blood.

I watched the glistening drops splatter onto his blue lips and slip like satin teardrops into his mouth. Drop by drop, I watched and doubted whether my blood could ever feed him life.

"*Your* blood?" she laughed, harsher this time. "Rachel, you are such a ninny."

Before I could reply with some very un-ninny-like words, a sound floated into the room.

So faint at first, I wasn't sure if I was hearing a song or a mosquito buzzing near my ear. The sound came closer, became louder. It was thick-tongued chanting.

An Cuan Eirinn o hì

Muir ag èirigh o hò

Abruptly, Scarlett's hold was broken. The chanting pulled me, Rachel, up into my body, as if the singers had reached down their hands and drawn me from the black depths of the grave. My wicked Other clawed and fought her way through my insides, as she was tramped down.

An Cuan Eirinn o hì

Muir ag èirigh o hò

'S cha bu lèir dhuinn o hì

Nì fon ghrèin ach na neòil

Her power over me crumpled like rose petals coming apart at the stem, and I landed with a loud thump on the floor.

I tried to open my own eyes and was relieved when my lashes parted at my request. I could still hear the voices chanting.

Colin, Duncan, and the other Scotsmen from the Albion were standing in a half circle. Their bodies blocked the door, and they sang together while keeping their eyes on me.

Their words were of the Irish Sea and how it was rising, and I understood, that I, Rachel, was the "Irish sea".

I was clueless how I could grasp their language, for it was becoming obvious they were not who they claimed to be. Neither was I. And, neither was Magda. She stood among them singing the words as if the song had been her childhood lullaby.

Rolling onto my stomach, I pressed my palms against the wooden floor and unsteadily pushed onto my knees. My short captivity within my body had left me an unsure director of my limbs. Unsteadily, I got both feet planted and stood.

My glance lit on Angus, twisted in the sheets.

Staggering to his side, I faced the damage I had done. They didn't try to stop me, just shadowed my movements, keeping a ring of their bodies blocking my escape.

The blood at Angus' neck was no longer oozing from the wound, but there was a horrifying amount staining the sheets. Touching his chest with a trembling hand, I hoped for the rise of a breath or the beat of a heart. Yet, his chest remained cool and still beneath my cold fingers.

I had killed the ox from my dreams. Gut-wrenching regret tore a hole in my being and a cry from my stiff lips.

I longed for Angus to wake up and comfort me. I wanted his wide hand on the back of my head. I wanted to hear him "shushing" me. But I would never feel his hands on me again.

Tears rolled down my face and over my mouth. I licked my lips, accidently lapping the last of Angus' blood that was still smeared on my skin. Bringing my hand to my wet lips, I fingered them like I was the village idiot. They came away red with Angus' blood. The ironic taste of it burned like judgement on my tongue, crucifying the madness in my brain.

I shrieked and tried to run from the room, but my foot caught on Lennox's body. I tripped and slammed my shoulder into the wall. Dazed, I slid down to the floor to find myself facing Lennox's bloodied face. His head was turned my way under the sheet, his one open eye a red globe of burst blood vessels. His death mask was a mocking mirror of my twisted mouth as I screamed in horror. The sound of my terror climbed in pitch until I was sure I would shatter like crystal.

The others moved in, closing the half-circle while increasing the tempo of their chanting. Each word drew pieces of grief from me. Each note swathed me in a sense of calm, floating me into a guilt-free state of mind. I could still see Lennox sprawled lifeless on the floor, but as they continued to sing, my emotions drained away leaving me numb and pliant.

They called to me, those impostors, demanding me to speak.

And I answered with foreign words that spilled from my mouth.

"Chì mi gun dàil an t-àite san d'rugadh mi. (I see straight away the place of my birth). Is fanaidh mi tacan le deòin. (And I will willingly remain there for a long while)."

Magda squatted before me and lifted the lid of my eye, peering at me like a doctor checking a concussed patient.

My tongue lay immobile within my mouth, languishing in the aftertaste of Angus.

She appeared satisfied. Clutching my arm in a rough grip, she yanked me onto my feet.

Speaking to Colin, Magda commanded, "Get it cleaned up. I'll meet you at the airport, once I get her settled."

My friend's voice was sharp and military, her speech clashing oddly with her cleft chin and heart-shaped face.

Colin gathered Angus' clothes from the chair in the corner. Three of them wrapped Lennox tightly in the white sheet, grunting as they rolled his body across the floor. Duncan and Colin tugged Angus' heavy body to one side of the bed, and Magda pushed me out the door.

Chapter 31: Spies and their Lies

Faltering on the threshold of my basement apartment, I banged my hip on the door jamb and stumbled against Granny's old chesterfield. I was muted by shock on the ride to my apartment, but here in my home, the paralysis left my tongue

"I killed him," I whispered in wonder.

"It was his destiny," Magda spoke as if she was telling me the price of a market hen.

She pushed the bolt across the inside of the front door and then moved by me to put on the kettle.

Turning from the stove, she gave me a calculating look. "You need to wash. I'll take those clothes and burn them."

"I killed him."

My brain was caught in a replay of the horror like a scratched record.

Magda let out a hushed curse and lit a cigarette. "Christ! Listen up, cause I'm only going to tell you once. The first born male McNab of every century's third generation is destined to bring out The Fergus She. Angus knew it from birth. We all did."

"The Fergus She?"

My 'alter' twisted and grasped at my guts, trying to climb up my entrails and tell me something. I pressed her down with will power grown strong over the many years of fighting her.

Magda looked at me as if I was a retard.

"The Fergus She?" I repeated, not understanding why she would name my alternate personality, or why Angus had anything to do with her.

"You're so dense." Her voice was scathing.

"I need to know," I begged.

"You're the Fergus She. She's in you."

I moved my head back and forth, still not understanding what she was saying.

Magda was enjoying her role of all-knowing deliverer of truths. "Angus was here to do a job. He had seven days after your eighteenth birthday. The job was you."

"Angus knew?" I left the support of the couch and shuffled towards her. "He knew I'd be... that she would do that?"

Magda sneered at me, basking in my pain. "He wanted her to rise. He wanted her to take you over."

She popped a few smoke rings out into the air between us, and I thought back to grade nine when she had shown me how to make them.

"Who are you?" I asked, feeling duped.

"Magdalen McNab, at yer service, m'lady," she curtsied low, looking at me with mocking eyes.

Her Scottish accent, which she had used as a joke in the past, rang authentic.

"You're Angus' wife?"

She barked out a laugh and choked on the smoke. "You're so insecure, it's pathetic."

"Who then?" My voice was louder. Stronger. I made it to the kitchen table and leaned heavily against the painted rose gracing the tabletop. "Who are you?"

She smirked. "He's my cousin." Her eyes dropped as the smile faded. "He was my cousin," she mumbled.

"Your cousin..." I slumped into a kitchen chair.

"Angus was the cure to what ailed you, Rachel." Magda, the Canadian, was back. "You don't have to fight anymore. Just let her take over. You've royally screwed up your life, now it's time to let her have hers."

I carefully, deliberately swallowed that pill of truth.

"Seven days..." Patrick had made me promise to wait seven days. He had made me vow, no fights, no sex, no men... seven days. Seven days in exchange for a normal life. If only I'd listened...

"It will be easier, this way." She dropped her cigarette onto my kitchen floor and ground it out beneath her black Peter Pan boots.

I should have hated her for her casual acceptance, but I was too busy trying to not come undone. If I lost it now I knew all the King's men would never be able to put me together, again.

"And Angus..." I dragged in a ragged breath before forcing out the question. "Is it easier for him, now?"

Finally, she let her hatred show. "It's *you* who's done this."

She turned her back on me while she washed her hands in the sink, speaking the whole time the water ran. "You and your family hosting that ungodly filth inside your DNA for centuries."

She turned around, drying her hands on the tea towel as if she were wringing my neck. "You are demon filth."

My eyelids were sweating.

"Worse, you're not even purebred. I trained all my life, and I didn't even get a purebred." She shook her head at me.

"I..."

"Your people could have ended this curse long ago. You could've killed yourselves off." Her mouth was twisting like a rubber band, exaggerating her words. "You could have stopped having babies, stopped giving the She a line to live in... but "oh no", you ignored the truth. You play the victims, and you blame *my* family...?"

Her eyes were brimming with angry tears.

I closed my mouth and swallowed.

She threw the tea towel at me. It landed on my shoulder.

"You're as stupid as Angus. He lived to serve the queen bitch that's going to take you over Rachel."

I couldn't believe Angus, the ox, had lived his life waiting to be slaughtered. Surely, he had a plan...

But, he was dead.

Dead men don't get to finish their plans.

Angus had spoken highly of destiny. He had encouraged me to embrace it.

Odd grunt-like noises were bubbling up, breaking free of my mouth in uncontrollable gasps. Shaking my head to the sound, I waited for someone to tell me it wasn't true, to tell me this wasn't happening. Black dots skipped before my eyes.

Magda broke into her Gaelic song, spitting the words out with a vengeance. She yanked me out of my chair with those angry hands. I cringed as she ripped away my clothing. When she was done stripping me, I stood, naked and trembling, my elbows pressed together over my breasts, my hands clasping my mouth to hold the grunts in.

A hard push forced the stiffness from my knees, and I obediently climbed into the metal shower stall.

Impatient, Magda leaned in and started the water. The cold pellets were like ice on my hunched back.

"Wash off the blood," she ordered, then added as an after-thought, "I won't be here when you get out."

I took a last look at the face of the person I had thought was my friend. Like the final piece to a puzzle, I saw her eyes were Angus' eyes, only lighter. How had I not noticed the resemblance before?

She slammed the door, trapping me alone with my trembling limbs.

The water warmed up, then became hot, burning dashes of liquid striking my breasts. My brain struggled to find reason and logic, it struggled to hold to something, anything that would make sense.

Its struggles resurrected frightening images, memories that did not belong to me, or this life. Memories of a promise made centuries ago; made to The Fergus She, who had once been a living, breathing woman.

A woman so powerful, she had compelled an entire clan to do her bidding for eternity.

Chapter 32: Surrender to Survive

Time pushed out, squeezing reality into a glass-bowl shape. I slipped down the edges, sliding away from my life.

I stood with my back to an old, stone tower that tilted against a brilliant, blue sky. The crest of the hill rolled away from my feet, spreading out into miles of rich, green carpet below. The grass was the colour of Canadian forest moss after a spring rain. The green pasture was dotted with grey and black rocks and white sheep and snaking through was a ribbon of indigo water reflecting the flawless sky above.

"The Fergus She'll not let us live, if we don't agree," a Scottish brogue declared.

"Has she sworn that peace will be left to the night if we agree to her terms?" another voice asked.

"Are we sure her word can be trusted?" a third, lower voice added.

In the tower behind me, the chieftains of the clans had gathered—the Campbells and Stewards, Clan Gregor, Clan Farlane, the MacNaughtons and the McNabs. They had joined together in the McNab's ancestral castle, to decide what could be done with The Fergus She.

Though they were enclosed within the stone tower, and I stood on the hill with the wind in my ears, I could hear their discussion as clearly as if I were seated beside them in one of the great carved chairs.

I could hear defeat in their sighs, and in the pauses between their words, and in what wasn't there at the table. Hope was missing. Bravery had fled. She had already won.

They would agree to the binding of her life to a clan's pedigree. They had only to decide which clan would sacrifice their future generations.

The men came out to the hilltop with their decision, not wanting to invite her into the castle. They were big-boned, with full, scraggy beards, and ruddy cheeks. All except MacGregor, who seemed to be a shadow of the others with his tall, willowy build and straight, black hair.

"We'll meet your terms," Old Man MacFarlane growled through his white beard.

"Who," the She demanded, her voice ringing like crystal next to the gravelly tones of the Highlanders. "Who will meet my terms?"

"Tomorrow will tell," MacFarlane scowled against the cold wind and turned to re-enter the castle.

"Tomorrow," another Highlander finished the statement, "we will hold the warrior games."

A shout echoed from those hearty hearts, "The warrior games!"

The excitement rippled through the chieftains and spread like fire to the men, women and children watching from the castle walls.

"The losing clan will meet your terms," MacGregor had said, feeling braver as the thrill of the caber toss filled his mind.

The She had nodded and smiled but had hidden her inner thoughts. She would not be taking the vow from the losing clan.

The next morning, the McNabs had won the games, and the She had bound the strongest clan to her bloodline.

SHARING MY "OTHER'S" memories brought recent events into clarity. She wasn't my split personality. Casbus had been wrong.

Casbus... the conversation on the tape... him calling her Mistress.

Casbus hadn't been wrong. He'd been duping me. He was a servant of hers.

Not only wasn't she my split personality, she wasn't even human. Predatory and vicious and long-lasting, but not human.

A revelation forced my eyes open. Though I could not see through the white steam of the shower, I was no longer blinded.

"I'm not crazy," I whispered.

I hadn't been crazy all these years.

And this time I repeated it louder, "I'm not crazy."

"I'm not crazy!" I shouted to the cobwebs drooping with water droplets above my head.

I'd never sought help outside of Casbus, because I'd been so afraid they would lock me up and throw away the key. Just as they had done to my mother.

I'd had no idea what I really should have been afraid of.

"All these years..." I whispered.

Tears rolled down my cheeks and dissolved into the steam condensing on my face.

The tears should have been for Angus, but they were for me. I was crying for the little girl I had been, who had withstood terrifying nightmares of death and blood and war and maiming. And when I had tried to share those horrors, the shock on my friends' faces had told me I was not normal, and I should keep my dreams to myself.

As a child, many teachers had cruelly struck my knuckles with sharp-edged, wooden rulers because I had not been paying attention. My focus had been on fending off the horrors in my mind, horrors they shrank from. I allowed them to convince me I was a sick little child who was in danger of hurting others. But it hadn't been me. It had been her... It was her. It was the She.

My self-pity bowed down to rage and my tears burned against my skin, as years of hurt and frustration found a target.

Magda.

When I had met her, I was overjoyed to have found a friend. Magda had accepted me, she enjoyed listening to my gory tales, had asked me to share my nightmares. She had studied my dreams, providing guidance in the form of "readings". Interpretations I now realized were for her purpose, to manipulate me into being a player in this ancient lore.

Magda had been one of the few people I had been able to be real with. Now I had to accept nothing had been real about our friendship. She had known what was happening, had known about The Fergus She and my heritage, and had encouraged my belief that I was insane. And in her sadistic way, I know she had enjoyed it.

I pushed my face under the shower's spray, holding my grief deep in my chest with my air until stars sparked behind my lids.

Up until now, I'd had some control over the She. I had been able to stop her from taking over. Sure, she had surfaced during some sexual encounters, and a few times when I had been a kid. But, she'd always been my inner voice.

She'd even had a name...

The word rose in my conscious like a hand thrusting from a grave, intrusive and frightening, and covered in filth.

Scarlett.

"I have your name," I whispered.

Scarlett had killed my childhood enemy, Timmy, in the park.

I closed my eyes tight against the memory of Timmy's little "o" face as he fell from the monkey bars. It had been Scarlett who'd done it, and my mother had paid to protect me.

I leaned my forehead against the shower stall in an effort to still the tremors.

I couldn't breathe. There was too much horror, too much pain and death suffocating me. My lungs collapsed on themselves. I turned off the hot water and cranked the cold. The change in temperature shocked me into gulping oxygen.

I warmed up the water and opened my mouth to the shower, letting the water wash my molars. The excess ran out over my lips and down my chin.

Scarlett wouldn't stay down. Now Angus had released her, she was strong, much stronger than before. She was everywhere, peeking over my shoulder, causing my skin to break out in goose bumps, listening in on my thoughts, whispering desires into my ear. I was emotionally exhausted and alone.

I couldn't fight her. I didn't have the strength.

With a sense of weary acceptance, I acknowledged Scarlett would devour me. Magda was not here with her song to stop her. Angus wouldn't be coming. It would happen soon.

As if on cue, she made her presence known. A stiffening started in my ankles and rose as Scarlett gathered my leg nerve like she would roll up spilled yarn. I could feel her moving inside of my body, her parasitic crocheting weaving around my vessels, one by one.

I wanted to scratch the word "Rachel" into the metal shower stall—leave some reminder that I had existed before I was completely consumed.

Over the sound of the water, the rustle of cloth whispered, followed by a sharp intake of breath. A hazy vision of my landlord, fed by Scarlett's awakening skills, danced behind my eyes. I growled low in my throat as my suspicions were confirmed.

The landlord *was* watching me, but not over the top of the shower as I had always assumed. He was standing on his side of the basement, leaning over, peering through a little hole he had drilled into the corner of my shower stall. He was not two inches away from my naked body, digging into his pants with a shaking hand.

The landlord was another imposter in my life, pretending to be the righteous keeper of my home, and here he was, spying on my nakedness.

I was surrounded by liars and deceivers! A mother who could not protect me. Magda who had pretended to be my friend. Angus who was willing to sacrifice my life and his to fulfill his destiny. My doctor who had never been on my side. And Patrick... Patrick was the worst. He had said I was a 350-year-old problem. He had known, and he hadn't stopped it. He had failed me more than anyone.

Each person I mentally recited reinforced what I already knew. No one remained for me to be stupid enough to trust.

I choked on a sob under the shower's spray.

Angus and Lennox were both gone. Lene was useless, she couldn't even help herself. I had no one. There was no one who could save me from my fate.

Magda had said she would be gone when I got out of the shower. And guess who would be blamed for the murders? Magda would make sure she and her cousins got home to Scotland by leaving a tip with the RCMP on where to find the real killer.

It was as Scarlett had said, there was only one person to blame, for there was only one person who had killed Angus.

I was looking at life imprisonment. Or worse. I would end up wrapped in one of Dr. Casbus' straightjackets, bunking down the hall from my mother.

The water cooled as cold despair filled me.

Suddenly, my spinning thoughts snagged on a spark of hope.

In Angus' room, Scarlett had said, "I can always keep us safe."

She was a huntress. She was a survivor. She would never let anyone cage us.

Determination dried the tears in my eyes. I wasn't going to end up under Casbus' care. Not if I was the "Mistress".

My ear's honed in on the sound of the landlord's moan as it caught in his throat. My eyes narrowed. I sensed his budding orgasm.

Scarlett was coming on whether I liked it or not, and she and I shared two common goals—a desire to survive and a yearning to punish the landlord. I wanted to because he was an asshole who deserved to pay. Scarlett wanted to because he was prey and blood flowed through his veins. That was enough for me.

"Might as well make it a party," I whispered, not caring anymore.

Closing my eyes, I released myself to the demon within.

She climbed up my larynx and grabbed my conscious thought in a vice of slivered metal and screeching death. Her control hooked into my spinal column like a wicked spider twanging the threads of her web.

And then we were up—skimming over the top of the shower stall in a fluid movement of slippery flesh.

The landlord twisted his face in terror as we dropped on him from above.

I latched our teeth into his neck.

He fell to the cold concrete floor, his legs kicking wildly.

His struggles thrilled me, but Scarlett's reaction fired in the range of spiritual glory.

The landlord's thrashing caused his flaccid dick to flap on the edges of his zipper like a flag of surrender.

A small twist of my head and his throat opened wide, pliant and willing to accept my darting tongue. I gulped his pathetic existence with greedy swallows. The heat of his blood washed away my emotional agony and cleansed my regret until there was nothing, but warm satisfaction left.

As the landlord's cries reached the pitch of a Scottish piper's call, a wailing beacon lured me to Scotland. Home of the McNabs, where Magda smug and victorious would return with a hero's story of how she had conned me.

I lifted my face from the nest of torn flesh between the landlord's ear and his shoulder. The air cooled my wet chin.

Magda.

A red bubble burst on my lips as Scarlett's laugh of anticipation rippled out of my mouth.

Chapter 33: Scarlett Appropriates my Face

T he last wavering note of the landlord's moan echoed against the concrete walls of the gloomy basement. Or maybe the trembling octave only seemed to echo as it reached into the fleshy cavern where I resided, so deep was I buried in my own body.

The landlord's leg kicked out, shaking his beige work boot at the end of his Levi jeans. One last complaint against death, before his body lay still in the small pool of blood that had escaped my hungry mouth.

My mouth? Scarlett's mouth?

Scarlett stood, naked under the single hanging light bulb. She held my body in the pose of an Amazon Queen, ramrod straight with victory. The water drops evaporated from my skin cooling the flush of the kill. I would have shivered, but she arched my back and stretched my arms to the ceiling above, fingers straining for the cobwebs that laced together the old, wooden floor joists above her.

My life-long battle with the she-bitch for dominion over my body was finally over. A feather stroke of relief at not having to fight her anymore caressed me.

Scarlett slipped back over the open top of the shower stall like an otter sliding over a river bank. She made sure my belly never touched the rusty edges. The hot water tank had been emptied of its warmth, just as the landlord's body had.

She stepped into the spray and the water struck my shoulders with an icy pelting. It washed the blood off my pebbling skin, churning it around my feet like the stirring of a witch's cauldron. A glutinous clot caught on my big toe, glistening black against the fire engine red of my toe nail polish. In disgust, I tried to shake the slick blob off, but my legs did not respond to my brain's order.

I was existing as some sort of back-seat driver to my body. I didn't have control of the wheel, the brake, or the gas. I could see and feel, yet I had no choice but to ride along. Acting separately from Scarlett was no longer possible. I could not even begin the process of moving my personal choices along my nerve stems, for the moment a command to move started in my mind, it was met with a void of disconnect. I had now become the "Other".

To escape, I detached completely from her and my body. I buried myself in a muffling emptiness, deep-deep, deeper until my awareness of Scarlett faded to an irritating ticking like the pincers of a beetle snapping together.

She was still there in the background, but from this underground depth in my subconscious, I couldn't read her. I couldn't see what she was doing. I couldn't feel what she was doing. I left her alone with my body.

Scarlett stepped my body out of the shower. She dried my skin with a stiff, frayed towel, which she tossed onto the floor. As she walked to my closet, I floated with purposeless buoyance, unanchored within myself.

But it didn't last. I couldn't lie down and die, and I certainly couldn't be a passive passenger in my life. I slipped back into position of observer.

Scarlett rifled through the closet hangers, pushing them with such force along the metal pole, I was sure sparks would fly from the friction. Hidden in the very far corner of my wardrobe Scarlett found the perfect outfit for a villain—a three-quarter length, black satin skirt and jacket. The shoulders were padded with "Dynasty" power, and the skirt hem rippled out with a 1920s school-ma'am delicacy. Scarlett paired them with a white, high-necked blouse, softening the outfit with a touch of romance. She pulled on my black leather boots, and cut the ankle chains off with a knife. The links clinked as they fell to coil like metal snakes on the rug.

When she stepped in front of the mirror, my thoughts folded in on themselves. Here she was, my mental illness incarnate standing before the reflection. Where was my psychiatrist now to see my "dissociation" in all her glory?

My face stared back with a calm, self-satisfied expression that in no way matched my emotions of shock, disbelief, and confusion. She controlled the appraising lift of my eyebrows, the confident tilt of my lips.

Moving my hands with unaccustomed grace, Scarlett twisted my long, blonde hair up into a painful knot. She stabbed the unruly curls into place with my 'hand-painted' chop sticks.

Another awkward reminder of her peeping became clear for the she-bitch knew where all my make-up was. The cotton balls, the hairbrushes, everything. She gathered it in front of the mirror, and then she used my fingers, which were clumsy and unsure, to dab and brush and stroke make-up onto my skin with practiced motions.

Her actions heightened my cheekbones and subdued my nose. She skimmed a rich, blood red lip liner along the outer edge of my lips, enhancing the pouty fullness of them.

The colour recalled Angus' blood.

She ran a finger slowly over the high arch of my brow bone, sharing in the memory of draining Angus. A satisfied smirk emerged on lips that used to be mine.

When she was finished outlining my eyes in black, she stepped back from the mirror, turning my sharp jawline to the left and the right to observe her handiwork.

I didn't recognize the woman before us. The light foundation dropped my bone structure into the background, bringing my eyes and my mouth to the fore. The brown of my irises shimmered like the sweat-shined flank of a chestnut horse under the sun. Instead of a hard line of tension, my mouth now begged with yielding softness to be scoured by a man's bristling whiskers.

Scarlett had taken what I had accepted as mediocre looks and had created a six-foot-tall, stunning woman who could fire the heart of any man. It was the Venus flytrap of make-overs.

Still baffled over my new image, I almost didn't notice Scarlett digging up my meager savings. I tried to speak to her in my mind, but only succeeded in converting those beetle taps into information—her thoughts. She intended to leave, before the landlord was found mangled in his basement. And she wasn't packing. She was stealing my college fund.

"I don't think so," I had control of my mouth before she knew I was coming up, and the words came out harsh and forceful in my voice.

The familiar pressure of our battle pressed in on me, but this time the sensation was different. This time, I was the rising force, the weaker entity and she was keeping me down.

We raged inside my body, like ships fighting in an organ sea, and in minutes I was tossed and broken, as if ground ashore. Bruised and punished, I shrank, while Scarlett checked her lipstick in the mirror. Then, she marched us out of my home, leaving the door swinging open behind us.

The sun was dropping quickly behind the row of stately Victorian houses on my street. The elongated branch-fingers of Maple tree shadows stretched over the light, grey asphalt of the road. Twisted phantom limbs clutching at the hem of my skirt as Scarlett walked out onto the quiet, empty street.

She put her hands on her hips, looking up and down the empty road, before turning to face my apartment. A slow smile spread as her glance took in the landlord's red Firebird convertible parked in the lane. Swinging my slim hips, she sauntered to the car. Her touch on the car's panel was light and delicate, a butterfly proboscis hesitantly tasting the bright red paint. She purred like a cat, opened the door, and slipped into the black, leather driver's seat.

A Phoenix was airbrushed on the car's hood. Its sharp beak pointed at the windshield, at my chest. The wings were streaks of flaming feathers, raised up and dropping curling grey ashes onto the shiny red paint. So like the frayed remnants of my life, charred and aimlessly drifting from the impact of Scarlett's resurrection. But unlike me, the bird appeared poised, ready to tear itself from the metal of the hood.

My desperate thoughts did not affect Scarlett. She ran a soft hand across the radio buttons, slid one long finger into the tape cassette port, pressed a sharp nail into the vinyl dash. She drew in that "new" smell of sun warmed leather. I had always loved that smell, but with Scarlett doing the breathing, there was a history woven into the scent. A second sniff and a collage of blurry images materialized with the odor: pictures of green grass, of black hooves clomping forward, towards the slaughterhouse where hides were torn from the cows to fashion seats for cars.

Sickened by the gory memories in the leather, I cleared my unsettling thoughts, but the temptation to read more of the scented messages from the vehicle was overwhelming. I was compelled to unravel each scent: the blood of a car plant worker who cut his hand when putting on the doors, the pungent semen spilt in a moment of release on the back seat, the smudge of waxy lipstick on the visor mirror, and the tang of dog shit snuck onto the front rug on the bottom of an unassuming shoe.

Scarlett was interested in these images but regarded them without the wonder I was experiencing. Like a detached scientist, she collected data without emotion, archiving knowledge that would help her survive in this modern world.

A traitorous thought surfaced. I shielded it with an imaginary cupped hand. It wouldn't do for Scarlett to find out I wasn't completely beaten.

Apparently, our switch in power had heightened some of my special talents, talents which I now figured out, were hers. My ability to track, my reading of shadow colours. These "talents" weren't delusions like my psychiatrist said they were. They were demon skills, leaking out of the she-bitch and into my tool box.

Scarlett was out of touch. At most, she'd only observed life. I was a child of the 70s, I had lived my life, and I knew way more about this world of rock 'n roll and rising world powers than she did. Maybe, just maybe, using what I knew of this world and her skills from whatever hell-hole world she came from, I could find a way to level the playing field and get my life back.

A quick mental check showed Scarlett was too wrapped up in the car seduction to care about my thoughts of liberation.

Scarlett tightened her grip on the wheel, twisting the leather binding with barely contained excitement. She smiled as she tapped her red nails against the steering wheel three times and whispered some mumbo jumbo. The car's powerful engine roared to life, the rumbling quickly followed by George Thorogood's voice grating "Bad to the Bone" out of the car's speakers.

I couldn't drive standard, but apparently, Scarlett could. She hit the shifter with her palm, and the car squealed as it reversed out of the driveway. She hit third gear and the Firebird's tires burned. The sound of screeching tires scared the songbirds out of the maple trees, their flighty shadows mixing with the crooked-limbed, shadow-fingers on the road. The tires finally gripped the pavement, yanking the car out of its fishtail and launching it down the street

Scarlett sped away from my life, trailing Thorogood's stuttering B behind us.

Chapter 34: The Firebird Burns Away

It was eerie, viewing the road from the driver's seat, feeling the pressure of the gas pedal beneath my foot, but having no idea of the destination.

I tried and failed to decode that tick-ticking a second time, so I didn't know where Scarlett was driving us. It wasn't until I saw the sparse lawn in front of Angus' house, that I realized she was taking us back to the place of her "birth".

Scarlett pulled the Firebird too close to the curb, causing the tires to squeak an announcement as they rubbed up against the concrete barrier. The sun was almost down and there was a stillness to the neighbourhood, broken only by the idling engine. Scarlett slammed the car door, strode up the sidewalk. Apparently, she wasn't sneaking in. She was drumming the marching beat of an approaching army with each step, and she'd left the engine running, just in case.

Returning to the scene of Angus' death terrified me. This house was the place of ultimate betrayal, where both my lover and my friend had thrown me to the she-bitch. I didn't know why Scarlett was here, but if it was to lap up the remaining blood that had pooled around Angus' body, the last of my stability would give, destroying me forever.

I couldn't stop watching as Scarlett stopped in front of the house and peered through the windows. She was checking to see who was home, listening, smelling, waiting. That much I could understand by the way she tilted her head, sniffed the air. Cautious yet eager, as only a predator can be, she took her time making sure the house was still.

With a glance back at the Firebird, she killed the engine from afar, and I knew we were going in.

The fear of seeing the carnage of Scarlett's resurrection had me trying to persuade the she-bitch to reconsider before barging into the Scotsmen's den. I knew from experience that my panic would only feel like a little flutter in her belly. My evil twin brushed a hand along the side of my head, smoothing the curls escaping the bun. She walked confidently up to the cheap, hollow wooden door. It swung open before she touched it, clearing the way for her to enter.

The living room was exactly as we had left it. No personal objects, no persons. Unbidden, I recalled Magda's orders to the others to get the place 'cleaned up'. That confirmation of Angus' death seemed engraved into the wood paneling of the house like a haunting. I didn't want to be here. I didn't want to be faced with what I had done. I didn't want to think of Angus, or his betrayal, or his death. It was all too painful.

Are you here to gloat? I pressed the question into our shared space, not knowing if she would answer.

Scarlett ignored me, perching on the arm of the couch I had sat upon only six hours before. She pulled up my satin skirt to reveal as much leg as possible then leaned back, placing her arm along the back of the couch. She could have been posing for a Vogue model shoot. Her stillness became unnatural as she stared down the dark hallway.

A door clicked from the direction of her gaze. Somebody was still in the house.

A sudden concern for my safety alighted in my thoughts. Two men had died in this house, and though I was sure Magda and her clan had removed Lennox and Angus' bodies, I could pay the price for the evidence left behind.

Scarlett could take care of the cops, but now that I was a fiend, there were worse forms of justice, like staking. Scarlett deserved it, but it would be into my soft flesh that Magda and her Scottish groupies would drive their sharp wooden spears.

A floorboard creaked, I fluttered an S.O.S. to Scarlett, as a man staggered out of the bathroom. He was wiping his face with a towel, oblivious of the threat watching him. His bangs draped over his hands as he scrubbed his face. His body was naked above his jeans, and Scarlett ran her hot glance over the six-pack beneath his elbows. I knew that body, intimately. But then again, so did she.

Scarlett drawled in her Southern accent, "Forgive me for not making my presence known sooner, Mr. McNab."

Angus ripped the towel away from his face. His eyes widened, and his mouth dropped open as he stared at Scarlett sitting there in my black satin skirt, curling up her blood red lips.

His square chin was shaven, and I swear it quivered.

He knew who he was talking to. He knew I was gone, replaced by the she-bitch he had released as part of his family "destiny". I should have hated him for what he had done to me but seeing him standing there set angels singing in my heart to the tune of a momentous truth: My Highlander was still alive!

I waited for Angus to ask about my welfare, or maybe even ask for my forgiveness, but he stood silent.

Scarlett's laugh came out like a triumphant purr. She uncrossed her legs and stood up, the movement as smooth as velvet. His green eyes narrowed, as she sashayed toward him.

The shadows under his cheekbones grew darker as if being near to Scarlett was increasing the gaunt look in his face.

"Aren't you going to offer a lady a drink?"

Scarlett's taunting glance dropped to his neck where a sloppy bandage rolled away from his ravaged skin. The fact she had driven my teeth into his flesh lent a sinister undertone to her question.

The spicy scent of fear drifted off him like a dark tide promising treasures in the deep. Scarlett pretended to look around.

"Now where 'o' where are all of your friends?" she whispered.

Silence was his only answer. His fists clutched the towel like a lifeline. His hard breathing pushed his pecs up to glisten with sweat under the light.

Scarlett stepped closer. Angus stepped back, bracing himself against the wall. She stretched out her hand to touch his bare skin, but Angus sucked his stomach in, pulling himself as flat as he could against the paneling. He even turned his head to the side.

Scarlett paused, leaving her hand in the air between them. It was a delicious hesitation, even I could appreciate.

"Don't tell me they abandoned you here?"

Angus squeezed his eyes shut. A shudder skittered over his belly. Scarlett sensed it. She was feeding on his reactions, delicacies to her palate. She licked the succulent aftertaste of his alarm off my lips.

I was sorry Magda, his own cousin, had left him for dead.

Scarlett echoed my sentiments. "My, my, what a fickle family you have, Angus."

Family was everything to the Highlander. Hell, he'd been willing to sacrifice my freedom to pay his family's debt. Her insult hit a nerve.

His head spun to face her. His chin came up, jutting out below his grim mouth. "Leave."

C'mon Angus, I silently cheered him on. Let's see the ox in action.

He pushed off from the wall and walked away from her. She didn't stop him. He disappeared into the bedroom.

Scarlett feigned indignation, pretending to fan herself, "Well, I never!"

"Ye ne'er what?" Angus came charging out of the room taking Scarlett by surprise. Wrapping his hand around her throat, he pulled my face right up to his. "What did ye ne'er do? Ne'er hurt? Ne'er ruin?"

He was growling through his teeth with a reckless fury that made me worry for my body's safety.

Scarlett let me up as effortlessly as blowing dandelion fluff into the air. I floated into my rightful place, face-to-face with my lover, the man who had destroyed my life and who was now trying to take it.

Chapter 35: Duty is the Dagger

"Angus?" My voice squeaked past the strangling hold he had on my larynx.

I gently wrapped my fingers around his wrist, imploring him with my eyes to let go.

At my touch, he became still. But then, he yanked his hand from my throat as if burned. Conflicting emotions flickered across his face.

With a slow, disbelieving shake of his head, he asked, "Is it truly ye, Kit?"

At the sound of his pet name for me, I crumbled. His dry hands cupped either side of my face.

"Kit?"

"It's... I'm me."

I turned my face into his hand.

"Ach!"

He pulled me into his arms setting my skin alive with tingling warmth and a soaring sense of giddiness in my heart that could lead me to laugh and cry, all at the same time.

Angus stroked my hair, and even though I wasn't uttering a sound, he murmured, "Shhhhhh".

I clutched at his back drawing him even closer, wishing we could stay like this forever. Scarlett was snickering as she eavesdropped on our moment. I tried to ignore her, but her mockery reminded me I was hugging my executioner.

Angus' legs began to shake, his knees banging against mine. I pulled back to look at him. His hair stood out in stark contrast to his skin, which had paled to a sickly grey.

"Are you going to be okay?" I asked.

"I'll be fine."

He cut a sidelong glance my way, without lifting his head.

He won't be fine, Scarlett whispered into my guts.

I jumped, startled by Scarlett's intrusion.

"It's ye I'm worried about."

To avoid Angus' concerned gaze, I gingerly lifted a corner of the bandage away from his neck. His skin was angry and swollen around the jagged edges of the slash, a slash made with my teeth. I averted my gaze and rubbed my nose.

"I'm so sorry, Angus!" My voice cracked on his name.

"None o'that," he admonished taking both of my hands in his. "We had a role tae play. We didna have a choice."

"We always have a choice."

He leaned weakly against the wall. "We're back tae that, are we?"

Unbidden, Magda's explanation of Angus' actions came to my mind. I slowly pulled my hands from his. He sighed and stared off into the dark hallway.

"Explain it to me, then."

I stared down the hall thinking something was there, but I guess it was only his past, because he said, "I'm Angus McNab of the clan McNab, and I was born tae a burden that comes with my birthright."

I knew if he could, he would have spoken his name with pride.

"Yoo're ..." He searched for a word.

I ground my teeth together, waiting.

"The Fergus She cursed my family hundreds of years ago..."

"Angus, why am I paying the price for your family's curse?"

His eyebrows drew together, creasing the skin at the bridge of his nose. "Who, lass, do ye think the *She* is?"

Scarlett snorted, and I pressed her down with a warning.

"She's not me, Angus!"

He wiped his lips with the back of his hand. His lips, no longer soft and full, no longer lips to make a woman swoon.

"Yoo're bound tae carry her. I'm bound tae raise her. no matter how far she goes, no matter what year she lives in, the McNabs must follow."

I was shaking my head, denying what he was about to say.

"And, yoo're the woman. Yoo're the line!"

"No..."

He spread his hands out in a helpless gesture. "Ye cannae deny yer birthright."

"No..." My voice trembled. "No, this is a mistake. She's just some demon bitch who hooked herself ... because I ... did something..."

"I kin yer life has no been easy."

I looked away from his pity.

"But we're still beholden tae kindle the demon."

I turned back to study his face. "How?"

His green eyes darted to the bedroom and back to me, guilt making them lighten.

I pointed at the bedroom where we had come together. "That's what you call it... kindling?"

I stood up and walked across the living room, pretending to stare out the window at the street. "Where I come from, we call it sex and usually it means two people like each other."

His footsteps approached me. A warm hand brushed my shoulder. "I do like ye."

I looked at him through the window reflection. "Is this what you do to people you like?"

He ran his hand through his hair. The movement reminded me of our first night together at the Albion. I turned around.

"Why couldn't you just... not do it Angus? Why couldn't you just let me be?"

He stared at me in silence.

My arms were trembling with the desire to punch him in the face. "Like...don't do your duty! Did that thought ever occur to you?"

"Aye, it did." His eyes darkened with his own storm of emotions. "It occurred tae me after I met ye."

He reached out to cup my cheek, but I shrunk back, banging against the window.

He stuck his hands in his pockets instead.

"I thought when I arrived, yoo'd ken who I was. Yoo'd ken what had tae be done. But...ye were ignorant." He frowned and shook his head. "I didna kin it. I had been told from the time I was a wee lad what my role would be."

"And Magda, did she know from birth she was going to be a deceiving bitch-friend?"

"She was necessary. It used tae be one McNab could do the job." He winced at how that sounded. "We track yer line. Magda was placed in yer life long before the calling came."

Ironic that he was the man I had started trusting. How foolish I had been. My life had taught me that hope and love were not options. I should never have wanted or believed I could have more.

You will always have me, dah-lin' Scarlett's sarcasm licked at my entrails.

"I didna expect ye." He took my hand in his. "An independent, wounded lass, prickling with pride and aching tae be loved."

I blinked away the tears, not wanting him to know how his words affected me.

"After I saw ye struggling, I realized ye have been fighting her all yer life."

He gave me a tight smile that didn't quite reach his eyes.

"Never in the stories had I heard of sech a thing—ye holdin' off the She. It was then I decided, I wasn't going tae see ye again, Lass. Not after ye left the restaurant with Lennox."

The image of Angus pounding Lennox into a bloody pulp came unbidden to my mind. I pulled my hands away from his hot grip.

"Lennox..."

Angus held up his hand to silence me, and I flinched.

"Lennox." The name caught in his throat. "He was willing tae risk his life tae warn ye."

My chin quivered. "And you killed him for it."

He hit the wall with his palm. "Aye!" The window rattled loosely in the old wooden frame. "Once things got out of control, I couldn't stop. The same as ye couldn't stop!"

Shame burned my face, for he was right. I hadn't stopped, even after Lennox was cooling on the floor, I had opened my body to Angus.

I wiped my nose, roughly.

Regret was etched on the lines of his face. He needed my forgiveness. But, I couldn't give it.

"Rachel, I was going tae avoid ye...end the curse," he pleaded with me to believe him. "Free my family...even if it meant I had tae die."

His eyes were shimmering, and I wondered if he was going to cry for me.

"Then why are we here?"

The dark circles under his eyes became more prominent as he paled.

"Och, lassie, I have tae sit down."

I set my jaw and took a step towards him. "Why? If you were going to end it, why didn't you?"

He slumped against the wall. It hadn't really been him who'd sought me out. It was Magda who had invited me to Angus' house. He had been here, in his bed, half-unconscious, and I'd come to him because she had encouraged me to.

Magda had betrayed us both.

"It was her," my voice rose. "She did this!"

"She's been trained fer this, lass," his voice was so low I barreled right over it.

"That hellacious..." I stuttered for a word bad enough, "...skank!"

"Nae..."

"She got in my life." I threw up my hands. "She pretended to be my friend!"

"It was her job."

"Her job?" The rage boiled out of my mouth. "Her JOB?"

I wanted to hate him. I wanted to curse him forever, but it seemed I was running low on hatred and making room for more sadness.

"You Scottish bastards ruined my life!" I yelled at Angus, the man I loved, the man responsible for liberating my inner demon.

He grimaced as if in pain, staggering away from my anger to lean against the wall. Scarlett, eavesdropping on our conversation trilled like a madwoman from somewhere deep inside of me.

"You screwed me over Angus. Now, you fix it!"

He rubbed his big hand down over his handsome face, his green eyes overcast with regret.

"It cannae be undone," he said.

It

Cannot

Be

Undone

His words were like the twists in a hanging rope.

His heart is faltering, Scarlett warned from behind my spleen.

"I don't care!" I hollered at the voice Angus couldn't hear. "He didn't care about me!"

Angus groaned, and staggered to the couch, half-falling onto the cushions.

Rachel, can you feel him fading? Scarlett wasn't snickering anymore.

I needed time to think, time to sort all of this out. I ignored her and moved away from Angus. Leaning against the far wall, I slid down into a squat on the floor and folded my hands in front of my mouth.

There is no time.

Angus had a strong heart. I knew how strong his heart was for his muscled flesh had imprinted on my mind, when we had come together. He was so alive and so powerful, the perfect man to carry out such an important deed. He had beaten Lennox to death with his bare hands, like a gladiator.

No, not a gladiator. Angus was the kind of man who became King. The kind of man who put duty before love, and love before life. The kind of man who would die before bringing dishonour upon his family. The kind of man you never want to fall in love with, because he would always leave you wanting.

And then there was my best friend, Magda. Another person I had been stupid enough to trust. They had all worked together to trap me, and yet I had gotten out, because fighting is what I do best. Survival is my game, not saving others. I'd never had to save anyone but myself. That's how love makes us weak. And until I could kill that love, Scarlett would use it.

I lifted my head and tried to appear uncaring. It didn't matter. He wasn't watching me. He was leaning forward, his elbows on his knees, his head in his hands. A shock of his dark auburn hair draping his fingers.

I knew how silky that hair was, and I knew how demanding those hands could be.

After Scarlett's release, her skills had been spilling into my abilities. As I stared at Angus, her talents allowed me to see the light flickering around the outside of his body. It glittered on and off, like a sputtering candle burning away his life force.

His shoulders slumped, and he tipped forward, quickly moving his feet farther apart to steady himself.

Come to me, Scarlett called. *Give yourself up to me, willingly, and I will save him.*

Come to her meant diving down inside and letting the she-bitch take over my body, take over my life, knowing I may never get free again.

Angus coughed, once. A dry, hacking sound.

I tried to harden myself against him, willing the ache in my chest to stop. I could let him die. Pay him back for what he did to me. Try to keep Scarlett down, and go back to my life as if none of this had ever happened.

He leaned against the back of the couch, his chin up to reveal the sloppy cotton taped against his throat. As I watched fresh blood blooming on the stained pad, Angus tipped to the side, collapsing to lie with his legs hanging down.

Big man brought down, I thought, hardening my feelings.

He can be your big man, again, she wheedled. *I can save him.*

From where I crouched on the floor, I couldn't tell if Angus was still conscious. I was almost at the point where I didn't care. Scarlett couldn't take credit for this talent. This, deadening of my emotions was my superpower and it had come in handy over my shitty lifetime.

Slowly, Angus' arm slipped to hang down from the couch, his lax fingers pointing at the floor. The light from the window cast shadows along the twisting muscles of his arm. I knew this pose.

Angus was like Adam in Michelangelo's Sistine Chapel painting. I knew the painting from the first pages of my mother's Bible. Often, when I had been locked up and ordered to read the scriptures, I would stare at the picture, memorizing the curves and dips of the muscular limbs.

Angus' hand was pointing to the floor just as Adam's had stretched out for God's touch.

I had touched this flesh.

I had loved this man.

The ache in my chest bloomed into life as I failed to suppress my emotions. Angus had ruined me, in more ways than one.

It was useless! I blew hot air out of my nose in disgust and pushed off the floor to move to his side.

Leaning close to Angus' ear, I inhaled the scent of forest trees and man musk. Mixed with his heady smell was the raw scent of blood from the wound I had torn in his neck.

"You did this to me, you bastard," I hissed. He didn't move, didn't make a sound. "Now, you better come find me and reverse it."

Scarlett squealed in delight at the idea.

"Hear me?" I pulled away and punched his shoulder hard. "You... fix... this!"

His body barely moved under my assault.

Come Rachel! She beckoned.

Dropping down into myself, I sought Scarlett as one would grope in the darkness for the source of a voice. Concentrating on connecting with her, the awareness of my outer surroundings shrunk down to the size of a black pinhole and closed completely.

I found myself "inside", the one who was now buried alive.

Don't forsake me Angus, I prayed.

The only response was the scratch of Scarlett's scorn as she consumed my will.

The End

The Story Continues with Master of Madhouse[1]

Get it now at http://www.cherylcowtan.com or read the following excerpt.

---

1. http://www.cherylcowtan.com/thefergusshe

MASTER OF MADHOUSE: *Book 2 of The Fergus She*

Rachel has survived being the dysfunctional daughter of a religious fanatic, the childhood playmate of a demon, and a Highlander's cast-off in the most heart-breaking romance of her life. She even survived the betrayal of her best friend, Magda. But now, she's possessed by The Fergus She, and her resilience is wearing thin.

Determined to escape her destiny as host to a blood-sucking demon, Rachel regains control from her possessor, Scarlett. Little does she know, some of Scarlett's demon-magic has rubbed off on her. In her panic, Rachel runs headlong into another century, and into the arms of Gräfen, Lord of the Vampires. He's an evil Mr. Darcy, dashing but deadly, and when he discovers Rachel has oppressed his demon-wife Scarlett, his lust turns to predatory rage.

Trapped in a century out of history, held prisoner in a Gothic mansion, and surrounded by a bedlam of servants, Rachel suffers Gräfen's gas-lighting torments until her will begins to weaken.

Though Gräfen is cruel and arrogant, Rachel's lifelong dysfunction is serving his game. With alarm, she realizes she must escape Gräfen's clutches soon, or become eternally obedient to his voracious and unnatural demands. But in the Lord of the Vampire's serfdom there is nowhere to run, no place to hide, no one to help. The only way to survive is to let Scarlett up, which will put Rachel down, possibly forever.

Is escaping a madman worth the cost of her freedom?

An excerpt from Master of Madhouse:

Book 2 of The Fergus She

Gräfen's chin pushed forward from the shadows, cresting the flame's orange glow. I leapt back, stepped on the hem of my nightgown and fell hard to the floor. Gräfen stood incredibly tall by the fire, his shadow bending, black-hole black, where the ceiling met the wall. Shuffling into the corner where the fireplace stone met the wall, I cringed in horror.

"You should not run from me, my dear," he said, his voice like gravel.

"Leave me alone."

"Oh, but I cannot," Gräfen's tone held the tenor notes of the emotionally tortured. He moved past the fire with unhurried grace, his cloying presence casting ahead of his body.

"Your pulse elicits an uncommon rapture in my core," he whispered. Like an owl, he swooped silently to the floor, landing with his hands on either side of my ankles. I blinked in surprise, then shivered as he began to crawl up my body.

I tried to shuffle away from him, but the wall stopped me.

"The throbbing of your blood's journey casts a reedy rhythm into the air to revive the melody of my lifecycle long past. His hand came down on the outside of my hip. I blocked him with my knee against his chest.

"Your life places genesis within this lifeless grotto."

"Lifeless because you're dead!" I accused.

"No, alive." He drew out the word. "Animated and pulsing for want of your soul..." His hand slid up the inside of my bare thigh, and gently pressed it to the side making way for his advancing torso. "...to have you, to consume you..."

"No..." I whispered, but it was a weak protest, and now he gazed down at my breasts, their form glazed beneath the clinging sheen of butterscotch satin.

"You are a vision," he purred, his eyes unblinking and predatory, "a visionary apparition, and your visage amasses in my consciousness until I feel I must pluck it out... or surrender..."

He drew the s' out like soft serpents caressing the air, and the sounds drew my will out of my mind leaving nothing but the lapping waves of rhythm he was fashioning in the space around us.

My wrists lay upon the floor, my hands conquered and open. My knees sprawled wantonly. Resistance was futile and over before it had begun. And still, he was not satisfied.

His eyes bore into mine through the black curtain of his hair. "Ask me, Rachel."

I could hear my own heady, heavy breaths brushing the air like the sounds in a diver's world.

"Ask me to come on."

There are no words under the sea.

Undeterred by my silence, Gräfen continued advancing until the proximity of his sniff against my cheek brought each unblemished pore in his skin into focus.

"Sultry." The timber of his voice made me float.

Then his lips were at my ear, and he growled, "Succulent."

Something about the word reminded me I should be fearful. I pressed back against the stone wall, the cold in stark contrast to my chest, which was on fire from his presence.

"Do not conceal your desire from me." His hand gently clasped mine, and he brought it to his chest. "Let it ripen, Rachel. Let yourself become what you were born to be."

I felt his heart quicken beneath my touch. A man's heartbeat. *Was he a man?*

He looked down at my hand and back to my face, and his eyes morphed into endless depths. The pressure from his hand was gone, and yet, I still held my palm pressed against his chest. I could not remove it.

"There is considerable enticement that I resist. There is a side to me that I save you from."

Protector?

Savior?

Resist.

"But when I am alone, with only my observance, my commemoration of you, your actions, your image..." A flame started up deep in those hole-eyes, and I watched its brightness grow as his tongue snaked out to wet his lips, and his voice dropped to a deep thrum.

"The things I do to you."

The fire in his pupils writhed orange, the heat scorching my face. A scream rose in my throat....

Then his dark feathery lashes covered the threat, freeing my soul from damnation.

"The things I could do to you." His voice caught in his throat like a sob. "The things I wish to do to you, Rachel."

His lips pressed against the side of my face. "Oh, what I could show you...teach you."

Now I quivered before the wolf, but not with fear. I shivered with longing to experience all that a devil could do.

Purchase to keep reading at http://www.cherylcowtan.com

Words from the Author

THANK YOU FOR READING Book 1 of *The Fergus She*.

I would love to hear your feedback on my work. To make sure I see your comments, use Twitter hashtags #TheFergusShe & #GirlDesecrated or @NspiredMe2Write.

If you can, please provide a review. Reviews are valuable gifts for writers, and I would appreciate a simple rating or review.

You can find my social media links at http://www.cherylcowtan.com.

Scarlett is a character with so many plot possibilities, and I'm excited to explore other journeys she might take to other centuries. But first, Rachel gets to run the course through a few more novels.

The second book, *Master of Madhouse 1894*, continues with Rachel jumping out of the frying pan and right into the sadistic arms of Scarlett's vampire husband, Gräfen.

Buy Book II while the story is still fresh in your mind, or read the first chapters for free, and put *Master of Madhouse* in your Goodreads' "to read" folder.

For Book Clubs

And curious reader
And blossoming writers!

EVER WONDER HOW AUTHORS come up with this stuff? Want a deeper reading of *Girl Desecrated* so you can impress your friends, post nuggets of insider information, and enrich your enjoyment of vampire literature?

This resource is fabulous for librarians, book clubs, teachers, students, writers and readers who want to grow and exercise their brains and squeeze every drop from this and other vampire stories.

In this enhanced reading guide, you'll find:

- lost Man-Boy chapters
- the history behind the setting
- detailed examples on designing a vampire from *Twilight*, *Dracula* and Anne Rice's novels.
- essays on vampire history and lore
- an in-depth explanation of literary devices and techniques used in *Girl Desecrated,* and more...

Impress Your Book Club for *Girl Desecrated* is available at Cherylcowtan.com. **Get it now.**

Author Newsletter

IF YOU WANT TO BE THE first to know when new *Fergus She* books are being released, sign up for my *Novel News* newsletter at CherylCowtan.com². Through the newsletter, you will receive notice of give-aways, contests for cool and original items, be given access to more pictures of Scarlett and Rachel's antics, and get sneak peeks of new writing and much more.

Dedications

MY HUSBAND, CHRIS, and my two sons, Nathan and Aaron, have been extremely patient over the past few years as I stole time, here and there, to write my novels. They understood when I needed to write, edit, design and market. I'm sorry for all the packaged meals and for making you sort your own socks. Truly, I love you guys!

I'm blessed to have published writers in my family, and each one has helped get me to the point of being published through personal encouragement, industry-relevant advice, editing assistance, and role-modeling, which includes them cranking out novel after novel. I am so proud to be related to and cared for by the following:

My mother, Dianne Ferris-Doekes writes Women's Fiction, capturing Canadian culture and history with her stories. From the time before I could form letters, my mother was encouraging me to write, ordering *Writer's Digest* magazine (which she still buys and passes my way) and submitting my work to contests. She's been a fabulous advocate for me. You can connect with her on twitter at @DJFerris and read more about her writing journey and her novels at https://authordiannejferris.wordpress.com/.

My aunt, Gloria Ferris, writes Mystery with a dash of hilarity in the *Cornwall and Redfern Mysteries* and *Cheat the Hangman*.

---

2. http://www.cherylcowtan.com

You can read more about her and her work at http://www.gloriaferris.com/ or connect at @GloriaFerris.

My Aunt Donna is an editor, who writes fast-paced crime thrillers. You can find her blog at http://djwarnerconsulting.blogspot.ca/, read more about her writing at http://www.donnawarnerauthor.com/, or connect with her on Twitter at @DWarnerLiterary.

How Did the Novel Evolve?

THE FIRST QUESTION I should answer is "Why did I write a psychological thriller with horror undertones"? Blame my father, Jerry Cowtan, or praise him if you love this genre. My dad was an avid reader of Asimov, King, Burroughs, and he rarely missed *Star Trek* and *Dr. Who*. Dad was a strong believer in imagination and the power of the mind. We'd be driving down the dirt roads of Belwood in his construction truck, tools rattling in the back, and he'd be playing classical music on the radio and encouraging us kids to visualize images to the rising and descending melodies. Even before the X-files, our dinner conversations contained the question, "Is there life out there?" Oh yes, I was raised to write *The Fergus She* series.

One thing I learned while writing *Girl Desecrated* is that a novel is never the work of one person. I had many encouragements and much assistance along the way.

Dania Lynne, my colleague and literary editor offered to read my novel when I thought it was done, and from there, she guided me through a series of literary edits that improved my writing beyond anything I had done before. I cannot thank her enough, and I truly believe *Girl Desecrated* would not be published if it were not for her, and her tireless efforts to polish this manuscript.

In 2014, award winning author Jeffe Kennedy selected *The Fergus She* (which was what *Girl Desecrated* was originally called) for a Twitter pitch competition called #NestPitch. The novel didn't go on to get an agent or a publisher, but this nomination went miles towards building my confidence in getting my book finished.

Between 2014 and 2016, two acquisition editors, Penny Barber of Lyrical Press and Kathleen Kubasiak of Curiosity Quills, took the time to tell me what they liked about *The Fergus She* when I was submitting, but more importantly, they told me what I needed to do to make the book better. Their advice took my book much further towards publishing quality.

Along the way, I had some "cheerleaders" and a "street team" of beta readers. Karen Cummins' ongoing enthusiasm for my writing inspired me on those days when I wanted to eat chocolate and give up. It's nice to know I have a champion in the neighbourhood.

Joanna Zurowski's support of my children's book, as well as *Girl Desecrated* made me feel like a "real" writer. She also provided detailed feedback on my manuscript drafts.

Others who weighed in with advice or who never failed to ask how I was coming along with the novel include Erin Britton, Kim Duquette, and Kelly Howes, David Spencer, Eve Hanninen, Julie Jacobs-Furlong, Gwen Gielfeldt, Lindsay Kirkpatrick, Karen Gardner, Mahshid Sarsangi, Justine Shim, and Alba Zilli.

Even just knowing you were there and had not defriended me and my irritating posts about my writing journey helped me get to this place—a published novel writer.

Imagine that!

Image Copyrights

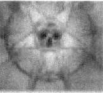

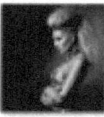

Author Bio

CHERYL IS AN AWARD-winning educator and fantasy author who loves to write on the wild side, digging deep into the unspoken secrets of society's seedier sins.

She is currently focused on putting the fangs back into vampires and resurrecting the monsters in Canada, one story at a time. The rest of her days are spent being a good wife, a good mom, and a good teacher. Every day's a good day, eh? http://www.cherylcowtan.com

How to Write a Book Review in 3 Minutes

IT TAKES ME ABOUT THREE years to write a novel. It can take a reader about three minutes to write a review.

It's great if you connected to my work, but I'll never know if you don't write it down. Reviews are the perfect format to share your response to a book.

I'd love to hear your reaction to this novel.

Your review will also help other readers decide whether my book is for them.

Please leave a review at the bookseller of your choice and Goodreads.

Not sure how to structure a review? Never fear:

1. This book made you feel _____.
2. The best scene/character/event was _____.
3. It reminded you of film/book _____.
4. This is a series/writer to follow.
5. You do recommend/will read another/can't wait...

Thank you so much for the review!

Also by Cheryl R Cowtan

The Fergus She
Girl Desecrated: Vampires, Asylums and Highlanders 1984
Master of Madhouse: Sadists, Mansions and Mayhem 1894

The Precious Quest
The Precious Quest: An Epic Fantasy of Love, Identity and Power

Watch for more at www.cherylcowtan.com.

www.ingramcontent.com/pod-product-compliance
Lightning Source LLC
Chambersburg PA
CBHW031419240626
47154CB00001B/107